W9-CED-965

Love and the Single Corpse

ANNIE GRIFFIN

BERKLEY PRIME CRIME, NEW YORK

LOVE AND THE SINGLE CORPSE

A Berkley Prime Crime Book / published by arrangement with the author

PRINTING HISTORY
Berkley Prime Crime edition / August 2000

All rights reserved.
Copyright © 2000 by Sally Chapman.
This book may not be reproduced in whole or in part,
by mimeograph or any other means, without permission.
For information address: The Berkley Publishing Group,
a division of Penguin Putnam Inc.,
375 Hudson Street, New York, New York 10014.

The Penguin Putnam Inc. World Wide Web site address is
http://www.penguinputnam.com

ISBN: 0-425-17612-6

Berkley Prime Crime Books are published
by The Berkley Publishing Group,
a division of Penguin Putnam Inc.,
375 Hudson Street, New York, New York 10014.
The name BERKLEY PRIME CRIME and the BERKLEY PRIME CRIME
design are trademarks belonging to Penguin Putnam Inc.

PRINTED IN THE UNITED STATES OF AMERICA

10 9 8 7 6 5 4 3 2 1

To my husband, Jim

Special thanks to the following people for all their help:

Margo Rohrbacher of the San Rafael Police Department,
Caroline Lundmark, Darren Keller, Chris Rauen,
Dave Thoeny, Paul Guttman, Velma Chapman
and Celia Bearce.

ONE

꙳

$\mathscr{A}$ DEVILISH MARINE BREEZE BLEW across Hill Creek's town plaza, chilling the prosperous locals as they sat on teak benches, sunning their toes in their Birkenstocks and sipping organic roast, fat-free lattes. The wind dipped and danced about them, riffling the liberal, soon-to-be-recycled newspapers they halfheartedly read, but they hardly noticed the pages fluttering. The locals did not come to the plaza to learn about the world at large. That was much too dreary and complex. It was their own microcosm they found fascinating, for Hill Creek, a suburban village a half hour north of San Francisco, was its own special kingdom, unique and endlessly intriguing, with every other place in the world a few rungs below it. All the locals coveted the benches on the plaza where they could watch with eager attention as the politically correct, inner-child sensitive, totally organic, and karma-attuned world of Hill Creek passed by.

The mischievous breeze swirled and sauntered, finding its way to the plaza's edge, at last performing a suicidal plunge into that dark yet thoroughly explored abyss between the silicone breasts of Kiki Goldstein and causing her to emit a high-pitched "ooh" from the sudden chill. Looking down at her goosebumps, she noticed the feathers rimming her sweater's plunging neckline fluff in a way she considered most alluring.

Granted, it was a nippy day for such a low-cut top, but Kiki felt suffering for beauty to be one of life's necessary sacrifices, and at the age of sixty she was willing to sacrifice with the fury of ancient Incas in order to look more seductive. As she rearranged a few feathers to enhance the effect, a crafty one escaped confinement, drifted upward, and lodged itself in her thick false eyelash.

"Oh, piddle," she muttered, squinting as she tried to remove it, but her long fake fingernails impeded progress.

"I have to admit, I'm impressed," her sister, Hannah Malloy, said, her voice lowered with concentration. With arms crossed, Hannah locked her eyes on the admirable object standing on the opposite side of the plaza, the corners of her mouth turned up in ardent approval. "After all these years, so strong and handsome."

"Oh, yes," Kiki answered with a dainty grunt as she managed to remove the feather and join her sister in this adoration. "I didn't think you'd notice."

Hannah narrowed her eyes to sharpen the view. "How could I miss it? There are some things in this world that are always evocative, always moving, and this is such an example."

Kiki's frothy bleached blonde head bobbed eagerly. "I'm moved. I'm really moved."

"Such symmetry."

"I'll say." Kiki's enthusiasm mounted.

"Grandeur, even."

"Ditto."

"And sensuality."

"You betcha," Kiki replied in slow, low drawl.

"Yet playfulness as well."

Kiki shrugged, a little confused. "Yeah, that too, I guess."

"Hung with little—"

Kiki's head jerked toward her older sister. "Oh, I don't think so. Look at his shoes. They're huge. Size eleven, at least. Trust me, one kiss on the ear and we're talking Louisville Slugger."

Hannah arched an eyebrow in disgust. "I was going to say 'hung with little berries.' I'm talking about the lovely strawberry tree."

Kiki's face scrunched. "Trees, schmeez. You're always fixated on silly plants and flowers. I'm talking about flesh and blood. I'm talking about Ron."

Hannah switched her attention to Dr. Ronald Gilman, recently widowed from a wealthy wife. He stood next to the tree, talking with Lillian Granger and Vera Brown, all of them old high school friends of Hannah and Kiki. The two sisters had been walking across the plaza to join them but stopped when Kiki fell off her gold platform sandals with the three-inch soles, an accident that inevitably led to other adjustments.

Hannah noticed the small portable picnic table standing between her three friends and the half dozen champagne flutes glistening in the lemony sunlight. The plaza backed up to the patio of the Book Stop, the bookstore and café that, together with the plaza, served as Hill Creek's nerve center, bounded on four sides by narrow streets lined with old graceful trees and quaint boutiques. That day, as usual, the streets were filled with BMWs and Volvos, and the plaza bustled with bearded New Agers and harried soccer moms, everyone in a rush to attain the life perfection they all felt certain they deserved. But in spite of their busyness the sight of this small champagne party caught everyone's attention.

As Hannah eyed Gilman she admitted silently that he was quite handsome, although she would never express it in such a base way as Kiki. But then, the two sisters had from birth been polar opposites. Hannah's tall, auburn-haired elegance and unflappable calm was as much like Kiki's short, plump form and impulsive brashness as a crème brulee was like a Popsicle. Still, the sisters had happily lived together and depended on each other for the past fifteen years.

"How typical of you to be focused on the contents of the closest boxer shorts," Hannah said. "Try to restrain your animal appetites. Poor Ron has been widowed only a few months."

"Which means there's no time for putzing around. A man like him will get snatched up in no time."

Hannah knew it was true. Gilman was not only single and available, he was a doctor and over sixty, which made him the current alpha male in Hill Creek's senior citizen love tribe, a man who could provide a lucky woman with prestige, regular sex, and free hormone supplements. These qualities obviously weren't lost on Lillian, whom Hannah could see edging closer and closer to him. Lillian, like Kiki, wasn't going to let any grass grow under her feet now that Gilman was a free man. No woman their age could afford to, Hannah supposed.

Kiki emitted a loud "humpff" and crossed her arms, the gesture sending another feather flying. "Just look at her," she said, carefully checking Lillian for visible defects. "She's always throwing herself at men."

"Like you haven't tossed yourself in front of any Y chromosome in your path."

Kiki slapped her palm against her chest, ejecting three more feathers. "That's so untrue!"

"Dear, half your sweater is flying around your head."

"Darn it," Kiki said, trying unsuccessfully to grab a feather out of the air. "I've had this top for close to twenty years and the feathers are coming loose. But this flouncy look is back in style, don't you think?"

"Only if avocado is back as a good color for refrigerators," Hannah said with a wicked smile. She noticed Kiki's goose bumps. "Do you want my jacket? You must be freezing."

"No, thanks. I'm not covering up my sexy sweater. Whether you like it or not, it's just the thing to catch a man like Ron."

"Only if he's attracted to molting pheasants." To make up for the comment, Hannah gave her sister a good-natured pat on the shoulder.

Kiki opened her mouth to let out a retort, but just then she and Hannah spotted their next-door neighbor Naomi heading their way. Dressed in loose ankle-length pants and a knee-length tunic, her long dark hair plaited into a thick braid twisted over her scalp, Naomi carried three canvas shopping bags overflowing with vegetables. Being ecologically correct, all the hip locals sported canvas shopping bags around town, or if one was into high eco-chic, a quaint wicker basket, so that the minimum of trees would be destroyed or land defiled in the pursuit of one's day-to-day necessities. Hannah smiled when she saw a package of tofu placed strategically on top of one of Naomi's bags, suspecting that her friend had tucked her favorite spicy sausage near the bottom safely from view. Hill Creek was one of those places where everybody claimed to be vegetarian but could occasionally be caught with a Big Mac on their breath.

"What synchronicity! I knew I'd find you here," Naomi said with her inherent cheerfulness. "I want to whip up a cheese and grain casserole this afternoon, and I need to use your oven."

"Of course," Hannah said. "You don't need to ask." Enduring termite repairs in her kitchen for the last month, Naomi had been running over to Hannah and Kiki's house at least three times a day to use the stove for tea and tofu.

"Thank you," Naomi said with a sigh, brushing back a loose strand of hair. "The construction's been so stressful, it's disturbed my spiritual balance. Luckily the fresh air is rejuvenating my chi." Chi, as Naomi loved to tell, was an Oriental term for life force energy. She was always informing her friends how their chi needed rejuvenating, when in truth, the women in their circle had so much life force energy they were to the point of bursting.

Naomi drank in the air, sucking in as much chi as she could. "What a scrumptious day!"

"Gorgeous," Hannah replied. "Just look at Mount Tam. The outlines are so sharp."

Naomi turned to look at the lush green mountain towering between Hill Creek and the Pacific Ocean and bowed her head in reverence. She was a well-known local psychic who channeled the spirit of Red Moon, a five hundred-year-old Hopi snake shaman. For fifty dollars an hour, Red Moon, speaking through Naomi, delivered life advice buried in metaphysical Indian metaphors. Whenever Naomi felt her psychic powers waning, she hiked up the mountain and partook of its mystical powers, sometimes in the nude, if the park rangers weren't around.

"The day feels pregnant with possibilities!" Naomi pronounced.

At that moment the women heard a squeal of salutation and, turning, they found Wanda Backus flying toward them at warp speed, her Bruno Magli mules slapping the pavement. With one well-moisturized, stick-thin arm she carried her wicker basket and with the other her new poodle, Zeno, the little dog looking highly annoyed, his long ears bouncing as she jogged. "Thank God, I found you!" she said, panting from the exertion. "Something remarkable has happened!"

The first thing Hannah thought was that maybe her husband, Walter, had given up vodka, but then she quickly decided that was unlikely. Not when he had to live with Wanda.

"Take a deep breath and calm down," Hannah told her. "You'll have a heart attack." She knew from experience not to take Wanda's self-created melodramas too seriously. Wanda was typical of many of Hannah's friends in that her life ran so smoothly she had to busy herself with self-concocted personal problems, digging into every crevice of her psyche with an archeologist's fervor.

Wanda put down little Zeno, placing her foot on his leash. Closing her eyes, she took a deep breath, sweeping her arms upward as she inhaled and then downward as she let out the air. Ferociously aware of her chi, Wanda was one of Naomi's best channeling clients, with Red Moon advising her on everything from her sex life to car repairs, the advice for both being similar. "Thank you. I feel centered now."

"Please, Wanda, tell us what happened," Naomi said, filled with curiosity. The women stood at attention.

Wanda's eyes popped open and she glanced furtively around the plaza as if her news was so hot, spies were tailing her. Titillated, the women stepped closer.

"Well," she began. "The other day Zeno and I were in the living room listening to Bach, and suddenly he bumped against the stereo's power button and turned it off. Then later that day Walter was eating a pastrami sandwich and Zeno jumped on his lap and took the sandwich right out of his

hand. And then," Wanda said, the drama in her voice building to a big finish, "Zeno made a wee wee on my photograph
of Grandpa Harvey. Isn't it fantastic?" It was apparent by
the vacant looks of her listeners that they failed to grasp the
event's magnitude. Unthwarted, she forged on. "Six months
ago my favorite relative, Uncle Marv, died in the bathroom
in New Jersey. Uncle Marv hated Bach, loved pastrami, and
loathed Grandpa Harvey. You realize what this means?" Her
friends' silence indicated continuing noncomprehension.
"Zeno is the reincarnation of Uncle Marv!" she announced,
throwing up her arms as if she had just shouted hallelujah.
"I've suspected it for days, but now I'm sure. The timing is
right. I checked, and Zeno was born the very day Uncle Marv
died, or at least close to it."

Wanda looked down and, seeing Zeno expressing his sexuality on Hannah's ankle, gasped, finding the inexorable
proof she required. "Hannah, don't you remember how Uncle
Marv groped you at my *Women Are Venus, Men Are Mars*
party three years ago?" Smugly pursing her lips, she gestured
to the maniacally humping animal. "Do you need more evidence?"

Hannah grimaced. She was an animal lover, but she had
her limits. "What I need is for you to get your dog off my
leg."

Wanda squatted. "Bad Uncle Marv, ooh, naughty doggie,"
she said in a baby talk that made the other women shiver.
Wanda shook her finger at the dog. "You haven't changed a
bit."

Hannah gave her foot a gentle kick but Zeno remained
determined. At last Wanda picked up the poodle, the animal
responding with an indignant growl. Naomi always said it
was karma that caused all Wanda's pets to be neurotic and
impossible to housetrain.

"Would you like some tea, Wanda? You seem frazzled,"
Hannah said in the tone she would have used with a mental
patient claiming to be Marie Antoinette. It seemed sad to her
that Wanda, having exhausted the limited possibilities of her
own psyche, now stooped to investigating those of her dog.

"They have some new jasmine tea at the Book Stop that would be very soothing."

"No time for tea," Wanda replied briskly. Just then she lifted her surgically sculpted nose and sniffed the air. Lowering her gaze, she saw Zeno relieving himself. Hannah noticed with puzzlement that this seemed to delight her. "Ooh, good, good doggie, I mean Uncle Marv. Going outside, very good. Mommy so proud of ooh!" Wanda mewed with a clap of her hands, apparently not disturbed by the dog's deposit being on her shoe. She took a plastic baggie from her pocket and picked up the odorous mound. Not cleaning up after one's dog was considered a major faux pas in Hill Creek, right up there with smoking, wearing furs, and drinking rosé.

"Anyway, I'm just so thrilled. I've called the pet psychic," Wanda explained. "And she said she could give me a phone session at five-thirty, so I've got to run." She squeezed up her shoulders with excitement. Caught up in the moment, Wanda dropped the packaged poop in her Gucci handbag instead of the trashcan behind her.

Apparently the only one who noticed this, Hannah chuckled. "Wanda—" she said.

"Sorry, Hannah. No time for chitchat."

Hannah pointed to Wanda's handbag. "But—"

"Got to scoot!" Wanda said, and with a fling of her hand, took off toward Center Avenue, Zeno biting his leash and barking nastily.

"Do you really think Zeno could be the reincarnation of her Uncle Marv?" Kiki asked as they watched Zeno pull Wanda around the corner.

Hannah cast a skeptical glance at her sister.

"Of course, it's possible," Naomi said, nodding philosophically. "Although normally spirits don't move down the food chain like that." Naomi looked in the direction Wanda had gone, thoughtfully tapping her chin with her finger. "Interesting what Wanda said about the phone psychic session. I need a way to package my own psychic skills so they're a bit more accessible to the general public. I'm developing such an expertise in chi counseling. It's a shame I can't share it with more people."

Kiki nodded. "It's so true. Remember when I was feeling sluggish last spring and you figured out that I had low liver chi?"

"You had allergies," Hannah said, always doubtful of Naomi's psychic snake shaman mumbo jumbo.

"It was her chi," Naomi said with firmness. "If only there was some way I could bundle up my natural healing powers."

The edges of Hannah's mouth curled upward. "Maybe you could put it in a can and call it Chi Whiz."

Naomi gave her best "I'm spiritually elevated and you're not" expression, which consisted of half-closed eyes and a Buddha smile.

A sudden loud laugh grabbed the women's attention, and they all looked in the direction of Gilman, Vera, and Lillian. Lillian was whispering something in Gilman's ear that he apparently found exceptionally amusing. Kiki glowered as Lillian rubbed against him in a manner reminiscent of Zeno on Hannah's leg.

Hannah noticed Vera silently watching Lillian and Gilman from only a few feet away. Small and chinless with soft gray hair waving around her face, Vera stood pigeon-toed, both hands stuffed in the pockets of her long cardigan sweater. She wore her usual kindly smile, but her eyes looked hurt that she wasn't included in the joke. *That's the way it's always been,* Hannah thought. Gilman and Lillian the center of attention, still the football hero and prom queen, with everyone else looking on, quietly envious. Everyone except Kiki. Kiki did a lot of envying and she never did it quietly.

"I've got to get over there before Lillian ruins my chances," Kiki said, glancing around to make certain no one was looking, then giving her breasts a gentle shove upward. "It's five o'clock and time for us to start, anyway."

"But Geraldine's not here yet," Hannah said, eager for any excuse to delay the inevitable collision between Lillian and her sister.

"You snooze, you lose." Kiki rummaged through the bottomless canyon of her handbag and pulled out a travel-sized plastic bottle of hair spray. She gave her poufed hair three short blasts. "Does the back of my hair need more spray?"

"No. You're the only woman I know whose hair comes in regular and extra crispy," Hannah said with a grin. She loved teasing her sister, especially since she knew Kiki was oblivious to it.

Naomi giggled. Kiki kept her eyes on Gilman. "Make whatever jokes you like," Kiki said. "But I'm going over there to save Ron from Lillian's clutches."

"Please stay and talk with me and Naomi," Hannah urged.

Kiki looked at her sister with suspicion. "Why do you care if I set my sights on Ron? I could be a doctor's wife. Think how proud Mother would have been."

Hannah paused, trying to come up with a suitable white lie, but opted for the truth. "I know our high school days were eons ago, but I can't forget the awful rivalry between you and Lillian when you two were cheerleaders. The way you squabbled over Ron back then."

Naomi's eyes glinted with interest. "Really?" she said, drawing out the word into several syllables. "What happened?"

Kiki stiffened. "One little scuffle in the girls' bathroom. It was nothing. It only took a week for Lillian to get the glue out of her hair. Besides, things are different now. I'm more mature than when I was sixteen."

Hannah seriously questioned that. She tried another route. "You know, Kiki, you really should give a recent widower like Ron time to grieve."

Being softhearted, Kiki wore an expression of thoughtful concern that lasted a good three seconds until Gilman let out another raucous laugh.

Kiki pulled her Tahiti Pink lipstick from her purse with the same ominously assertive movement as if it had been a revolver. "I think Ronnie's grieving period is over."

"He's probably using some sort of laughter therapy to help him deal with the pain," Naomi suggested, always ready to believe the best in people.

Hannah watched Gilman perform his barnyard strutting. He now spoke with animation to both Lillian and Vera, smiling and winking at them, his arm slipping briefly around Lillian's narrow waist. Hannah had to admit he was bearing up awfully well under his tragic loss. But then, Lillian was making it easy for him. Hannah studied Lillian as she coquettishly straightened Gilman's collar. It would be no surprise if he were attracted to her. Lillian had always been beautiful, although over the years she had become that brand of Marin County woman who was more manufactured than born, every part of her exfoliated, massaged, bleached, fluffed, and sculpted into taut perfection.

"I don't understand what's going on. Why the champagne?" Naomi asked. "Is there a party?"

"It's the annual Botany Club meeting," Kiki explained.

"Botany Club?" Naomi tipped her head to one side. "I thought you and Hannah were in the Rose Club."

"We were in the Botany Club back in high school," Hannah explained.

Naomi looked surprised. "The club still meets? But your high school days were over forty years ago."

Kiki bristled at the arithmetic. "The club doesn't really meet, silly. We like to get together once a year under the tree we planted when we were in school, when I was a junior and Hannah and the others were seniors."

"Oh, yes, that lovely strawberry tree," Naomi said. "It brings such earth energy to the plaza."

"Every year the old Botany Club meets by the tree on the anniversary of the planting, and we have champagne to celebrate," Kiki continued, the prospect of telling a story momentarily distracting her from Gilman. "And today's the day. I never miss them."

Hannah blinked, since Kiki had rarely attended any. The only reason for her presence that day was Ron Gilman being her *man du jour*. But Kiki had never won Gilman's heart back in high school, and Hannah didn't think much of her sister's current chances. Gilman seemed as entranced by Lillian now as he had been over forty years ago, and Hannah worried that it would open old wounds for her sister. To Kiki, Lillian had always represented everything she wasn't. Lillian was tall, slender, moneyed, and sophisticated. The first three qualities had eluded Kiki by fate and genetics, and although Kiki did her best to feign a cosmopolitan air, she was irrevocably down-to-earth, and worldly only in the sense that her physique was globular.

"It's odd how things don't change," Hannah said thoughtfully.

"What do you mean?" Naomi asked. "The world is constantly under transformation."

"But people stay the same," Hannah replied. "Look at the Botany Club. Even after all this time, Kiki's still the bouncy cheerleader." Pleased at this description, Kiki patted her hair. "Gilman is still the sought-after male prize," Hannah continued. "Lillian's still acting like a prom queen, managing to look regal even in that tennis outfit. And look at Vera standing there so shyly, just as she always did. I remember a saying from high school. They said that girls fell into two categories, flowers and pots. Kiki and Lillian were flowers. Vera, I'm afraid was a pot."

"And which were you, Hannah?" Naomi said, giving her a playful poke in the ribs.

Hannah smiled. "I was a cactus growing off somewhere by myself."

"But the kind of cactus with no thorns," Kiki said with affection.

"And the kind that flowers," Naomi added. "But there's one thing that must have changed. Surely you had more than five members in your club."

"We did, but most everyone moved away over the years. Now there's only Ron, Lillian, Vera, Kiki, and me. And of course, Geraldine Markham. She was our teacher and one of the club sponsors."

"Hannah was always the teacher's pet with her," Kiki said. She pointed to the far corner of the plaza. "Here she comes, late as usual."

Twisting around, Hannah saw Geraldine walking up the plaza. She had on her usual mannish brimmed hat, shirt, and pants, and wire-rimmed spectacles. She wore her thick, dark hair in the same blunt chin-length cut with sharp bangs she had worn ever since Hannah had known her.

It occurred to Hannah that Geraldine's appearance hadn't changed that much over the years, which by Hannah's measurement was an excellent thing. Hannah liked all her old Botany Club friends, there being a special affection between people who had known each other so long. But there had always been a special place in her heart for eccentric Geraldine. Hannah seldom saw Gilman, Lillian, or Vera any more, but she had worked to keep up the friendship with her former teacher. Not that they had ever been close. Geraldine was a private woman who, much like Hannah, preferred books and plants to socializing. But at Hannah's instigation they had met at the Book Stop every few months for tea and lively discussions of their mutual hobbies—writing poetry and growing roses.

"She doesn't look old enough to have been your teacher," Naomi remarked.

"She's not much older than us," Hannah explained. "We were her first class at her first teaching job."

"Darn that Lillian," Kiki said. "She's whispering in his ear again. I'm going over." Not waiting for any protest, she shot toward Gilman with the fury of a nuclear warhead.

With a sigh, Hannah watched her sister tramp across the plaza, teetering on the thick platform sandals that belonged on a sixteen-year-old. She turned to Naomi. "Why don't you join us? One of the club members might need some channeling."

She made the last remark jokingly, but she knew Naomi would jump at the chance of rounding up a new client or two. Hannah always gave her any assistance she could, even though she was basically a nonbeliever when it came to Red Moon.

"Always interested in making new friends," Naomi said with gratitude as she gathered up her groceries. "And I wouldn't turn down a touch of bubbly either, just for stress reduction, of course."

Hannah helped Naomi with her shopping bags, and together they reached the small group just as Gilman popped the cork from the champagne.

"Here you are," Lillian said in a voice smooth as lotion. As Hannah clasped Lillian's hand, she gave the woman an appraising look. Tan and muscular, Lillian wore a short tennis skirt that showed off her legs and a blue cotton sweater that brought out her eyes. Since she was a teenager, Lillian had worn the confident air of a woman who knew what she wanted and knew how to get it, even if she had to snatch it from you. Hannah shook off this negative thought, reminding herself of Lillian's tireless volunteer work.

Hannah introduced Naomi, quickly finding her friend's reputation already well-known, since both Vera and Lillian immediately asked her a dozen questions about Red Moon. Naomi lapped up the attention, dispensing a few Hopi metaphors and managing to discreetly give out her phone number and business hours.

Always savvy, Kiki used Lillian's distraction to plant herself at Gilman's side, standing so close to him their arms touched. Gilman sidled a few steps from her.

"It's nice to have an addition to our little party," he said, giving Naomi a nod. "I've brought two bottles of a fine vintage, so there's plenty of champagne, especially with old Hannah being a teetotaler."

As he handed out the champagne glasses, Hannah studied him, not understanding what Lillian and Kiki saw in him. She appreciated a handsome man as much as the next woman and basically she liked him, but he had always seemed so self-impressed. That afternoon, for instance, she felt certain he had purposely overdressed, with his double-breasted sport coat and his silly cravat. And the way he took control of every little thing, making himself the center of attention. Hannah's opinion of him that day was the same as always— nice box, no cereal.

"Please, Ron, don't call any of us old," Vera said with a laugh as she passed out paper cocktail napkins. "I like to think of us as being a fine vintage, just like your champagne."

"I don't consider myself old at all," Kiki said, directing the comment at Gilman and pushing out her chest. "I'm what I call fully ripened."

Lillian's eyes shot to Kiki, and suddenly aware that Kiki had invaded her turf, she placed herself on Gilman's other side. In a countermove, Kiki edged in even closer to him until he was wedged between the two women.

A quarter pound of beef between two not-so-fresh poppy seed buns, Hannah mused, observing this human sandwich. She felt the old familiar anxiety, not wanting Kiki to embarrass herself, but she knew there was nothing she could do. Love made a person irrational and Kiki was almost always in love. Since Kiki's second husband, Cecil, died and she moved in with Hannah, Hannah had resumed her old role as her sister's counselor and protector. There was only a year's difference in their ages but several light-years in their levels of good sense.

Hannah's eyes connected with Geraldine's, and they exchanged a smile. As far back as high school Geraldine had been telling Hannah not to worry so much about her sister.

Hannah started to speak to her, but Geraldine's gaze had shifted to the ground. Geraldine looked consumed with thought, and Hannah noticed that she had twisted her paper cocktail napkin to shreds. It wasn't until then that Hannah became aware of Geraldine's atypical quietness. Her friend seemed distraught and pale.

"You're looking lovely as usual, Hannah," Lillian said, smoothing her sleek cap of streaked hair. "You always manage to dress with such a simple elegance." Lillian slid her eyes to Kiki. "And Kiki, you're looking so—" She paused for effect. "So festive. But you must be freezing." Her eyes darted to Kiki's goose-bumped cleavage.

Kiki's smile tightened. "I'm just dandy. But what about you? With that skimpy tennis skirt your buns must be ice cubes."

The gauntlet had been thrown, and everyone knew it.

"Vera, did you bring the sparkling cider for Hannah?" Geraldine quickly asked, breaking the tension. Hannah gave her a grateful smile.

Vera cast a concerned glance at Lillian and Kiki as she pulled the sparkling cider from her "Save The Sea Otter" tote bag. Vera had always hated discord, and was the first to smooth over an argument.

Gilman filled Hannah's glass with cider and everyone else's with champagne, then lifted his glass for a toast.

"Once again, friends, let's drink to the Hill Creek High

School Botany Club of nineteen fifty-five. May we all be as rugged and healthy as this tree we planted forty-five years ago."

"A lovely statement," Geraldine said.

"And may we continue meeting every year," Vera added with a smile. There were echoes of approval as everyone clinked glasses and drank.

The stress of her termite repairs apparently taking its toll, Naomi downed her champagne in two gulps, and Gilman, playing the host, refilled her glass.

"If I could ask a question," Naomi interrupted after emitting a dainty burp to equalize her inner harmony. "How have you managed to keep up this party for so many years?"

"It's not like we've met every year since nineteen fifty-five," Lillian said. "For the first twenty years or so we didn't meet at all."

"But then I think we all got nostalgic for the old days," Vera chimed in. "Hill Creek started changing."

Hannah laughed. "I think we're the ones who started changing and we didn't like it, so we decided to hang on to the past."

"Hannah, you may be the town poet but you're remarkably free from sentimentality," Gilman told her.

Geraldine looked at Hannah with affection. "Always one of her strengths. She's made of steel and velvet."

Geraldine was about to say more, but Lillian cut her off. "We're the only members of the Botany Club left," she said to Naomi. "I don't remember whose idea it was, but it was a good one. Our little get-togethers are always fun."

But it didn't look like Geraldine was having a bang-up time, at least not to Hannah. Her expression worried, Geraldine no longer listened to the chatter, her gaze directed at some point in the distance.

Hannah placed her hand underneath Geraldine's elbow. "Are you feeling all right?"

Geraldine looked startled for a second, then smiled.

"I'm fine. I never did well with champagne. I'm not the type, I guess."

Hannah glanced at her full glass. "You've only had a sip.

Would you like to sit down?" Geraldine shook her head.

"What are you girls whispering about?" Lillian asked. "I think we should have another toast." She raised her glass. "To old friends," she said, shifting her eyes to Gilman. "And to our futures."

Everyone again raised their drinks, Vera's hand stopping before hers reached her lips. "Look at that limb," she said, stepping closer to the tree. Reaching up, she held a leaf in her fingers. "The leaves are all mottled."

The rest of them moved in closer. Lillian jerked off a leaf. "It looks like it has a disease."

"Ridiculous," Gilman said. "I specifically chose an *Arbutus unedo* because it was disease resistant."

"You never chose the tree, Ron," Geraldine told him. "The club made the decision as a group."

Obviously not liking to be corrected, Gilman shot her a barbed look.

"I remember quite clearly that Ron chose the tree," Lillian said, taking his arm. "You're not always right, Geraldine."

An awkward silence settled on the group, and Hannah couldn't help wondering if age had made her friends cranky. No, that couldn't be it. They had been cranky even as teenagers. Yet she felt some new discontent brewing, and she couldn't imagine its source. She didn't think her friends even saw each other that often, except for Vera and Geraldine, who had remained close over the years.

"Let's freshen up our drinks," Vera said with forced cheerfulness. She grabbed the second open bottle off the table, pouring champagne in Gilman's glass and then Naomi's and Kiki's. Unnerved by the unpleasantness, her movements were jerky, and as she poured the liquid into Lillian's glass, it sloshed onto Lillian's sweater.

"Be careful," Lillian snapped.

Looking surprised by the harsh tone, Vera pulled the bottle back so quickly she knocked Lillian's hand, spilling more champagne.

"I'm so sorry," Vera said, flustered.

"I know, but this sweater is new," Lillian said with exasperation, dabbing at her sweater with her napkin.

"I didn't mean to do it," Vera told her, then adding sharply, "It's not like it's going to melt you."

Gilman laughed, which aggravated Lillian further. "Just get away from me," she said to Vera.

Kiki caught Hannah's eye and tipped her head in Lillian's direction, mouthing the word "bitch."

"It's not a disease," Naomi said, the gentleness of her voice grabbing everyone's attention.

"Of course it isn't," Lillian said, looking at Naomi with shock. "Vera's just a little clumsy."

"I'm talking about the poor tree," Naomi said. "It could be out of primal balance."

"Primal balance?" Vera repeated, her eyes wide with interest.

Suddenly looking as if his underwear was chafing, Gilman downed the last of his champagne. "There's nothing wrong with that tree's balance. What are you talking about?"

"It could be suffering from inharmonious influences, feeling out of sync with the universal whole," Naomi explained, ignoring his gruffness. Gilman looked at her with an expression suitable for a patient who had suggested performing his own rectal exam. Naomi turned up her palms. "There's an easy way to find out."

"How?" Vera asked eagerly.

Naomi grinned. Hannah, noticing that Naomi's ears had turned bright red, realized her friend felt the effects of the champagne. "We'll just ask it," Naomi said with a squeak, confirming Hannah's suspicions.

"This isn't a good time for a channeling session," Hannah told Naomi, not wanting her to frighten anyone. When Red Moon supposedly took over Naomi's body, her voice changed to a man's, and the first time you experienced it, it was downright ghoulish.

"It's okay, I'm not going to call forth Red Moon completely. He's just going to help me communicate with the tree. You know, he always says that a tree's sap is the blood of our ancestors, and that the rustle of the leaves is our ancestors' voices. I'm just going to take a little listen and see what our ancestors have to tell us. I'll be done in a jiffy."

Everyone watched as Naomi approached the tree. After circling it a few times, she placed her hand on its trunk, closed her eyes and began to mutter the string of Hopi phrases she always claimed to have learned from Red Moon.

Newly invigorated, Vera moved next to Hannah. "This is so fascinating. What's she doing?"

"Having a chat with the leaves and the sap," Hannah replied.

Knowing all eyes were upon her, Naomi played to the crowd, hugging the tree and pressing her ear to its bark. There was a long moment of silence while she remained in this position. Suddenly she pulled back, jerking her hands from the tree trunk as if it were red hot.

Vera let out a distressed gasp. "What is it?"

"The tree is disturbed," Naomi said, holding up her index finger. "It told me the strangest thing. It said that reality here isn't as it appears."

"How did it speak to you?" Vera asked.

"I communicated with the tree's earth spirit," Naomi said, still eyeing the tree's trunk.

Gilman laughed. "What a lot of hogwash."

"I agree," Lillian said. Hannah silently agreed also, but did notice that Naomi stared at the tree with an honestly perplexed expression.

"Was the tree referring to itself?" Vera asked Naomi, unaffected by her friends' incredulity.

"This is California," Geraldine said, sounding more like her old self. "The tree probably wants to undergo an operation because deep inside it feels it's really a flowering shrub."

"Now don't be sarcastic," Kiki said with a wag of her finger. "Naomi's almost always right about these things."

Hannah and Geraldine exchanged a knowing smile. Then Geraldine's expression turned thoughtful, as if an idea had just popped into her mind.

Naomi ran her hands over the tree's bark, shaking her head. "The tree feels suspicious and afraid."

"Okay, who's hiding limb cutters?" Hannah joked, but no one laughed.

"I'm serious, Hannah," Naomi said, too absorbed in the

tree to take offense. "There's a negative vibration around it. It's giving me a funny feeling right here." She tapped at the base of her throat with her finger.

There was nothing like a neurotic tree to put a damper on a party. Hannah laughed off Naomi's claims about the tree, but everyone else looked disconcerted. After a few meager attempts at conversation, they downed the rest of their drinks and made hasty excuses about important errands they had suddenly remembered. Hannah was coaxing Kiki away from Gilman when she felt a hand on her shoulder and saw Geraldine. Geraldine pulled her away from the others.

"Hannah, I'd like to talk to you."

"Of course," Hannah replied. "Let's sit down on that bench."

"Not here."

Hannah detected a slight shaking in Geraldine's voice. Over her shoulder she heard Gilman shout good-bye and watched him walk across the plaza with Lillian on his arm. Kiki glared after them a few seconds, then began talking to Naomi and Vera. Hannah turned her attention back to Geraldine.

"What is it?" she asked. "You're not yourself today."

"I need your help," Geraldine said. She hesitated before getting out the rest. "I think I may be in some trouble."

"What do you mean? What kind of trouble?"

"I've found out about something, something illegal, and I want to take what I know to the police."

"So why don't you?"

"I don't want them to think I'm crazy. I know you've dealt with the police before. If I could discuss it with you, get your opinion, then maybe you could support me when I talk to them. Come with me, even."

"What's this all about, Vera? How is this connected to trouble for you?"

They heard Kiki's voice rise as she complained about Lillian.

"We can't talk here," Geraldine said. "Too many people around. Can you come to my house tonight?"

"I'm working with a new group this evening," Hannah

replied. A cancer survivor herself, Hannah had begun volunteer work with a breast cancer support group one night every two weeks. She had new participants scheduled for that evening and she couldn't cancel, but the look on Geraldine's face bothered her. "Maybe I can get someone to fill in for me."

"No, of course not," Geraldine said. "Those women need you." She smiled, seeming more relaxed. "We can put off our talk until tomorrow morning. It can wait until then. How about nine at my house?"

Hannah took her friend's hand. The skin felt cold. "Are you sure you're feeling all right? Maybe we should stop Ron, so he can take a look at you." Hannah spotted him at the very edge of the plaza, about to turn onto Center Avenue. She raised her hand to flag him, but Geraldine stopped her.

"No," she said, her tone urgent. "I'm fine."

"Can I drive you home?"

Geraldine shook her head. "I have my car. I'm fine, really. A little tired, maybe. Think I'll go home and take a nap." Her hand squeezed Hannah's. "You've always been a good friend to me."

Hannah started to speak but heard Kiki call to her. With a quick good-bye, Geraldine walked away.

"That darn Lillian," Kiki spat as she stomped up.

"What about her?" Hannah asked, her eyes still on Geraldine. She couldn't imagine what kind of trouble her friend could be talking about.

"That hussy managed to snag away Ron right out from under my nose. She told him she needed a ride home."

"The shameless slut," Hannah joked.

"Naturally he couldn't say no. It wouldn't be polite."

"What happened to Naomi and Vera?"

"They went to the Book Stop for a decaf. You know, I think Ronnie's interested in me. He didn't talk to me much, but I could feel this animal heat coming from him. He's going to fall in love with me, I just know it." There was a short silence. "If only I can figure how to keep that Lillian out of the way. Hannah, you're not paying attention."

"I'm hearing every word. Did you notice anything funny

about Geraldine? She doesn't seem quite right to me."

"She's always been a weirdo, if you ask me, the way she keeps to herself and dresses in clothes that look more like a man's than a woman's. But now that you mention it, she was quieter today. She usually jokes around." Kiki considered it a moment. "She seemed bothered about something, sort of like the tree."

Yes, just like the tree, Hannah thought, trying her best to squelch the apprehension growing inside her.

Two

"IF A WOMAN WANTS TO catch a man, she's got to have a battle plan."

Kiki pounded the small wooden breakfast table for emphasis, stimulating her Velcro hair curlers into a feverish tremble. This declaration made, she returned her eyes, already laden with makeup at seven-thirty in the morning, back to the open book in front of her.

If Hannah's second cup of coffee, strong as bat's blood, didn't fully awaken her, the sight of Kiki did, her sister's fluffy pink chenille robe and matching bunny slippers vivid against the cozy kitchen's cornflower blue walls. She watched Kiki's face scrunch with concentration, her eyes fixed upon the dusty Hill Creek High School yearbook from nineteen fifty-five.

Hannah was dressed in trim dark slacks and a white hip-length sweater. Her shoulder-length auburn hair was pulled back into a low ponytail and twisted into a haphazard knot held in place with hair sticks. Her only jewelry was a pair of large gold hoop earrings. After dipping a slice of bread into a bowl of beaten egg, she plopped it on the griddle, where a small dab of butter sizzled. Reaching for the knob of the old gas stove, she turned up the heat just slightly.

"What about letting things happen naturally?" she asked, smiling when she felt a nuzzling at her leg. Her pet pig, Sylvia Plath, and dog, Teresa S. Eliot, stood at her socked feet, their expressions showing they were hopeful of getting a taste of French toast. They knew she was a soft touch.

Kiki glanced up from the yearbook. "Are you nuts?" After giving Hannah a cold eye, she held up the open book beside her head. "Look at this picture of me when I was seventeen and look at me now." She pointed to the book and then her face. "This is an example of what happens naturally, and, personally, I think it stinks."

She shook her head at her sister's ignorance, but since she had the attention span of a gerbil, this annoyance quickly disappeared, soon replaced with sentimental delight as she flipped through the book and came to another picture of herself. In a cheerleader skirt and sweater, a teenaged Kiki stood with her feet wide apart, shaggy pompoms held high, a gargantuan grin on her face, and, as only Kiki knew, two pairs of bobby socks stuffed in her bra.

"Maybe I haven't really changed all that much," she said wistfully. "I'm a little plumper now, but I've still kept my figure." Cheered by the delusion, she flipped through a few more pages. "Here's the group picture of the Botany Club. Look, Hannah, we're all so young. I've never understood why you wore that beret over your eyes and stuck that silly cigarette in your mouth just before the photographer took the picture."

"I was a rebel back then, or at least trying to be."

Kiki turned another few pages. "And here's one of Geraldine." She pulled the book closer to her face. "It's amazing, but she doesn't look that much different now than she did back then.

After flipping over the toast, Hannah, spatula in her hand, approached the table and looked over Kiki's shoulder.

"I was thinking the same thing yesterday," Hannah said. "She's aged, of course, like all of us."

Hannah studied the photograph, the uneasiness she had felt all morning still gnawing at her. The photo was a standard passport-sized headshot, Geraldine staring straight at the camera with a knowing smile. Geraldine always had a confident steadiness about her, Hannah thought, which made their conversation the day before that much more troublesome.

Hannah's worrying jag started as soon as she and Kiki arrived home from the party the previous evening. She immediately made a round of phone calls to find someone to fill in for her at the support group, but no one was available. She finished up the group after eleven, too late to call Geraldine, but the image of her friend's face so pale and careworn, and the idea of her wanting to go to the police, were still on Hannah's mind when she woke up at six this morning. She waited until seven, then phoned. There was no answer.

"Part of the reason Geraldine looks the same is because she hasn't changed her hair in all these years," Kiki said with the disapproving tone natural to a woman who changed her hairdo every week.

"I don't think she's ever cared much about her looks. She's concentrating more on her inner life than her outer one."

"Oh, don't start a lecture. Geraldine never had any outer life to concentrate on. She's a nice person, but let's face it, she's always been a dull spinster. Absolutely no sizzle in that woman's bones. And do you want me to tell you why?"

A slight burning smell drew Hannah and her highly sensitive nose back to the stove. "No," she said over her shoulder as she turned the toast.

Kiki put the book in her lap. "Because she never had a man, that's why. And she never had a man because she never got aggressive about it. When you come across a man who gives you that special feeling, you've got to take action."

Still facing the stove, Hannah rolled her eyes. The special feeling her sister talked about usually involved feather boa feathers and a vibrating bed.

"A woman's got to seize control of the situation," Kiki continued. "She's got to make things happen."

Sylvia snorted in apparent agreement, but Hannah knew the pig only wanted a treat. Sylvia, on a constant diet, loved food, but unfortunately everything she ate went straight to her hips.

Turning off the stove, Hannah started to reply to Kiki's last statement, but thought better of it. In a triumph of hope over reality, Kiki still believed she had a chance with Ron Gilman. Hannah thought she had a better chance of flying the space shuttle, but didn't have the heart to tell her. It wouldn't have done much good anyway. Once Kiki got an idea in her head, getting it out again was about as easy as nailing Jell-O to a tree.

"Kiki, you and I are too old to be chasing after men," she said, opening the cabinet and taking out one of her mismatched garage sale plates.

"The truth is, the older you are, the more you have to chase them," Kiki told her. "What are we supposed to do, sit around and do old lady things before our time?"

Hannah chuckled as she put the plate on the countertop. "What old lady things do you mean? Gardening? Reading? Volunteer work?"

"I mean making tissue box covers out of yarn, wearing terry cloth house slippers, and putting rubber flower decals on the bathtub so we don't slip. I won't do it. I'm going to stay young, and to do that, I need something to keep my hormones fresh. That means a man."

Kiki's hormones were well past the sell-by date, but Hannah had the good sense not to mention it. After feeding a few bits of toast to the pets, she sprinkled powdered sugar on the remaining two slices and carried them to Kiki, whose eyes grew large with joy at the sight of her favorite breakfast.

"You'll never learn," Hannah said, putting down the plate with a small whack that communicated more than words. "I know how this will turn out."

"No, you don't. Where's the syrup?"

"If you don't watch your calories, we're going to have to pay property taxes on your hips. Kiki, I'm serious."

Her sister looked hurt. "I think of it as a Renoir-style plumpness."

"I was joking about your hips. You know you always look good. What I'm serious about is Gilman. In the past, your—

how can I say this tactfully?—quests for love haven't ended well," Hannah said, generously understating the string of debacles that comprised her sister's long romantic ground war.

"This is different," Kiki replied, grandly enunciating each word. Realizing that the syrup would not be brought to her, she went to the refrigerator, opened the door, and stuck her head inside.

As Kiki rattled around looking for the syrup Hannah had thrown out four days earlier (when Kiki split the seams of her size 14 petite capri pants), Hannah rinsed the skillet, her mind returning to Geraldine. She could have been out for a walk, Hannah reasoned, and that's why she didn't answer the phone. But Geraldine always took her walks in the evening.

In an attempt to calm her mind, Hannah looked out the kitchen window at her garden. It was Hannah's pride and joy, a sumptuous blend of silky lawn, vine-covered cedar fencing, and curved flower beds, with one section dedicated to her prize-winning roses. Even in November she still had a few blossoms, one of the benefits of northern California's mild climate. It was time to start cutting back some of the plants for winter. The hydrangeas especially, she thought. Just then she saw Naomi rush across the lawn, having let herself in through the side garden gate.

The back screen door slammed. Barefoot, Naomi sailed into the kitchen, wearing her red silk robe, the one with the embroidered pop-eyed dragon crawling up the back. Hannah wondered why no one but her was ever dressed before nine.

"Bad, awful, utterly horrendous news!" Naomi announced, bracing herself against the kitchen counter like Bette Davis in some old black-and-white movie. Sylvia and Teresa trotted over and greeted her with friendly sniffs.

Hannah put down the skillet and turned off the faucet. "What is it?"

"My contractor came by last night and said the termite damage is worse than he thought. He's going to have to rip out another wall."

"I'm so sorry," Hannah said with her most heartfelt sympathy, understanding money difficulties.

"Are you sure he knows what he's talking about?" Kiki

asked, now back at the table. Kiki didn't realize Hannah was watching when she mouthed something else to Naomi, who was too absorbed in her troubles to notice. Hannah resumed work at the sink, wondering what secret was going on between them.

"I trust him completely," Naomi said, pulling a banana from one pocket and a small carton of low-fat organic soy milk from the other. "I need your blender, dear. My stars, this is going to be expensive. How can I afford it?"

"We could loan her a few hundred dollars, couldn't we, Hannah?" Kiki asked, after swallowing a bite of French toast. "If we didn't do the weekend in Monterey we planned?"

"Of course," Hannah said. After drying her hands, she got the blender from the cabinet and placed it on the counter.

"That's so sweet and generous, and the very offer is karma enhancing, I'm sure," Naomi said. "But a few hundred dollars isn't going to do it. My contractor says it will cost three thousand."

Hannah and Kiki's mouths dropped open at such a large and unobtainable sum.

"You see my problem. I've just got to come up with a money-making concept," Naomi said, her gaze drifting off as she peeled her banana. "I must get my creative energies flowing."

"I'm sure you'll get them flowing in no time. Now Naomi, on another subject," Kiki said, her voice low and earnest. "What about the, you know, thing you were going to get for me?" Naomi gave her a questioning look. Kiki exhaled with aggravation. "You know, the *thing*."

"Oh, the love potion," Naomi said with a flamboyant wave of her banana that sent its top half flying to the floor. Sylvia quickly gobbled it while Teresa looked on with curious brown eyes, amazed at the things the pig would eat. Naomi dropped the remainder of the banana in the blender.

"The what?" Hannah asked.

"The love potion," Naomi replied, adding the soy milk. "I'm anxious to give it a try. It could turn out to be a lucrative side business for me, which Lord knows I could use." She flipped on the blender, and it came to life with a high-pitched whir.

Hannah worked hard to suppress her laughter. "Kiki, don't you have enough confidence in your own womanly charms?"

Swallowing the last bite of French toast, Kiki drew herself up. "Of course I do. It's just that with Lillian chasing after him—she's so pushy sometimes—I think a little extra help couldn't hurt. And you're always saying I should expand my interests. This is just like science."

"It certainly is. This potion is the best in the business," Naomi said, pouring her smoothie into a glass. "I found out about it from a good friend in L.A. who's a psychic who got it from a certified witch who does spells for movie stars. How do you think Nicole Kidman got Tom Cruise?"

"Just imagine, a love potion recipe that comes from the witch to the stars," Kiki said dreamily.

Hannah looked at Naomi with wariness. "What's in it?"

"I'm not sure yet, but my friend said it's a recipe from the twelfth century," Naomi explained, her tone important. "It uses ancient mystical powers, and it comes from crone women who live in stone huts in the mountains of Montenegro. My friend's going to e-mail it to me."

Hannah shook her head as she put the skillet in the rack and dried her hands with a dish towel. Although she loved Kiki and Naomi dearly, they occasionally exhibited the analytical skills of plankton.

While Kiki and Naomi chatted excitedly about the potion, Hannah again phoned Geraldine. She let it ring eight times, then hung up, filled with even more worry. What if Geraldine had hurt herself or was too sick to call for help? On the other hand, she could just as easily be running an errand. Their appointment wasn't until nine, so there was no reason for her to panic about Geraldine not being home at eight, Hannah told herself. After considering it a moment longer, she made a decision. She sat down at the kitchen table and pulled on her crepe-soled flats with arch supports.

"Where are you going?" Kiki asked.

"To Geraldine's."

"But you're not supposed to meet her until later," Kiki

said. "Don't you want to stay with us and talk about the love potion? There are some rituals we're going to have to do. It all sounds so exciting."

"Hannah's not interested in the least," Naomi said. "She has no sense of the mystical or spiritual. She only believes in what she can hear and see."

Hannah moved to the kitchen doorway. "You're both grown women, and if you want to spend your time on something as absurd as a love potion, that's your business. Personally, I believe in rational thought, facts, and data," Hannah said, then turned and walked out the front door to pursue the instinct she felt swimming in her gut.

Hannah pulled the gold 1972 Cadillac Eldorado convertible in front of Geraldine's house on Cypress Avenue, the old car letting out a groan and a shiver after she turned off the engine. The Cadillac was famous in Hill Creek, an anomaly in the Marin County world of sleek Mercedes and BMWs. It had come to Hannah along with Kiki, and she had grown to love it. It was every inch a woman's car, roomy with comfortable seats, smelling of perfume and pressed powder, and it drove more like a yacht than a car, never moving so fast that you couldn't change your mind about which turn to make. Machine and woman had bonded, the two being a lot alike—showing some wear yet still stylish, cantankerous at times but dependable in a pinch.

Hannah got out of the car, smoothed the front of her slacks and glanced up and down the street. The neighborhood was older, half residential and half commercial, sitting on the edge of town about a mile from Highway 101. It had been a long time since she had been there because she and Geraldine preferred getting together at the Book Stop. Hannah was surprised at how the neighborhood had improved, with many of the formerly run-down buildings smartly remodeled. It had been one of Hill Creek's less desirable neighborhoods, but in recent years the real estate values had shot upward, and Geraldine's small house was now probably very valuable.

Hannah headed up the uneven brick sidewalk. In spite of

the spruced-up neighborhood, the house was in the same slightly shabby state that she remembered, a sweet and tired-looking two stories covered with gray wood siding, the windows trimmed with peeling white shutters. The garden, filled with white potato vines, purple lavender, and pink shrub roses, appeared neglected. Its poor state surprised Hannah, and she made a mental note to come back with her clippers and do some trimming.

She reached the front door, her foot knocking into one of the dozen plants in chipped terra-cotta pots scattered around the porch. They all looked like foundlings that Geraldine had rescued. *How typical,* Hannah thought with a smile. Geraldine was always saving things from destruction. In some ways she had even saved Hannah so many years ago. Hannah had been rebellious and unhappy when she reached high school. Friends and activities had come naturally to Kiki, and observing her sister's social ease made it that much harder for Hannah, who never seemed to fit anywhere. But Geraldine had taken an interest in her, talking with her, helping her realize that uniqueness was a source of pride and not despair, and, best of all, seeding in her a love of poetry and books that stayed with her the rest of her life.

Hannah knocked on the door. No one answered. She rapped twice more, her anxiety growing when she still received no response. She peered into the window, but with the blinds halfway closed she saw nothing.

"Excuse me." Hannah heard a voice behind her and turned, finding a woman at the end of the walkway. She was about in her forties, had cropped hair, and wore blue jeans and a sweatshirt. She held a cardboard box that looked too big for her to be carrying. "You want Geraldine?"

"Yes. Do you know where she is?"

"Yeah, I do," the woman said, her tone apprehensive. She lumbered up the sidewalk, panting from the weight of the box.

Hannah met her on the steps. "Can I help you with that?"

"No, I'm okay. It's good for my arm muscles. I'm starting to get that wiggly wobbly stuff underneath." She rested the box on the railing. Hannah noticed her eyes, a clear gray rimmed with thick black lashes. "You're the second person who's come looking for her today. I'm Judy, her neighbor." She noticed Hannah glance at the small office building next door. "No, I live in the house on the other side. Listen, Geraldine got sick late last night. I saw the ambulance take her."

Hannah's previous misgivings hardened into something much worse. "What happened?"

"I'm not sure. I think she had trouble breathing or something. I checked a little while ago. She's in Marin Valley."

Hannah thanked her and hurried back to the Cadillac. The engine started smoothly, sensing that Hannah had no time for moodiness.

Marin Valley, a private hospital, wasn't far and Hannah arrived within ten minutes. After checking with the information desk she rode up in the elevator, emerging on the third floor into a short, wide hall. Walking briskly, she turned the corner into a longer hallway lined with patients' rooms. A nurse brushed past her, and Hannah followed her to the nurses' station at the far end of the hall. There several nurses in blue smocks busied themselves behind the desk, a uniformed young man whizzed by, pushing a metal cart, and an older man in street clothes, his arms filled with flowers, leaned over the counter, barking at one of the nurses. It was on the other side that she spotted Gilman. Wearing a white coat, he stood by the long L-shaped desk, reading the contents of a manila folder. Hannah hurried to him

"Ron, what's wrong with Geraldine? How is she?"

His eyes darting up from the papers, he looked irked at the interruption, but on seeing Hannah, his expression eased. He closed the folder.

"Hannah, I'm glad you're here. Her heart was racing last night and she dialed 911. The emergency room docs decided to keep her overnight for tests. I'd just come off the ward this morning when I found out she was here."

Hannah's insides clenched. "Was it a heart attack?"

"No, but they gave her an echocardiogram and didn't like the results. Apparently she's had mitral valve prolapse for years."

"Speak English."

"A heart valve problem, and it's gotten worse."

Hannah thought about the sorry condition of Geraldine's house and garden. She probably didn't have the strength to keep things up.

"They're going to replace the valve. She's scheduled for surgery first thing tomorrow morning, so they're keeping her overnight." He shook his head philosophically. "You know, I thought her color was off yesterday."

"Will she be all right?"

"Calm down, Hannah. Heart surgery is safe these days. Gerry's got a fine surgeon who does this kind of operation every day. Some patients are back playing tennis in a few weeks."

"How long has she known about the problem with her heart valve? I never knew about it."

"Neither did I, but I'm not her doctor. I haven't kept up with her other than our annual get-togethers, and you know how closed mouthed she always is about anything personal." He gave Hannah's shoulder a comforting squeeze. "Geraldine will be fine. A heart valve problem like hers is serious, but it can be repaired. Now go see her. She's in 324, down the hall on the left. She's been asking for you, and pretty insistently. I think she's getting tired of Vera and Lillian fussing over her."

"How did they know she was here?"

"I was on the phone with Lillian this morning just after I found out, and she called Vera. I just called your house a little while ago and left a message with Kiki. I apologize for not calling you first thing." He looked sincere. "My day's been hectic."

"It's okay, I understand." Gilman had his superficial flaws, but Hannah knew he had always been very caring when it came to his friends. She gave him a smile and he returned it. Only then did she notice his neatly slicked-back hair and the elegant red tie peeking out of his white jacket. Giving the air an exploratory sniff, she smelled his cologne, the subtle, rich kind that costs fifty dollars at Nordstrom's. She could save him a lot of time and money, she thought, and tell him that, from the way Lillian made goo-goo eyes at him the day before, he could skip bathing a week and dab cow manure behind his ears, and the woman would still be entranced by him. She would have to think of a gentle way to break the news to her sister.

Hannah located Geraldine's room, pausing in the doorway to gather up her most optimistic attitude before walking in. She peeked inside and saw sun streaming through the window, casting an angle of light on the floor.

Geraldine was awake, tucked beneath a blue blanket with only her arms, head, and shoulders exposed. A metal tray stand had been pulled in front of her, and on it sat a plastic cup with a lid and a bendable straw. Hannah tensed at the sight. It reminded her of her own hospital stay when she had her mastectomy. At the foot of the bed stood a nurse, her head bent over a chart. Vera sat in a chair by the wall, her face fretful, her fingers twisting the cotton of her skirt. Lillian, dressed up in a pantsuit and pearls, sat perched on the bed's edge, a compact in her hand, applying powder to Geraldine's cheeks.

"I don't want it," Geraldine said, not seeing Hannah. Lillian continued dabbing at her face with a small makeup brush.

"You need blusher. You already look much better," Lillian said with the forced exuberance she would have used with an eight-year-old.

"If you don't stop trying to make me look like a two-bit tart, I'm going to take the thing and throw it out the window," Geraldine told Lillian, the words tough but her voice without its usual vigor. The nurse lifted her eyes from the chart and looked at Lillian with disapproval. The nurse was pretty—youngish, black-haired and dark-eyed, about thirty-five. She was moving protectively in Geraldine's direction when Hannah interrupted.

"May I come in?" Hannah asked, stepping into the room.

Lillian looked up. "Hannah, please do."

Putting her handbag on a chair, Hannah went over and stood next to Lillian. A good look at Geraldine's face stunned her. She didn't know if Geraldine was really that pale or if it was only the contrast against the heavy circles of rouge on

her cheeks. If Hannah hadn't known better, she would have
thought Lillian intended to make Geraldine look ridiculous.

Vera must have seen Hannah's expression because she got
up out of her chair, grabbing a tissue from the box on the
nightstand.

"You put on way too much, Lillian," Vera scolded, reaching between her and Hannah and making ineffective swipes
at Geraldine's face.

"I did not. She needs color," Lillian said. "She's white as
a sheet."

"Well, she's pink as petunias now," Vera shot back.

Geraldine grabbed the tissue. "Will both of you leave me
in peace? And stop talking about me in the third person, like
I'm a corpse."

"I'm sorry, but it's time for all visitors to leave," the nurse
said firmly.

"I want Hannah to stay," Geraldine said. She looked anx-
iously at Hannah. "I need to talk to you." She raised up on
her elbows.

Out of the corner of her eye Hannah saw concern on the
nurse's face, and it made her think that Gilman had under-
stated the seriousness of Geraldine's condition. But she noted
with relief that Geraldine wasn't hooked up to oxygen or
monitoring equipment, which she took as a good sign.

"You must lie back, Mrs. Markham," the nurse said to
Geraldine, her manner gentle but firm.

Geraldine smiled. "Ruth takes flak from no one."

"Please listen to her, Gerry. You're very sick," Vera said,
her hands pressed together like she was praying. "And Ron
said that you must rest."

"Yes, you should follow Ron's instructions to the letter,"
Lillian said.

"He's an internist, not a cardiologist, and he's not even
my doctor," Geraldine told them, giving Lillian and Vera a
look that said she wished the floor would open up and swal-
low them both. She took hold of Hannah's wrist. "We need
to talk, Hannah. Alone."

Lillian went rigid. Vera sank back in her chair, looking
surprised.

"Well, of course, if you need to be alone, we'll be glad to leave," Lillian said tartly, standing. "You realize that Vera and I drove all the way over here and you've barely said a kind word to us."

"Leave her alone. If she wants to talk to Hannah, that's her business," Vera said, rising to her feet and gathering her coat and purse. "I see Ron. Come on, Lillian. Maybe he could have coffee with us in the cafeteria."

Lillian needed no more encouragement, the mention of Ron sending her fast as a bullet to the hallway, with Vera straggling behind.

The nurse walked to the door. "Five minutes, okay?" she said.

Geraldine nodded. Hannah pulled a chair close to the bed and sat.

"Thank God, they've gone. I know I was rude, but I've got a lot on my mind," Geraldine muttered. Her expression darkened. "I'm so glad you're here, Hannah. You have to help me." She pulled her body upward. "It's even more important now."

"Take it easy," Hannah said, gently pressing Geraldine back onto the bed. "Vera was right. You need to rest."

Geraldine relaxed into the pillow. "I'm not dead yet, you know."

"You're also not ready for a triathlon, either. You're having major surgery tomorrow."

Geraldine shrugged. "These days it's like changing a spark plug. Odds are I'll be back at the Book Stop swilling espresso within the week." She paused. "Still, there's always the chance something could happen."

"Ron said it's safe."

"The surgery's got a five percent mortality rate. I checked. That's why we have to talk."

"I'm ready when you are. I want to know what you were talking about yesterday."

Geraldine twisted on her side, her hand straining for the metal nightstand.

"What do you want?" Hannah asked. "Let me get it."

"My purse. Top drawer."

Hannah opened the drawer and pulled out a well-worn leather handbag that she handed to Geraldine. Geraldine unzipped it and pulled out a small ring of keys.

"I'll tell you everything, but first I need you to go to my house," she said, pressing the keys into Hannah's hand. "There's a wooden box sitting on top of a chest at the foot of my bed. Inside it is an envelope. You can't miss it. I want it here with me, and it'll help me explain things. Could you get it and bring it back to me? And please don't show it to anyone. It's private."

"Of course, but what's this all about? I'd like to hear about it now."

Hannah saw Geraldine's brain percolating, weighing what she should tell now and what should wait. Geraldine glanced away a second, and when she looked back at Hannah, her eyes signaled that she was going to spill it all, but a knock at the door caught her attention. Gilman stepped into the room.

"Gerry, you've really hurt Vera's feelings, and Lillian's in a snit. I know you're under a strain, but please apologize and make both our lives easier. You know how they are."

He didn't wait for a response, assuming his request would be obeyed. With a smile he turned to leave, but stopped in the doorway to chat with the nurse.

"We'll have to talk later," Geraldine said quietly, tipping her head toward Gilman, who was within eavesdropping distance. "They're doing tests on me today and they said I wouldn't be done until around four. Can you come back then?"

Consumed with curiosity, Hannah didn't want to wait for Geraldine's story. Her first impulse was to press her and get the whole thing right then, but she realized she shouldn't put pressure on someone with a heart condition. "Of course. Can I get you anything else while I'm at your house? How about a book and a fresh nightgown?"

"Don't fuss over me. It makes me feel like I'm ninety years old with a fractured hip. I just want the envelope. It's too risky to leave it at the house, even for a few hours."

Hannah heard Vera and Lillian's voices joining Gilman's in the hall as she stood to leave.

"And remember," Geraldine said, her eyes sliding briefly to the hall. "This is between us. Promise me."

"I promise," Hannah assured her. She said good-bye and walked into the hall.

"I'm going to be here first thing in the morning. I'd like to talk to Dr. Lee before she goes into surgery," Gilman said to Vera and Lillian as Hannah approached them just outside Geraldine's door. "And it will make her feel better if she has friends around."

"You're not telling us everything," Vera said. "You're trying to protect us. Gerry's really sick, I know it. She looks so awful."

"Vera, I can assure you—" Gilman started, but Vera didn't let him finish.

"You reach a certain age," she said with emotion. "And friends and family start dying."

Hannah listened to this with sympathy, knowing that Vera's husband had died a few years earlier.

"Please, Vera," Lillian said. "You're overreacting."

"I don't care what you or anybody else thinks," Vera said. "I'm coming back here and spending the night."

Lillian sighed. "It's not necessary."

"I'm spending the night," Vera said with firmness. "Gerry doesn't have any family, and regardless of what she says, I know she's frightened. She'll feel better if she knows someone is here."

Gilman opened his mouth to protest, but then stopped. He put his hand on Vera's shoulder, a gesture that didn't escape Lillian's notice. "I understand what you're feeling. You're a good friend."

"I'm going to stay tonight, too," Lillian quickly chimed in, and it was obvious that she said it only so Vera wouldn't outshine her in front of Gilman. Vera cast Lillian a disparaging look, then noticed Hannah.

"What did Gerry want to talk to you about?" Vera asked in an anxious tone that matched her expression.

"Yes, we're dying to know what was so secret," Lillian said.

"A secret means that you don't tell it," Hannah replied. Lillian responded with a pinched look. "It's just a simple errand," Hannah added, noticing the queasy feeling in her stomach she sometimes got when she told a lie. It was the truth, in a way, but deep inside she knew there was something very odd going on with Geraldine, and she was as interested as Vera and Lillian to find out what it was.

THREE

$\mathscr{T}$HE CADILLAC BELCHED GRAY SMOKE as Hannah pulled away from the stop sign, with Hannah on the verge of belching smoke herself, she was so rankled by her sister's fixation on love potions.

It being a fine sunny day, they drove to Geraldine's house with the convertible top down. Hannah never minded if her hair got mussed, but Kiki was fresh from the hairdresser and had that week's coiffure, a meringue-like helmet dyed a pinkish blonde not found in the human gene pool, wrapped in a long, narrow scarf, the ends flapping behind her like two wind socks.

"I'm going to say this again," Hannah said, gunning the engine and cutting over to the next lane.

"You've already said it ten times," Kiki replied, her tone blithe as she inspected her lipstick in her compact's mirror.

"But this time I want you to watch my lips, because I don't think you're getting it. There's no such thing as magic."

Still engrossed in her reflection, Kiki made kisses in front of the small mirror, then smoothed the edges of her lipstick with the tip of her little finger. "You're just grumpy because Geraldine's sick, but I'll tell you, hon, she'll probably be just fine, so try not to worry. She's strong as an ox." She snapped her compact shut. "I take your advice on a lot of things, but when it comes to the spirit world, you're just not in the know. Naomi's an expert on this stuff, and she says there's magic everywhere. No kidding, Hannah. She says it's in the food we eat, the air we breathe, that it's in trees and furniture and just about everything."

"Naomi also once said that she was getting alien signals through her hoop earrings."

"You know she was on pain medication for her sprained ankle when she said that, and we can't be sure it didn't happen. Besides, you can just take a chill pill." A grin on her face, Kiki cocked a thumb at her chest. "Because this old girl's in motion on the potion whether you like it or not. Ronnie will be all mine in a couple of days. He'll never know what hit him. Naomi got the E-mail from her witch friend, and we're going to start on it as soon as she's done at Wanda's."

"So that's where she is. I tried to call to confirm her for the poker game tonight."

"She's still on for the game, even though she's tied up almost all day. She and Wanda are talking to Zeno, I mean Uncle Marv."

As she made a right turn, Hannah jokingly wiggled her finger in her ear as if it needed unclogging. "Excuse me?"

"Oh, Hannah, it's so thrilling, like something you'd read in the *National Enquirer*. After talking it over with Wanda, Naomi's decided that Zeno really is the reincarnation of Uncle Marv. And Naomi needs extra cash, right? Well, it turns out that Uncle Marv was an investment counselor back in New Jersey. A real good one, and, according to Wanda, he made tons of money in computer stocks or something like that. So she and Naomi are getting investment advice from him. Naomi says they're going to get rich."

Hannah stopped the car at a red light. "Naomi's grasping at straws, she's so desperate for money, poor thing. She'd be better off just living with the termites. And exactly how are they planning to communicate with Uncle Marv?"

"Naomi said that first they're going to scratch his stomach and hand-feed him a little pastrami so he doesn't think they're only interested in money. Then they're going to label rubber balls with different stocks and investments, and see which one Uncle Marv chooses."

Hannah screwed up her face as she visualized this scene. The light changed and the Cadillac lurched forward. Kiki rubbed her hands together in anticipation. "I can't wait to get to Geraldine's."

"I still don't understand why you wanted to come with me. I'm just running an errand. I thought you had an appointment at Lady Nails this afternoon."

"I don't have an appointment exactly," Kiki said. "I was just going to hear the gossip, but I changed my mind."

Hannah found this very curious. Kiki normally loved gossip at Lady Nails the way a drunkard loves happy hour, and she rarely missed a chance to park herself in one of the pink vinyl chairs and catch up on the latest Hill Creek minutiae. Hannah hadn't told Kiki about the envelope, only that she was picking up something for Geraldine, and she knew Kiki assumed it was something simple like a nightgown. What could be so fascinating? Hannah asked her.

"I'll get to see her house and all her things," Kiki explained. "I love to look inside people's houses. You learn so much about them. I've known Geraldine for ages, but I haven't ever walked through her front door. There was always something a little mysterious about her."

"I'd just call her private."

Kiki leaned closer to her sister. "There's scuttlebutt around town. You want to hear it?"

"No."

"They say she got hurt by a man when she was really young and never got over it, and that the trauma left her sexually agnostic."

"You mean celibate."

"Don't correct me. I meant just what I said."

"So what if she is? It's none of our business and it doesn't change the way we feel about her."

"Of course. But still, it's interesting. Makes me want to take a peek in her lingerie drawer."

"You think she's going to have No Trespassing stamped on her panties?"

"Go ahead and joke, but you can tell a lot about a woman by looking at her underwear."

A few blocks before reaching the freeway Hannah turned left on Cypress Avenue, drove another two blocks, and parked at the curb in front of Geraldine's. After making their way up the sidewalk, Hannah pulled Geraldine's keys out of her purse, inserted the brass key in the lock, and opened the door.

They stepped into a darkened living room filled with fraying but comfortable furniture and aged oriental rugs on a wooden plank floor. A large bookcase covered the entirety of one wall, its shelves filled with old hardbacks. Hannah knew that Geraldine scavenged for them at garage sales the way she herself scavenged for old dishes. They had even gone garage sale shopping together a few times.

Going to the window, Kiki opened the shade, light spilling into the room. She turned just as Hannah closed the door. "That's strange."

"What?"

Kiki pointed to the door. "She has three bolts plus the chain."

Hannah looked at the heavy brass bolts, two of them gleaming with shiny newness. They had been recently installed. There hadn't been any rash of crime in Hill Creek, so why would Geraldine suddenly be so concerned about a break-in? Hannah remembered what she had said about being in some trouble, the idea sending a shiver up her neck. Yet it seemed unlikely that anyone would want to hurt Geraldine.

"I'm going to get the things she asked for. You wait here," Hannah said. She went into the bedroom. Pale yellow wallpaper covered the walls, and a scarred antique dresser sat opposite the bed, its top scattered with personal things—watch, hairbrush, a rumpled nightgown. Against the adjacent wall stood a desk covered with papers. The bed was unmade, and a depression in the pillow gave her the eerie feeling that some invisible person was lying there. A small table by the bed held a glass half full of water, a squeeze bottle of hand lotion, and a paperback novel. Hannah ran her hand over the white bedspread and touched the ruffled pillows. The room was frilly, so unlike Geraldine. Maybe Kiki was right, Hannah mused, and intimate possessions revealed the true woman. It made her curious about the contents of Geraldine's lingerie drawer.

Hannah heard a small crash from the living room. "Kiki, are you snooping?"

"Just bumped into something," Kiki called out. Hannah knew she was fibbing. She took the nightgown from the top of the dresser to make Kiki think it was what she had come for.

It was then she noticed the large, battered wooden chest sitting at the foot of the bed, and a much smaller walnut box sitting on its top. She opened the lid of the small box and found a white envelope, just as Geraldine had described. It rested on a pile of curled old black-and-white photographs. Without examining the box's contents, she slipped the envelope in her purse and started to close the lid, but the photograph on top of the pile caught her attention. She felt a powerful urge to take a closer look at it, but decided she shouldn't. She was there only to pick up something for a sick friend, not to rummage through the friend's things. She paused, curiosity getting the best of her. Her hand inched toward the photo.

"Is the little girls' room in here?" Kiki asked from the doorway. Hannah's hand jerked back. She knew that Kiki just wanted to check out Geraldine's bathroom, yet she could hardly criticize her sister for snooping when she was about to commit the same crime herself. She glanced guiltily in her sister's direction.

"I see it," Kiki said cheerfully, traipsing past Hannah into the bathroom and closing the door.

The briefest little peek at the photographs wouldn't hurt, Hannah told herself. She picked up the yellowed photo and was astounded by what she saw. Geraldine stared back at her, but not the Geraldine she knew. This was the deluxe model, fully loaded and with all the options. She looked a lot younger, twenty to thirty years minimum, and her eyes were heavily made up, her lips rouged. She wore a low-cut dress that showed off her breasts, dangly earrings, and a strand of pearls around her neck. She leaned back sensuously against a tree, her head tipped slightly downward, eyes aimed seductively at the camera.

Hannah jumped when she heard the sound of Kiki pawing through Geraldine's medicine cabinet, most likely looking for jars labeled "Sexual Abstinence Cream." Now that the crime of snooping had begun, Hannah resumed with fervor, eagerly looking through more photos. She found several with rickshaws in the background and strange writing on the shop signs that told her they had been taken in Asia. Geraldine posed with the same man in several of them, a dapper-looking guy in a sport coat and slacks, Geraldine usually draped against him. In another photo the camera caught them sitting at a table holding sparkling martinis, looking giddy and in love, the kind of love that blossoms from a person's third cocktail. Her man was a handsome one, with an even nose and a strong chin. And lust in his eyes, Hannah thought, feeling a tingle of pleasure. It looked like Geraldine wasn't quite the dull spinster everyone had thought.

Something hit the bathroom floor. "I can hear you," Hannah said loudly, fully aware of her hypocrisy. Still, a person's medicine cabinet was different. "It's very tacky."

The door opened. "I think she's got stomach problems. There are lots of antacids," Kiki said, then remembered herself. "I was just looking for an aspirin. I think I'm getting a headache."

"Since you're intent upon prying, I have proof that Geraldine isn't sexually agnostic, as you call it."

Kiki hurried over to her sister. "You've been through her underwear?"

"Of course not, but look at this. Geraldine had a boyfriend, and it was when she was middle-aged." She held up one of the pictures. "This doesn't say agnostic to me. This says praise the Lord and hallelujah."

Taking the picture, Kiki studied it. "Ooh, la, la," she said, a lurid smile spreading across her face. "Our Geraldine did know some men."

"She knew this one, that's for sure. I suppose it could have been a onetime adventure."

Kiki shook her head. "If it was a onetime experience, she'd have an embarrassed, silly look on her face. But here she looks really confident."

Hannah took the photo from her sister and gave it another look. "Yes, she's showing the learned eye of a connoisseur." She put it back in the box and closed it. "We've got to go. I told Geraldine I'd see her around four."

Due to Kiki applying a full array of Revlon products in the car, in hopes of seeing Gilman, Hannah had to drive at a snail's pace and they arrived late at the hospital. When they reached Geraldine's room, they found her bed empty. A tall and imposing nurse told them that Geraldine's tests had been delayed and that she had just gone in for them a few minutes earlier. The nurse said it would be pointless to wait, since Geraldine wouldn't be done for a couple of hours, and by that time visiting hours would be over. When Hannah mentioned that Lillian and Vera were spending the night in the waiting room, the nurse assured her that even they wouldn't be able to see Geraldine until late the next morning, after her surgery.

Geraldine had insisted upon such secrecy regarding the envelope that Hannah didn't feel comfortable leaving it, so she kept it in her purse. As she and Kiki rode the elevator down to the lobby, she felt an anxiety that her sister couldn't help but notice.

"It's okay, Hannah. We left the nightgown. You did what she wanted."

But that was just it, Hannah thought. What *did* Geraldine want from her? She had told Hannah that she was in trouble, and the more Hannah considered it, the more she felt that it wasn't a coincidence that there were two new bolts on her door. And what was in the envelope that was so important that Geraldine was afraid to leave it at home?

FOUR

"I'LL SEE YOUR EARRING," KIKI said, her eyes glinting with bare aggression. The tension in the air was as thick as pancake makeup on a fifty-year-old hooker. Kiki pulled the dangly beaded earring from her earlobe and slapped it on the table with a melodramatic whack. Nostrils flaring, she leaned forward menacingly, giving Naomi a chilly stare. "And raise you *an outer garment.*"

The other three women at the old polished oak table emitted shocked gasps. Not that these Wednesday night poker games had ever been tranquil, especially when Kiki mixed up a batch of peach margaritas, as she had that evening. There had always been minor spats, a couple of cards thrown, a few accusations hurled, and that infamous time when Kiki, having overindulged a bit, puked up three Moon Pies and half a cheesecake all over Hannah's royal flush. That was part of the fun. But never had such raw, unconstrained excitement filled Hannah's rose-colored dining room as it did that evening. An outer garment for Kiki meant at most a blouse. For caftan-clad Naomi, it was the whole enchilada.

Having already folded, Hannah grabbed a Milano Mint cookie from the antique buffet table, snapped it into small pieces, and surreptitiously fed bits to the dog and pig under

the table. She felt certain that her sister's bravado was
founded on vapor. Poker confused Kiki, and she seldom remembered what hands beat what. But it had been her decision to forgo their normal ten-cent-per-bet limit and sail into
the risky seas of strip poker, these waters made more treach-
erous by an addition Hannah made to the stakes—at the end
of the evening they would take a Polaroid of the player with
the least clothes and pin it to the bulletin board at Lady Nails.
If Kiki lost her blouse on this hand, she could be the butt of
jokes over the manicure table for months to come.

Lauren, who was Hannah and Kiki's twenty-eight-year-old
niece, completed the poker foursome. Sweet Lauren was a
timid accountant doted upon by her aunts since her mother's
death ten years before, and she currently suffered from her
recently dashed romance with Detective Larry Morgan, a
member of Hill Creek's police department. Normally Hannah
wouldn't have approved of anything as silly (and potentially
perilous) as strip poker, but tonight she was willing to try
anything to distract Lauren, not to mention that she needed
a little distraction herself.

Ever since her discussion with Geraldine that morning and
her subsequent retrieval of the envelope, the idea of Geraldine's troubles and the bolts on her door had been a rash on
Hannah's brain that wanted scratching. She chided herself
for not putting up more of an argument with that nurse and
maneuvering her way into seeing Geraldine. She had been
spineless to allow herself to be stopped by some silly hospital
rules when she had promised Geraldine she would come back
that day. Hannah stared at her purse on the buffet, knowing
it contained the envelope, longing to know what was inside,
but not feeling right about looking. Yet in spite of this she
had managed to win most of the poker hands and was still,
along with Lauren, fully clothed.

Playing with skill and caution, Hannah was mindful to not
lose her blouse. When she had her double mastectomy eight
years earlier, she had forgone reconstructive surgery, accepting the scarred landscape of her chest. But a few months
earlier, without telling a soul, she went to San Francisco and
had a garland of ivy and flowers tattooed where her breasts

had once been. She had shown it only to Kiki and to her boyfriend, John Perez, and it had taken her a while to get the nerve to show it to them. She wasn't ready to display it to anyone else.

"Maybe you should fold," Lauren said nervously to Naomi, her cheeks flushed from the game's high suspense.

"No," Naomi replied, feeling confident because she was wearing her lucky turban, a twisted pile of white fabric with bright red splotches that made her look like the victim of some type of primitive brain surgery that hadn't gone well. She stared at her cards, then took a bolstering gulp of peach margarita, scrunching her nose from the icy cold. Hannah knew that Naomi had weighed her odds carefully. Naomi was already in the embarrassing position of having lost her queen-sized control-top support hose and a pair of Halloween socks, garments she hadn't been too keen on having her friends know she wore. No telling what surprises would emerge from under that caftan before the night was over.

"Okay, show me what you've got," Naomi said gruffly, the fresh tequila reaching her bloodstream.

With a delighted squeal, Kiki put her cards on the table, displaying three queens. Her mirth evaporated when Naomi slapped down three jacks and two aces.

Kiki's face crumpled with anguish. "That's not fair. You're psychic. Red Moon told you what cards I had."

"Absurd," Naomi replied. "Red Moon doesn't approve of games of chance." She cleared her throat. "Maybe you should turn up the heat, Hannah. Kiki may get chilly without her blouse."

Humiliated, Kiki unbuttoned and removed her blouse, revealing a blue velvet bra with "Maui" embroidered on the left cup, its engineering pushing her breasts upward so they looked like two breaching white whales in an azure sea.

"It's your turn to deal, Lauren," Kiki said, chin lifted with dignity as she pretended not to notice everyone staring at her bra with question marks in their eyes. They all knew she had never been to Maui. "What's your game?"

After a moment of inner turmoil, Lauren replied with "Indian," the game she always chose, one that required the players to hold their cards face out against their foreheads, allowing you to see every player's cards except your own. Lauren gathered up the cards and shuffled them.

"How are things going with Uncle Marv?" Hannah asked Naomi, a sly smile spreading across her face.

"I hear the sarcasm in your voice," Naomi said. "Scoff if you like, but he recommended a European commodities fund that I have great hopes for."

"How does Uncle Marv tell you which fund you should buy?" Lauren asked, dealing the cards.

"It was ticklish at first," Naomi said. "But Wanda and I came up with a system. We pick out some recommendations from this investment newsletter Walter gets."

This alerted Hannah's suspicions since Wanda's husband Walter, though amiable, was normally filled to the gills with vodka, and, as far as Hannah knew, had never made an honest nickel. They lived off Wanda's lavish divorce settlements from previous, more ambitious husbands.

Naomi continued. "Then we write down the names of the investments on yellow sticky notes and put them on identical red rubber balls. Whichever ball Uncle Marv bites is the fund we go for. This afternoon he bit into that European commodity fund and took it right under the bed, so I'm feeling especially optimistic."

Lauren finished dealing and everyone picked up their cards and, without looking at them, held them face out against their foreheads. The players, much more interested in the conversation than in poker, didn't even glance at each other's hands.

"Where are you getting money to invest?" Lauren asked.

"I'm tapping into my IRA."

Hannah frowned. "That's very foolish, Naomi. Is it too late to get your money back?"

"You're such a worrier," Naomi told her. "You've been in a snit all night."

"Aunt Hannah, you do seem a little down," Lauren said. "Is anything wrong? You're not worried about Larry and me, are you? Because if we're meant to be together, I'm sure it will happen."

At this intriguing allusion to Lauren's hampered love, the

women focused a laserlike attention on her, saw she had three tens pressed against her forehead, and immediately all folded.

"Don't worry, dear," Naomi said, tossing down her cards. "I'm making a love potion for Kiki, and I'll just double the recipe for you."

"Hannah's worried about Geraldine," Kiki said, still cranky. She couldn't understand why she was so unlucky at cards. If her bad luck continued, she would be bared down to her underwear in half an hour. She had to figure out a way to escape playing altogether. It was her turn to deal, and she swept the cards toward her.

"I'm so sorry, Aunt Hannah. I'd forgotten. But, you know, heart surgery is so common these days," Lauren said, looking at Hannah tenderly. "I'm sure Geraldine will do well."

"I'm concerned about the surgery, naturally. But you see, there's something else," Hannah said, immediately regretting the admission.

"What is it?" Kiki asked.

"I just think there's something very peculiar going on with Geraldine," Hannah said.

"Sure there is," Kiki replied. "Her ticker's going kaplunk."

"That's bad enough, but there's more. I have the strongest feeling—" Hannah stopped in mid-sentence, knowing she shouldn't discuss it, but she had gone too far.

"What, Aunt Hannah?" Lauren asked. The women all stared at Hannah with the keen-eyed expectancy of a bird spying a particularly plump worm.

"I have a feeling there's something else very wrong with Geraldine. Something unrelated to her heart problem."

Naomi leaned forward, eyebrows raised. "When you say 'feeling,' do you mean you think it in your head or you feel it in your body?"

Hannah didn't have an answer and wasn't especially interested in analyzing it, since in the previous sixty seconds she had decided that she was definitely going to the hospital to see Geraldine and was going right then. Silly hospital rules about visiting hours were no reason not to fulfill a promise made to a sick friend. But if she directly announced her intention, she would have to endure a half-hour of questions, complaints, and impassioned entreaties to stay home, since the women at the table weren't impressed by reasoned decision-making. On the other hand, if she claimed that unseen spirits were talking to her or that aliens from the planet Veezob were giving her psychic instructions, it would be accepted without question.

Closing her eyes, Hannah placed her hand on her stomach. "I guess I feel it here. It's a tightening sensation, like an invisible cord pulling me." She barely opened one eye and saw everyone looking at her with rapt interest.

Naomi turned up her palms. "That's it, then," she said excitedly. "Hannah, it's a personal breakthrough. You're having a psychic experience and you have to tap into that energy. You must look inward. You must heed the message. What's it telling you to do?"

"To go see Geraldine," Hannah replied. She stood up.

Naomi sat back in her chair and crossed her arms with professional satisfaction. "It's so rewarding to provide fellow souls with guidance."

"You're going right now?" Lauren asked, looking skeptical. "It's after ten."

"She must," Naomi said.

"I must," Hannah echoed. "Just play without me." When she went to her bedroom to get her coat, she heard Kiki behind her.

"I'm coming, too," Kiki said, buttoning up her blouse. "I don't think you should go out so late by yourself."

"That's fine, but you'll have to wait in the car," Hannah told her. She knew that Kiki wanted any excuse to avoid having her picture taken in her underwear, since she had recently gained ten pounds, and Hannah was happy to oblige.

The game broke up, with Lauren and Naomi staying to clean up the mess. After a round of good-night hugs, Hannah and Kiki put up the convertible top on the Cadillac, it being a chilly night, and headed for the hospital with Hannah behind the wheel. When they arrived, Kiki refused to wait in the car. Hannah didn't blame her, the parking lot being empty and poorly lighted, so she allowed her to come along on the condition that she would wait outside the room if Geraldine wanted to have a private conversation.

Together they walked up to the hospital's main entrance and found the doors locked and no guard in sight.

"Darn it. I guess we'll just have to come back tomorrow," Kiki said.

"Don't be so easily discouraged," Hannah replied. "Follow me." They went down the walkway along the side of the building, turning left at a red-and-white-lighted sign that read Emergency Entrance. There, automatic double glass doors slid open and they stepped through. Kiki gave Hannah a questioning glance, but followed her into a plain white-walled room with uncomfortable-looking gray chairs lined against the walls, all of the chairs empty. It was a weeknight, a slower time for any emergency room, but especially for Marin Valley, since most people in the area preferred the larger hospitals in the county for emergencies.

They hurriedly tiptoed through the emergency room lobby, Kiki freezing when they saw a doctor and two nurses in an adjacent room huddled over a man thrashing on a gurney. Hannah took her hand and pulled her forward. The doctor and nurses were too busy with their patient to notice the two women.

"Is this illegal?" Kiki asked once they were safely in the elevator.

"Of course not. We're bending the rules a little, that's all."

"So why do I feel like this is an arrestable offense?"

"It's not," Hannah told her. "On the other hand, it would be better if no one saw us."

"And what does Geraldine want to talk to you about that's so secret?"

"Just a personal issue, that's all. Now be quiet."

The elevator doors opened on the third floor, the hall's stillness filling Hannah with trepidation that matched her sister's. She and Kiki turned down the corridor, reaching the next hallway and the patients' rooms. They started down the hall, then, hearing footsteps, ducked inside a linen closet. When the sound disappeared, the two women slipped back into the hallway. Nervous from that close call, they hurried to Geraldine's room and found the door half-closed.

"What if she's asleep?" Kiki whispered.

"We'll just wake her."

"She's going to be excited to see us. It's like a slumber party."

Hannah knocked gently on the door, then opened it, and she and Kiki stepped inside.

"*Hellooo,* Geraldine," Kiki said in a singsong whisper. "Wake up, sleepy head. You have visitors."

Hannah stepped close to the bed, and with her next inhalation her throat constricted, her earlier misgivings congealing into cold fear. Geraldine was dead. Hannah couldn't have said exactly how she knew. Geraldine's eyes were closed, her face relaxed and undisturbed, but there was a thick air of death in the room that Hannah felt in every nerve and artery. She pressed her fingers to Geraldine's wrist, hoping desperately she was wrong.

"Why are you doing that?" Kiki asked, her tone panicky.

Geraldine's skin felt warm, but Hannah detected no pulse.

"No," she pleaded softly, feeling bile rise in her throat.

She heard Kiki's shoes against the linoleum floor as her sister went to the other side of the bed. Looking up, Hannah saw her sister's face frozen in horror. Kiki tended to be a few beats behind on things, and Hannah assumed that the truth of Geraldine's condition had just hit her.

"Yes, she's dead," Hannah said, her voice breaking. Kiki, too stunned to speak, looked at her sister with wide, fearful eyes. Kiki violently shook her head, her dangly earrings slapping against her cheeks. "I know it's hard to accept, sweetie, but it's true. I checked her pulse."

Hannah's foot brushed against something soft. She looked down and saw a pillow on the floor. It was halfway under the bed, but it stuck out enough so that she saw a pink streak on the white casing. Hannah knelt down and examined it. The pink smudge was makeup. Hannah remembered Lillian putting the heavy blusher on Geraldine earlier that day.

Straightening, Hannah noticed Kiki still on the other side of Geraldine's bed, but now with one hand pressed against her mouth like she was going to throw up. Kiki frantically jabbed downward with her index finger.

"How can you think such a thing?" Hannah said, tears starting to well up. "If there's a heaven, I'm sure Geraldine will go there."

Removing her hand from her face, Kiki opened her mouth, but only impotent peeps came out.

"What is it?" Hannah asked, receiving only a flailing of hands in response. Kiki waved her over. Hannah took a couple of steps and then let out the horrified yell that her sister couldn't.

On the floor a white-coated orderly lay on his back, his body twisted, one arm flung out to the side. His eyes were open and dully staring upward, his lips parted as if just on the verge of a scream, and a gleaming pair of scissors was plunged deep into his blood-soaked chest.

FIVE

*I*T AMAZED HANNAH HOW RATTLED the hospital staff became over the sight of a dead man. Her own panic was understandable, but surely these medical professionals had seen so much death in their careers that one more corpse would hardly be worth a notice, but the sight of the deceased orderly sent the whole night shift into barely controlled hysteria. Of course, it was the scissors in his chest causing all the fuss.

Hannah stood in the hallway, hands trembling, fighting the urge to cry. She didn't have the luxury of falling apart. Kiki, Vera, and Lillian had already usurped that privilege, and they left Hannah too busy ministering to them to deal with her own misery.

The furor started as soon as Hannah saw the dead man on the floor, for, after she screamed, Kiki's vocal capabilities returned with the force of a tidal wave. Hannah, being experienced with hospitals from her surgery and volunteer work, hit the Code Blue emergency button near the bed, but it was Kiki's howl that brought two nurses running. The first nurse screamed when she saw the orderly, but the second one kept her head and pushed Hannah and Kiki out of the room to make space for the doctor and additional nurse who quickly arrived. The commotion soon brought Vera and Lillian from the lounge in the adjacent hall, more hospital staff, and several patients dragging their IVs behind them. Within minutes more people from other floors turned up to see what was happening, and the hall outside Geraldine's room became chaos.

As soon as Vera heard that Geraldine was dead, she shoved past a nurse, caught sight of the man lying bloody on the floor, ran back into the hallway, and promptly threw up. Hannah held a wastebasket under Vera's head while Lillian shrieked, Kiki sobbed, and a team of doctors and nurses worked furiously on Geraldine as well as the orderly.

Hannah told Kiki and Lillian to take Vera to the ladies room, then she secured a spot in the hallway and watched while the doctors and nurses tried unsuccessfully to resuscitate Geraldine and her unwitting companion. Hannah couldn't see what was going on, but it didn't take long for her to surmise with grief that both of them were beyond help. Seconds later more hospital staff arrived, some entering Geraldine's room, others trying to calm the rest of the patients. Everyone had sick looks on their faces.

Kiki, Vera, and Lillian returned from the rest room, with Vera pale, her hair wet from splashing her face with water, and Lillian popping Valium, yelling out her fears that a mad killer was loose in the building. Hannah thought she had a point. Hannah put an arm around a still crying Kiki, and within a few seconds she had a sobbing Vera in her other arm. Once Hannah heard a doctor confirm the death of both Geraldine and the orderly, she warned the gathering crowd to stay out of the room until the police got there. They didn't have long to wait. Already having been called, the police arrived within seconds and immediately cordoned off the room. Detective Larry Morgan, Lauren's heartthrob and Hannah's friend, arrived with the second group of officers. His mind on other things, he brushed past Hannah without noticing her.

A few minutes later, after an officer led Kiki away for questioning, a second officer took Hannah into an empty office and questioned her on what she was doing in the hospital after visiting hours, and what she had seen in Geraldine's room. She explained everything as truthfully and completely as she could, including what Geraldine had said about being in trouble and uncovering something illegal. But when she came to the envelope, she held back. Geraldine had asked her not to tell anyone about it. The bizarre circumstances around her death would make such a promise moot if the information could help explain what happened to the orderly. But Geraldine had given no clue regarding the envelope's contents. What if it contained personal information that she wouldn't have wanted made public? It could be an old love letter, financial information, poetry she had written. The last thing Hannah wanted was to withhold information from the police, but it seemed disrespectful to her friend to tell the police about what was in the envelope without at first taking a look at it. She decided to open the envelope as soon as she had some privacy, and then, if necessary, give it to an officer.

When the initial questioning was over, the officers left Hannah and Kiki at the nurses' station, where the sisters were instructed to wait. They sat in ergonomically correct chairs with Kiki sobbing, telling Hannah over and over how they should have stayed home and played poker, even if they had to strip buck naked and have their photos posted at Lady Nails. Barely hearing her sister, Hannah sat quietly, her hands in her lap, the reality of what had happened grinding into her.

She got up, leaned over the counter, and looked down the hallway at Geraldine's room. She saw an officer with a video camera turn the corner, followed by two men wearing county sheriff's department jackets and carrying blue vinyl bags. The sight made Hannah feel nausea. Geraldine was a thing now, a depersonalized object to be examined and videotaped. She wondered if the police had seen the makeup smudge on the pillowcase.

She felt a hand on her shoulder, and turned to find Kiki with big tears running down her face, most of her makeup washed away. The sight of Kiki crying always turned Hannah to mush, and she put her arms around her sister and held her close.

"This is so awful. Poor, poor Geraldine," Kiki said. "I mean, how did that dead man get in her room? It's all so tacky." Kiki looked at her sister with pleading eyes. "What was he doing there?"

Hannah didn't want Kiki to know what she was thinking. She supposed Geraldine could have gotten makeup on the pillowcase as she slept, but when Hannah walked into the room, Geraldine already had a pillow under her head.

Gilman saved her from answering Kiki's question. "What happened?" he asked as he approached, voicing the same question on everyone's lips. He wore a stunned look.

Hannah shook her head. "We found her. That's all I can tell you. How did you find out?"

"I was in the lab looking at X-rays and heard the emergency code. I don't understand any of this."

Hannah glanced at her Seiko. It was close to midnight. "You work this late?"

"Not usually, but I'm on call tonight and got beeped around nine-thirty. I came here to work with a patient in emergency, and when I was done, I thought I'd finish up my notes on some X-rays so I could be with Geraldine early tomorrow." He paused. "Before she went into surgery." He looked down the hall toward her room. He shook his head with confusion, then moved his eyes back to Hannah. "How did you get in here at this late hour?"

The police hadn't asked nearly so politely. Hannah was about to explain, but Kiki interrupted by flying to Gilman's side.

"Oh, Ronnie, I'm just crushed," she said, hanging onto him with an iron grip. She leaned her head against his shoulder.

He looked uncomfortable. "We have to be strong."

"I feel so much better with you here," Kiki replied with the frail girlish voice she had been using on men since she was thirteen. Hannah wondered if Kiki realized she had cried off all her makeup and had big gray circles around each eye. As Kiki gazed up at Gilman, looking like a lovesick raccoon, she ran her hand up his arm and he placed his fingers on top of hers. This Kodak moment was shattered by Lillian march-

ing up with Vera in tow. Vera looked pale. Lillian had fresh-
ened her lipstick.

"I have a good mind to sue this hospital," Lillian said,
looking straight at Gilman as she deftly pushed his hand off
Kiki's.

"You can't blame the hospital," Vera said, a tissue pressed
to her nose.

"And why not?" Lillian said. "It's their lax security that's
responsible for this tragedy. A stranger murdered in Geraldine's very hospital room, for God's sake. Obviously, the
sight of it killed her."

Kiki nodded, her hand inching back toward Gilman. "With
her weak heart and all."

"You think that somebody chased an orderly into Geraldine's room and murdered him while she watched?" Hannah
asked with disbelief.

Vera let out a woeful groan and looked like she might
throw up again. Everyone backed a few paces away from
her. Lillian offered her a Valium, which she refused. Lillian
then offered the drug to the rest of the group, but no one
took her up on it except a stressed-looking nurse who happened to be passing by. She took two.

"But he wasn't an orderly," Gilman said. "I heard the
nurses talking. Nobody recognized him, and he didn't have
a hospital ID."

"But he was wearing an orderly's jacket," Hannah said.

"He could have easily gotten it from a local uniform store,
or he could have stolen one here in the hospital," Gilman
said. "Drug addicts sneak into the hospital to steal drugs. It's
rare, but it happens."

"If he was a drug addict, maybe his drug dealer followed
him into the hospital and killed him," Kiki suggested. "He
could have owed him money."

"But I definitely saw scissors in his chest," Hannah replied.
"No drug dealer would use scissors as a weapon."

"But Hannah," Vera said. "Somebody could have stolen
them just like someone could have stolen the jacket."

"What other explanation could there be?" Lillian said,

sounding shrill. "Do you think Geraldine killed the man, then a few minutes later died from the shock?"

"No, of course not," Hannah answered.

"How come the nurses didn't know when Geraldine died?" Vera asked, her voice now thick with tears. "Aren't buzzers supposed to go off when someone stops breathing?"

"Only if they're hooked up to one of those machines," Lillian said with a know-it-all tone. "And Geraldine wasn't."

Hannah saw Detective Morgan coming down the hallway, his baby face weary. He wore rumpled khakis and a T-shirt topped with a leather jacket, and Hannah knew he had gotten out of bed to come there. Her heart went out to him when she saw the grim look on his face. He was a worrier, and, in Hannah's opinion, way too sensitive for such a harsh profession.

He approached the group with no salutation. "Mrs. Malloy, I need to talk to you, please." His tone came out flat and professional. Kiki cast a worried glance at her sister. Hannah gave Morgan a nod and followed him around the corner, stopping near a water cooler.

"You and your sister are going to have to come to the station to give a formal statement," he said. "I believe we already have your fingerprints on file."

"Are we suspects?"

"Everyone in the hospital tonight is a suspect. The fact that you and your sister sneaked in here after hours doesn't look great."

"We didn't sneak in anywhere," Hannah told him, drawing herself up. "We walked right in through the emergency room door. Surely there's a security camera that will confirm it. No one tried to stop us and we didn't evade anyone." This last part wasn't quite true, but she didn't want to confuse him with unnecessary details, especially when they could be incriminating. She took a step, lessening the distance between them. "Do you know how Geraldine died?"

"We don't have a handle on it yet."

"Have you identified the murdered man? I heard he wasn't a hospital employee."

"I can't say. Listen, I've got to get back."

"Please, wait." Hannah looked around to make sure no one could overhear. "I saw the pillow on the floor and the makeup on the case," she whispered. "Was she smothered?"

He gave her a hard look. "Did you touch anything in that room?"

"I kicked the pillow a little when I was taking Geraldine's pulse, and I told the other officer about it. But other than that, I don't think so."

He took a paper cup from a metal cylinder on the wall, filled it with water from the cooler, and offered it to her. When she declined, he downed it, then tossed the cup in the trash.

"Is there anything at all you can tell me?" she asked, her voice quiet. "Geraldine was an old friend."

Morgan relaxed a little. "Listen, Mrs. Malloy, you know how much I respect you, but I can't give out that information. I'm sorry, but I've got to do my job." He walked a few steps away, then stopped. "How's Lauren?"

"She's fine. She's coming to our house for dinner tomorrow night. You want to join us?" Hannah had no actual plans for dinner with Lauren the next night, but plans could be arranged.

"I have a feeling I'm going to be busy this week with this case." The words stuck in his throat a minute before he got them out, and Hannah realized with a jolt that he probably couldn't have dinner with a murder suspect. He looked at Hannah, and she could see a new idea forming in his head. "You know, you might be able to help with something. Wait here."

He left, returning a moment later carrying a small plastic bag. He held it out to her. "Do you recognize this picture?" he asked. It held a photo, about one by two inches. She examined it through the plastic and realized she had seen the same one earlier that day.

"This is an old picture of Geraldine. It's from a forty-five-year-old high school yearbook."

Morgan took the bag back. "I thought it was probably her, but I wasn't sure." He gave his head a small shake. "I don't get it."

"What do you mean? Where did that come from?"

Morgan leveled his eyes at her. "From the murdered man's pocket."

At four in the morning a sad stillness had settled over Hannah's rose-covered cottage, an agitated quiet she felt in her bones. Wrapped in her flannel robe, she sat in her favorite squishy chair by the window, staring out into the darkness, finding it hard to shake the image of Geraldine's yearbook picture from her mind. She found it even harder to figure out how it had gotten into the dead man's pocket.

She and Kiki had spent a long hour at the police station. Kiki had cried when they first arrived, but when she laid eyes on the good-looking male officer, she dried her tears and combed her hair. The sisters were each taken to a different room. Hannah knew the police had separated them so, just in case they were cold-blooded murderers, they could have their cover stories tripped up under questioning. But Hannah knew that Kiki's story, though perhaps embellished, would match hers. That would be in their favor.

Hannah's statement was tape-recorded. She answered the questions calmly, trying her best to help where she could. Except for the envelope. That she had continued to keep secret because she hadn't had any time alone to look at it. She felt guilty not mentioning it, but she knew she could bring it to the police later, claiming that in her distress it had slipped her mind. The police would believe her. It was one of the advantages of being a middle-class woman in your sixties. People almost always underestimated you.

Her face shiny from cold cream residue, Kiki padded into the living room, wearing a ruffled pink nightgown made of a silk-simulating synthetic. "Are you okay, Hannah? Why are you sitting in the dark?"

"I'm just thinking, that's all. You go to bed and get a few hours' sleep."

"You want some cocoa?"

"No thanks."

Kiki came closer. "If it will make you feel better, I thought of a positive aspect of this terrible thing that's happened."

"What?"

"Just that, at least Geraldine didn't die alone. There was someone there with her."

"But who was he?" Hannah asked softly, not too certain that his presence was a reassuring thing. "What was he doing there, and who killed him?"

Kiki leaned back against the window ledge. "The police will figure it out. Try not to be so upset. At least Geraldine had a better life than we thought. Those pictures proved it. She had some fun." Kiki reached over and stroked Hannah's hair. "Try to forget about it for a while and get some sleep. Things will look better in the morning."

Kiki gave Hannah a kiss on the cheek, then left for bed. She was wrong, Hannah thought. It was already morning and things looked awful.

The truth was, Kiki didn't feel things as deeply as she did. Even when Kiki's second husband, Cecil, died, Kiki had wept a few weeks and then bounced back with a new hairdo and a liposuction appointment. At that moment Hannah envied her sister's resilience. The loss of Geraldine weighed heavily on Hannah, a dozen self-recriminations thrashing inside her head. If only she had agreed to see Geraldine the night before, as Geraldine had wanted. Geraldine would have told her what was going on, and perhaps she could have helped. Maybe even saved her life.

Although she hadn't voiced it to anyone, not even Kiki, Hannah felt certain that her friend had been murdered. Perhaps the stabbed man had tried to save Geraldine and gotten the scissors in his chest for his trouble. But why did he have that old photo in his pocket?

Geraldine's envelope sat alone on the small round table in front of Hannah, its whiteness catching the moonlight from the window. It spoke to her as if it had its own voice, gently reminding her that it had a story to tell. But she hadn't wanted to open it until Kiki was safely in bed. If she was guilty of delaying evidence, she didn't want her sister involved.

Hannah picked it up, running her finger against the slick paper. After a moment's hesitation, she untucked the flap and pulled out a white sheet of paper. She expected to find something momentous on it, but the information was very simple.

The words Hunters, Inc., 5671 Gibraltar Drive, Novato were written on the page in neat handwriting. After that was a list of five names.

Six

"DOUBLE HOMICIDE AT MARIN HOSPITAL?" Her red rhinestoned reading glasses perched on the end of her nose, Kiki read the headline with bewilderment. Shifting the newspaper away from her face, she gave her sister a horrified look. "Geraldine was murdered, too?" She put the newspaper down. "But I . . . I thought Geraldine died of a heart attack or something nice and normal. Nobody said anything last night about her being murdered." She pressed a trembling hand against her cheek, then her eyes grew large. "Poor Geraldine. And my God, Hannie. We were practically in the middle of it. We could have been murdered, too."

Her leg bouncing nervously under the table, Hannah had her nose buried in the *New York Times* crossword puzzle, but spasms of distress, and now Kiki's upset, made concentration impossible. She and her sister sat at their usual table at the Book Stop, a primo position next to the arched windows where you could see the town plaza as well as the hubbub in the small café.

Kiki took off her glasses, never wanting to leave them on a second longer than she had to. "This is all just too awful. I've felt sick all morning."

Hannah considered the veracity of this last statement, since

it seemed to her that Kiki's built-in self-protection mecha-
nism had kicked in full throttle as soon as she woke up that
morning. In spite of only a few hours' sleep, Kiki popped
out of bed, put on a pink jogging suit, a pound of fake gold
jewelry, and a thick layer of makeup. In contrast, Hannah
awoke still in shock, barely able to get through her morning
routine.

"You think people know we were there?" Kiki asked, her
forehead furrowed. "It's not good to have our names asso-
ciated with a double murder."

Hannah hadn't broken it to her sister that they were probably at the top of the suspect list. Better to wait until she
knew for sure, since Kiki would surely get hysterical. "We
found the bodies. There's no shame in that."

"Except that we weren't supposed to be in the hospital in
the first place, as that cute policeman pointed out over and
over again last night." She gyrated a finger at Hannah. "That
was your doing, missy. Now everyone's going to think we're
criminals."

"How was I supposed to know there would be two murdered people in the room?" Hannah said with rising agony.
"Besides, we weren't mentioned in the newspaper and probably no one will find out."

"Wishful thinking," Kiki replied in an agitated whisper.
"Look around. Everyone's talking, and you know you can't
keep anything secret in this town."

Hannah realized it was true. Normally at this hour café
customers were performing the Ritual of the First Espresso,
where they sat in complete silence, taking repeated sips from
tiny cups until the precious caffeine hit their system. But
today the café hummed with manic energy, people huddled
together, heads nodding and mouths moving.

Randy, the seventeen-year-old who worked the counter,
came up to the table, carrying a bran muffin and a double
espresso for Hannah, and a Lemon Lift tea and iced cinnamon bun for Kiki. He glanced down at Kiki's newspaper.

"Two dead people at the hospital. Can you believe it?
Whoa," he said, setting down the tray and placing the food
and drinks on the table. "I mean, hospitals get, like, dead

people, you know. But people murdered?" He slapped the heel of his palm against his forehead. "I mean, like, whoa."

Hannah thanked him, and Randy, his Nikes shuffling, returned to the counter, where he could share his lucid commentary with others. Kiki took a big bite of cinnamon roll, having a tendency to stress eat. Hannah couldn't eat a thing. It had been a mistake to come to the Book Stop. Normally she and Kiki had their breakfast at home, but Hannah felt too stressed to make even the simplest meal, and Kiki was hopeless in the kitchen even on her best days. Hannah thought that going out for breakfast would take her mind off things, but as soon as they arrived at the café they were hit by the headline on the front page of the paper.

"The thing to do is to not discuss what we saw at the hospital with anyone," Hannah said. "We keep it to ourselves."

"Oh, yes, Hannie, I agree."

Just then something large and green flapping in the café doorway caught Hannah's attention, and for one irrational second she thought a giant banana plant was flying through the door. A closer look revealed Naomi, wearing a green caftan, whisking straight for the two sisters. Wanda, with the figure of a starving cat, could just barely be seen behind Naomi's billowing dress.

"Great Buddha, have you heard?" Naomi said as she reached them, she and Wanda plopping down in the two empty chairs, not needing an invitation. "You might have been the last people to see Geraldine Markham alive."

Hannah and Kiki exchanged a look, then Kiki stuffed the remaining half of the cinnamon roll in her mouth, her cheeks puffed up like a gorging hamster's.

"How do you know we were there?" Hannah asked

Naomi pressed her heavily ringed hand against the base of her throat. "Dear, as soon as I read the newspaper I felt this throbbing in one my chakras, and I knew the tragedy was somehow linked to those close to me."

"Ellie called and told her first thing this morning," Wanda explained, breathless with excitement. "She heard it from her neighbor who's a nurse on the night shift."

"Well, that only confirmed the messages of my inner voice," Naomi said.

Kiki swallowed. "The truth is, we didn't see Geraldine alive," she said in a grand whisper. Hannah shot her a look. So much for secrecy. "We must have gotten there right after it happened," Kiki continued. "We found Geraldine and that man both dead as doornails."

Wanda sucked in air, and Naomi's hand jerked up to her lips. "Such evil," Naomi said, her voice low and throaty. She looked first at Kiki, then at Hannah, then suddenly she shivered, as if she had received a mild electrical shock. She reached into her large handbag and fished around, finally coming up with a small glass bottle with a screw top. After pouring some of its contents into her palm, she dipped the fingers of her other hand into the liquid and began flicking drops onto Hannah and Kiki.

"What are you doing?" Hannah asked, shielding her face with the newspaper.

"This is purified water mixed with essence of hyssop," Naomi said. "Your auras have a dark cast about the edges that I don't like at all."

"Oh, my, I see it, too," Wanda said, squinting at Kiki.

Grabbing the newspaper away from Hannah, Naomi flicked the liquid with increased vigor. "Without a good aura cleansing you might have some spiritual blockage."

Thinking that sort of blockage could be painful, a whimpering Kiki leaned closer to Naomi for a more complete dampening. When a drop hit Hannah in the eye, she gave Naomi's wrist a slap.

"Our auras are fine," Hannah said sternly.

Naomi let out a derisive laugh. "What piffle. You can't fool me." She gave the sisters another hearty sprinkle. "Normally I charge ten dollars for this, but for you, sweet troubled ones, Naomi cleanses gratis."

Wanda beamed with admiration. "You're a saint."

"No, just a good friend." Naomi looked at Hannah and frowned. "Oh, my, I can see the pain you're in," she said with sincerity. "You must have cared for Geraldine very much."

Hannah nodded. Naomi's sympathy, though appreciated, only made her feel worse, and for the moment she didn't dare speak for fear of crying.

"There's a bad wind blowing through our little burg," Naomi said, eyes darting around the room with mistrust. "I felt it in the tree day before yesterday. It wanted to say more to me, but it was constrained by something or someone."

"Lillian, probably," Kiki said sourly. "She constrains everybody."

"The gossip is certainly flying," Wanda said, eager for her turn to talk. She leaned her elbows on the table. "I heard at the pharmacy this morning that Geraldine was in some sort of pagan cult that worshiped the full moon, and that she was killed because she was going to reveal cult secrets."

"That's the dumbest thing I ever heard," Hannah told her.

"Of course it is," Naomi replied. "If there was a cult in this town, I'd know about it."

One corner of Hannah's mouth turned up slightly. "You'd be leading it."

Ignoring the remark, Naomi held up her index fingers on either side of her face and closed her eyes. "Yes, I can feel it. It's definite."

"What is?" Kiki asked, worried.

"A vortex of negative energy swirling around us." Lowering her hands, she opened her eyes. "It's affecting everyone. I had a channeling session with Wanda this morning and something happened that's never happened before."

"Red Moon wouldn't come out. He wouldn't speak. Wouldn't say a thing," Wanda blurted, Red Moon's affliction obviously not contagious. "We just sat there for an hour, then gave up."

"Oh, my God," Kiki said. She grabbed Hannah's muffin and bit into it like it was an apple. "What do you think is wrong?" she asked, her mouth full.

"Red Moon's a spoiled child sometimes," Naomi said. "He's pouting because I'm communicating with Uncle Marv."

"Five hundred-year-old snake shamans can be so possessive," Hannah said dryly.

"Tell me about it," Naomi replied, missing the sarcasm. "It's a fine time for him to clam up when I've got bills out the yin yang." She cast Wanda a frosty look. "And Uncle Marv's investment advice is proving less than fruitful."

"Our investments took a little dip today, but they'll go back up," Wanda replied defensively. "Marv was never wrong."

"But that was in his previous incarnation. My worry is that since he's inhabiting a new physical vessel, we're not interpreting his communications correctly," Naomi said with worry. "We invested in those European commodities because Zeno—excuse me, Uncle Marv—lifted his leg on that ball. But he could have been making the opposite statement."

"But he ignored the technology fund ball completely," Wanda said. "Granted, lifting his leg was an avant garde way of choosing, but as far as I'm concerned, he was showing a positive communication toward the European opportunity."

"But urinating on something is a universally negative statement." Naomi said this in a high tone, as if she were the world's expert on the subject.

"Uncle Marv was always special," Wanda replied.

Naomi lifted her shoulders. "But how do we know he just didn't aim properly?"

Wanda bunched her lips, her expression thoughtful. "Now that you mention it, I remember Aunt Estelle always complaining how he used to miss the bowl."

Naomi's lips parted, her mouth poised for strong commentary, but her eye caught something over Hannah's shoulder, and she smiled. "Heads up, ladies. Here comes our handsome John Perez."

The three women gave Hannah pregnant looks. Her romance with John Perez had for months now provided them with food for the most mouth-watering speculations. As he neared, they all tightly pressed their lips, suppressing the girlish titters they knew would embarrass Hannah.

In spite of her current misery, Hannah felt a flutter of happiness as soon as she saw him. She kept waiting for her infatuation with him to wear off so she could once again be her old cynical self, but just the sight of him in his faded blue work shirt sent her heart into a spin.

He's forgotten to comb his hair again, she thought fondly, noticing a thick strand of wavy gray across his forehead. As if reading her mind, he distractedly pushed the strand back. Her pleasure at seeing him dimmed when she caught his serious expression. He had to know about the murders even if he hadn't read the paper. Perez had retired as police chief of a neighboring town only a few years before, and the local police frequently called him, if not for direct advice, then for his general take on a given case. At that moment it occurred to Hannah that this must have been one of the reasons why Geraldine had wanted her input on whatever illegal goings-on she had uncovered. A discussion with her could have led indirectly to advice from Perez.

He had probably received a call about the case first thing that morning. That meant he had what she wanted most. Information about Geraldine.

He greeted the women and pulled up a chair, squeezing in next to Hannah. Cradling her chin in her hand, Kiki stared at him with the rapturous, half-delirious look she always wore when any good-looking man was within grabbing distance.

He glanced down at the newspaper headline, then looked at Hannah. "Are you okay?"

"Of course," she replied. Unlike her sister and friends, she was never the type to immediately spill out her feelings, but his direct gaze melted her defenses. "Not really."

Kiki opened her mouth, but Naomi, using the psychic powers available to most women in this situation, interrupted before she got the chance to speak. "Got to scoot. So much to do," she said, standing up. "Come, Wanda. And Kiki, why don't you let me give you a lift home?"

"But I haven't finished my tea," she said, her smile still fixed on Perez.

"Forget the tea. We can work on that recipe," Naomi said, putting a special emphasis on the last word.

Kiki appeared confused a moment before the lightbulb switched on and she remembered the potion. "Oh, right, the recipe! See you later, Hannah, John." With a wave, she scurried out of the café behind Naomi and Wanda.

"What do you know about the murders?" Hannah asked him as soon as the women were out of earshot. On another occasion she would have edged up to the question, but that day she was too upset for pleasantries.

"Good to see you, too," he said wryly.

"Sorry. Geraldine was an old friend."

"I remember you mentioning her. I've lost some good friends myself, and I know it's hard." He slid his hand across the table until it barely met hers. He wasn't the touchy-feely type in public, which suited her just fine. She knew he cared about her, even though she didn't always understand why. He could have had any number of younger and less difficult women. For years she thought that her mastectomy would scare off any man, and she never let one near her. But Perez had been persistent, the knowledge of her surgery not fazing him. In fact, she thought perhaps he cared for her more because of it. His wife had died from breast cancer years before.

"So Geraldine was smothered?" she asked. She watched the cop in him tighten.

"How do you know that?"

She hadn't known for sure, but his response confirmed her suspicions. The sick feeling in her stomach worsened. The part of her muffin that Kiki hadn't eaten still sat in front of her, and she pushed it away, suddenly unable to stand the smell of it. "I saw the pillow on the floor last night and there was smeared makeup on the case. What happened, John?"

"I don't know. I'm retired, remember?" Bracing his hands against the table, he raised up from his seat. "I'm going for coffee. You want a refill?"

Her eyes locked on his. "There's no point in playing games with me. You know more than you're telling."

"Why do you say that?" he asked, sitting back down.

"Because you know I was at the murder scene last night and gave a statement, or you wouldn't be here this morning. You never come to the Book Stop this early. You always say it's too crowded. You also have that look on your face."

"Okay, so you're right. Morgan called me first thing. He was up all night." He paused, pulling on his ear. "Chief Bradley called, too. They filled me in on some details."

"Like what?"

"General things. You probably know more than I do. They told me how the two people were killed. The results on Geraldine Markham are still preliminary, but they expect the pathologist to confirm it today. I also heard about the photograph."

"That's the part I don't understand," she said, voice lowered. "What was that man doing with a photo cut out from an old yearbook? It makes me think someone sent him to protect Geraldine."

Perez looked at her with astonishment. "Protect Geraldine? Hannah, it's more likely he was sent there to kill her." She felt the color drain from her face. Perez squeezed his eyes shut for a second. "I'm sorry. I shouldn't have said that so abruptly. Let's drop this subject."

"We're not dropping it. Tell me everything."

"Hannah, I shouldn't." His eyes caught hers. She saw him weigh his options. "Okay, I can give you some information as long as you promise not to pass it on to anyone."

"You know I won't."

"I know." He took a moment to get his thoughts in order. "They ran the guy's fingerprints through the computer. His name was Ray Mendoza. He was a gang member in South San Francisco and he had a record. Drugs, assault. And there was something else in his file that was interesting."

"What?"

"A year ago somebody paid Mendoza to kill someone. At least that's what the San Francisco cops thought."

"Then why wasn't he in jail?"

"The charges got dropped. I don't know why. Maybe they didn't have enough evidence or they screwed up somehow."

Hannah sat back in her chair, trying to digest this incredible information. "So the police think Mendoza was paid to kill Geraldine?"

"It's the most likely explanation for the photo in his pocket. They'll check his bank account, if he has one, and search his place. They'll do tests to see if there are fibers from the pillowcase on his hands." He saw the despair on her face. "I know this is hard for you, and I know how you fixate on things. You need to let this go for a while. Let me make you lunch at my place. I'm planning another climb and I'd like to tell you about it."

She found it ironic that he accused her of fixating on things when he had decided in his sixties to take up mountain climbing. Looking at his earnest expression, she wanted to tell him about the envelope, but he would pitch a fit because she hadn't already turned it over to the police. She fully intended to drop it off at the police station that morning.

"Lunch sounds great, but not today," she told him. "I've got a lot to think about."

"The police are on top of this."

"But John, if someone paid this Mendoza person to kill Geraldine, it had to be a friend of hers, someone who knew her in high school. Morgan showed me that picture from Mendoza's pocket, and I recognized it. It came out of our school yearbook from forty-five years ago."

"I heard that," he said, puzzled. "It's very weird that the killer didn't have a more current picture."

"I thought about it all last night. I was assuming he was there to protect her, but even if the opposite is true, it still makes sense."

"What does?"

"Unless a person gets his picture in the newspaper, and I don't think Geraldine ever did, it would be very hard to get a generic photo of someone."

He considered it. "But if you think one of her friends hired Mendoza, wouldn't a friend have pictures of her?"

"A personal photo could be connected to its owner."

"The person could have taken a new picture of her."

"Too risky. Someone could have seen them take the picture, or maybe the police could trace the photo to a specific camera. The photo needed to be generic, and the only generic photo of her I know of was in the yearbook. The police should check the old yearbooks at the high school as well as the ones belonging to her friends. I'll turn in mine to the police this afternoon."

"But Hannah, the yearbook picture was ancient. You think it did Mendoza any good to have it?"

"Yes, I do. Geraldine had very distinctive features and she always kept the same severe hairdo. She looked at least similar to the way she did back then. Maybe the photo didn't identify her completely, but it had to have helped. If he watched her house and saw her come and go, the photo was enough to confirm who she was. But it means that whoever hired Mendoza had to be someone local. There's no other explanation. Who else would know about the yearbook picture?" She hesitated before saying the next part. "And there were three high school friends of Geraldine's in the hospital that night. Lillian, Vera, and Ronald."

"Hannah, I don't think one of your high school buddies would hire someone to kill Geraldine and then stick around the hospital to watch the guy do it. It would make more sense for whoever hired him to keep their distance."

"I know. I also can't believe any of them capable of such a terrible thing, much less have a motive. But it has to be considered. Geraldine became ill so suddenly. Her going into the hospital would have put a kink into the killer's plans. Whoever hired him might have thought it would look funny if he or she stayed away when Geraldine was sick. Being at the hospital would be the best way to divert suspicion."

"Do any of them have motives to want her dead?"

"Not that I know of, but they're logical suspects. So am I. So is Kiki." There was an awkward silence. "Do they know how Mendoza got into the hospital?"

Perez shook his head. "He didn't come through the emergency room that night. They think he got into the hospital during visiting hours and hid out somewhere. They're still going over all the security tapes."

Forehead furrowed, Hannah stared down at her empty coffee cup, her brain in overdrive. "We've been so busy talking about Geraldine, and there's another big question." She raised her eyes. "Who killed Mendoza?"

"They don't know yet."

"What about the scissors? They looked medical to me, so wouldn't that implicate a hospital employee?"

"They were for cutting sutures, although apparently they get used around the hospital for different things. One of the nurses said she had used that pair earlier in the day to cut her cuticles. She also told us they were sitting on the desk in the nurses' station, so anybody who walked by had access to them. The police will question the hospital staff."

"Any fingerprints on them?"

"Only partials because the scissors are so slender. The lab's working on them, but the scissors got used by a lot of people."

"What about fingerprints on the photo?"

He shook his head. "Only Mendoza's."

"I guess Kiki and I are at the top of the suspect list for killing him. He couldn't have been dead that long when we found him."

"Only a few minutes, and Geraldine hadn't been dead much longer. But that's lucky for you. Because of it the police don't think you're connected to either murder."

"I don't understand."

"They know exactly what time you walked in the hospital because it's on the security videotape. They went over it in the wee hours this morning. They also know what time you hit the Code Blue button. You and Kiki didn't have time to go to Geraldine's room, see Mendoza, go back to the nurses' desk, get the scissors, and then kill him. It had to be someone already in the hospital."

"What if I hired Mendoza to kill Geraldine? In that case I might have already known he was there. I could have picked up the scissors on my way to Geraldine's room, then killed him."

"The timing would still be tight. But for the sake of argument, let's say you did that. It still doesn't make sense. If you wanted those two people dead so badly, then why did you push the Code Blue button to try and save them? It doesn't add up. Which is what I told the Hill Creek police this morning."

"Thanks."

"Any time I can save you from prison is my pleasure," he said without smiling. He shifted in his seat. "Listen, I've told you more than I should have because I know Geraldine was your friend, but the truth is, none of this is your concern. The police are investigating. You shouldn't get involved." She didn't respond. "Are you listening to me?"

"Of course I am," she answered, bristling. He spoke to her like she was a teenager getting the keys to the family sedan. "But you can't expect me not to ask questions. I feel some responsibility. Geraldine wanted to talk with me the night before she died, and I didn't have time for her. She said she knew of something illegal going on."

"Did you tell the police this last night?" Hannah nodded. "Then you've done your duty. Hannah, I'm going to repeat this because I care about you. Stay out of this murder investigation. There was a paid killer involved. The situation's dangerous."

"The paid killer is dead, John. He's hardly a danger anymore."

"If you won't listen to that reasoning, then listen to this," he said, his tone growing harsher. "The police have their work to do, and you can get in the way." He gave her a long, hard look and must have realized that he had offended her. "Listen, you said that you weren't able to get together with Geraldine before she died. That's called fate. Things like that happen for a reason."

Hannah knew he couldn't understand how she felt. Nobody could. She gave him a nod and managed a small smile to discourage further conversation on the issue. He slid his hand under the table and held hers.

She knew he was right about this much. The police had the resources to handle the investigation, and the last thing she wanted was to get in their way. Yet the idea of Geraldine being murdered by a hit man was gnawing a hole inside her. She believed in fate, only she wasn't sure if fate was moving her away from Geraldine's tragedy or propelling her closer. One thing was for certain, and Perez's opinion on this didn't matter—one of the finest women she had ever known had been murdered, and she wasn't going to rest until the person behind it was identified.

SEVEN

WHAT WAS QUICKLY DUBBED THE "Hospital Homicides" sent a rumble of terror through normally sedate Hill Creek. The town's baby boomers paid top dollar for health care, willing to shell out whatever was necessary for the latest high-tech tests, probes, and punctures to keep their aging bodies youthful and fit. In addition to high-priced medical care, they jogged, rolfed, took herbs and vitamins, detoxed, cleansed their colons, and drank wheatgrass juice, which tasted like liquid compost. And to think that after all that, you could check into the hospital and be murdered there like any fool on a dark street. The hospital had to call a special meeting to deal with the irate locals.

But that afternoon, while Hill Creek feverishly churned with the news, while the townspeople ranted and gossiped, critiqued and theorized, Hannah Malloy quietly took action. After arriving home from the Book Stop, she took the list of names from the envelope and tried looking them up in the local phonebook, not finding a one. She called information and tried them in all the different northern California area codes, but still couldn't get even one number. The people had to live in other states or at least other parts of California.

Close to noon, she finally became hungry and fixed herself

her favorite quick sandwich of brie and sliced red peppers. As soon as she finished, she climbed the ladder stairs into the attic and dug out all the old Hill Creek High School yearbooks. The photo of Geraldine found in Mendoza's pocket had definitely come from the nineteen-fifty-five edition, the first year Geraldine had taught high school. Hannah confirmed this because Kiki, a year younger, had graduated in fifty-six, and in that yearbook Geraldine had worn a different blouse in her photo. Each of the sisters had bought her own yearbook, so Hannah now had two copies of the fifty-five version, hers and the one that Kiki had in the kitchen the morning after the Botany Club party.

Satisfied that its contents weren't personal, Hannah slipped the original envelope inside a larger one and took it, along with the yearbooks, to the police station. She asked for Detective Morgan. He was out, so she wrote him a note and left the items for him, but not until she had copied the envelope's contents and tucked the copy in her purse. She told herself that it was merely a precaution in case the original document got lost. She had heard stories about police misplacing evidence. But in the back of her mind she knew there were other reasons she wanted to hang on to the information.

After leaving the station she got in the car and turned left at the end of the block. She was heading toward the Urban Farmer Nursery for a bottle of dormant oil for her dwarf cherry trees, but when she arrived, she didn't turn in to the parking lot. She kept on driving, perhaps pulled down the road by one of the unseen, powerful spirits Naomi loved to talk about, and before she knew it, she was halfway to Novato and to Hunters, Inc.

She never intended to go there, not consciously. Being a sensible person, she completely agreed with Perez that investigating Geraldine's murder was best left to the police. She had a dozen pressing things to do that day. Her poems were published twice a month in the *Marin Sun,* and she had a new one she needed to finish and turn in. And there was that new brochure for the cancer support group that had to be proofed, and she badly needed to cut back her hydrangeas. But curiosity about Hunters, Inc. had taken hold of her, and her mind had become a beehive of questions and conjecture. Before she knew it, she was halfway to Novato and had pulled off the freeway to consult her Marin County street map. She decided it wouldn't hurt to drive past the address and take a look. It wouldn't accomplish much. On the other hand, it couldn't hurt anything either, and she thought it would help ease her mind. No one, not even Perez, could find fault with that.

On a normal day, when the murder of a friend wasn't fresh on her brain, she would have relished the sight of the golden hills lying like lion's paws in front of her as she headed down the highway. This day she kept her eyes on the road, focused on somber thoughts. The Cadillac sputtered as she pressed her foot against the accelerator and changed lanes, passing a sluggish truck. It was time for the car's tune-up. For budget reasons the job would have to be put off until next month, but no longer. An old car required regular maintenance.

"Don't we all," she said out loud, giving the dashboard a pat. After pulling off at the Randall exit, she went two more miles, again consulted her map, then turned left onto Gibraltar. It was an industrial neighborhood made up of low office buildings and small warehouses, all bearing names of companies she had never heard of. California was the land of entrepreneurs, and this was where they got their start, she supposed, in cheap office space. If anything in northern California could ever be cheap.

She glanced down at the address she had hastily scribbled, then drove slowly down the street, checking the numbers on the buildings and pulling to the curb when she found the one she was looking for.

She turned off the ignition and remained in the car, studying the one-story building's gray wood facade. Backing up to a marshy area that led into one of the several small bays that linked off San Francisco Bay, the building sat at the end of the street apart from its neighbors, distinguished only by large parking lots on each side. The lots were empty except for two cars. When she had earlier checked the phone book, she hadn't found Hunters, Inc. listed, which probably meant the business was fairly new. She took another look at the banal building, wondering what it held inside.

She started up the car to go home, then turned off the ignition. As long as she was there, it wouldn't hurt to walk inside the place and take a look around.

During impulsive youth you plunge toward trouble in single grand leaps. When you get older and more cautious, you do it inch by inch, a small but rash decision here, another one there, and pretty soon you've baby-stepped your way to calamity. Taking a baby step, Hannah got out of the car.

She headed up the sidewalk, spotting double glass doors bearing the name Hunters, Inc. in fat black lettering. Nothing gave a clue to its business. She decided to go inside and ask a couple of questions. After that she would go home, write poems, and whack back the hydrangeas with a freer mind.

She gave the door a push and entered a reception area about big enough for her dog and pig, as long as they sat really still. It held a desk and two vinyl-upholstered chairs on either side of a small coffee table. Fake wood paneling lined the walls, and the vaguely blue carpet was the thin commercial variety you saw in the bargain bin at Home Depot. Everything looked new but cheap, she thought, as if they didn't expect many visitors. The lack of a receptionist confirmed it. She pushed the buzzer next to a door that she assumed led to the rest of the office.

Waiting for a response, she picked up one of the glossy one-page brochures stacked on the table and saw a photograph of an ostrich. Underneath the picture it read, "Hunters, Inc. provides exotic meats from around the world, fresh to your door." Below that was a long list of available animal flesh, including antelope, kangaroo, emu, and snapping turtle.

"Can I help you?"

Startled, Hannah looked up and saw a girl in her mid-twenties in the doorway, one hand pressed against the door-jamb. Petite but sturdily built, she had a pretty face and long, bleached blonde hair piled into curls on top of her head.

"I'm sorry, did I scare you?" she said with a big display of teeth and a heavy Southern accent that was a rarity in California. Hannah couldn't help smiling. The girl had a cheerleader bounciness that reminded her of Kiki when she was that age.

Fighting a growing nervousness, Hannah tugged on the hem of her sweater and cleared her throat. "I'd like to see the manager, please."

The girl's face grew wary. "Are you a salesperson?"

"No," Hannah answered. She took a breath and held it. A piece of barbecued kangaroo wouldn't have stuck in her throat more completely, but she finally forced out the words. "I, um, want some meat." Hannah hadn't eaten the flesh of a mammal in over thirteen years. The words "I want some meat" were the last ones she ever expected to spill out of her, right after "No, John darling, not tonight, I have a head-ache," and "I'll pass on the cheesecake."

The words had a soothing effect on the blonde. "My name's Sandy, and I can help you with that," she said, re-suming the gargantuan smile that reminded Hannah of a grin-ning doll. Sandy was wasting her talents in that small office. She should be a tax auditor or work the returns desk at Macy's. Sandy opened the desk's side bottom drawer, bend-ing over and making her skin-tight skirt crease at the thigh. She pulled out an order form, handing it to Hannah along with a ballpoint pen. "Just look this over and decide what you want," she said, then pointed a finger at the form's top line. "And don't forget to check off the type of delivery."

The print was small, and Hannah had to get her round tortoiseshell reading glasses from her purse and put them on. She saw an even longer list of meats than on the brochure, the options expanded to include bison, gazelle, ostrich, and buffalo. She emitted a silent "ugh," and took off her glasses. "If you don't mind, I'd really like to see the manager before I make my decision." She used her kindest but most firm 'I could be your grandmother, so don't give me any crap' tone, the one that usually got her what she wanted. Usually. Sandy's smile lost some wattage, her round blue eyes turning steely.

"Mr. Berger doesn't see customers."

"He could make an exception," Hannah said, heating up her voice a few degrees.

The blonde didn't retreat. "I just don't think so. But why don't we sit down and go through the order form together? I'm sure I can answer all your questions."

Hannah said she would study the information at home and come back another time, and Sandy readily accepted this, looking relieved to get rid of her.

A few yards down the sidewalk, Hannah turned and stared at the words Hunters, Inc. painted on the glass door. She jealously guarded her own privacy and had the same respect for the privacy of others. If Mr. Berger didn't want to see people, then that was his prerogative. The intelligent thing was to go home and work on her poem, proof the brochure, and then chop back the hydrangeas while pretending they were Sandy. She had given the name of Hunters, Inc. to the police, and they were well equipped to find out if the company was doing anything illegal that Geraldine might have stumbled onto. John Perez, who was the single best thing that had happened to her in years, would applaud such a reasonable decision. On the other hand, she knew that, being a woman in her sixties, she could get more information out of this Mr. Berger than the police ever could. But in order to wheedle anything out of him she needed face-to-face contact. The problem was how to get past the Sherman tank in a miniskirt.

Hannah walked back up the sidewalk. Building up courage, she waited a few minutes, then opened the door. The tiny reception area was empty. She went in and, instead of ringing the buzzer, quietly opened the door that led to the offices and peeked inside.

The rest of the place was as bland as the reception area, with the same cheap paneling and thin blue commercial carpeting. Sandy stood at the end of the hallway, her back to Hannah, softly singing "The Way We Were" as she made coffee at a small kitchen area.

Hannah slipped through the door, and spying an empty office, ducked inside it to give herself time to think. If Sandy caught her, it would be awkward, and she had a feeling that little Sandy could get nasty when ticked off. She heard the girl pouring water into the coffeemaker, followed by the sweet sound of footsteps moving away. Relieved, Hannah looked into the hallway, noticing four open doors, two on each side. She peeped inside the first one and found a small room with Formica-topped counters and cabinets running along both walls. The next two led to empty offices that looked unused. With the fourth door she hit pay dirt, finding a man sitting behind a desk, typing on a computer.

"Mr. Berger?" Hannah said softly so Sandy wouldn't hear. He looked up, dismayed to see a stranger. He was a big-boned man in his forties with black hair clipped close to his head, a salon tan, and broad flat features, the total effect reminding Hannah of a Rottweiler that used to live down her street. She smiled and walked confidently into his office, although the biggest part of her felt like dashing for the Cadillac. "I'm so glad I caught you. I've been looking at your brochure, and I have a couple of questions."

He went rigid. "Didn't Sandy help you?"

"Yes, of course, Sandy was very helpful." Hannah paused, keeping her best smile beaming while she thought up her next sentence. "I'm thinking of placing a large order."

Berger looked at her with more interest. "A commercial order?" He picked up a plump black pen and rolled it back and forth between his thumb and index finger.

"Yes."

He motioned for her to sit, and she took one of the two vinyl upholstered chairs in front of his desk. She introduced herself, using her real name, since she didn't trust herself to remember a fake one.

"I'm David Berger," he said. "The owner and manager."

Looking him up and down, Hannah noticed his crisp white shirt and striped tie. He looked like he jogged every day and took handfuls of expensive vitamins.

He began tapping the pen against the desk. "Are we talking about a restaurant order?"

"Yes," she said, grateful for the idea since she was currently running low on them herself. "For Café Lucca."

"I know that place." He gave her a frown, the staccato tapping of his pen adding an anxious rhythm to their conversation. "It's Italian, lots of pasta."

"They're thinking of expanding the menu, making it much more upscale." Hannah had known Paulo, the owner of Café Lucca, for years and wondered what he would do if a hundred pounds of emu meat arrived at his door. "His business is booming, and he's adding more restaurants."

Berger didn't display wild enthusiasm at this potentially profit-making news, and it bothered her. Here she was dangling a lucrative arrangement in front of him, and although he was being polite, she got the impression he'd prefer to get rid of her, which only increased her determination to stay. To let him know she was in for the long haul, she repositioned herself in her chair and crossed her legs; it would have been impressive if the chair seat hadn't let out a windy sound when she shifted her hips.

The pen stopped tapping. "So what are your questions?"

What *were* her questions? Hannah's mind raced. "I was wondering, how is the meat packed?"

"Dry ice, of course," he replied. Hannah saw a questioning glimmer in his black Rottweiler eyes. He looked over her shoulder. Twisting around, she saw Sandy in the doorway, hands on hips.

"I told her you didn't see customers," she said with high irritation. "I thought she left." The air of familiarity in the girl's tone and the intense way she looked at Berger put the notion into Hannah's head that their relationship was more than just professional.

Berger told Sandy it was all right and waved her away. "She's protective of me," he said with smugness. He leaned back in his chair, giving himself enough space to cross his ankle over his knee. "What else can I answer for you?"

"Well, let's see now. What's the delivery time?"

"Usually a week. Depends on the type and size of the order."

"And how long have you been in business?"

"Two years."

"And how long in this location?"

He paused before answering. "Six months."

"And some of the meats you had listed, like kangaroo. Are

those meats legal?" As soon as the words flew out, she cringed. She had flubbed it, and she knew it.

The edges of his mouth drooped. "You're not here to order anything for a restaurant, are you?"

She felt a pinging sensation somewhere around her sternum. "Of course I am," she said with a modulated firmness supposed to convey confidence, but the attempt fell flat.

"I don't think so. You haven't offered me a business card. You haven't asked about terms, portion size, or delivery guarantees. You're sitting there nervous and fidgeting, clutching your purse in your lap. You take no notes, and you don't look at all like someone in the restaurant business."

So who's perfect? she asked silently, trying to calm her jangling nerves. He spoke in a gruff monotone, but his eyes gave away nothing, staring at her with the blandly earnest gaze of a passport photo. But what his eyes didn't broadcast, his hands did. He put down the pen, and with one hand he pulled on the knuckles of the other, a sign of nervousness she had seen before. In Hannah's many years as a secretary to a series of CEOs at the same corporation, she had observed a hundred executives in hundreds of meetings. She had seen them ooze confidence and take control of a room with a glance, observed the sweat on their starched shirts when they got fired, watched them lie with cool dispassion about their failures. And experience told her that a man who fidgeted with his fingers that way was hiding something.

"Who are you?" he asked. "What do you want?"

She didn't know what else to do except tell the truth. What was the worst he could do? Have her arrested for impersonating a restaurant employee?

"A good friend of mine just died," she said. "Geraldine Markham." She saw the recognition on his face when he heard the name, and it wasn't a flash of joy. More like a cattle prod had just touched his backside.

"I should have known it," he said, pushing his chair back with an ear-jolting scrape. "She's going to haunt me after death." He looked at his lap a moment. When he raised his eyes again he seemed more human. "I'm sorry. Forgive me. I read about Miss Markham in the newspaper this morning."

Hannah caught that he distinctly and deliberately said "Miss" and not "Mrs." or the politically correct "Mizz." She wondered if and how he knew Geraldine had never married.

"It's a terrible thing," he continued. "Hard to believe. I mean, what's going on in this world when people can get murdered in hospitals?" He shook his head philosophically, then looked at her a long moment. "You know that she and I weren't on the best of terms?"

"What was the problem?"

"If you don't know, then why are you here?"

Hannah hesitated. "I'm trying to clean up some things for Geraldine's family. Gathering up her important papers, making sure her bills are paid."

"A little soon for that, isn't it?"

"It takes my mind off things. I saw the name of your company on her calendar. It looked like she had an appointment here."

"Then why didn't you just call and cancel it?"

"I wanted to know what it was about."

"Why?"

"Naturally nosy, I guess."

He started working his fingers again. "For your information, she and I didn't have an appointment. But you already know that." He was showing emotion now. He pressed his lips together and sniffed a few times, giving her an Arctic glare. Then some switch inside him flipped over. He inhaled, then ballooned his cheeks as he let out the gush of air. He held up his hands, palms out. "Listen, I've got nothing to hide. We import meat, exotic stuff, and sell it here in the U.S., mostly by phone. We have a catalog, a web site. Everything we import is legal and farm-raised. But Miss Markham got it in her head that we shouldn't be in business."

"Why?"

"She's an animal rights activist. *Was* an animal rights activist. If you're her friend, you should know that."

"She mentioned it a few times," Hannah told him, inwardly flinching at yet another lie. They were starting to pile up like rubbish.

"She was harassing us, making lots of phone calls, tying

up our fax machine. She complained to the police, customs, the SPCA, and the Food and Drug Administration, which naturally came to nothing, but it caused us headaches. Then she got hold of our customer list somehow and sent out letters saying we were being cruel to animals." His temperature began rising again. "I have a good business here, and she was out to destroy it."

Hannah didn't respond. He looked like he wanted to talk, and it was best to just let him roll. He rose from his chair, walked a few paces, glanced out the window, then turned back to her.

"Listen, killing animals is cruel, okay? But I see a leather strap on your watch, you're probably wearing leather shoes, and your face cream very likely has animal fat in it. So what's the difference? People have been eating meat since the beginning of time. I didn't need that wacko, militant vegetarian making trouble for my business." He put his hands on his desk and leaned toward her, his face turning crimson. The man definitely had a temper.

"I can assure you—" Hannah began.

"You can play innocent with me, but I know why you're here, lady. I have a good business, a damn good business, and if you think you're going to pick up where she left off, I can promise you more of a fight than you're bargaining for."

He didn't take his eyes off her when he shouted "Sandy!" so loudly that Hannah jumped. Sandy came in with the confident trot of a well-trained pony, and Hannah noticed a sly smile on her face. "Show Mrs. Malloy out."

When Hannah got back in the Cadillac, she rolled down the window for a parting look at Hunters, Inc. Berger had been so threatened by her, and she couldn't understand why. She never said she wanted to harm him. So why would a businessman with a successful company react so strongly to a benign sixty-one-year-old Hill Creek matron?

There was more about her visit that unsettled her. Something about the place bugged her, and it wasn't the fact that Berger had thrown her out. She put the key in the ignition, and the engine came to life with a groan and sputter.

She took a last glance at the building and saw Sandy at the edge of one window, looking at the Cadillac and scribbling something on a pad. When she saw Hannah looking her way, she disappeared. "Berger told her to get my license number," Hannah said out loud, the idea of it rattling her.

She shifted into Drive, and then it hit her. It wasn't what was there at the Hunters, Inc. office. It was what *wasn't* there. Berger bragged about his great business, but his office had almost nothing in it: no stacks of papers, no file cabinets, no framed certificates on the walls.

And most intriguing of all, she had been there for almost half an hour, and although Berger said they did most of their business by phone, she didn't hear it ring once.

"Hello? Yes, sorry. I couldn't tell if you were on the line. Well, I don't want to give my name. Oops, wait a second." Hannah picked up the dirt-covered gardening trowel she had dropped on the floor, leaving a spray of soil across the linoleum. She had decided to make the call right in the middle of transplanting a fuchsia, and was dressed in her gardening clothes and covered with dirt. "No, I can't give it to you." Pause. "Because this is an *anonymous* tip for the investigation regarding Geraldine Markham." Hannah felt a cheap thrill from using the words "anonymous tip." It was so invigorating, and no one would know that she had called it in. Berger might tell the police that she had met with him, which would send Perez into a barking sweat, but she would deal with that if and when it happened. "Check out a man named David Berger. He manages a company called Hunters, Inc. It's in Novato. Ms. Markham was causing trouble for his business. You should look into it. 'Bye now. Good luck."

She placed the receiver back on the cradle. Even though the police would talk to Berger anyway, the additional information would hopefully make them pay closer attention. A small, satisfied smile crept over Hannah's face, but it quickly vanished. It was a good lead for the police, but it could easily go nowhere. She had to come up with more leads, more ideas that would help. Repositioning her tattered straw hat, she went back outside to renew her work with the fuchsia, knowing there was nothing like gardening to stimulate one's thinking.

EIGHT

$\mathcal{J}$T TOOK HANNAH A GOOD five minutes to scrape the garden dirt off her only pair of decent black pumps. She was in the back garden looking for her reading glasses when she saw the aphid convention on her favorite Mr. Lincoln rosebush. Her gardener's nature wouldn't allow her to leave it, and in the process of hosing off the insects, she muddied up her shoes, which was why she arrived last at the Cadillac. Normally she would be the first one in the car, honking for the others to hurry up. By the time she arrived, Kiki was already in the front passenger seat, with Lauren and Naomi in the back. It was a first.

"Sorry I'm late," Hannah said, the words coming out in a rush as she arranged herself in the driver's seat. No one would ride with them if Kiki drove. Rummaging through her purse for her keys, she tossed an apologetic smile at her passengers, then did a double take.

Lauren was appropriately sedate in her dark accountant's suit and white blouse, the outfit she wore every day that, to Hannah, made her look like a nun on a power trip. On the other hand, Kiki and Naomi were dressed more like they were attending a Shriner beer bust than Geraldine's funeral. Kiki sported a black knit cocktail dress, its scoop neck lined with a fat ruffle made of the same material. To her credit, her bosom was almost completely covered, but the dress was at least two sizes too small, causing it to bulge in places where it shouldn't have been bulging.

Naomi, in contrast, had fabric to spare, wearing a caftan made up of so much sparkly green material that with a few strategically placed poles she could have provided shelter for a Boy Scout troop. She wore one of her older turbans, but had draped it with gold chains.

Hannah understood Kiki's outfit, knowing that she planned on flirting shamelessly with Gilman at the funeral. Kiki would never let death interfere with her love crusade. Naomi's flamboyance was a mystery.

There was never much time to plan one's funeral outfit, Hannah rationalized. They had found out only the day before, on Thursday, that the coroner had released Geraldine's body and that the funeral was planned for Friday afternoon. Hannah had been working in the garden when Kiki burst out the back door with the news. Hannah spent almost all day Thursday working in the flower beds, assuming the physical work would boost her cogitation on Geraldine's murder. While she pruned and dug, she went over everything she knew about Geraldine, but came up with nothing useful. To stave off hopelessness, she kept reminding herself that the police were working on the case. To avoid her constant questions, Perez was doing an all-day hike on Mount Tam. Instead she called the people around town who were known for always having the latest breaking news, mainly Wanda and Ellie, the owner of Lady Nails, but neither of them had heard of any progress made by the police. This worried Hannah, and it stayed on her mind all night, and was still fresh the next day as she turned the key in the ignition and took off for the funeral home.

In the rearview mirror, Hannah saw Naomi give Lauren a nudge. "So, do you think your cute Detective Morgan will be at the funeral?" Naomi asked.

"It's of no interest to me whether he's there or not," Lauren said sullenly, her arms crossed. "I'm over him."

Hannah detected the wavering in Lauren's voice and remembered that last night was *Cops* night. Ever since the end of her brief dalliance with Morgan, Lauren religiously watched *Cops* on television, curled up on the couch and crying into a bag of barbecue-flavor Doritos.

"Naomi, when do they tear out the wall in your kitchen?" Hannah asked, wanting to change the subject for Lauren's sake.

"I'm not sure when I'll be able to afford it. My investments took another plunge yesterday and today. Such a disaster. Looks like I've lost half my money. I'm beginning to think my belief in that flea-ridden dog's reincarnation was in error."

"You don't say," Hannah said with sarcasm.

"That sort of negative chi is so bad for the bowels, Hannah. Positive energy brings positive results. I'm such a wonderful example," Naomi said. "You see, I've come up with a much more creative way to break through my financial barriers. A way that will develop the path to divine guidance for so many people."

"How?" Lauren asked, always interested in money matters.

Naomi paused to let the drama build. "I'm going to offer our community Red Moon's spiritual tutelage via the modern miracle of telecommunications."

There was a brief silence while each of the car's passengers did her own quick translation.

"A web site?" Lauren asked.

"Don't be silly. Naomi can't use a computer," Kiki said. "It's got to be a psychic hot line."

"That term's a bit vulgar," Naomi replied, confirming Kiki's guess. "What I'll be doing for people via telephone will be so spiritually empowering, so healing." Pressing her hand against her chest, she took a deep, dramatic breath. "I felt like Hill Creek needed neutralization of the negative energy flows, with these murders and all. You can just feel the anguish in the air. Plus I think it could be a real moneymaker." Her voice gained an excited edge. "I'm going to charge two bucks a minute, and I'm taking credit cards!" The unbridled enthusiasm of this last statement caused her to bounce, sending the chains on her turban into happy jingles, not unlike the sound of a cash register. She reached into her handbag and pulled out a stack of green business cards, slipped a few from under the rubber band, and passed them out.

Stopped at a red light, Hannah read the card.

Is Your Chi Choked? Your Mantra Missing?

Let an Ancient Shaman Soothe Your Soul

Let's Get Metaphysical!

At the bottom of the card in smaller print were a 900 number and the available hours, between one and five in the afternoon.

Lauren seemed puzzled. "Can you get Red Moon to speak over a phone line? Can a five hundred-year-old Hopi snake shaman even know what a phone is?"

"Red Moon is quite receptive to technology, especially when I explain it to him in buffalo metaphors," Naomi told her. "He's counseled Wanda over the phone several times. You remember when she had that last brow lift and for a few days she couldn't get her eyes to close? Every night Red Moon performed the Song of the Evening Bird over her speakerphone to guide her down the pathway to slumber. So you see, I already know how to do it. I'm going to start taking calls this afternoon."

"How did you get a 900 number set up that fast?" Hannah asked.

"The planets are so aligned on this, it was easy. I was at Wanda's this morning when we learned our European commodities had gone in the toilet, and Walter was there. He heard me telling Wanda about my idea for phone sessions, and he mentioned that he has a friend who does psychotherapy over the phone with a 900 number. It turns out he's not getting much activity in the afternoons, and Walter had the great idea of the two of us sharing the line. I get it the whole afternoon and Walter's friend's clients will call during the evening. Such synchronicity!"

"And such an opportunity," Kiki said gleefully. "You'll make a fortune."

"Naturally my main priority is to uplift the spiritual center of our wonderful little town," Naomi said.

"There could be lots of people at the funeral who'll need spiritual cleansing," Kiki told her.

Naomi's head bobbed. "Exactly why I brought my cards with me." She began digging around her purse. "And while I'm thinking of it, Kiki, let me give you my nail scissors so you have them handy."

"Why do you need nail scissors?" Hannah asked as she pulled the Cadillac into the funeral home parking lot.

"For the potion," Kiki said, her tone blithe. "We need some of Ronnie's hair."

Hannah cut off the ignition and, wearing a stern expression, turned to her passengers. "Ladies, let me remind you that we're attending the funeral of a beloved friend. Naomi, you will not hand out business cards. Kiki, you will not cut off any of Ron's hair."

"We're not children," Kiki replied haughtily.

Worse than children, Hannah thought. At least children you could spank.

Hannah waited impatiently while Kiki touched up her makeup, Naomi closed her eyes and repeated her soul work affirmations, and Lauren gathered up her courage to possibly face Detective Morgan. At last the women exited the car and walked through the lobby of the Westmoreland Funeral Home, pausing in the door of the main chapel to survey the crowd.

"Look at all the people," Hannah said with surprise. "There must be a hundred."

She knew people had flocked there because they were intrigued by the circumstances of Geraldine's murder. If someone had murdered the woman in an angry rage, that would be a scandal people would love to chin-wag about, but they would avoid any personal involvement. Angry rages were too emotional and messy. But someone hiring a hit man to murder Geraldine, now *that* captured Hill Creek imaginations. Even though the crime was unspeakably awful, the guilty party showed goal orientation, shrewd use of capital, and a willingness to delegate—all qualities admired by the upwardly mobile in a service-oriented economy.

But it was more than the number of people at the funeral that amazed Hannah. It was also the opulence of the room. The chapel's front platform was filled with huge bouquets of flowers and flanked by a six-foot candelabra with all the tapers lighted. And an organist had been hired, the sounds of Bach drifting through the room.

"Who paid for this?" Hannah asked. "Geraldine couldn't have left much money."

"Didn't you hear?" Kiki said. "It was Ronnie. I heard Vera chipped in, too, but I think Ronnie paid for most of it. See the coffin?"

With an inward ache, Hannah noticed the gleaming wood-and-brass box on the center of the platform, its lid open.

"I heard it's the BMW of coffins," Kiki said, obviously impressed. "No veneer. Solid walnut."

Hannah knew that Geraldine wouldn't have cared if she had the BMW or the Yugo when it came to her coffin and wouldn't have approved of such an expense. It seemed odd that Gilman would spend so lavishly on Geraldine's funeral when he hadn't paid that much attention to her when she was alive. The usual motivation for that sort of behavior was guilt, but he said at the hospital that he had hardly seen her over the past years. Perhaps that was what he felt guilty about.

Hannah glanced at Lauren a few steps ahead of her and noticed the girl's lips trembling. At first she thought her niece was moved by the coffin and the flowers, but following Lauren's line of sight, Hannah's eyes fell on Detective Morgan, standing in the aisle near the front of the room, speaking earnestly with a woman about Lauren's age. He wore a dark suit and his hair was slicked back like a schoolboy's on Sunday.

"Detective Morgan *is* here," Kiki whispered so their niece wouldn't hear. "Do you think he came to see our Lauren?"

"More likely he came as part of his investigation," Hannah whispered back, watching him. She was anxious to talk to him and find out if there was progress on the case. "He may think there's a killer in this room. He could very well be right."

A pall settled over their little group, the silence soon broken by Lauren's sniffling.

"Aw, sweetie," Kiki said, giving her a hug. "You'll get him back." She broke into a smile as she pulled the nail scissors out of her handbag with a magician's flourish. "We'll get some of his hair and do a potion."

"No, you won't," Hannah said.

"Oh, be a wet blanket." Kiki frowned, putting the scissors back.

"Come on, Kiki, let's circulate and see if anyone's got chi blockage," Naomi suggested. The two women hustled down the aisle, Hannah and Lauren following at a slower pace.

Hannah winced when she saw Kiki and Naomi make a beeline for Gilman, who stood near the right bank of pews, talking somberly with Lillian. Lillian wore a sumptuous black suit accessorized by a fat strand of pearls. Within seconds Kiki was hanging on Gilman's arm. Hannah saw Lillian's eyes leveled at Kiki and felt she could almost see Lillian's thoughts whirring. Lillian was like a swan, all grace and elegance, but you knew there was frenzied paddling going on where you couldn't see.

Hannah saw Naomi hand her business cards to both Ron and Lillian, as well as a few strangers who passed by. To vex her further, Hannah glimpsed the silver nail scissors peeking out of Kiki's clenched hand.

Hannah headed in their direction to protect Gilman, but he suddenly excused himself, abandoning Kiki and Lillian. Their prey having escaped, Kiki and Naomi went in the direction of the casket, leaving Lillian behind, looking frustrated.

The crisis averted, Hannah moved toward Geraldine's casket, stopping when she got within a few feet of it. She took a fortifying breath, then approached it, standing next to Kiki and Naomi.

"She looks fabulous, doesn't she, Hannah?" Kiki said, teary-eyed.

With one hand on her hip and her nose scrunched, Naomi bent over Geraldine and examined her as if she were discounted broccoli in a grocery bin. "A little heavy on the blusher, I think."

"It's just too pinky," Kiki said. "With her coloring she needs earth tones."

"She'll be getting earth tones soon enough. Would you two stop it?" Hannah whispered angrily.

"I haven't done anything wrong." Kiki put a hankie to her nose and blew. "I just think Geraldine looks good, considering she's dead."

Naomi exhaled with exasperation. "Don't say 'dead.' She's not dead."

"She's not exactly ready for Roller Derby, now is she?" Kiki replied with testiness.

Naomi turned up both palms and looked upward. "She's only passing through to another form."

"Why don't you two pass on?" Hannah said, completely losing patience

"That attitude is crass in this solemn setting, dear," Naomi told her.

Hannah narrowed her eyes. "An ironic comment coming from someone who's handing out business cards."

"I'll have you know that people have been very receptive," Naomi said. "One gentleman said he would call this afternoon."

Hannah turned to Kiki. "And you, writhing against Gilman like a python in heat."

"So hostile," Naomi said. She put her hands on the casket and leaned close to Geraldine. "We'd like to apologize for this squabbling, but naturally we're upset. If there's anything you'd like to communicate, I'd be more than happy—"

Hannah gave her a hard nudge. She wouldn't put it past Naomi to slip one of her business cards into Geraldine's hand as an advertising gimmick. "Go sit down," she said.

Hannah rarely issued commands, but when she did, friends and family obeyed. Naomi and Kiki moved sulkily down the center aisle and slipped into the pew next to Lauren, who sat sniffling, her leaking eyes still glued to Detective Morgan.

Hannah made a mental note to gently suggest to Lauren that staring at a man and blubbering was not the most effective way to attract him. Fortunately, if Morgan saw Lauren's distress, he would probably assume it was grief for Geraldine.

Wanting to catch Detective Morgan alone to query him on the investigation, Hannah was just about to head his way when he started a conversation with a cluster of people near him. She felt sure he was avoiding her.

She turned back to the casket, and looked down at her friend.

"It's so disgusting that this happened."

Hannah heard Lillian's voice and found herself flanked by her and Vera. "To have your life end in such a terrible and pointless way."

"She didn't deserve it," Vera said.

"Like someone else would," Lillian replied.

Vera gasped. "I didn't mean that."

"We know," Hannah said kindly. While Vera stared at Geraldine, Lillian gave Hannah a pregnant look.

"Can I speak to you alone?" Lillian mouthed the words so Vera wouldn't hear. "Let's take a look at that huge bouquet in the corner. So many lilies," Lillian said out loud, directing the statement at Hannah. "I wonder who sent them." Lillian cocked her head toward the corner and Hannah followed her.

"I need to talk to you about something that's bothering me," Lillian whispered as soon as they were alone.

"I had no idea Kiki was going to wear that outfit until it was too late for her to change," Hannah said quickly.

Lillian's nostrils flared. "That's not what I meant, although for the record your sister could use some remedial fashion consulting." She saw the reprimanding look on Hannah's face and faked a smile. "But of course we all still adore her." She leaned her head close to Hannah's. "I heard that this will be in the newspaper tomorrow, and I wanted to let you know so you wouldn't be too shocked when you read it. The man who was stabbed in Geraldine's room. He was a paid killer."

Hannah tried to look astonished, not wanting to let on that Perez had already told her. She was wildly curious how Lillian had gotten the information. "How do you know?"

"The hospital administrator found out because the police questioned him for hours about how the man got into the ward. I say 'man,' but actually he wasn't much more than a boy. They think he came in during visiting hours and hid in a supplies closet. Ron found out about it and told me." She paused. "We have no secrets."

Hannah thought he might have at least one. Over Lillian's shoulder she saw him talking with Ruth, the pretty young nurse from the hospital. Gilman looked at her, his eyes glazed over with infatuation. She considered telling Kiki about this new development, but decided not to. Even though Gilman looked very interested in the nurse, the nurse might not be interested in him. And it was a good sign in a way, since it could mean he wasn't irrevocably attached to Lillian.

"I hate to say what I'm about to say," Lillian told Hannah with an energy indicating the opposite. "It pains me to have it pass my lips."

"I'm sure it does," Hannah said, getting impatient because she saw Kiki eyeing Gilman and the nurse, Kiki's expression reminding her of those nature shows where the lion stalks the crippled wildebeest. "What is it, Lillian?"

"I believe our dear Vera had a motive for wanting Geraldine dead."

Hannah's attention snapped back to Lillian. "What do you mean?"

"I mean that Geraldine kept Vera out of Stanford."

"What are you talking about?"

"She flunked her in senior English. Don't you remember? It was such a fluke that everybody knew. But most people didn't know that Vera lost a scholarship to Stanford because of it."

"Lillian, that was forty-five years ago."

"Vera's never forgotten it or forgiven it, as far as I can see."

"But Vera was Geraldine's friend."

"On the surface, yes, but that doesn't mean that Vera wasn't harboring deep resentments. She's the quiet type, but believe me, she remembers the Stanford incident like it was yesterday."

"How do you know?"

"Because a few years ago Vera's oldest granddaughter was deciding on a college, and I remember Vera pushing her toward Stanford. She and I met for lunch, and Stanford was all she talked about. How she wanted her granddaughter to have the chance she missed." Lillian fingered her pearls. "There was such regret in her voice, Hannah. Such bitterness. It broke my heart."

"Did Vera's life turn out so badly?"

"It's been no picnic. You know she married Sam right after she graduated from high school and got pregnant a few months later. She ended up not going to college at all. And then Sam turned out not to be the best of husbands."

"I have to admit, I never heard a good word about him."

"He was a drunk. Vera never said it out loud, but I think she was glad when he died."

Hannah observed Vera, now chatting with Dr. Westmoreland, who would be giving the service. The conversation ended and Vera walked back to the casket, looking so harmless and prim in her navy blue dress with its lace collar. She appeared hardly the type to hold a grudge for forty-five years, certainly not one strong enough to have someone killed. Hannah looked back at Lillian, whose radar had picked up on Gilman and the nurse. Lillian hastily excused herself and went to restake her property.

Hannah walked back to the casket where Vera stood, now alone. Unaware of Hannah's presence, Vera stared at Geraldine, her lips moving. To Hannah's surprise, she heard Vera whispering. Hannah wasn't trying to eavesdrop, but she couldn't help overhearing at least part of what Vera said. Hannah felt certain she heard Vera mutter, "You paid the price for honor." The comment intrigued Hannah.

"Do you think she can hear you, Vera?" Hannah asked softly.

At first Vera looked surprised that she wasn't alone, but then smiled. "Some people would say it's silly, but I think she can."

Hannah smiled. "I'm sure of it."

"We have to find out who's responsible for this," Vera said. "They should be punished."

"The police are working on it, and they're already making progress," Hannah told her, then hesitated before continuing. "Vera, I couldn't help but hear what you said just now about Geraldine paying the price for honor."

Vera turned pink. She played with her gold necklace for a moment, her eyes intense. "I knew Geraldine better than anyone. She had a strong moral code and she stuck by it. If she was murdered, it was because of that."

"What do you mean?" Hannah asked. She was anxious for Vera's answer, but before she could get it, Dr. Westmoreland announced that the service was about to begin.

Vera gave Hannah's hand a squeeze and then hurried to a seat next to Lillian and Gilman. What had Vera meant? Hannah wondered, afire with curiosity.

Westmoreland now stood in the lectern. He looked directly at her and cleared his throat. Not only was she still at the front of the room, she was the only person not sitting, other than him. Embarrassed, she scanned the room for Morgan so she could sit next to him, but couldn't find him fast enough, so she hurried down the aisle and slid into the pew next to Lauren, Naomi, and Kiki. As she settled herself, she let out an "ouch," causing heads to turn. Lifting herself up, she saw a couple of Naomi's business cards sticking straight up between two pew cushions directly beneath her. She noticed others placed strategically along the pew.

With Hannah finally seated, Dr. Westmoreland, dressed in an Italian-cut gray suit, looked gravely at his audience and with solemnity spoke of how many friends and loved ones Geraldine had left behind, and how happy Geraldine must have been at that moment, looking down from heaven. Gilman and Vera had obviously chosen a traditional service, which Hannah preferred even though she wasn't religious. Marin County was always on the cutting edge of cultural fashion, and local funerals ranged from Irish wakes to druid rituals. Hannah found such a solemn occasion disconcerting enough without the other attendees praying to pagan gods or tap dancing.

Hannah heard a *psst*. Kiki cupped her hand over her mouth and leaned over a still sniffling Lauren. "Maggie Thomas's son Arnold is sitting two pews back. It's been years since I've seen him. He's had a nose job, and I hear he's divorced. His skin's all cleared up, too."

Hannah didn't want to give in to such a base impulse but she couldn't help looking, not because Arnold was divorced and available, but because she had to see his nose. To make it attractive would have taken an engineering feat equal to suspension bridges. But when she turned, she didn't even notice him. Something else grabbed her attention—an old man's face. It was a stranger's face, and yet she had seen it before. Hannah stared at him a moment, then quickly turned back around.

Kiki leaned over Lauren. "So what do you think?" she whispered to Hannah, making sure Lauren heard. "His nose looks like Tom Selleck's, doesn't it?"

Hannah shushed her. Judging from Lauren's demeanor, the girl wouldn't have been interested in Arnold if he looked like Tom Selleck and Tom Cruise combined. Hannah finally spotted Morgan. It wasn't hard, with Lauren staring at the back of his head in a dripping-eyed, lovesick torpor. Hannah glanced at Naomi to make sure she wasn't tossing up business cards over the pews like confetti, and instead found her neighbor sitting very straight, her eyes closed and her fingers pressed trancelike against her temples. Hannah knew it was all for show to impress potential hot line clients.

Kiki made a *hmmpf* sound and folded her arms. "Just look at Lillian sitting so close to Ronnie. She's practically in his lap. You know she's had tons of plastic surgery."

Naomi's eyes popped opened. "Like what?" she whispered.

"Like everything. She's got so much plastic on her I hear she's got a stamp on her that says Made by Mattel," Kiki said with a devilish smirk. "We're talking implants in both cheeks and her chin, and fat injections in her lips."

Hannah shushed her again.

Naomi emitted a silent *ooh* and stretched her neck to get a better look at Lillian.

"What is important in this earthly world," Westmoreland said from his lectern, "if not love?"

The last word caused Lauren to let out a pained gulp and a spout of fresh tears. The other three women all reached over and gave her comforting pats.

Westmoreland opened a large, leather-bound Bible. "Remember, O Lord, thy tender mercies and thy loving kindnesses."

Hannah couldn't concentrate on his words with Lauren noisily weeping, Kiki continuing with the *hmmpf* sounds as she watched Lillian, and Naomi now emitting an annoying humming sound that Hannah recognized as "om." What unsettled her even more was the image of that man sitting a few pews behind her. She knew she had seen him somewhere. She closed her eyes and visualized his face, then stole another quick glance. Then it hit her. He was the man she had seen in the old photographs at Geraldine's house.

"Remember not the sins of my youth, nor my transgressions," Westmoreland continued. "According to thy mercy remember thou me for thy goodness' sake."

Stealthily sliding down in her seat and twisting around, Hannah gave the man a furtive stare. Yes, it was definitely him. He was much older and somewhat shrunken, now in his seventies at least. His thinning white hair was flattened with pomade, his suit was too large, his bow tie out of fashion. He caught Hannah's stare and returned it, his expression stony.

"Pay attention, Hannah. This is the good part," Kiki said. "Ronnie's going to give the eulogy."

Westmoreland exited the stage, and Gilman stepped behind the lectern. He spoke of Geraldine's kindness and intelligence with a sincerity that made Hannah teary, and then he told a couple of funny stories about her teaching days. When he finished, Hannah noticed Kiki wiggle her fingers to get his attention, then blow him a kiss.

Hannah leaned over Lauren and slapped Kiki's hand. "This is a funeral home, not a singles bar."

"That's the lettuce calling the cabbage green," Kiki whispered back. "I saw you staring at that man back there, though Lord knows why. He looks a hundred."

After Dr. Westmoreland led a prayer, everyone stood up to exit the chapel and make the short drive to the cemetery. Searching the throng of people, Hannah saw the old man pushing through the crowded aisle, using his to cane to knock the ankles of those who got in his way.

She pushed past Kiki and Naomi, and squeezed through the crowd, catching up with him just as he reached the exit.

"Excuse me, sir." He turned and faced her. "I'd like to talk to you."

"What about?" The simple question came out sharply.

"Geraldine was a very old friend of mine. She was an old friend of yours?"

"I don't go to funerals for strangers." He turned and continued through the chapel door, his feet shuffling. He moved slowly, favoring his right leg, and Hannah easily caught up with him. "How did you know her?"

He looked at Hannah with distaste. "And pleased to meet you, too. My name is Harry Stanley. Your manners stink." He pinched his nostrils together with two gnarled fingers.

Hannah held out her hand to him. "Excuse my rudeness. I'm Hannah Malloy."

He took her hand and gave it a brisk shake. "Hello, Hannah Malloy. You can walk with me if you like."

He didn't wait for a reply, turning and shuffling off. She walked beside him.

"Are you going to the cemetery? I have a car."

He kept his eyes to the ground as he walked. "I prefer not to see dirt thrown on dead people."

"Mr. Stanley—"

"Call me Harry."

He quickened his pace, moving along the walkway in front of the funeral home. Hannah put her hand on his arm. She did it gently, but he stumbled and shot her an angry look. "Is this a mugging?"

People swarmed past, jostling them. "I saw a photograph of you at Geraldine's house. I'm interested in your relationship to her."

He gave her a quizzical look. "I'm not inclined to give you any information about Geraldine that she wasn't willing to give you herself."

"Even after her death?"

He tapped Hannah's ankles with his cane. "Especially after her death."

"But she was murdered."

"I read the newspaper."

"I want to find out who's responsible."

"So don't waste your time with me."

"I just want to talk to you."

"I don't especially want to talk to you. Nice to meet you." He turned to leave.

"Wait," Hannah said. He stopped. She pulled a pen and notepaper out of her purse, scribbled down her phone number and handed it to him. "Call me."

He stuffed the paper in his pants pocket, turned, and headed off down the sidewalk.

"Who is that man?"

Hannah spun around and saw Naomi, Kiki, and Lauren. Lauren had asked the question.

"He's too old for any of us," Naomi said.

"I don't know," Kiki told her. "I got a better look at him, and he's kind of cute."

"You think any man who can keep his false teeth in his mouth is cute," Naomi replied.

Hannah didn't hear the rest of it. She looked around for Morgan, spotting him just as he got in his car and drove away. It looked like Vera also had left.

"I guess we should go to the car," Hannah said. Just as they reached the Cadillac she heard her name called. Turning around, she saw Jim Kaitowsky, a Hill Creek lawyer whom she knew from the Rose Club, hurrying toward her.

"Hannah, could I talk to you alone for a minute?" he asked, his face red from the exercise. They had been all out of small sizes when they made Jim. He was six-five with a large head and a girth to match, and it always amused Hannah that he grew only miniature roses with dainty little blossoms no bigger around than his thumb. Hannah unlocked the car for the other women, then followed him down the sidewalk a few yards. "Two things," he said. "First, I tried that mixture you suggested with the bone meal and the Epsom salts, and it worked wonders. I've never had so many blossoms in September. Thanks for the tip. Second, I need you to come by my office this week."

"Why?"

"It's Geraldine. She's left you something in her will." He saw the shocked look on Hannah's face. "I don't think it's much. Her only real asset was her house, which she left to charity. There are only a few odds and ends she left to friends."

"What sorts of odds and ends?"

"It's nice, when you think about it. Favorite books and records, some potted plants, a painting, a few clothes of good quality. It's like she wanted to give pieces of her life to those close to her."

"What on earth did she leave me?"

"Let's see now." He took his reading glasses from his pocket along with a folded piece of paper. He balanced the glasses on his nose and gave the paper a look. "She left you a wooden box and its contents." He pointed his eyes at Hannah. "I think she described it in her will as the small box that sat at the end of her bed."

$\mathcal{N}$INE

You GO THROUGH LIFE THINKING eventually you'll learn something. That the years will add up like course credit and one day you'll wake up some kind of Zen master, calm and infinitely wise. It doesn't work that way, Hannah thought as she sat on the edge of Perez's bed and slipped off her shoes. The years added up only into arithmetic, and the person inside stayed confused, emotional, and ignorant. On the other hand, it would be infinitely worse to wake up one morning and realize you knew everything, that you had nothing left to learn. Maybe that was the real definition of death. The end of not knowing.

She switched off the bedroom light and began to undress while Perez took his beloved spaniel for a before-bed walk. Setting her shoes in front of his mirrored armoire, she removed her clothes—socks, pants, then blouse. The amber light from a street lamp came in through the window, illuminating the roses, lilies, and ivy cascading across the level plane of her chest. She studied them in the mirror. She hadn't wanted the tattoo to hide her scars. It had been her way of celebrating them. It took a few years, but she discovered that the cancer had given as much as it had taken away. From it she had learned the value of health, of family, and of time.

Time, most of all. She had learned gratitude for every moment, the ticking seconds of each day becoming a precious rhythm she lived by.

That was the part of Geraldine's murder that ate into Hannah's heart. Someone had wrenched time away from her friend. Geraldine had only been in her sixties, with so many good years left, maybe the best years. They were turning out to be the best for Hannah, so why not for her? And whoever had her killed had probably been at the funeral that day and had publicly lamented her death, pretending to pray for her soul.

"Whoever you are, I'll find you," Hannah said aloud, her eyes filling with tears. She started at the sound of the door opening, followed by the friendly clatter of the dog's paws in the entryway, then she slipped between the sheets of Perez's bed.

"Hannah, you're embarrassing me. Get your fingers off my tush," Kiki said, swatting behind her at her sister's hands.

"There's so much of it back here, it's hard to avoid." Hannah stopped to catch her breath. "How else can I get you up the hill? If you'd take off your high heels, you could do it yourself."

Kiki had bad knees to begin with, and wearing high heels caused her to walk a little stooped, with short geisha steps. For her to walk up a steep hill was impossible, but she always refused to wear sensible crepe-soled flats like Hannah, calling them "old lady loafers."

"The sidewalk would rip my pantyhose. You don't have to stand right behind me and use two hands like you're shoving a mule."

Hannah resumed pushing in precisely that fashion.

"I've been trying to get someone to grab me back there for three years," Kiki said. "And wouldn't you know the first person I get would be you."

"I see the retirement home up ahead. It's not much farther," Hannah said, puffing. "I don't see why you're complaining. I'm doing all the work." She knew that Kiki was jealous that Geraldine had left her something in her will, while Kiki received nothing. "It's just a box with some old photos. It's not like it's valuable."

"You were always the teacher's pet with her. She never liked me."

The last part was untrue, but Hannah had no desire to rehash an old argument. She preferred to set her mind to a more provocative issue—why Harry Stanley was suddenly so eager to talk to her about Geraldine. The day before, at the funeral, he would rather have had a tooth pulled. Hannah awakened that morning determined to talk to him whether he liked it or not, and she was finishing her coffee and about to call information for his number when the phone rang. It was him, offering to meet with her that afternoon. Hannah was puzzled by his change of heart, but also delighted, since he might provide crucial information about Geraldine's past.

The information wouldn't be coming too soon, for all the outward signs told Hannah the police weren't making substantial progress. The previous night she had gone to a movie with Perez. He knew she was depressed over the funeral, and convinced her that a movie would take her mind off things. It didn't end up that way. Hannah whispered questions to him throughout the film, and continued them over coffee later. He told her nothing. He claimed it was because it was private police business, but after an hour of fruitless wheedling, she came to the conclusion that he was keeping mum because there was no new information to tell. The prospect of the police reaching a standstill on the case made her sick at heart, and even more determined to dig up evidence on her own.

She and Kiki trudged up the remainder of the hill. Reaching the top, they found themselves in front of a one-story cube of glass and stucco. In front stood a wooden sign that read Redwood Forest Retirement Home.

Kiki tugged on her skirt and smoothed her hair. "I don't know why I'm here in the first place."

"I need your assistance. I want you to observe this man, see if you think he's hiding information. Your intuitions are so keen."

Kiki scrutinized her sister, certain there must be another

agenda lurking behind the flattery. Her suspicions were well founded. In reality Hannah preferred to meet with Harry Stanley on her own, her purpose in bringing Kiki along being solely to get her away from Naomi. That morning Kiki and Naomi had spent two hours at the kitchen table burning something that smelled awful, and then Kiki dropped a burning match and almost set the dog on fire. Once the burning part was completed, they mashed up the ashes with secret ingredients and Naomi tramped around the backyard muttering some witch's chant that gave Hannah the creeps. When the potion was done, Kiki called Gilman and invited him to dinner the next evening. After he accepted, she hung up the phone and shouted that the potion was a miracle, and got so worked up, she begged Naomi to whip up batches to work with several other men in town, including the postman, who was thirty years her junior.

"You owe me a favor for this," Kiki told her. "Naomi says that if the love potion is going to work completely and totally, I have to concentrate all my thoughts on Ronnie. I should be at home concentrating right now."

As if she were capable of concentration, Hannah thought but didn't say. Kiki's mind didn't just wander, it evacuated. "What's in the potion?" Hannah asked. "It stank up the kitchen."

"Some herbs and stewed tree bark, some secret witch ingredients Naomi wouldn't let me in on, and, of course, Ronnie's hair."

There was a chilly pause. "How did you get that?" Hannah asked.

"At the funeral when you weren't looking. Naomi told Ronnie his aura looked funny and that he needed an emergency spiritual cleansing. You should have seen him, he looked so worried. So the three of us slipped out into the lobby, then Naomi said she needed tactile contact with his cranial energy. He looked like he was going to back out, but before he could get away, she got him in a head lock and I clipped off some hair real quick."

The story reinforced Hannah's decision to keep Naomi and Kiki apart. She opened the entrance door, a medicinal odor sweeping over her. *It actually smells of old age,* she thought, the idea of it jarring. The lobby was large with a low, suffocating ceiling and steel handrails lining yellow walls. A foursome of men who looked to be in their eighties played cards on a spindly metal table set up in one corner, their movements slow and deliberate, but their conversation lively, punctuated by gruff laughter.

"My God, Hannah," Kiki said softly as she looked around. "Is this where we'll end up one day?"

"Life's a round trip ticket. This is the ride home."

"Don't depress me."

"Look at the bright side. There will be a lot of widowers for you to chase, and you'll be the sexiest woman around. And I hear they serve three meals a day at these places. We won't have to cook anymore." Hannah said it in a joking manner, though she found the retirement home just as distressing. She put an arm around Kiki's shoulder and gave her an affectionate squeeze. "Anyway, we'll share a room, like when we were kids. I'll even let you borrow my sweaters." This elicited a smile from Kiki.

Hannah politely interrupted the card game and asked the whereabouts of Harry Stanley.

"You don't want him. We're men enough for you two gals," the oldest-looking man said, taking in Kiki's short skirt and red spike heels. Hannah noticed he was still in his pajama top. Once the men stopped their sputtering laughter, they directed Hannah and Kiki to room 162.

The women headed down a long corridor with aging green carpet that smelled like cleaning fluid. They dodged an old man in an electric wheelchair spinning down the hall at what seemed to Hannah an imprudent speed. Kiki watched him careen around the corner.

"It seems to be all men here."

"I've noticed," Hannah replied. "It must have some veterans affiliation." After turning down another hallway they reached an open area where two white-haired men sat on a weathered couch watching *Judge Judy.*

"Hey there, honey," one of them said, his eyes directed at

Kiki. He scooted over and patted the seat next to him. "Got room for ya." His friend told him to shut up.

"There must be Viagra in the water cooler. You men are just animals," Kiki told them appreciatively.

"You've finally found nirvana. Come on, let's go," Hannah said, but Kiki walked slowly, wagging a finger at the men and batting her eyelashes until Hannah finally took her arm and steered her down the hallway.

They found Harry's room halfway down on the left, the door partially open. Hannah saw him hunched over an electronic chessboard. She tapped on the door.

"You're late," he said without looking up. Hannah checked her Seiko.

"Only ten minutes. We had trouble parking. This is my sister, Kiki. Kiki, this is Harry."

"Nice to meet you. So sit." He nodded toward a twin bed pushed against the far wall, its tan chenille bedspread pulled and tucked with military tautness. His room was small and spotlessly clean with a table, television, and recliner in addition to the bed. A few framed prints hung on the walls, but Hannah saw nothing personal, no framed photographs or mementos. It could have been a motel. Harry wasn't as neat as his room, his slacks and shirt rumpled, his face sporting a couple days' growth. The white stubble made his face appear ashen, as if he had been stuck in a closet for a few years.

Hannah moved his cane to the bed's far side, and she and Kiki sat down, putting their purses on the floor at their feet.

"Thanks for seeing me," Hannah told him.

"Don't thank me," he answered, remaining in his chair. "Do you know what it's like to spend day after day in this stinkhole with nothing to do but watch yourself rot? I woke up bored stiff today, and you were the only entertainment I could think of. So what do you want?"

"I want to find out who's responsible for Geraldine's death."

"Isn't that what the cops are paid for?"

"Well, yes, but I want to help all I can."

Kiki pointed a finger at her sister. "She's nosy."

He smirked. "I know the type." He kept his gaze on Hannah. "I'll make your trip worthwhile. An old army buddy of mine has a son on the San Francisco police force, and he's been getting bits and pieces for me. He said they found fibers on Mendoza that came from the pillowcase. It proves he killed her. He was a crack addict. He also had a gun on him. They figure he went into the hospital at night thinking he could shoot her and no one much would be around. When he realized a nurse could come walking by any minute, he got the idea of using the pillow. They also found a couple of thousand in cash in his apartment."

"But why did he take the risk of killing her in the hospital?"

"Crack addicts tend to lack patience, not to mention brain cells. The cops have been talking to his druggie friends. Mendoza owed a lot of money, and the people he owed it to were getting pushy about getting paid back. Things were getting physical. Mendoza told them that some rich person in Marin was paying him to off somebody. The cops figure the money in his apartment was the down payment, and he was expecting more afterward. That's why he took the chance at the hospital. He was desperate to get the rest of the money. What if she stayed in there for a week? What if she died of natural causes and he didn't get the money at all?"

The details put the sensation of a lead brick in Hannah's stomach, and there was a lull in the conversation while she got her emotions in check. She wondered if Perez had known this new information about Mendoza. Surely he did. He probably kept it from her so she wouldn't get more involved.

"I'm sure they'd also like to know who killed Mendoza," Hannah said.

Harry shrugged. "I don't see why anybody should care, a punk like that. Good riddance."

"I'm sure his mother doesn't feel that way."

"The piece of scum was a murderer. Whoever killed him was doing the rest of us a favor. So now, what do you want from me?"

"I've seen pictures of you and Geraldine taken in Asia maybe thirty years ago."

"Interesting pictures," Kiki added, her mouth turning up at the corners.

"I doubt we were naked," he said with a scowl. "She got murdered less than a week ago. What does something that happened thirty years back have to do with it?"

Getting a good long look at him, Hannah realized that Harry got out of the retirement home more often than he let on. She had seen him at the hospital the afternoon before Geraldine died. He had been at the nurse's station, holding a big bouquet of flowers.

Hannah rose from the bed, pulled a spindly chair to the table and sat down. "I want to know more about Geraldine's past."

"Why?"

"It may help us find out why someone wanted her dead."

Pain washed over his face. "I don't see the point of digging that stuff up. It's too late. Gerry's gone. How can any of it matter now?"

"It does matter, at least to me. It could matter to the police," Hannah told him, sensing her opportunity. "It should matter to you, too. None of us were there to help her when she needed it; the least we can do is find out who's responsible for her death."

She watched him mulling over her words, and she knew she had gotten to him. He stared at the chessboard a few moments before he looked up again.

"And make them pay for it?" he asked Hannah.

"Yes."

"What do you want to know?"

"Where were those pictures taken?"

"Bangkok, in the mid-sixties."

"What were you doing there?"

"Civilian job with the military. I was a security expert. Burglar alarms, security systems. It paid pretty good and I didn't have to get close to the fighting much." He leaned forward as he spoke, his words taking on new vigor. This was what he needed, Hannah thought. A purpose. It was what everybody needed.

"How did you meet Geraldine?" she asked.

"Hold your water. I'm not on trial here." He got comfortable in his chair, the simple movement so slow and cautious Hannah expected to hear his bones creak. But though his body was sluggish, his mood had turned cocky at the opportunity to tell a story. "It was late July, about eight in the morning and already hot as hell. I was wandering through the fish market looking for shrimp. That's when I saw her. There weren't many American women around then, especially in civilian clothes. I caught her eye, and she flashed me a look that lit up those fish as bright as neon lights." His mouth widened into a smile, and Hannah noticed even, white teeth she guessed were false. "She was a pistol, you know. Gave me one of those sexy come-hither looks." He gave his rendition of a come-hither look, which consisted of moving his shaggy gray eyebrows up and down. Then he whispered, "She wanted me right from the start."

"Really," Kiki said, drawing out the word. She got up from the bed and pulled a stool to the table so she wouldn't miss anything.

"Oh, yes, how she did," Harry said. "We were scrambling the sheets before evening. Made Chinese fireworks seem dull in comparison."

"Ooh, this is good," Kiki said breathily, her hand pressed against her chest.

"I was in love with Gerry. Crazy in love with her. We weren't young even back then, but we felt like teenagers. She taught me things, you know. Exotic things. Best sex I ever had."

Kiki's mouth dropped open. The two sisters exchanged a look.

"We're talking about Geraldine Markham?" Kiki asked. "The one who dressed like Groucho Marx?"

"She didn't in Bangkok. She was the sexiest woman I've ever known. I never got over her." His tone grew pensive. "Couldn't ever get her out of my mind. Now I'm seventy-five and sick and all alone in this stinkhole. Maybe if she hadn't left me, my life would have been different."

"She left you?" Kiki asked with incredulity; the idea of a

woman voluntarily giving up a sexually active male was completely alien to her.

"About two months after we met. Told me she was leaving one day, then vamoosed. I knew she had to go back to the States and teach school, but I hoped she might stay a while because of the good work we were doing." Hannah gave him a questioning look. "We worked with Thai kids. Illegitimate ones, orphans. A lot of those poor kids were treated no better than dogs."

"Why?" Kiki asked, her face crumpled.

"Because their fathers were American soldiers who were long gone. The locals resented the kids, and sometimes their mothers didn't want them either. Couldn't afford them even if they did. So a lot of them, some as young as ten, ended up as slave labor in factories or as prostitutes in Bangkok."

Hannah looked sickened. "That's horrible."

"Gerry thought so, too. She found out about it the first time she visited the country, and got involved with a group that helped find homes for them in the States. She even got me working for them, doing a bit here and there. She could manage trips to Thailand only in the summers, when she wasn't teaching, but she helped out on the U.S. end of things the rest of the year."

"How did you end up living so close to her?" Kiki asked. "It's such a coincidence."

"No coincidence. I wanted to be near her." As soon as the words were out, he looked like he wished he could take them back. He gazed down at his hands as if ashamed. When he raised his eyes again, Hannah studied them. They were a clear, powdery blue, the color of weathered glass you pick up on the beach. She imagined Geraldine looking into them so many years ago, and wondered if her friend ever returned his passion. For his sake, she hoped so.

"So I came here," he continued. "But she didn't want to have anything to do with me. Said she didn't want a heavy relationship with anyone. There wasn't any other place for me to go, so I ended up staying. I guess I hoped she'd change her mind."

Kiki mewed with sympathy and patted his shoulder. He

still loved her, Hannah thought. After all the time that had passed, this poor man's love for Geraldine seemed freshly painful.

"The two of you must have kept up," Hannah said. "You knew she was in the hospital. I saw you there."

That revelation unsettled him. "That was a fluke. I hadn't spoken to her in fifteen years. But she called me a few days ago out of the blue. Said she needed to talk."

Hannah straightened. "About what?"

"I never found out. I guess I flew off the handle, told her if I hadn't been good enough for her the last fifteen years, then I wasn't good enough now. Then I hung up."

"What day was that?" Hannah asked him.

He thought it over. "Monday. Monday afternoon. I remember because Monday we have bingo after lunch. I hate bingo. Listen, I want you to know, I felt pretty bad about it afterward. I shouldn't have talked to her that way. She sounded worried. I went to her house the next day, and the neighbor told me she was in the hospital."

Hannah remembered Geraldine's neighbor saying that someone else had been looking for her that morning. She thought of those new bolts on Geraldine's door and had an idea of why Geraldine might have wanted to talk to him. Advice on security. She couldn't afford to call a commercial security service, so she sought advice from an old friend. Only the old friend wouldn't help.

Clasping her hands in her lap, Hannah considered all that Harry had told her. It was interesting, even fascinating, but the big question remained unanswered.

"Harry, do you have any idea who would have wanted her dead?"

Pain fell across his face as he slowly shook his head. "No. Who would want to hurt my Gerry? She was the best woman." His hand shook, and he knocked a few chess pieces to the floor. "You're right about what you said before. We have to find out who paid Mendoza to do it."

"It's going to be okay. Hannah will figure it out," Kiki said, trying to soothe him. "When it comes to investigating things, she's a freight train. You can't stop her."

"What about this work Geraldine did with the orphans?" Hannah asked him, interrupting what she considered a huge overstatement of her abilities. "Could there have been some trouble with that? Could someone have held a grudge against her?"

"That was all over twenty years ago, lady. Water under the bridge." Harry shook his head. "It had to be something else."

Hannah considered whether she should mention Hunters, Inc. Geraldine had asked her to keep it secret, but by giving the company's name to the police she had already broken that promise. There was a new promise to Geraldine now, to find out who paid to have her murdered.

She shared the information with Harry. "The company imports meat from wild game," Hannah told him at the end of it. "Exotic animals—gazelle, kangaroo."

"You never told me about this," Kiki said.

"Up until now I've only told the police, and it's information you shouldn't pass on to anyone else." She returned her attention to Harry. "The manager, David Berger, told me that Geraldine was trying to close him down. Did Geraldine mention anything to you?"

"No, but that's my girl," he said, smiling. "Always out for the underdog. That's it, then. That's why she wanted to talk to me, to help close those bastards down. Who would eat a kangaroo?"

"It's so repulsive," Kiki said, her face puckered.

Hannah stood up and walked to the window. She looked out over a small patio with mildewed lawn chairs and a couple of metal tables. "I think you're right, Harry. Her crusade against Hunters, Inc. could have been what got her killed."

"But who killed that Mendoza person?" Kiki asked.

"Mendoza was in a gang," said Harry. "That meant he had enemies. Somebody with a grudge could have followed him into the hospital and killed him."

"But why wouldn't they kill him in the parking lot?" Hannah asked. "Why take the risk of following him into the hospital?"

"Who knows how these gang types think?" he said.

"Maybe the guy thought Mendoza was going into the hospital to steal drugs and wanted to take the drugs off him. You know, kill two birds with one stone."

It was a possibility, Hannah admitted. She sat back down.

Harry gave Hannah and Kiki a cagey look. "You may need protection, you know. Whatever's going on here, it's dangerous. Nice girls like you could use a man around."

Hannah fought back a chuckle. First, they were hardly girls, and second, Harry looked too frail to protect anyone.

"I appreciate the offer, but I'm sure we'll be fine," she told him, then stood up. "We've bothered you long enough. Thank you for your help."

While Kiki got their purses, Harry grabbed his cane off the bed and limped to the door, blocking it.

"It's because you think I'm too old, is that it? Because I use a cane?" he said, shaking it in their faces. "Let me tell you something, sister, age is a state of mind. There's a ninety-year-old down the hall who thinks I'm a young stud because I'm only seventy-five."

"Harry, your age has nothing to do with it," Hannah fibbed. "It's just that you may be right. There could be some danger."

"I knew it!" Kiki said, her fists punched into her hips. "We shouldn't be running around asking questions."

Hannah had intended the statement only to scare off Harry. She regretted getting Kiki into a snit, but the damage was done.

"What do I care about danger? You think this is worth living for?" he said, sweeping his hand around the room. "To lie around this dump where the only thing to look forward to is roast beef on Sundays?"

There was momentary dead air. "I love roast beef," Kiki finally said, her tone soft. "And Hannah won't let me have it."

"Okay, you've got me," Harry said, holding up his hand. "The truth is, not only do you need me, you can't go much farther without me." He moved back to the table, and using his cane to steady himself, lowered his body into a chair. "You see, I haven't told you everything."

"What do you mean?" Hannah asked.

"That I lied, simple as that. I'm sorry, but I don't know you, and I had to be careful."

"Lied about what?" Kiki asked.

"I did talk to Geraldine a week ago," Harry said. "I mean, really talked to her. She said she'd gotten herself into a mess."

Hannah felt a tingling at the back of her neck. "What kind of mess?"

"Some of the people Geraldine and I worked with in Bangkok had called her a while back. They knew that animals in Thailand and Laos were being killed and the meat and skins shipped to the States. We're talking wild animals that are supposed to be protected. Monkeys, baby elephants."

"That's too horrible," Kiki said. "I can't believe that would happen here."

"If that's what Geraldine wanted help with, then why didn't she call the authorities?" Hannah asked.

"She planned to get enough information to prove what was going on, then hand it over to the feds. If you just give them a suspicion, they assign some two-bit flunkie and nothing comes of it. We saw it all happen when we were helping those kids in Bangkok."

Hannah wasn't convinced. "You said only a few minutes ago that Geraldine's work in Bangkok couldn't have had anything to do with her death."

"Like I told you, I had to be careful. You grab me at a funeral and expect me to tell you private details? For all I knew, you were one of the bad guys. It took me a few minutes to size you up, but I think I can trust you. Gerry would like the idea of us working together."

"Are you nuts?" Kiki blurted. "We're not getting involved in anything like this. We could get hurt or killed or worse. Come on, Hannah, let's go."

She tugged on Hannah's arm, but Hannah didn't budge. She stood there looking at Harry, her devouring curiosity and desire to help overcoming reason.

"Hunters, Inc. has to be involved," Hannah said. "We

could turn up enough new leads to get the authorities interested."

"Sure, and right after that we'll cure cancer and then whip up enough casseroles to feed the starving people in Africa," Kiki told her. "Forget it, Hannah. We're talking about smuggling, gangs, hit men, all the things Mother warned us about. We can't get involved."

"Mother warned us about men who played saxophones and not eating enough roughage. We're not going to get involved," Hannah explained. "We're just going to see what information we can find and then turn it over to the federal authorities."

"Bingo," Harry said, turning his focus to Kiki. "Stop worrying. Would I let anything happen to a gorgeous doll like you?" He gave her a wink.

Kiki pondered this a second, but her survival instincts won out over her thirst for flattery. "I don't like it."

"Where do we start?" Hannah asked Harry.

"This club I know in San Francisco. There's a woman who owns it. She used to live in Bangkok and she was one of Gerry's main contacts. She'll know who Gerry was talking to in Thailand. We could go tonight. You have a car?"

"Yes," Hannah answered.

"Good. Pick me up around eight-thirty."

Moments later, outside, Kiki stomped down the steep hill, so mad at Hannah she refused all help, teetering with every step.

"It's going to be okay. We'll just spend a few days on this," Hannah assured her. "And if we come up with anything, we'll turn it over to Detective Morgan. He'll know what to do with it."

"I know you. You'll get us in up to our necks."

"I won't, I promise. But I really think Geraldine would want me to do this. The day before she died, she said she had found out about something that she needed to tell the police about. Now it's up to me to finish up what she couldn't."

Kiki halted, the abrupt movement causing her to wobble until her sister steadied her. "Listen to me, Hannah, I feel terrible about those baby elephants or whatever getting eaten, I really do. But if someone in Thailand paid to have Geraldine killed over this, and then we start digging into it, that same person could want us dead, too. Are you listening to me?"

"My quietly nosing around a couple days won't incite someone to send a hit man after us," Hannah told her, fully believing it. But there was something else bothering her that she didn't want to tell her sister. She didn't trust Harry Stanley. The revelation about his conversation with Geraldine seemed too well timed to be true, but he was the only good lead she had, and that left her no choice but to follow it through.

$\mathscr{T}$EN

$\approx$

$\mathscr{K}$IKI'S DISTRESSED GASP DIDN'T FOOL Hannah one bit. A petite exhalation of horror, it erupted from Kiki as soon as they drove around the corner from the retirement home. Born with a short attention span, Kiki found her distress over potential danger in a murder investigation rapidly replaced with the expectation of benefits that same investigation could provide. Looking at her fingernails with feigned shock, she claimed she had no idea they were in such a sorry state, and that she needed a manicure immediately. But Hannah knew what Kiki really needed was to swap gossip at Lady Nails.

Their visit to the Book Stop a few mornings before had netted the latest news on the murders, but that news was now stale as old toast, especially with the succulent details of Geraldine's past that Harry had just delivered. Armed with such valuable contraband, Kiki intended to get to Lady Nails as quickly as possible. In terms of rumormongering, the difference between the Book Stop and Lady Nails was the difference between grade school tetherball and the Olympics. You went to the Book Stop to get the general lowdown on any local event, but if a person wanted the inside coughs and spittle, Lady Nails was the only place. There a woman could park herself for hours and verbally spelunk into the darkest caverns of Hill Creek existence.

"I hope Ellie can fit me in," Kiki said with urgency, her high heels clicking a brisk tempo as she and Hannah walked down the tree-lined sidewalk toward the salon.

"I don't want you telling anything you heard about Geraldine today," Hannah warned. "It's not for public discussion."

"I wouldn't dream of telling a soul," Kiki replied, wearing the smug glow that comes from possessing gossip so juicy it could squirt you in the eye. Hannah knew her sister would blab the whole story.

"I'll come inside a second to make sure Ellie can take you," Hannah told her. "If she can, I'll do the grocery shopping and pick you up in an hour."

As she pushed open the salon door, Hannah smiled at the sign that read One Hand Clapping. Ellie, the owner, had changed the name earlier that year, hoping the salon would sound more trendy, but her aging clientele refused to call it anything but Lady Nails.

The door's Buddhist prayer chimes tinkled a cheerful greeting as the sisters entered the salon's blur of pink—pink walls, pink floor, pink chairs filled with pink-tinged women. It felt like reentering the secure rosiness of the womb, except in the womb you had to keep your mouth shut, while in Lady Nails you got to say anything and everything you wanted.

Once inside, Hannah paused and inhaled the heavy scent of lavender and cedarwood. To maximize hipness, Ellie offered aromatherapy with her manicures, so while you had your nails done you could also take the sniff cure for a wide range of ailments, which, according to Ellie, included insomnia, anxiety, and underactive thyroid.

Long and narrow, the salon had a wider area with wicker chairs and magazines at the front that served as a waiting room. But most clients found that part of the salon too isolated and instead grabbed a free manicure chair when they had to wait.

That day the salon buzzed with activity, the high-pitched chatter rising over the voice of Cher on the stereo. Every one of the pink vinyl chairs was filled with someone Hannah and Kiki knew, including Wanda, who was getting a pedicure from Shiloh, Ellie's twenty-something assistant. Seeing Shiloh, Hannah chuckled. The girl wore a lacy blouse, a long flowered skirt, platform sandals, and a flower in her long straight hair, the exact style Hannah had worn thirty-five years earlier.

The salon's cackling chatter quieted as soon as the two sisters walked in, convincing Hannah that murder was that day's discussion topic.

"Hello, ladies," Ellie said. She sat on the other side of the manicure table from Bess Harper, who ran the card shop down the street. Once everyone got a good look at the sisters and found no startling changes in them from stumbling across two corpses, the heart-to-heart chats resumed. "Shiloh and I are both swamped, but I think I could get you started in about fifteen minutes if you don't mind being on the assembly line. That okay?"

"Take your time, sweetie," Kiki said to Ellie with a waggle of her hand, then sashayed over. "Love your hair today. It's got lots of lift."

"Thanks," Ellie said, giving her hair a pat. "I woke up looking like a dog's dinner and wanted to do something special, so I took your advice and used that strong gel along with the mega-hold hairspray."

"It's fabulous." Conversational foreplay concluded, Kiki sidled closer. "Any news?"

"Nothing good. How about you?" Ellie asked hopefully. Listening in on this exchange, Hannah noticed Bess watching with anticipation.

Kiki nodded and curved out her arms in front of her in the gesture that meant "buckets," then quickly lowered them, seeing her sister's reprimanding look.

"Hannah, I've got some gardening magazines you might like if you're going to wait," Ellie said, obviously hoping to distract her so Kiki could unload the latest, unimpeded by her sister's moral authority.

Hannah was about to say she was going grocery shopping when she noticed Vera sitting in a manicure chair near the rear of the salon. She had tried calling Vera several times to continue the tantalizing conversation they had begun at the funeral, but hadn't been able to reach her. And now she had even more reason to talk to the woman. Vera might be able to confirm some of the things she had heard about Geraldine over the past few days.

"Could you fit me in for a manicure?" Hannah quickly asked. Both Kiki and Ellie shot her suspicious looks. Hannah almost never got a manicure. It was a holdout from her radical feminist days when, as a personal protest against the oppression of women, she refused to shave any body hair, put on makeup, or wear undergarments. Painting one's fingernails was out of the question. Once she got a little older and made her way in the world, she realized that a little lipstick and a pair of silky bikinis weren't necessarily bad things, and that a woman could maintain her integrity with shaved legs and underarms. Still, she had resisted manicures, but at that moment she decided a manicure was precisely what she needed.

"If you don't mind waiting around a while, I can get to you in a few minutes," Ellie answered, watching Hannah with bird eyes.

Waiting was exactly what Hannah had in mind. She saw Wanda sitting next to Vera, so she took the chair on Wanda's other side. Wanda's toes, blood red, as if she had just tiptoed through a slaughterhouse, looked almost dry, and Hannah hoped to take her seat as soon as she left.

"Where's Zeno today?" Hannah asked Wanda, making small talk.

Dressed in a white silk knit DKNY jogging outfit suitable for almost any occasion except jogging, Wanda eyed Hannah over the top of her *People* magazine. "You mean Uncle Marv. At home with his new dog nanny," she said, adding with pride, "She's Swedish."

"Maybe he'll pick up a foreign language," Hannah joked.

"How droll," Wanda said, glancing at Kiki, who chattered away at the salon's other end, already gathering a small crowd around her. "So it looks like you and Kiki have gotten yourselves in the center of all the attention once again, finding poor Geraldine."

"You sound almost envious, which is very silly," Hannah said. "It was horrible."

"Could we not talk about it?" Vera asked, her voice breaking. Wearing peach cotton slacks and a sweatshirt that read Keep Tuna Dolphin-Free, she looked down at a glossy magazine open on the manicure table in front of her. Hannah saw her chin tremble.

"We're sorry," Hannah said. She gave Wanda a nudge with her elbow.

"Yes, Vera, I'm so sorry," Wanda said with sincerity. "Naturally, you're still grieving. You know, when my Uncle Marv died, Naomi took me up to the deer trails at the very top of Mount Tam. It was right at midnight, and we asked for blessings from the moon, and then I stripped nude and Naomi tossed cornmeal all over me. After that I felt so healed." Vera looked a little stunned, and Hannah gave Wanda another nudge. "Oh, well, of course, it's not for everybody," Wanda quickly added. "I hardly knew Geraldine myself, but I always heard the nicest things about her."

They were all grateful when the clicking of Kiki's high heels interrupted.

"Vera, sweetie, how are you holding up?" Kiki said with a waggle of her hand, her voice full of sympathy.

"A little better each day," Vera replied.

"I'm glad. Poor Ronnie's still so devastated," Kiki went on. "He's coming to dinner tomorrow night. He absolutely insisted on being with me. He said it was the only way he could bear up under the strain."

Hannah sucked in her cheeks. That morning she had heard Kiki begging Gilman, pleading with him to come over for dinner. Potion or no potion, there was no way the man could have said no, and she knew that Kiki was telling Vera this fib only so it would be repeated to Lillian. Vera nodded with what appeared to be pleasant surprise at Kiki's news.

"*You're* dating Dr. Gilman, the internist Dr. Gilman?" Wanda asked.

"Yes," Kiki said, pulling back her shoulders. "He's crazy about me."

"I thought he was dating Lillian Granger," Wanda said.

Kiki couldn't refute that since Vera was sitting right there, so instead she simply lowered her fake eyelashes and smiled, the same expression worn by Princess Di in the eight-by-ten black-and-white glossy that graced her altar. Lady Nails patrons created the Princess Di altar the week after Diana's death. Including a photo and a commemorative Princess Diana teacup, it sat on a small table along with a candle and some fake flowers.

Kiki's artful expression had the desired effect on Wanda, whose face now puckered as if she had just gotten a whiff of some foul odor.

Hannah smiled inwardly, knowing that Wanda detested the possibility, however remote, that Kiki might marry a doctor. Like Kiki, Wanda had a competitive nature, and though she considered herself superior to Kiki in every way, since she had a husband and packets of money, and Kiki had neither, she knew she could never count Kiki out. Kiki might be plump, a fashion fatality, and usually up to her ears in some embarrassing situation, but she had an amazing way of falling into a pile of horse shit and coming out smelling like Chanel.

"I'm so happy for you," Wanda said.

"Actually," Vera said softly, "I saw him flirting with that nurse outside the funeral home."

Kiki's head snapped to Vera. "That's impossible. She's too young for him."

"I'm sure you're right," Vera replied.

Hannah saw torment flash across her sister's face.

"Just because he talked to her doesn't mean anything. Besides, after tomorrow night he won't be thinking of any woman but me. Trust me," Kiki said with a confidence Hannah knew she didn't feel. At that moment Hannah felt a little sorry for Gilman. No telling what Kiki had in store for him.

Wanda hastily slipped on her sandals, said her good-byes to everyone, and made a quick exit, probably to make a dozen calls on her car phone to get the inside skinny on Gilman's love life.

Hannah slid into Wanda's chair. Kiki planted herself in a chair at the other end of the salon, as far away from Hannah as possible, so she could gossip about Geraldine. Ellie was tied up on the phone, so Vera and Hannah were alone. They exchanged a few comments about the funeral before Hannah got down to essentials.

"Vera," Hannah said at low volume, "do you know if Geraldine was ever involved as an animal rights activist?"

Vera had been looking at her magazine, but at the question her eyes jumped to Hannah. "Why ask such a thing?"

"Um, just curious," Hannah said, fumbling with the words. "I've been thinking a lot about her lately, asking myself questions."

Vera gave her an ardent look. "You're helping the police, aren't you?"

"Not helping them in the strictest sense."

"At least not so they know about it, you mean?" Hannah's tendency to snoop into police issues was well known.

"Yes," Hannah said, scooting her chair closer to Vera's. "I need to find out everything I can about Geraldine."

Vera's small, dark eyes searched Hannah's. To reassure her, Hannah reached over and touched her hand, careful not to disturb the still damp manicure. Vera glanced about the room to make sure no one was listening. Kiki had begun disgorging news in a heated whisper, so everyone else was distracted. "To tell you the truth, I'm glad you're looking into it. You're so smart. You must have found out about that meat company and that terrible man."

"You know about David Berger?" Hannah asked with surprise.

Vera nodded. "I know that Geraldine didn't like him. He gave her a lot of grief."

"From his point of view it was the other way around. He said she was harassing him and trying to disrupt his business."

"He's a despicable man. Geraldine thought he was doing something illegal. She never told me exactly what it was, but

I think he was selling meat from protected animals."

"What else did Geraldine tell you?"

"Not much. I just knew she was angry about the whole thing. Wealthy people can be so awful, willing to buy something that's wrong, just because it's different and expensive. And Berger cashed in on that."

"Did Geraldine go to the police?"

"Yes, when his business was in San Jose. She also went to a couple of government agencies, but nothing happened. They looked into it, but said they couldn't find anything illegal. She told them they needed to look harder. They wouldn't do it, and after that they treated her like she was some batty woman. See, Berger made them all think she was crazy. He moved the business a few times and finally he came to Marin, right into her own backyard. At first she was livid, but then I think she was afraid of him."

"She thought he might hurt her?"

Vera nodded. "He had a lot of money at stake, so he didn't like Geraldine interfering."

"Is that what you meant at the funeral when you said that Geraldine had paid the price for honor? Were you talking about her dealings with Berger and Hunters, Inc.?"

Vera nodded again, a gleam of fright in her eyes. "From what Geraldine told me, he's a depraved man who would do anything for money."

"Have you told the police this?"

"No. I'm ashamed of myself for not doing it, but what if he found out that I'd told them?"

"But the police have to know."

Vera chewed on her lip. "You're right, I know you are. But Hannah, I'm afraid."

"Then give the information to the police anonymously," Hannah suggested, thinking of the anonymous tip she had made. "You can phone them and not give your name."

"That's a good idea. That's what I'll do," she said, sounding like she was trying to convince herself. Just then Ellie walked past on her way to the coffeepot. "I'll finish you up in just a sec, Vera," Ellie said.

Hannah pressed on. "Did she ever mention her trips to

Asia and about helping orphaned children there?"

Vera hesitated. "It was something she didn't like to talk about. In fact, she always kept it a secret."

"Why?"

"Apparently, in order to help the children she had to do some things that weren't quite legal, so she preferred that no one know what she was doing. Also, she said that the children were starting new lives here and might not want people knowing where they came from, especially as they got older. Some of these poor children were prostitutes and hooked on drugs when they were just little things. She told me all this a few years back. But it happened eons ago."

"Is there any chance she could have started up with it again?"

"Oh, I don't think so. We got pretty close the past few years, and lately she was too busy fighting David Berger to have the time for anything else."

"Did she ever mention Harry Stanley to you?"

Vera hesitated. "She used to talk about him a little. She knew him in Bangkok. I think he actually stalked her for a while, years back, before people called it that. How do you know him?"

"I recognized him at the funeral."

"Recognized him from where?"

Hannah wondered why Vera was so interested. She didn't want to go into the story about Geraldine, the envelope, and the old photos. "I saw him at the hospital," Hannah told her. "He visited Geraldine."

Vera sucked in some air and held it. "I'm frightened, Hannah. I'm starting to think that you shouldn't investigate any of this. What if something happened to you?"

"I'll be fine," Hannah said, trying her best to give Vera a reassuring smile, but Vera didn't look like she was buying it.

"David Berger is an evil man. And Harry Stanley, I wouldn't trust him either, if I were you." Vera laid her hand on Hannah's wrist. "Geraldine was a strong woman. If she was afraid of something, she had good reason."

Vera's hand tightened, and then, remembering herself, she

released it. "Oh, darn," she said, seeing her manicure wrecked. Shaking her head and making a distressed clucking sound, she gathered up her belongings.

"Vera, please, I have a few more questions."

"I've told you everything I know," Vera whispered. "I'll call the police, I promise, but other than that, I want to stay out of this." She walked out of the salon.

Ellie was on her way to Hannah when she saw Vera hurry through the door. She shook her head sadly. "Now what got into her? She didn't let me put on her top coat."

"She's upset about Geraldine," Hannah said.

"That's a shame. I could have done some aromatherapy on her that would have fixed her right up. But I guess we're all upset about it. Of course I hardly knew Geraldine, since she didn't get her nails done, but still . . ." Ellie tilted her head toward Hannah. "I heard a lot about her." Raising her eyebrows on the word "lot," she examined Hannah's nails and frowned. "Look at those cuticles. Don't you wear gloves when you garden? Listen, since Vera's gone and Kiki looks busy"—she glanced at Kiki, who was still busily delivering a monologue to half a dozen women—"I can fit you in right now if you'll settle for just a clear coat and no color."

Hannah cast an anguished look at Kiki. She wanted to stop her sister from telling Geraldine's personal details, but the prospect of hearing the personal details that Ellie's tone of voice promised was too tempting. She assured Ellie that a clear coat was fine, and Ellie pushed a manicure table in front of her that held a bowl of warm water, cotton balls, and cuticle sticks. Ellie put Hannah's fingers in the water.

"You said you heard things about Geraldine," Hannah asked. "What kind of things?"

Ellie smiled slyly. "You're always telling Kiki not to gossip, and here you are dying for a little news, and old news at that."

"Old news?"

"Well, before Vera came in, we were talking about who hired that gang member to kill Geraldine. You know, the one who got stabbed. It was all in the paper." Ellie lifted one of Hannah's hands from the water and dried it with a towel.

"Anyway, it occurred to me while I was talking to the girls," she continued in a lowered voice, "that Lillian had an excellent motive for wanting revenge against Geraldine."

"Really?" Hannah said, trying not to look as rabidly interested as she was.

"You know, I shouldn't repeat all this."

Hannah gave Ellie a look that penetrated right into the woman's soul.

"Okay," she said eagerly. "You see, about twenty years ago Geraldine had an affair with Lillian's husband, Leonard."

The news stunned Hannah. That little bomb dropped, Ellie began pushing back Hannah's cuticles with an orange stick.

"Are you sure?" Hannah asked.

"Of course, I am. I remember because that was before I had my own salon and I was working at Yvette's place down on Hilldale, and Lillian's neighbor was Susie, my best client. She told me everything. Apparently Leonard wanted to leave Lillian for Geraldine, but Geraldine wouldn't let him. Geraldine broke off the relationship and Leonard pined away for her. The sad part was that Lillian knew it."

Hannah heard a gasp and saw Kiki only inches away from them, her eyes like saucers and her jaw dropped. "No, I simply don't believe it," she said, which was Lady Nails speak for "I suspected it all along."

"You shouldn't eavesdrop," Hannah told her.

"I wasn't," Kiki said. "I was on my way to the little girls room and just happened to catch a few words."

Hannah was skeptical. "Well, at least keep your voice down."

Kiki plopped into the empty chair next to Hannah. "That Geraldine! What did she have going for her? She looked so quiet and dowdy, and it turns out she was one hot mama."

"Still water runs deep," Hannah said.

"*I'm* still water," Kiki said.

Kiki's water was in a blender with the "frappe" button pushed, Hannah thought but didn't say. She turned again to Ellie. "But twenty years ago. That's a long time for Lillian to harbor a grudge."

"Maybe, maybe not. Lillian's marriage was never the same

after the affair because she knew Leonard carried a torch for Geraldine. Lillian never forgave her, blamed her for the whole thing. I heard that Leonard was asking for Geraldine right on his deathbed. Imagine how Lillian felt. She had to be bitter."

Yes, she did, Hannah thought uneasily. Perhaps bitter enough to want revenge.

ELEVEN

HARRY STANLEY'S AFTERSHAVE, AN AROMA
Hannah felt sure was bay rum with a dash of eau de dead
mackerel, wafted through the Cadillac as it chugged up the
steep hill. The car let out a vexed snort when Hannah hit the
brake at a stop sign. The aging vehicle wasn't meant for
driving in San Francisco, and neither was she. She loved the
city, but found the steep hills tortuous, holding her breath at
every stop, praying the car wouldn't roll backward into the
one behind her.

She hit the gas, and the Cadillac surged through the inter-
section without mishap.

"Turn left! Left right here!" Harry shouted, a bundle of
constrained energy. There was no need to yell. He sat right
next to Hannah, having insisted on being up front where he
could better give directions, but for some reason he felt com-
pelled to bark them out.

"You're awfully dressed up," Kiki said from the backseat.
"Are we going someplace special? You've been so secre-
tive."

"Nah, I just thought I'd spiff up a little, that's all," he said,
straightening his red bow tie. "Now turn right! Here!"

Hannah steered the car down a dim, narrow street, its neglected storefronts caged behind black iron bars. It was nine o'clock, the time when she usually wrapped herself in her flannel robe and curled up in bed with a book. She found it exhilarating to be just starting out at an hour when she would normally be thinking about bed. Still, Harry's demeanor, like that of a puppy on its first trip to the park, concerned her. The neighborhood concerned her even more.

"Are you sure you know where we're going?" she asked. "This isn't a nice part of town."

Kiki leaned forward and pointed to a small cluster of women on the sidewalk. "Are those hookers?"

A closer look confirmed for Hannah that they were.

Twisting in her seat, Kiki stared out the back window. "Hey, I think that tall redhead has on the same sweater I do."

Hannah felt sure there was a message there, but let the event pass without comment. She was too busy dealing with her own worries. "I don't like this neighborhood one bit," she said to Harry. "We could be mugged."

"Aw, don't get your panties in a wad," he replied, still looking at the hookers.

Hannah arched an eyebrow. "Excuse me?"

He faced forward. "I mean, don't worry, you're safe with me," he said more politely, then pointed to the left side of the road. "This is it! Park over there."

Hannah pulled the Cadillac to the curb and turned off the ignition. She gave Harry a penetrating gaze. "Now can you tell us where we're going?"

"I told you already," he said. "To see an old friend of Geraldine's. Her name's Lila Sue. Geraldine and me knew her in Bangkok."

"And she lives on this street?" Kiki asked with disbelief.

"Aren't we hoity-toity? Geraldine used to come here all the time. She and Lila Sue were real good friends. If Geraldine's problems were connected to the old days, Lila Sue will know about it. You two coming or not?"

Hannah and Kiki got out of the car and followed Harry down the sidewalk. Limping along as fast as his cane allowed, he turned the corner, and the women found themselves in an alley, a dark concrete gash between two dilapidated, soot-covered buildings. At its dead end they saw a blinking neon sign, the tawdry pink light reflected in the muddy puddles spotting the pavement. It depicted a scantily clad woman jerkily leaning over to pat a French poodle. Each time the woman reached the dog's head, he pulled down her bra with his teeth. Hannah felt a powerful urge to go home.

To her chagrin, Harry stopped in the doorway just beneath the neon woman/dog combo. Beneath the door's streaked glass porthole was painted lettering that read Lila Sue Rak's Famous Poodle Dog Lounge.

"Are you one hundred percent positive that Geraldine came here?" Kiki asked. "I mean, are we talking about the same person?"

"The one in the casket, right?" Harry said sharply. "Sorry. Shouldn't have said that." He ran his eyes over the building's chipped stucco facade. "I guess the neighborhood's gone down a little."

"A little?" Hannah said.

He looked insulted. "Hey, we've all got a few miles on us, don't we, sweetheart?"

"And you're sure this Lila Sue person is here?" Hannah asked. "You called first and told her we were coming?"

"What is this, an inquisition? She's a good friend of mine. She'll be here." He shoved the door, and it swung open.

Following him, her hand gripping Kiki's, Hannah found herself engulfed by a smoky gray light, the smell of stale beer filling her nostrils. On the left she saw a dark wood bar running the length of the large room, and behind it a wall of shelves holding hundreds of liquor bottles, their yellowed labels peeling. A leather jacket with what looked like a bullet hole hung over the bar next to a torn American flag. At the back wall she saw a low stage set aglow by pink track lights, two firemen's poles running floor to ceiling on each end. To the right of the stage stood an ancient chrome-trimmed jukebox. At the table next to it sat a haggard, youngish man, his lips wrapped around the long neck of a beer bottle, his stringy hair bouncing as he slapped his thighs to one of Hannah's favorite songs by The Doors.

Two more patrons hunched over glasses in the opposite

corner, bringing the number of Saturday night customers to a grand total of three. The whole place, along with the people in it, looked like it needed a good scrubbing and a few years of career counseling. Hannah had never stepped foot in such a foul and disreputable establishment.

"The place looks good," Harry said. Hannah and Kiki exchanged a glance. "You gals get a table. I'll round up Lila Sue."

Harry walked off, and Hannah made her way through the tables, trying to locate one that didn't look too sticky.

"You think we can catch a disease in here?" Kiki asked, staying close to her sister.

"Try not to touch anything. I hope Harry isn't scamming us." Hannah stopped near the stage at a small table that looked cleaner than the others.

"Scamming us how?"

"I'm not sure. This doesn't feel right."

After the women sat down, Harry emerged from a doorway at the back of the room. As he headed to their table, it looked to Hannah like he had lost some of his enthusiasm.

"Lila Sue's on her way out," he said, sitting next to Kiki. "Damn, it's good to be back here."

A petite Asian girl carrying a cocktail tray sidled lazily up to their table. A skirt the size of a dinner napkin clung to her childish hips and a stained T-shirt exposed a soft, flat midriff. Wearing a bored expression, she put down the tray and pressed her hands against the table's edge, shoving out one hip.

"Two-drink minimum per person," she said, making it sound like a threat.

"Hi ya," Harry said to her. "You're one gorgeous babe. You know that?"

She looked at him like he was something a dog threw up. "I don't have all night."

Hannah sat very straight in her chair, her hands folded in her lap. "I'll have a Coke."

"White wine for me," Kiki said.

Harry chortled. "This isn't a white wine kind of place."

"I agree," Hannah said, her tone wary. "Just have bottled water."

"Water?" Harry looked at the waitress and pointed a crooked finger at Kiki. "She and I'll have tequila shooters. Little Miss Priss can stick to her Coke. And bring the bottle of tequila to the table. The best you've got."

"Ooh, tequila," Kiki said with a lustiness in her voice that Hannah feared. Kiki was a notoriously bad drinker, and her history with tequila was especially loathsome. Hannah remembered an incident with Kiki and tequila in college. The campus police had found her in a fraternity laundry room, wearing a scuba mask and little else. Or was it the semiconscious frat boy who wore the mask? So hard to remember that far back.

They sat silently a few minutes, listening to more Doors music on the jukebox and a bitter argument over the Forty Niners that had erupted at another table. Hannah's uneasiness grew with each passing moment, and she wished she had heeded her misgivings about Harry.

The waitress returned with a can of Coke, a bottle filled with gold liquid, two shot glasses, and a saucer of cut limes. After placing the Coke in front of Hannah, she put the empty glasses in front of Harry and Kiki, then filled them.

"Twenty-six dollars," she said. Frowning at the amount, Hannah reached for her handbag, but Harry insisted on paying. He pulled a tattered wallet from his inside coat pocket, handed the waitress a twenty and a ten, and told her to keep the change. She stuck the money in her pocket and left.

"You know how to do tequila, don't you?" Harry said to Kiki. "Suck on the lime, then straight down the hatch. Watch an expert." He picked up one of the glasses, bit on the lime and tossed the liquid down his throat. He winced, then coughed. "Tasty," he said weakly.

Kiki raised her glass. "Down the hatch." She sucked on the lime, emptied the glass with the ease of a sailor, then daintily wiped her lips with her pinkie. "That was just awful," she said with a satisfied grin. Hannah's eyes narrowed with apprehension.

The music changed to a louder, faster beat, and the other

three customers began clapping halfheartedly. Purple light drenched the stage and the waitress, sans cocktail tray, oozed onto it, wearing a bikini consisting of a few strings attached to three small triangles of sequined fabric. Upon reaching the center, she gyrated her hips without perceivable enthusiasm, her face maintaining the same expression of colossal ennui she had worn when serving the drinks. After grabbing the pole at the front left quadrant of the stage, she wrapped one of her legs around it and slowly slid up and down, her eyes aimed no where in particular.

"This is revolting," Hannah muttered.

"I'll say. I mean, you like to see a little more oomph put into it," Harry complained.

"I mean the fact that this poor young girl is displaying herself as a sex object," Hannah said, fighting the urge to kidnap her and enroll her in community college. Hannah looked to Kiki for moral support, but her sister didn't appear to share her pique. On the contrary, Kiki swayed in her chair to the music, wearing a dreamy, tipsy look. Harry's eyes were glued to the dancer.

"You realize, of course, that you're old enough to be that girl's grandfather," Hannah told him.

Wearing a wicked smile, Harry kept his eyes on the stage. "I don't know about that."

"You have hemorrhoids older than that girl," Hannah said. "I'm beginning to question your motives for bringing us here."

"Hold your water. Lila Sue's gonna be out in a minute."

At that moment a rotund shadow cast itself over their table. When Hannah looked up she saw an Asian woman, middle-aged and fat as a cow, swathed in a shiny red floor-length kimono. Her black hair was pulled into a knot on top of her head, and her painted red lips, full and misshapened as punched pillows, sucked greedily on a cigarette clamped into a long plastic holder.

"So, Harry, you stinking lousy bastard," she said, her voice slow and thick, her black almond eyes as watchful as a lizard's. "You finally come back to see Lila Sue, you stinking piece of puke?"

Hannah's eyes slid to Harry. "This is your good friend?" she whispered. He didn't answer. He looked too afraid to speak.

After a long, awkward moment, he braced himself with his cane and rose from his chair, his free arm outstretched. "Lila Sue, sweetheart, it's great to see you." He gave her a two-second hug, then quickly pulled back as if he feared for his safety. "You look great."

"I look like shit," she responded gruffly, giving the cigarette another drag. "You look like shit, too." Her eyes moved to Kiki and Hannah, and Hannah hoped their appearance wouldn't be likewise assessed.

Harry introduced them, stumbling on their names, then he pulled out a chair for Lila Sue. Once settled, her black eyes lingered on Harry and, after a moment, softened. She reached out a sausage-shaped finger and tickled underneath his chin.

"It good to see you, Harry, baby," she said, her voice melting into a girlish coo. "You not been by for ten years. Lila Sue miss you."

Harry leaned back in his chair, increasing the distance between them. "Yeah, well, I've missed you, too."

The visage of Lila Sue had captivated Hannah and Kiki's attention, but a few boos from the small audience drew their attention back to the stage, where, despite the fast tempo of the music, the waitress swayed with the vigor of someone about to lose consciousness.

"Come on and move it, baby!" a man yelled with a drunken slur.

With apparent dedication to customer satisfaction, Lila Sue raised up in her seat and gave the dancer a steely eye. "You do some dancin', girlie, or you don't get paid," she shouted. "You shake that thing or old Lila Sue get up there and show you how to do it." She followed this with a hearty laugh that erupted into a coughing fit.

The dancer/waitress pivoted, facing the back of the stage. With one quick movement she threw herself forward from the waist, putting her head between her ankles and looking directly at the audience. She did it with such swiftness and flexibility that Hannah and the other customers were suitably impressed, and there was a smattering of applause. The girl looked at Lila Sue from her upside down position, then shoved her fist in Lila Sue's direction, her middle finger extended.

Lila Sue's eyes flashed with anger, but the customers' laughter quickly soothed her. "That girl, one day I gonna fire her ass."

"She doesn't seem too committed to her work," Hannah said dryly "Why do you keep her on?"

"Have to." Lila Sue grunted. "She my daughter."

"That's little Tulip?" Harry asked with disbelief.

"She look good, huh?" Lila Sue said with pride. "Last time you saw her was right before you left Bangkok, and she come to your knee." Leaning a bulbous elbow on the table, she sidled closer to Harry, resting her chin on her hand. "We had good times back in Bangkok."

"That's what we want to talk to you about," Hannah said, wanting to get the necessary conversation over as quickly as possible so they could leave. Lila Sue ignored her, keeping her eyes on Harry. Hannah tried again. "We want to talk to you about Geraldine."

Lila Sue's head twisted in Hannah's direction. "You come here to talk about that woman?" She made a spitting noise, then turned to Harry. "After all these years, it still Geraldine. I love you, but you don't care. You too busy chasing Geraldine all over Bangkok." Lila Sue turned her attention to the stage, where Tulip hung onto the pole, barely twitching her hips. "You shake it, girlie!" Lila Sue shouted angrily.

Harry put his hand on Lila Sue's arm. "Geraldine's dead."

Lila Sue faced him, squinting. "When?"

"A couple of days ago," Hannah told her.

"Dead from what?"

"She was murdered."

Lila Sue took a long, anxious drag on her cigarette, holding in the smoke a moment before letting it curl out through her nose. "They know who did it?"

"Not really," Hannah said. "We want to help the police find out. That's why we want to talk to you."

"I don't know nothing." Anxiety was audible in Lila Sue's

voice. "That Geraldine, she always push and push. Everything black-and-white. She make people good and pissed. This time she do it, and somebody up and kill her ass. Lila Sue knows."

"What do you know?" Hannah leaned forward over the table. "Who did she make mad?"

Lila Sue sat back in her chair and put one foot on a chair next to her. "I don't want no trouble."

"There won't be any," Hannah replied. "Please, tell us what you know."

"Listen, lady, me and Geraldine, we never got along. I don't owe her nothing."

Hannah glanced at Harry. "He said the two of you were great friends."

Lila Sue smiled and ran her index finger up Harry's arm. "Harry, he always tells whoppers. Geraldine and I know each other a long time ago, but we never like each other. We work together some. We help kids get out of Thailand and to the States."

"How long did you and Geraldine do this?" Hannah asked.

"Right after the war and a few years after."

"Why did you stop?"

Lila Sue shrugged. "Couldn't keep up with all the kids. Not enough people to help. Besides, after Geraldine stole Harry from me, I don't help her with nothing."

"She didn't steal me from you," Harry said.

"Hah!" she shot back, slapping her foot on the floor. "You and me were lovers until she came along. She put a spell on you."

Kiki sat up straighter. "You mean, like a love potion?" Hannah detected a slur to Kiki's words and noticed that her shot glass was half full. Kiki had been drinking the tequila when Hannah wasn't looking.

"You were telling us about Geraldine," Hannah said.

Lila Sue shrugged. "Geraldine come into the Poodle Dog fifteen years ago when I first open, and I throw her out. That's why I think something funny's going on when she come back a few weeks ago asking favors."

Harry looked very surprised at this, which Hannah found odd.

"What did she want?" he asked.

"We sit right here at this table and she tells me she got problems, that somebody after her."

The words hit Hannah with a jolt. "Did she say who it was?"

"No. She just say somebody watching her house, that somebody try to break in. She thinks somebody wants to kill her. She wants to know if I know a bodyguard she can get on the cheap, and I say I don't know no cheap shit bodyguard. If I did, I hire one myself, the riffraff that come in this place."

Harry, now looking alarmed, fidgeted nervously with his empty shot glass. Even Tulip's writhing on the floor like a dying snake wasn't distracting him.

"Why didn't she go to the police?" Hannah asked.

Lila Sue turned up a palm. "That's what I tell her. I say, 'You pay taxes, girl. Go tell the coppers.' But she say she can't."

"Why?"

"She tells me our old friend François in Bangkok, he call her about a year ago and tell her he think somebody around here smuggling something from Thailand. He asks her to check it out. She does, and she tells the cops. The cops check it out, come back to her, and say she's crazy. Nobody smuggling nothing. But Geraldine, she don't give up. She keep bugging the cops. She watches, she listens. After a long time she finally figures out somebody smuggling something, but not what François said. François got it wrong. But she already cried wolf to the cops too much before. Now she can't go back until she got solid proof, because they think she's some nuts old lady. Same reason she can't tell the cops about somebody being after her until she got solid proof. She got herself a bad reputation."

"Did she say what was being smuggled?"

"She tried to tell me. She said she wanted to tell somebody real bad, that it sitting inside and wants to come out. But I say, 'Don't tell me, girl. I don't want to know nothing.' And she say, 'Lila Sue, that a good decision, because this thing, it so bad nobody going to believe it.' That's why she got to have proof, otherwise the cops, they going to still think she's a crazy old lady."

While Hannah digested this information, Lila Sue pulled her chair right next to Harry's so he had no means of escape. He didn't seem to notice, his eyes off somewhere, lost in thought. "I'm scared, Harry," she said in a baby voice. "Somebody may know Geraldine come talk to me and they may want to kill me, too. You protect me, baby, like the old days?"

It occurred to Hannah that in a match between Lila Sue and any would-be murderer, the smart money would be on her. She looked like she could crush a watermelon between her knees.

Lila Sue looked at Harry with soft, liquid eyes and sighed deeply, her huge breasts heaving like an ocean swell. For an instant Hannah saw her the way she must have been thirty years ago when she was still young and flushed with love. Lila Sue rested her hand on his shoulder. "I'm still a lot of woman for you, Harry. I got me a nice little room upstairs with a bed big enough for two."

The prospect shook him out of his stupor. "Gee, sounds great, but you know, I'm in a relationship now." Kiki's eyes grew to the size of Lila Sue's breasts as Harry put his arm around her and roughly pulled her to him. "This is my girl."

Lila Sue twisted up her lips like she was about to spit out a cockroach.

Kiki held up a finger. "Um, not really."

"Don't listen to her," Harry said, giving Kiki's shoulders a threatening squeeze. "She's just shy."

Hannah watched this scene with amusement, unable to remember the last time Kiki discouraged a man's advances or any time that she had been described as shy.

Lila Sue looked Kiki up and down. "You be good to Harry," she told her, then held up her cigarette in front of Kiki's face. "Or I come find you and put this out in your eye."

Kiki let out a fearful squeak.

"Time to fill her up," Harry said with forced cheerfulness as he poured more tequila into his glass. In need of a drink herself, Kiki filled her glass with tequila and tossed it down; Harry did the same. Now drinking for medicinal purposes, they both passed up the lime.

Kiki stood, handbag in hand. "I'm going to the little girls' room."

"I'll come with you," Hannah said.

Harry grabbed Hannah's arm and mouthed the words, "Don't leave me."

"That's right, hon, you stay here," Kiki said, her slurring getting worse. "I'll be dandy as candy. Now where is it?"

"Through that door, then second door on right," Lila Sue directed, pointing to the right of the stage. Kiki gave them a little wave, turned, stumbled, then wobbled her way toward the door.

Ordinarily Hannah wouldn't let her sister go anywhere on her own with a few tequilas in her, but she was anxious to ask Lila Sue more questions.

"Do you think Geraldine was helping Thai children again? Could the smuggling have been connected to that?" Hannah asked.

"No way," Lila Sue replied. "Now there so many kids being whores in Bangkok, you need a fleet of cruise ships to get them to the States." She finished her cigarette, pulled it out of the holder and tossed it to the floor, stamping it with her foot. "I tell you what Lila Sue thinks. I think half of what old Geraldine told me is hooey, and she really involved in drug smuggling, trying to make a little money on the side. That the only reason somebody up and kill her."

"Absolutely not," Hannah said, offended. "She wouldn't do such a thing. She told Harry it was animals being smuggled, and she was trying to stop it. Geraldine was an animal rights activist."

"You mean one of those people who don't like other people eating meat?" Lila Sue said, her eyes questioning. "Geraldine, she no animal rights person. Back in Bangkok, I never see anybody eat as much meat as Geraldine. When she here two weeks ago, she wants a burger, and I told her we only have chips. Any kind of chips you want, we got—sour cream, barbecue, everything. No burgers. She said that too bad, because that what she like best for lunch."

Hannah sat back in her chair and took a contemplative sip of her Coke. She didn't know if a person could risk her life for her work as an animal rights activist and still eat meat. Maybe Geraldine was only opposed to Hunters, Inc. importing endangered species, but David Berger had called her a wacko militant vegetarian. Wacko militant vegetarians didn't ask for burgers. They asked for tofu and then felt bad because a soybean had to die.

"Uh-oh," Lila Sue said. She elbowed Harry. "Your girlfriend took the wrong door. I say second door on right. She take second door on left."

To Hannah's amazement, Kiki stood at the right side of the stage, staring vaguely across it. Her brain, a bit like fruit salad to begin with, was now marinated in cheap tequila, and she couldn't make sense of her environment. Her eyes darted about wildly, searching for a stall where she could relieve herself and a mirror where she could refresh her Tahiti Pink lipstick. But all she saw was Tulip rubbing against a pole.

Slowly and fearfully, Kiki turned to the front of the stage. Her hands jerked up and covered her face in shame when she at last understood her mistake. She stood frozen, and Hannah looked on, equally flabbergasted and immobile. A wolf whistle from a drunken customer, followed by a shout of "Baby, you are looking gooood!," broke the spell. Kiki peeked through her fingers. A man sitting on the other side of the room jumped to his feet.

"Show us what you got!" he shouted, banging his beer bottle on the table. "You've got to be better than that other one."

Apparently ready for any excuse to leave the stage, Tulip spit out a curse and skulked off.

"How dare he speak to my sister that way!" Hannah stood up to rescue Kiki and then give the man a piece of her mind, but out of the corner of her eye she saw Kiki walking to the middle of the stage. Her eyes anxious, but with a curious sparkle, Kiki held her hands out from her side. When she reached center stage, she halted. She stared transfixed at the audience, and the audience stared back at her. After a suspenseful moment, she bumped her hip to the right, then bumped it to the left.

If Hannah's eyebrows had lifted any further, they would have been airborne. A smattering of applause struck her ears, and she watched Kiki swish her hips again, this time with increased energy and a growing smile. She then shimmyed her shoulders, sending her breasts into a fierce jiggling and every man in the room, including Harry, into shouts of approval.

Lila Sue cast a critical eye upon Kiki, then upon Harry, who was clapping wildly.

"Yeah, that girlfriend of yours, she got a bad shyness problem," Lila Sue said, her gaze sliding back to Kiki just as she began dancing the twist. "That shyness problem so bad she better go to the doctor and get some anti-shyness pills."

"This is, uh, a new side to her," Harry said, then turned to Hannah. "You think you should go get her?"

The rational answer was yes, but Kiki was having such a wonderful time, Hannah didn't have the heart to end it. Kiki pranced on the stage with primal abandon, swinging her purse on its strap and gyrating her shoulders. It crossed Hannah's mind that she never had a camera when she needed one.

Varying her repertoire, Kiki stopped in the middle of the stage, stuck out her left foot and left hand, pulled them back, then repeated the motions on her other side in some risqué version of the hokeypokey. Egged on by shouts and applause, Kiki resumed her saunter across the stage, shimmying and dipping, grinning like a madwoman. With one hand she grabbed the pole and swung her body around it, stumbling but quickly catching herself.

It was when Kiki turned her back to the audience, her high-heeled feet as wide apart as her tight skirt allowed, that Hannah realized what was coming. Leaping from her chair, she bolted past the tables toward the stage, but stopped at the stage entrance, astonished that Kiki had quasi successfully executed Tulip's head-through-the-ankles maneuver. Although Kiki had to put her hands on the floor to brace herself, she managed to get her head at least in the general vicinity of her ankles.

The small audience, including Lila Sue, applauded wildly, then Kiki collapsed.

Hannah rushed onto the stage, and, having retrieved her sister from this position many times, especially during their younger years, skillfully rolled her over, put her arm underneath her shoulder, and dragged her off.

"I was good, wasn't I?" Kiki asked, her words garbled, once Hannah got her into an upright position in the small hallway.

"You were fabulous," Hannah replied. "Everyone thought so." It occurred to Hannah that she should chastise Kiki for lewd public dancing, since she had earlier pronounced Tulip's dancing so offensive, but at Kiki's age it seemed more aerobic than lewd. Withholding criticism, Hannah steered Kiki back to the table, the hoots of approval still sounding in their ears.

"Hey, lady, you making real progress on that shyness problem," Lila Sue said as Hannah helped Kiki into a chair. "That good, because your boyfriend here, he don't like shy women." Lila Sue looked mischievous as she put a new cigarette in the holder. "Harry got the hots for women like Geraldine that throw themselves around."

"Geraldine never threw herself around," he said bitterly.

"She slept with half the Bangkok officials."

Absorbed in this drama, Hannah didn't catch Kiki drinking another tequila until it was already down her throat.

"She didn't!" Harry answered angrily.

"She did!" Lila Sue shouted back. "You're not the only man in her bed."

"If she did sleep with anyone, it was only because she didn't have money to bribe them," he said, breathing hard. "She only did it to help the kids."

Lila Sue made a spitting sound. "Yeah, she spread her legs to help mankind, to save the whales." She lit a match and touched the flame to the fresh cigarette. "That's why she stole those drugs, huh, Harry?"

"What drugs?" Hannah asked.

Kiki chose this moment to enter the conversation. "I wath faboolous, wathn't I?"

"What drugs?" Hannah demanded, but both Lila Sue and Harry had forgotten everyone else in the room.

"Yeah, that's exactly why she stole them," he shot back.

Her eyes ferocious, Lila Sue gripped the edge of the table, the cigarette holder stuck between two fingers. "And when she shot that guy dead, was that for his own good?"

Kiki slumped in her chair, semiconscious, while Hannah zeroed in on every word, her eyes bouncing from Lila Sue to Harry as they argued.

"She didn't mean to kill him. It was an accident. You were always jealous of her," Harry said, his face filled with despair. "Jealous of everything about her."

"Of that cow? She had nothing over me. That woman, she never loved you, Harry."

"That's not true."

"She used you," Lila Sue told him. "But I loved you."

"I want to know about the drugs and the gun," Hannah said loudly, thumping the table with her fist. "I demand to know, who did she shoot?"

Lila Sue aimed angry eyes at her. "You listen, lady, and listen good. I don't want nothing to do with you or that Geraldine. Now you get out of here. I'm throwing you out." She noisily slid back her chair and stomped away, her kimono flapping.

Harry took a swig of Hannah's Coke, then wiped his mouth with the back of his hand. "Let's go."

Hannah had no objections, since it looked like their conversation with Lila Sue had come to an abrupt halt. She helped Kiki up from the chair, and the three of them navigated through the tables toward the exit.

"Hey, lady, you got a dancing job here any time!" Lila Sue yelled with hoarse laughter as Kiki stumbled by.

They pushed open the door and walked out into the dark

alley. A heavy mist had settled, and it magically turned to
pink smoke each time the neon sign blinked.

"Now tell me what you meant about Geraldine shooting
someone. Tell me about the drugs," Hannah said. She had
her arm wrapped around Kiki's waist to keep her vertical as
they made their way down the alley. Harry's limp appeared
to have worsened, but he managed to stay ahead of them.
"Harry, talk to me."

He stopped. "I'm tired of talking. This was a mistake. If
I'd known we were going to rehash Geraldine like that, I
never would have come here."

"But that was the reason we came. You said Lila Sue could
tell us about her."

"None of that was true. Geraldine did call me and I did
hang up on her, and I did go to her house to apologize. But
she and I never had a real conversation. She never told me
that any animals were being smuggled or that she was in
trouble. When you told me about that Hunters, Inc. place, I
just played on a theme, and you bought it. It never crossed
my mind that Geraldine actually spoke to Lila Sue or that
anyone from Bangkok had called her."

"Why did you lie?"

"Because I wanted a night on the town with some women,
and the Poodle Dog has some memories for me. I never
figured on Lila Sue still being in that dump. You could have
knocked me over when the bartender said she was there."

"You were willing to waste our time so you could have a
few drinks in a run-down bar?" Hannah asked.

"You got what you wanted, didn't you? All that nice dirt
about Geraldine." They reached the Cadillac, and Hannah
made no move to find her keys. "Could you unlock the
door?" he asked.

"Not until you tell me about the gun and the drugs," she
said. "Is it true?"

"Yeah, it's true, but it's not as bad as it sounds."

"It's hard to imagine a kinder version," Hannah said, leaning her sister against the car. Her eyes half closed, Kiki
grabbed the front of Harry's shirt.

"Come on, big boy," she said. "Come to mama."

"I've had enough of women tonight," he answered, pushing her away. He turned back to Hannah. "Listen, I don't want you thinking anything bad about Geraldine. She did steal drugs, but it was only medicine for the kids. Some of them were sick by the time she got them. They had hepatitis, venereal diseases. She found a doctor who helped her get the medicine, but she didn't do it through legal channels and she didn't have the money to pay for it, so technically, yeah, she stole it."

"What about her shooting someone?"

"She shot a low-life pimp, so what? The world was better off without that scum, the things he was doing to little kids. And she never meant to shoot him. She said she only wanted to scare the bastard, to get this little girl away from him. But she'd never handled a gun before and her aim wasn't that great. She didn't know you were supposed to hold a gun with both hands. It was just bad luck."

"Everyone has off days," Hannah told him, not sure of what else to say.

Looking at the ground, Harry shook his head sadly. "It's funny how things turn out. I thought tonight I'd have a couple of drinks and some fun, but all it did was bring up bad memories. Made me realize I never knew Geraldine at all."

"Looks like I didn't either," Hannah said.

"Lila Sue was right. I've been kidding myself all these years. Geraldine never loved me. How could she? I've always been a screwup."

"Now don't start feeling sorry for yourself," Hannah said gently, then felt a slap on her shoulder.

"Let's go have a drink, huh, Hannah?" Kiki said.

"No," Hannah answered. "Please be quiet. I'm talking to Harry."

"We're done talking," he said, looking so dejected it touched Hannah's heart. "I apologize for wasting your time."

"You didn't," she said, trying to bolster him. "We accomplished a lot tonight, thanks to you, whether you planned it or not. We know for certain now that Geraldine was afraid for her life, that she thought someone wanted to hurt her. We also know that she definitely uncovered something about

Hunters, Inc., something different than what she originally thought Berger was doing. Those are great leads for the police. They can talk to Lila Sue and find out more about this François person. And I have some plans for tomorrow that I need your help with. I want you to go to Hunters, Inc. and see if you can wangle any new information from David Berger. I can't go back because he knows me, but you could do it. He's the type with a temper, and if you made him angry, he might let something slip."

Harry looked at her like she was crazy. "Listen, toots, I'm depressed but not suicidal. I want to find the bastard who paid to have Geraldine killed, but risking my neck isn't going to bring her back."

"I'm not asking you to risk your neck."

"I'm risking my neck if I go anywhere near that Hunters place. You heard what Lila Sue said. Geraldine was scared for her life. She wanted a bodyguard."

"But the police are involved now, and—"

"Police! Are you kidding me?" He tapped his knuckles against Hannah's skull. "Hello? Anybody in there? Geraldine obviously didn't think the police could protect her. Why should they be able to protect us?" He walked down the street, pounding his cane into the sidewalk. Hannah followed him.

"Where are you going?" Hannah called to him.

He stopped and faced her. "There's another bar right around the corner where I intend to get good and soused."

"But I need to get Kiki home."

"Be my guest. I'll take a cab."

"Please let me drive you home."

"No thanks. Good-bye and good luck," he said, then turned and walked away.

Hannah watched him as he hobbled along the littered sidewalk, his body stooped. She didn't like the thought of him going to a bar by himself, but she understood it. Sometimes it was better to plunge headfirst into your misery. At least then you had a chance of coming out the other end. She decided to call him the next morning. She walked back to the Cadillac, considering all that she had learned that evening and how she could use it to help the police.

"We had one heck of a night, didn't we, Hannie?" Kiki muttered, leaning against the Cadillac with her arms sprawled across the hood.

"Yes, we certainly did," Hannah replied, her expression pensive as she watched Harry disappear around the corner.

TWELVE

THE CREAKING OF OLD HINGES cut through the stillness as Hannah, using the key Geraldine had given her, slowly opened the front door. It was long after midnight, and the empty house felt cold; the living room's blackness, frightening. *Like a coffin,* Hannah thought, acutely aware that she had entered the house of a dead woman. She doubted that murdered women, especially feisty ones like Geraldine, slept peacefully in their graves. Would Geraldine's spirit, bitter and restless, pace these rooms?

A knot in her throat, Hannah began seriously questioning her impulsive decision to look inside Geraldine's refrigerator. After Kiki had gone to bed, she had sat for half an hour in the squishy chair by the living room window, thinking about everything Lila Sue had told her that night. For some reason her thoughts stuck on what Lila Sue said about Geraldine wanting a hamburger. The rest of Lila Sue's information, however fantastic, somehow made sense, but the idea of the hamburger nagged at her. It didn't fit with what she knew. That's when she remembered the key. She still had Geraldine's house key in her purse.

She could have waited until morning and simply called Vera or Lillian. One of them would have known if Geraldine ate meat. But Hannah was too antsy to wait, and although her suspicions were increasingly focused on Berger, she couldn't allow herself to forget that her friends were still suspects as well.

Force of habit made Hannah lock the door's main dead-bolt. She didn't dare turn on the lights, afraid that a neighbor might see them and call the police. Instead she turned on the small flashlight she kept on her key chain, aimed it safely at the floor, and made her way to the kitchen.

As Hannah moved soundlessly across the carpet, her thoughts ran with the riddle of Geraldine. The dark house felt full of her, as if her spirit lived in the walls, lingered in the stale air Hannah pulled into her lungs. Objects in the room—chairs, tables, books—that had looked so cozy and safe a week before now took on threatening shapes in the dark, as if the house were warning her not to trust the things she used to believe in.

She no longer knew what to believe about Geraldine. Geraldine hadn't been the chaste, simple spinster Hannah had always thought her, but a powerfully sensual woman. She had captivated Harry as well as Lillian's husband, and these men had pined for her the rest of their lives. She had been brave and adventurous, a woman who aggressively pursued life, who bribed and thieved when necessary, who had killed a man in order to save a child. Hannah wondered if, put in a similar situation, she would do the same. She decided that she would. She hoped she would.

Her crepe-soled shoes with all-leather uppers and arch supports squeaked against the kitchen's linoleum floor, the sound as brash as cymbals in the house's dead quiet. She opened the door to the Frigidaire, the light cutting a white swath through the blackness. Closing the door enough to minimize the light, she peered inside and found the evidence that proved Lila Sue had told the truth—an open package of franks, the fat, juicy kind with the barbecue sauce inside that nobody admitted they ate. Next to those sat a package of bacon and a half-full bottle of steak sauce. A blast of cold hit Hannah's face when she opened the freezer. Shining her flashlight on its contents, she discovered several pounds of frozen ground beef as well as three frosty packages of steaks.

Hannah closed the freezer door, her hand pressed against it as she considered the facts. Geraldine not only ate meat, she had half a cow in her refrigerator. If she hadn't been murdered, her cholesterol probably would have gotten her in a few years. The bottom line was that the woman couldn't have been the "wacko militant vegetarian" that David Berger claimed. He was trying to make her sound irrational, like she had harassed him simply because she didn't like him selling meat. But now Hannah felt certain that there had to be something else about Hunters, Inc. that forced Geraldine to butt heads with him.

A chill ran through Hannah as a horrible idea took shape. A few weeks ago Geraldine had contacted two people for help, Harry and Lila Sue, two people who had worked with her in Thailand in helping children. That couldn't be a coincidence. If the rest of Lila Sue's story was true, Geraldine told her that Hunters, Inc. was smuggling something so bad that no one would believe it. What if Berger was importing humans, bringing children into the United States for prostitution? That was the sort of evil that would have inspired Geraldine to keep after Berger, even if it meant risking her life. The names that Geraldine had listed along with the name and address of Hunters, Inc. could have been customers. Berger could have known she had the information and was about to go to the police. An excellent reason to want her dead.

"I think I've figured it out," Hannah whispered into the darkness. A cracking noise outside startled her. After taking a few yoga breaths to calm herself, she went into the bedroom. On her earlier visit she remembered seeing a small desk pushed against the wall underneath the window. She realized it wasn't enough to deduce that Berger had paid to have Geraldine killed. She needed proof. Maybe Geraldine had left something else that could be used as evidence or could at least give the police a new lead. When Geraldine had been a teacher she had always kept neat, organized files. People didn't change habits like that. Geraldine had pursued Berger for months. She might have kept a file on him.

Hannah thumbed through a small file cabinet next to the

desk, but couldn't find anything related to Hunters, Inc. or to Berger. A search of the desk drawers yielded the same results. She tried the oak chest next to the bed, finding only books and old sweaters that smelled of mothballs. She was about to try the living room when her flashlight shone upon a paperback book lying on top of the nightstand. Geraldine must have been reading it before she became ill, the final book in the life of a woman who had treasured them. Picking it up, Hannah expected to see a copy of *War and Peace* or a biography of the Brontë sisters, but to her surprise the cover bore a photo of a shirtless, muscular young man wearing a sheik's headdress and a smoldering expression.

"Geraldine, you continue to astound me," Hannah whispered with a smile. The book fell open to a page marked with a folded paper. After taking her reading glasses from her purse and putting them on, Hannah shone her flashlight on the page. The book was steamy erotica written for women, its prose describing a lusty woman named Miranda making love to two young Arabian sheiks, with one of them using sheep fat and a camel harness in the most inventive manner. Eyebrows raised, Hannah turned the page, eager for more, but before she could read further, something else captured her attention. Printed at the top of the paper that had been used as a bookmark was Ron Gilman's name and the address of his medical office.

Hannah unfolded the paper. It bore no date, but the paper looked fresh. Gilman had said at the hospital that he hadn't spoken to Geraldine in years other than at the annual Botany Club meetings. So why would he write to her?

"I offered you a good price," the note stated in a barely legible handwriting. "If you're waiting for more, don't waste your time. We had an agreement. Live up to that agreement or I'll do something about it. We'll talk tomorrow after the club. I expect to get the answer I want."

The note had no greeting and no signature, but the handwriting looked masculine and was the type of messy scrawl typical of doctors. And the reference to the club—was Gilman referring to the Botany Club meeting?

Her head jammed with questions, Hannah slipped the note

in the book and shoved both in her handbag. She exited the bedroom, pulling her keys from her purse along the way, and hurried down the hall to the living room. She was close to the front door when she heard the sound of metal against metal. She froze. The main deadbolt twisted open.

A shiver started at the base of her skull and crept down her spine. She assumed there was a back exit and was about to look for it when the front door began slowly squeaking open. She turned off her flashlight and dropped behind the sofa.

She heard the door open, then softly shut. Footsteps moved slowly across the carpet. Hannah remained crouched, not moving a muscle. Whoever it was didn't belong in the house just as she didn't belong, for he or she didn't turn on a light, and the footsteps were light and cautious. The person approached the couch, passed it, then paused, standing close to Hannah. She held her breath. She could see the bottom edge of a raincoat as its wearer hesitated, deciding where to go.

Hannah heard a jingling thud by her feet and realized with a sick dread that she had dropped her keys. The person gasped. Panicked, Hannah grabbed the keys, jumped up to run for the door but stumbled directly into a body. She caught herself, tried to push past, and in the process jammed the keys against the other person's face. She heard a yelp.

She bolted out the front door, tripping on the steps, catching herself on the porch railing. She flew down the walkway, then the sidewalk, her feet pounding against the pavement until she reached the Cadillac. Her heart beating in her throat, she took a quick look behind her and saw with relief that no one followed. When she at last got in the car, she started the engine and took off with a shriek of tires. Moments later, stopped at a red light, when her breathing slowed enough to let her brain function, she tried to remember what she could about the intruder. Height, weight, facial features. She hadn't been able to see anything. Male or female? She couldn't be sure even of that. Then it struck her that she had left more than a streak of rubber on the street when she left Geraldine's. Her keys had probably left a mark on the intruder's face.

• • •

"Oh, my God, I feel just awful," Kiki moaned, walking down the back steps and out into the garden. Every few steps she halted, pressed her hand against her skull as if to steady it, then took a bite of the waffle she held in her fingers, the frozen type she popped in the toaster. Thick, gooey red jam lay across the top of it. She was still in her pink chenille robe, though she had changed her house shoes for loafers as protection against the dewy grass.

Dressed in Japanese gardening pants, an old sweatshirt, and rubber clogs, Hannah crouched by her prized Mr. Lincoln rosebush, busily clipping dead blossoms. She awakened that morning with her head still swimming from the amazing events of the night before, as well as a dozen questions about the note on Gilman's stationery. As soon as she had downed her first cup of coffee, she had called the Hill Creek Police and left a message for Detective Morgan, asking him to call her. She wanted to tell him what she had learned from her meeting with Lila Sue. She wasn't sure she should tell him what happened afterward.

"What's the problem?" Hannah asked distractedly, her eyes on the bush. She felt rattled, her jumbled thoughts refusing to arrange themselves in a linear fashion. Spying a snail chomping on a rose leaf, she picked it up and hurled it over the fence into Naomi's yard, wondering if a snail felt the sensation of flying. Naomi didn't care if snails ate her garden. On the contrary, she liked to get down on her knees and commune with them.

"You know what's wrong. It was that tequila last night," Kiki said, shaking her head, then groaning. "It must not have been good quality. I've got an awful headache."

Hannah started to elucidate for her sister the evils of alcohol, but one glance stopped her. Kiki looked like a melting Martian, with some bright green goo slathered an inch thick on her face.

"Did you fall in the compost pile?" Hannah asked.

"Ha, ha. It's a papaya and avocado facial. I'm rehydrating. Ronnie's coming over tonight." Kiki tried to wink, but the goo stuck her eyelids together and it took a few facial con-

tortions to release them. That job accomplished, Kiki re-
warded herself with an extra-big bite of waffle. The mention
of Gilman caused Hannah's stomach to clench.

Kiki pressed one hand against the small of her back. "I
think I pulled something." She cocked her head with puzzlement. "Did I do any dancing last night?"

"On stage, with the men in the audience hooting."

Kiki's mouth twisted up. "Eeew. I had some fuzzy memories of something like that, but I thought I dreamed it." A
slight smile crossed her face. "How was I?"

Hannah thought it terrible that Kiki should have such a
night of abandon and then not be able to remember it. She
was about to refresh her sister's memory when she saw Naomi bustle through the garden gate and thought it best not
to tell the story in front of anyone else.

Naomi glided over, wearing a cloud of pink cotton. Lauren
was right behind, in blue jeans and a sweater.

"Look who I found just as she pulled up!" Naomi said,
her face beaming. She seemed especially ebullient that morning and Hannah wondered why. "What synchronicity!"

"I thought I'd drop by for a cup of coffee," Lauren said.
"They were all out of Sunday papers at the market. You've
got one?"

Hannah stood up, brushed the dirt from her knees and went
to Lauren, giving her a kiss. She then pointed to the Sunday
paper lying on the garden table. Lauren and Naomi sat down,
and Hannah, once she retrieved extra mugs from the kitchen,
sat down with them.

"Any news?" Naomi asked greedily. "There must be
something going on or Kiki wouldn't have that goop on her
face."

"I've got a date with Ronnie tonight," Kiki said. "Remember?"

Pouring coffee into Lauren's mug, Hannah saw her niece
wince. She knew it bothered Lauren that her sixty-year-old
aunt had a more active love life than she did. Of course, at
this point a cloistered nun was getting as much action as
Lauren.

"Ron's coming to dinner! That's right. The spell is still

working!" Naomi said, clasping her hands beneath her chin. "Why didn't you remind me earlier?"

"I left you a message on your machine," Kiki said.

"Oh, well, I haven't been keeping up with that, not since I started the 900 number."

"How's that going?" Hannah asked.

Naomi swallowed a gulp of coffee, then fanned her mouth. "Brilliantly. It was a little slow at first, but things are picking up. I put up some flyers around town." Naomi tried the coffee again, this time more cautiously. "There have been a few minor organizational problems."

"Like what?" Lauren asked.

"Nothing really," Naomi replied, her thick eyebrows knitted for a second. "It's just that, as you know, I'm sharing the number with Walter Backus's friend, and sometimes the calls get a little confused. But it's really going very smoothly, wonderfully well."

Hannah's instincts detected a turd swimming in Naomi's punchbowl of delight. Any other time she would have explored it further, but currently her mind was too focused on other issues.

Kiki sipped her coffee, holding the mug so her pinkie stuck out with a daintiness Hannah found ironic for a woman who had danced at a strip joint the night before.

"So, Naomi," Kiki said with a girlish lilt in her voice. "Is there something special we could do tonight for my big date with Ronnie?"

"You mean like knock him unconscious and tie him to your bedpost?" Hannah asked. It was hard to tell through the green goo, but she felt certain that Kiki frowned.

"I meant like another love potion or spell or something," Kiki said. "The last one was such a winner. But if you could make one that's a teensy bit stronger this time. . . ."

"Doing little witch potions isn't my metier, dear. I'm a channeler and a psychic," Naomi said with atypical haughtiness.

"That's right. Being a witch is so tacky," Hannah said. "But a psychic hot line, now that has class."

Naomi gave Hannah the best Buddha-type countenance

she could muster up, which was Buddha's expression when Buddha had just sat on some stiff, sharp object. "What I meant was, my telephone channeling looks so promising that I'm no longer exploring potion opportunities. But Kiki, why don't we do the Dance of the Summer Buffalo just before Ron arrives? It would help you get in touch with your primal emotional flows. It requires total nudity, of course, and we'll have to rub ourselves with chicken fat."

"Excuse me, ladies."

All heads pivoted at the unusual and welcome sound of a masculine voice coming from the side of the house. Hannah saw Detective Morgan behind the garden gate. She then heard two gasps, the first an especially loud one erupting from Kiki as she remembered the current condition of her face. Jumping up and knocking over her chair, she jogged into the house, little globs of green mush flying from her head. The second, more muffled gasp came from Lauren, who, upon sighting the man who fired her loins, sat immobile and saucer-eyed, as if someone had just smacked her.

"What a nice surprise," Hannah said, hoping Morgan hadn't heard the comment regarding chicken fat and nudity, since it could possibly be an illegal combination. She went over and unlatched the gate for him. He wore dark slacks with a blue shirt that looked like he had ironed it himself.

"I'm sorry to bother you," Morgan said. His eyes fell upon Lauren, and redness crept over his cheeks.

"Please sit and have some coffee," Hannah said. After hesitating, he nodded and approached the table. He and Lauren simultaneously grabbed Kiki's overturned chair to upright it, and there was a moment of shy smiles and "excuse me's." Hannah noticed Kiki peeking out the kitchen window. When Kiki saw Morgan sit next to Lauren, she smiled broadly, looking like a grinning cabbage. Hannah mouthed the words "make more coffee," and Kiki nodded and disappeared.

"I checked my messages this morning before I left for work," Morgan said.

"You work on Sundays?" Naomi asked.

"When there's a murder investigation." He looked at Hannah. "You said you wanted to talk to me." Both Naomi and Lauren gave Hannah meaningful looks.

Hannah had to think of some way to get Morgan alone. "Would you like to see my roses?" she asked him. He looked baffled at first, his mouth opening slightly. She nodded toward the far part of the garden. "I'd like to show you my Mr. Lincoln."

"I thought you drove a Cadillac," he said.

"It's a rosebush," Hannah explained, reminding herself that Morgan, although not always a rocket scientist, was still chock full of wonderful qualities.

Morgan excused himself from Lauren and Naomi, then followed Hannah to the rose bed.

"We could talk at the station," Morgan told her. "But your house is on my way to work, and I thought this would be easier for you."

And you were also hoping Lauren would be here, Hannah thought with satisfaction. Why didn't he and Lauren just admit to each other that they wanted to resume their relationship and get on with it? But she knew that Morgan's pride had been hurt because Lauren, foolish thing, had dumped him when she met someone else. Of course, it wasn't really an official dump, since Morgan and Lauren had gone out only a couple of times, but Hannah knew that a man's ego was delicate. All the more reason for her to help him with the case. Once he had solved it, it would restore his self-confidence.

"I have information," she said. It took her a good ten minutes to explain what she had learned about Geraldine from Harry and Lila Sue, including Geraldine's work in Thailand and her asking Lila Sue about a bodyguard. Morgan listened intently, making notes on the small steno pad he took from his shirt pocket.

"So we know that Geraldine was doing her own investigation of David Berger," she continued. "I'm not completely sure what she originally thought he was smuggling, but whatever it was, she told the police about it."

"I already know that. After we interviewed Berger, we spoke to the police in San Jose. They said that about a year ago Geraldine called them over and over again, claiming that Berger was smuggling animals, live ones—mostly monkeys she said. She claimed he was bringing them to the States, then killing them for some hormone."

"To be used for what?"

"To treat cancer or something bizarre. It had to be a scam. But the police never came up with any evidence."

"That's because by the time they looked into it, Berger had moved on to something else. I think she figured out that it had something to do with children. Whatever it was, Berger knew she was on to him, and we know that she was afraid of the man."

He nodded. "Somebody called in an anonymous tip saying the same thing." Hannah knew the tip had come from Vera. "We're checking him out. But how would Berger get an old yearbook picture of her? We've looked at every old yearbook in this town, including those kept at the school and the library. But not one of them is missing that photo."

"I've been giving that some thought. He could have gotten it through the publisher or maybe some kind of book warehouse. You should check the Internet," Hannah said. "There might be services who do searches for old yearbooks."

He nodded. "Good idea."

"I heard there was money found in Mendoza's apartment," she told him. "Have you connected it to Berger?"

"That's something I can't talk about."

"I suppose you've checked Berger's bank records?"

"I'm sorry, but I can't discuss that. Trust me, we're doing everything we need to."

Hannah thought his last statement was confirmation enough. "What about the names on the paper I gave you?" she asked. "Have you spoken to any of them? Have you found a connection?"

Morgan opened his mouth, closed it, then spoke. "Since you're the one who gave me the lead in the first place, I owe you something. I'll tell you this much. We haven't found a connection between the names, and we haven't been able to locate any of them. Not yet, anyway. That's all I can give you."

Hannah took a long look at one of the deep red roses, considering what she was about to say. "I have something else. Although Berger appears to be the strongest suspect, we can't forget that there are other people who could also have motives."

"We haven't forgotten," Morgan said.

"Of course, sorry. Anyway, I don't like to spread gossip," she said with sincerity. She glanced over his shoulder to see if Naomi and Lauren were watching them, and found it extremely odd that they weren't. Their attention was focused on the kitchen window. "But I think I should tell you a few things."

Hannah started by telling him about Geraldine's flunking Vera in English her senior year of high school. As she spoke, she saw Kiki in the kitchen window waving something, then she saw Naomi hurry into the house.

Morgan looked incredulous. "That happened a long time ago. Besides, if I hired a killer to get every teacher who flunked me in high school I'd—"

Hannah smiled. "Flunked that many classes, did you?"

Morgan looked embarrassed. "Just one, actually. Gym. But I flunked it twice. I hated basketball."

He found her other information more compelling. She shared the story about Geraldine's affair with Lillian's husband, then told him about the letter from Gilman. He asked to see it, so she went into the house. It took her a few minutes to find her purse, and when she started back outside with the letter in hand, she saw Kiki, still green-faced, looking out the kitchen window.

"Hannah, we may have a little problem," Kiki told her before she reached the kitchen door. Hannah looked out the window. She saw Morgan standing near Lauren and looking at Naomi with the strangest expression. Naomi had her hands in the air, one of them holding scissors.

Guessing what had happened, Hannah rushed out the back door and saw Morgan looking grim, standing with his feet wide apart, his hands raised, palms outward.

"Hand over the scissors, nice and easy," he said to Naomi.

"I most certainly will not," she replied indignantly, waving the scissors at him as she spoke, which didn't help things. "I wasn't trying to attack you. I was only trying to get a little clip of hair."

"Why would you want my hair?" he asked.

Lauren's face crumpled, and she ran past Hannah into the house.

With disaster looming, Hannah's brain raced. "To test your, uh, your inner—" She struggled for some New Age term.

At first Naomi looked confusedly at Hannah, then her eyes widened with comprehension.

"Your inner coyote. You have sadly neglected it, I'm afraid, Detective Morgan," Naomi said, lowering her arms and looking at him with feigned maternal concern. She studied him a few seconds, then shook her head sadly. "Have you been feeling a little vague lately?"

Hannah looked at Morgan, thinking that just then he looked pretty vague in general. Naomi continued. "Have you felt confused, sort of muddled?"

Morgan thought a moment. "My head's been a little fuzzy in the mornings."

"I knew it. I have a little test I do." Without waiting for consent, Naomi reached up and clipped off some hair. "I'll give you a call this afternoon with my analysis."

His forehead scrunched with concern. "I haven't been feeling quite myself lately." He looked longingly at the back door, through which Lauren had so recently scampered.

Watching him, her arms crossed, Naomi made a *tsk* sound. "It's so obvious that you're not expressing your inner coyote, that you're stifling your masculine energy. Red Moon can help with that."

Hannah rolled her eyes.

"Is that the thing where men get together and beat on drums?" Morgan asked with interest.

"No, no," Naomi answered with a "you're sweet but ignorant" chuckle. "Your inner coyote is that essence of you that's male and wild," she said with a dramatic increase in volume. "The part that wants to howl at the moon, to soar with the eagle and run with the buffalo. The part that yearns

for the female coyote." On the last part she slid her eyes
meaningfully toward the house. She whipped a business card
from her caftan pocket and handed it to Morgan. He stared
at it with perplexity, apparently concerned that he had left
his inner coyote so neglected for so long. "Call my 900 number," Naomi said, then added with a wink, "I give a police
discount."

Kissing her fingers at him, Naomi said good-bye, then hurried into the house, his lock of hair clutched in her fist.

The crisis averted, Hannah gave Morgan the letter. He
quickly got back to business.

"How did you get this?" he said once he had read it. "We
went through the house and didn't see it."

Probably because men were doing the searching and they
didn't feel comfortable flipping through a book with a nude
male on the cover, Hannah thought. Straight men in the Bay
area were hyper-sensitive.

"I went to her house to get a few of her belongings when
she was in the hospital," Hannah said, stumbling on the
words, even though they weren't a lie, only a misdirection.
She wanted to tell him about the person she encountered at
Geraldine's house the night before, but she shouldn't have
been there herself and didn't want Morgan to know she had
been practically breaking and entering. It would get her in
trouble with Perez as well, and she knew Morgan would tell
him.

"And you waited until now to give it to me?"

"I just found it yesterday. It fell out of a book." Now she
was definitely lying, which she hated doing, but self-
preservation required it. "Do you think it's important?"

"Very important. This letter is threatening. It suggests a
murder motive."

"On the other hand, you can't be sure it's from Gilman.
There's no signature. Someone else could have used his stationery."

"It will be easy to confirm with a handwriting sample."

"Maybe I should go back through Geraldine's house and
see if I can come up with anything else."

"No," he said firmly. "Thanks for all your information, but

I don't want you involved any longer. We can handle the investigation on our own." He refolded the letter and slipped it into his shirt pocket. After saying good-bye, he exited through the gate.

Once he left the garden, Kiki and Naomi sailed out the back door. "Isn't it exciting!" Kiki said. "Naomi got Detective Morgan's hair."

"Naomi, I thought you weren't doing love potions anymore," Hannah said.

"I had to make an exception. Lauren looked so stricken."

"Where is she?" Hannah asked. "Is she okay?"

"She locked herself in the bathroom," Kiki answered. "She's fine, or at least she will be when she knows we can make her potion."

"I wish you wouldn't. It's such nonsense," Hannah told her.

"I don't think so," Kiki said, with a singsong emphasis on the word "think." "It worked for me, didn't it? I can't wait to tell Lauren. Come on, Naomi, let's coax her out."

Naomi and Kiki went back in the house, leaving Hannah alone by the rosebushes to contemplate again what had bothered her all morning. The idea of Gilman, Vera, and Lillian all having murder motives left a queasiness in her stomach. There was evil loose in Hill Creek, and for the first time she truly considered the possibility that the evil could be very close to home.

THIRTEEN

AN HOUR LATER, ALONE IN the backyard, Hannah clipped off the last three roses from her Double Delight bush and examined them lovingly, knowing there would be no more until spring. Yellowish cream, tinged with bright pink, the large blossoms were sumptuous and showy, yet ladylike with their long, elegant stems.

Burying her nose in the blossoms, Hannah drank in their fragrance. She was a romantic at heart. All rose lovers were, which made November such a melancholy time, with the year's last blossoms picked, the leaves falling to the ground. It felt as if, after months of intimacy, the plants abandoned you, retreating within, holding secrets deep inside. Hannah put the blossoms into the vase filled with water that she had ready at her feet. Secrets had motivated Geraldine's murder, that much Hannah knew. Not just the secrets that Geraldine herself had kept, but the secrets of other people as well, maybe even people she had long considered friends.

She gathered up the fallen leaves and considered her next steps. She must talk to Lillian and to Gilman. Detective Morgan had warned her to stay away from the investigation, and she intended to, but she had an obligation to let her friends know she had given information about them to the police.

They wouldn't be happy about it, and for that reason she wanted to tell them in person and she wanted to do it that day.

Hannah held the roses once more to her nose, inhaling the perfume, but this time the blossoms smelled funny, the sweet fragrance mingled with a burning smell. Lifting her nose like a bloodhound, she sniffed the air and determined the smell was coming from the house. She saw the kitchen window open and thought that perhaps Kiki was cooking, but the smell was so odd that even Kiki's cooking couldn't have produced it. Then she remembered the love potion.

She entered the house, roses in hand, and found Kiki and Naomi huddled at the kitchen table, smoke curling from a bowl sitting between them. Kiki's face was cleaned up and she had changed into a bright yellow sweat suit. The dog and pig both lay near the table, full of hope that food was being prepared and that bits might come their way. Hannah leaned down and gave each of them an affectionate scratch.

"Are you burning Detective Morgan's hair?" Hannah asked.

"Shhh!" Kiki said, her finger to her lips. "Yes, and it has to be done in meditative silence."

"Is Lauren still here?" Hannah whispered.

"No," Kiki answered. "Once we got her all cleaned up and bandaged, she went home."

"Bandaged?"

Kiki nodded. "It was fate, really. Lauren ran out the front door the exact same time that Detective Morgan came from around the side of the house," Kiki said in her normal tone of voice, so interested in telling the story that she forgot all about the meditative silence. Naomi began chanting, her eyes on the smoke. "I guess being that close to him, him being so cute and all, she got flustered, and when she went down the porch steps, she tripped on your shovel."

Naomi stopped chanting and gave Hannah a reprimanding look. "You really shouldn't leave it out."

"It was leaning against the railing, completely out of the way," Hannah replied.

"Hmm, you're right, now that I think about it. We opened

the front door just as it happened. Lauren's knees sort of wobbled, then she fell into him," Naomi said. "She knocked him down, knocked over the shovel, then tripped on it, and hit her head on the porch railing."

"And she was hurt?"

"Just a scratch," Kiki replied.

Hannah put her hands over her eyes. "How humiliating for her."

"Oh, don't worry," Kiki said. "Detective Morgan was real nice about it. Though he did run off awfully fast."

"Like a gazelle fleeing a lion," Naomi added. "But it doesn't matter." Smiling, she pointed to the smoking ash. "Once we get this baby whipped up, he'll be putty in her hands."

"I hope it works better than it smells," Hannah said, walking to the telephone. Taking her address book from a drawer, she flipped through the pages for Lillian's number.

"Once I get it finished, it won't have much of an odor at all," Naomi said. "All Lauren has to do is rub it between her breasts, and voila."

"Yes, voila," Kiki repeated with enthusiasm. "Detective Morgan will come running to Lauren, just like my sweet Ronnie's running to me." She rested her chin on her laced fingers. "By the way, Hannah, could you be a sweetheart and make yourself scarce tonight?"

Hannah glanced up. "Why?"

"I want to be alone with Ronnie."

Hannah laid down the book. "I don't know if having him over is such a good idea." She cringed inside, not liking what she was about to say. "It's possible that Ron is moving up the murder suspect list."

Kiki looked at Hannah with the same dull noncomprehension the dog and pig would have displayed if you had shown them math flash cards. Naomi leaned forward eagerly. "What do you know, Hannah? Tell us everything."

Hannah didn't think it right to tell them about the letter, since possibly it meant nothing. "I don't know anything for certain. I have suspicions, that's all."

"Suspicions don't count," Kiki said.

Naomi gave her a curious look. "So you're willing to have a possible murderer over for dinner?"

"No man is perfect," Kiki replied.

With a worried countenance, Naomi pressed her hand against her chest. "I don't like this, Kiki. Maybe I should reverse the love spell."

"Don't you dare!" Kiki said. "Do you realize how few single men over sixty there are in this town? I can't afford to be picky."

"But Kiki, I'd never forgive myself if something happened to you as a result of this potion. This magic is powerful. It's too much of a gamble."

"Listen, women are so desperate they're writing love letters to San Quentin prisoners, and those guys have been tried and convicted," Kiki said. "Compared to that, a man who's only a murder suspect qualifies for Bachelor of the Year."

"Actually it would be wrong to cancel dinner with such an old friend just because of a suspicion," Hannah said. "And it's not even official."

"I guess you're right," Naomi replied, returning her attention to the burning hair.

"And, Kiki, I'm having dinner with John tonight, so you'll be alone with Ron. Just be careful. Don't talk about the murders."

"Don't worry," Kiki said with a sly smile. "I have other plans for him."

There was no real evidence against the man, Hannah reasoned. Only a letter that could perhaps be explained. Innocent until proven guilty. Gilman was probably the one who should be concerned for his safety, judging from the glint in Kiki's eye. And it would give her a chance to talk to him if she could catch him before she went to Perez's. Hannah continued thumbing through the address book and at last found Lillian's number. After she dialed it, an unfamiliar voice answered. "Could I speak to Lillian, please?" She listened to the response, then hung up.

Kiki observed her sister with high interest. "Why did you call her?"

"I need to talk to her about something."

"About what?"

Naomi's chanting again drifted into silence as she tuned in to the conversation. "She's getting higher on the suspect list, too," Naomi said. "That has to be it."

"She does have those beady killer eyes," Kiki added. "With kind of a crazed look in them. When are you going to talk to her?"

"Later this morning. That was her housekeeper on the phone. She says Lillian's out shopping, but that she's getting a mud bath at eleven. I can catch her at the Zen salon."

"I'm coming, too," Kiki said. "I want a body wrap, and if you're taking the car, we'll need to go together."

Hannah cast a wary eye on her sister.

"You can come along, I suppose, but I don't want you mentioning Ron to Lillian," Hannah warned. "It will upset her."

"I wouldn't dream of it," Kiki told her. "I just want a body wrap, that's all."

"Do you think it's wise for Kiki and Lillian to be in the same room?" Naomi asked Hannah.

"We won't be in the same room," Kiki said. "It's a big place. And I resent your implication. I'm a grown woman and I know how to behave."

"Of course you do," Hannah said with uncertainty lurking behind the words. "There's no reason for you and Lillian not to be civil to each other. Just remember, Kiki, my discussion with her will be private."

"You can question her all you want," Kiki said. "If it turns out she's a murderer, I hope you get the proof and see her put in jail. But I'm leaving that up to you. I want a little special pampering today, that's all. It's not like anything bad will happen."

A disbelieving smirk crossed Naomi's face.

Leaning an elbow against the glistening black granite counter, the young brunette cupped her chin in her hand, stroking the gold hoop in her upper lip with the tip of her index finger.

"Okay, Mrs. Goldstein, let's see. You want the Egyptian

water goddess oil of the Nile body wrap or the Ayurvedic elemental herbal cleansing?"

"The goddess wrap thing," Kiki replied, a gleam in her eye.

"And do you, uh, want to seek golden tranquillity or like, you know, excite your senses?"

"What kind of question is that?" Hannah asked. The brunette responded with a superior look. Hannah hadn't liked the Zen salon from the moment she stepped foot in it. The minimalist decoration was too sleek, the services too bizarre for comfort and too expensive for her pocketbook. She also didn't like the fact that Zen was cutting into Ellie's manicure business at Lady Nails. Kiki, on the other hand, was bursting with anticipation. She had been talking about a body wrap for years. Hannah wondered if her sister understood fully that "body wrap" referred to layers of gauze and not a Kama Sutra position.

"You get aromatherapy with the wrap," Kiki explained to Hannah, giving the brunette an apologetic smile for her obviously dense sister. "I'd like to have my senses excited, please."

"If you excite your senses any more, you'll be flammable," Hannah said under her breath.

"Hannah, are you sure you don't want something done?" Kiki asked.

"No, thanks. I'm only here to talk to Lillian." The truth was, Hannah couldn't afford to buy a Zen nail file. The cost of Kiki's body wrap would cause them to scrimp on essentials for two weeks, but it was such a treat for Kiki that Hannah didn't mind the splurge.

A short, pretty redhead with a gymnast's body walked in with a confident prance. "Ms. Granger says she'll see you, Mrs. Malloy."

Hannah turned to Kiki. "I'll meet you here in an hour, okay?"

Kiki nodded. The redhead led Hannah down a bright hallway, and with a muscular arm pushed open a heavy door. They entered a large room, the damp air warm and thick with eucalyptus. The walls were pale sea green with a matching tile floor, and along each side stood massage tables, half of them holding women wrapped in layers of gauze. Between some of the tables the tile rose to form oblong tubs filled with lumpy mud that looked to Hannah like steaming dung.

The girl gestured to the last tub on the left. It took a moment for Hannah to recognize Lillian, her towel-wrapped head sticking out of the dark ooze like some primordial beast. Hannah wondered what type of industrial-strength douching it would take to rinse the mud out of Lillian's orifices. The girl left. Hannah said Lillian's name, and her eyes opened.

"Hannah, there you are," Lillian said, her voice relaxed and dreamy. Her white towel was wrapped into a perfect turban, her lips painted a frosty peach. Even in a tub of mud Lillian managed to look elegant. "I was surprised when Susan said you wanted to see me. It must be urgent. Is it news about Geraldine?"

Hannah pulled up a stool and sat down. "No news," she said. Lillian looked disappointed. "But I need to talk to you. It's important."

Lillian's eyes lost their drowsiness. "What is it?"

Hannah shifted right, then left, on the stool, but every position felt uncomfortable. "I don't know of any way to say this except directly. You see, I heard that Geraldine had an affair with Leonard."

Lillian's mouth opened like a gasping fish. Her eyes darted about the room to see if anyone was listening. "Who told you that?" she asked, her voice hushed but furious.

"I don't want to say. I feel terrible repeating it to you, but I have to." Hannah steeled herself. "You see, I told the police about it."

"My God," Lillian groaned. Hannah heard the rustling of gauze as the other women in the room repositioned themselves for better listening.

"Lillian," Hannah whispered. "The police would have found out eventually. It's better to get it out in the open now."

"Why on earth would you say that?"

"Because it gives you a murder motive."

Her hand rising involuntarily to her mouth, Lillian inhaled

sharply, and in the process drew in some mud. Glowering, she spit it out. "All right, yes. Geraldine, that tramp," she said, ejecting the last word from her mouth along with a few bits of mud. "She slept with my Leonard, but it was twenty years ago. I barely remember it."

"That's not what I heard."

Lillian pressed her lips together. "All right, of course, I remember it. And I suppose I may have done a few things over the years, things that could be seen as spiteful."

The image of the numerous locks on Geraldine's door flashed through Hannah's mind. "Did you ever threaten her?"

"Of course not. Who told you that? It's a lie. All I ever did was, well—" The unfinished sentence dangled in the air.

"What did you do, Lillian?"

Lillian sunk a little lower in the mud. "I mailed Geraldine a few things."

"Like what?"

"It's none of your business."

"It's going to be the business of the police very shortly, so you might as well tell me."

Lillian contemplated this for a second before letting out a sympathy-provoking whimper. "I'll tell you, Hannah, if you'll help me. You're dating that man who used to be a police chief somewhere in Marin, aren't you? You have connections. If I tell you, will you talk to the police for me, Hannah? Help them understand why I did it?"

"Did what?"

"You see, Geraldine got pregnant."

"Twenty years ago?" Hannah said with disbelief. "She would have been in her forties."

"Mid-forties. The pregnancy was unexpected, needless to say. She was just entertainment to Leonard, you know. A mid-life crisis. It was always me he loved."

There was a hollow bitterness to Lillian's words that made Hannah not believe them.

"How did you find out about the affair?"

"When Geraldine got pregnant, Leonard confessed everything to me. He couldn't keep something like that secret. He wasn't that way." She paused. "He even toyed with the idea of Geraldine keeping the baby, but she went ahead with the abortion."

"What did you do?"

"I'm ashamed of it now. It was a terrible thing, but you have to remember that I was half-crazy, I was so angry. After the affair my marriage was never the same. We had been so happy, Leonard and me." She stopped. "Until Geraldine happened. I was the victim in all of it."

"Lillian, what did you do?"

Lillian sucked in some air. "I sent Geraldine photographs every year on the anniversary of her abortion."

"Photographs of what?"

Another foreboding silence ensued, and Lillian's bottom lip started quivering. "Aborted babies. I got them from a pro-life organization. They were all bloody and terrible looking."

"Lillian, why did you do such a thing?"

"She killed him," Lillian blurted, then quickly caught herself. Hannah heard more rustling of gauzed carcasses as the other women strained to hear something, anything. "After the affair, Leonard was never the same." Lillian spoke softly, and Hannah could hear the anguish behind her words. "He seemed broken. He had his first heart attack not that long afterward. You remember?" Hannah nodded. "His health was never good after that. It was Geraldine's fault. The stress killed him. His remorse over the affair."

From what she had recently heard about Geraldine, Hannah doubted it was remorse that did in old Leonard. More likely the excitement permanently weakened his heart. "But you kept coming to the Botany Club meetings every year when you knew Geraldine would be there."

"I wouldn't hide from her. I wouldn't give her the satisfaction."

"When she was ill, you went to the hospital and even spent the night."

"I couldn't let Ron know what had gone on. If I hadn't shown concern about Geraldine, he would have asked questions, and Vera might have told him the whole story."

"How did Vera find out?"

"I told her in a weak moment. But she's a good shoulder

to cry on." Lillian stopped, her expression suddenly thoughtful. "It was funny, though. When Ron told me Geraldine was in the hospital, I started thinking."

"About what?"

"About old friends," Lillian answered, her voice becoming gentle. "About what it means to have known people for so long. It's a kind of connection to the past you don't get anywhere else."

"I know what you mean. Old friends make you feel rooted."

"After Leonard died, Geraldine came to me. She said she regretted the affair, that it was wrong, and she asked for my forgiveness. Of course, I couldn't forgive her. But then she died so suddenly. At her funeral, I guess I finally did forgive her." She looked up again at Hannah. "But if the police find out about those photographs, it will look incriminating. Will you talk to the police for me, Hannah?"

"I don't see how my talking to them would help."

"They respect you. Talk to them, won't you, please? For an old friend?"

She looked at Hannah pleadingly, the ice queen melting under the heat of possible police questioning. There was something familiar about it. Where had Hannah seen that look before? An image from high school came back to her. Lillian and her in the hallway outside Geraldine's classroom, with Lillian wanting to use Hannah's class notes to study for the next day's essay exam, wearing the same pleading expression that Hannah never trusted. Any woman who could harbor enough bitterness to send those horrible photos was bitter enough to want somebody dead. And it would be just like Lillian to pay to have the murder done so she wouldn't muss her clothes. At the moment it seemed strangely appropriate that Lillian was up to her neck in mud.

"Hello, girls!"

Hannah turned and saw Kiki trotting up, wearing a white bathrobe and rubber flip-flops on her feet, a young female attendant scurrying behind her with an armload of gauze and a small pail. Upon reaching the table next to Lillian's tub, she patted its sheeted top, turning to the attendant.

"I'll take this table so we can all have a chat while I'm wrapped," Kiki said.

"Kiki, don't you want to relax in solitude?" Hannah said in a stern voice her sister couldn't possibly misinterpret.

"Not really," Kiki said with an innocent smile, avoiding Hannah's gaze. She untied her robe and let it fall from her shoulders to the floor, unconcerned about who should see her naked. Hannah averted her eyes. From the moment Kiki had been born she had never possessed any modesty, always willing to display her abundance of pink flesh to whoever was or wasn't interested in viewing it.

The attendant knelt down and, starting at Kiki's feet, wrapped her in thick, wet gauze strips about eighteen inches wide and yards long that smelled of flowers and herbs. Hannah and Lillian silently watched the process, each woman about to burst with things she still wanted to ask or say, but Kiki's arrival had closed off their conversation like a lid on a bubbling crock pot.

"She seems to be wrapping you awfully tight, Kiki," Lillian said.

"This is the Egyptian water goddess wrap," the attendant said. "A Zen exclusive. It's a mummy wrap technique and you want it snug. Now sit on the table, Mrs. Goldstein, and I'll do your top."

With the attendant's help, Kiki hoisted herself onto the table.

"This is so much trouble, but I suppose it's worth it," Kiki said with a fake, tinkling laugh. "But I want to look special for my date tonight."

Hannah recognized this comment for exactly what it was, the launching of the first Scud missile in a surprise attack. Lillian's radar went on full alert, and she fixed her eyes, red-hot as pokers, upon Kiki. Hannah gave her sister a full range of warning facial gestures—raised eyebrows, firmly set mouth, eyes opened wide. But Kiki ignored them all.

"A date? How nice for you," Lillian said in a voice with the icy smoothness of a silk scarf that had come straight out of the freezer. Lillian lifted one muddy arm and laid it on the tub's edge, her fingers tapping against the tile. Hannah knew she wanted desperately to ask Kiki who she was going out with, but wouldn't give Kiki the satisfaction.

"Yes," Kiki said, boldly returning Lillian's gaze. "I think it'll be the start of something really special."

"Now hold out your arms," the attendant told Kiki.

"Why? I want them wrapped with the rest of me," she replied.

The attendant looked doubtful. "Most people don't. They think it's too confining."

"Well, I want my arms all wrapped up. I want every single part of me silky smooth for *Ronnie*."

Hannah closed her eyes and said a silent *Oh, no*. War had been declared. Time for civilians to evacuate.

Hannah thought that if Lillian's eyes grew any more intense, they would explode right out of her head. Lillian sank lower in the tub, the mud coming up to her chin, watching Kiki as the attendant wrapped her torso until she looked like a huge sprained limb. Once she was wrapped to her neck, Kiki lay down and the attendant put a small terry cloth pillow under her head. Then, using a soft brush, she painted Kiki with more of the oil and herb concoction left in the pail, until the gauze was drenched. When she was finished, the attendant grabbed her pail and scurried off. Hannah wanted to scurry off right along with her, but felt she should stay as peacekeeper in case things got ugly. She didn't have to wait long.

"The word *date* might be a little strong, don't you think, Kiki?" Lillian said.

"He's coming over for dinner, just him and me," Kiki replied, her voice gaining a discernible edge. "That qualifies for a date in my book."

Lillian's eyes narrowed. "In your book a pelvic exam could qualify."

Kiki's head popped up as far as she could get it off the table, which was only a few inches. "Oh, really?"

"Ladies, let's not bicker," Hannah said gently, but Kiki and Lillian eyed each other with venom, their old cheerleader rivalry as fresh as if they had just suited up in bobby socks and pompoms. Fortunately age had placed certain constraints upon them. Lillian didn't want to lose the self-control she had so carefully created over the past forty-five years. Kiki didn't want to create a scene that would get reported to everyone in Hill Creek. Kiki stories had already become local folklore.

"What you don't understand, Lillian, is that Ronnie and I have always had something unique," Kiki said, her head straining upward. "He's always felt something special for me."

Lillian looked pinched. "Anything he felt regarding you happened in the backseat of his father's Chrysler."

Hannah winced. The remark was a low blow, however accurate. The despair on Lillian's face made Hannah realize how important Gilman was to her. She knew that to some women, men were everything, the only yardstick they used to measure their worth. Kiki chased men, but for her it was sport. For Lillian it was her lifeblood.

Kiki raised up farther, lifting her shoulders off the table. "Like you were the virgin. What was that phrase they had for you?"

"I was the Football Day Queen," Lillian said with haughtiness.

Kiki smiled. "More like Football *Lay* Queen."

Lillian bolted upward, causing bits of mud to splatter on Hannah's clothes.

"Now, girls, let's play nice," Hannah said, wiping a speck of mud from her trousers. "The truth is, I think in high school neither of you was exactly stingy with your sexuality." She couldn't help the chuckle that slipped out. "At least according to what was written on the wall in the gym."

Lillian's attention snapped to Hannah. "Oh, you, always so superior, even back then. Thinking you know everything. How many husbands have you had?" Lillian spat, flicking her fingers at Hannah and intentionally splattering her with more mud.

"Only two!" Kiki said in her sister's defense.

Insulted, but still in control, Hannah drew back her shoulders. "That practically makes me a Quaker by Marin County standards."

Lillian reaimed her guns at Kiki. "Ron's just using you. You're nothing more than a night's entertainment for him, just like you were in high school."

"Like he has any real interest in you," Kiki shot back.

"Ron's a sophisticated man with sophisticated tastes. Do you seriously think he'd want you over me? I'm a gourmet dinner, my dear. You're fast food."

"Oh, yeah? He seems to have developed quite a hankering for the Kiki special."

"Ladies, please, let's stop this right now," Hannah said, growing increasingly anxious.

Lillian exhaled loudly, picked up a handful of mud and threw it in Kiki's direction. In the line of fire, Hannah managed to dodge it, but the mud hit Kiki directly on the nose, splattering all over her. Her face, or at least what you could see of it, turned purple. She struggled to get her arms free from the gauze, but she twisted and kicked to no avail, her white form squirming like a demented larva. But although she didn't get her arms free, she caused the table to bounce toward Lillian's tub.

"I'll get you, you floozy!" Kiki yelled, throwing dignity to the wind, not caring who saw or heard.

"You were a tramp in high school and you're a tramp now!" Lillian shouted.

Hannah hurried toward the door to find an attendant to help her get Kiki out of the room, but before she reached the exit she heard more insults hurled, followed by a few thuds, a loud expletive yelled by Kiki, and finally a larger thud capped off with a shriek from Lillian.

When Hannah turned back to look, she saw Kiki's mummy, wrapped form facedown on top of Lillian.

FOURTEEN

"No NEED TO STARE AT me like I've got a second head growing out of my neck," Hannah said to Dolly at the cash register. Hannah took her change and dropped it in her coin purse. "Go ahead and ask me. Everyone else has."

Struggling against a grin and losing, Dolly leaned across the grocery bag. She had been checking Hannah's groceries for ten years and knew her favorite customer wasn't the type to pass on gossip, but this rumor was so delicious, she couldn't help asking. "I heard Kiki and Lillian Granger got into it today at the Zen salon and started flinging mud on each other. Is it true?"

"How ridiculous. The silly stories people tell in this town," Hannah said, following up with a gallant attempt at a dismissive twitter. But since she had little practice with such things, and it came out more as a gagging sound. With a quick good-bye she picked up the grocery bag and headed fast as a bullet for the Cadillac, glad that she hadn't lied, at least technically, about what had happened at Zen that day. What Dolly said hadn't been completely true, because the reality had been much worse than a little mud flinging. In her wriggling to free herself from the gauze, Kiki had fallen off the wrap table, facedown on top of Lillian. Pandemonium ensued, all the women in the room shouting, with Lillian and Kiki shrieking like mating cats. By the time Hannah and the attendant managed to pull Kiki from the tub, they were all covered with mud, and some additive in the lumpy stuff had given Hannah an itchy rash on her chest and hands.

After the day's freakish events, she looked forward to a peaceful dinner with John Perez. He was cooking the main course, and she had stopped at the Hill Creek Grocery on her way to his house to buy dessert. She had originally planned to get vanilla ice cream and hot fudge sauce, but that particular color combination reminded her too much of gauze-wrapped Kiki in the mud bath, so she opted for double Dutch ice cream, a jar of raspberry sauce, and a bag of Milano Mint cookies. In that short shopping time three people pulled her aside and asked for the down and dirty on the Zen incident. Hannah managed to evade the questions, finally dropping a carton of pistachio gelato on Bertha Malone's yellow cowboy boot when she got pushy in frozen foods. Hannah knew the story would be all over town by morning.

By the time she left the store, dusk had turned to darkness, and, realizing how late she was, she quickened her pace across the parking lot. It amazed her that after forty-five years Kiki and Lillian could still be squabbling over Gilman. But that was human nature, she supposed. Were any of them really different from when they were seventeen or eighteen, her included? They were essentially the same people they had been in high school—the same strengths and frailties, pursuing the same dreams, trying to heal the same hurts. It occurred to her that if Kiki and Lillian could still harbor grudges from the distant past, it was conceivable that Vera could still be bitter over missing her opportunity to attend Stanford, and could have blamed Geraldine.

Hannah checked her watch. She should have been at Perez's a half-hour ago. She had waited at home for Gilman to arrive, but he was so late she finally had to leave, deciding to call him in the morning. Hannah reached the car, put the grocery bag on the hood, and rummaged through her handbag for her keys, wondering for the thousandth time why her purse was always such a bottomless canyon.

A sudden grip on her arm startled her. She jumped, then spun around and saw David Berger. There was no question of exchanging polite hellos. He had changed from the first day she met him. She saw no confidence or professional air. He looked tired and raw, his nerves close to the surface. The vehemence in his eyes frightened her.

"Keep away from me and my business," he said, the words brusque. "Do you understand me?"

Blood rushed to her face. She looked frantically around the parking lot, but saw no one to help her, and the lot was mostly hidden from the street by trees.

"I don't know what you're talking about." She tried to sound self-assured, but her voice broke.

His fingers tightened around her arm. "You know exactly. You talked to the police about me."

It was Vera who had made the first call to the police, but Hannah would never tell him so. She searched his face for marks, thinking he had been the one the night before in Geraldine's house, but he had moved into a shadow, and the darkness obscured him.

"Let go of me." She tried to pull her arm away but he only jerked her closer. Her arm knocked into the side mirror, the jolt causing her groceries to fall from the hood onto the ground.

"You fuck with me—"

She could smell his breath and perspiration, felt his skin's clamminess.

"And what?" she asked.

The sound of gravel under tires surprised both of them. A car pulled a few feet into the lot. Berger let go of her. As the beam from the car's headlights washed over his face, Hannah looked again for marks but saw nothing. Still, it didn't mean that it hadn't been him. The keys could have scraped him on the neck and the injury was hidden by his collar.

The driver backed out, taking off in the other direction.

"You'll pay for it. You understand?" Berger pointed his finger in her face. "You'd better be afraid of me, lady."

The statement was unnecessary, since at the moment she

was scared to death. "I'll . . . I'll call the police."

"You already have, but see, they can't help you." He smiled slightly. "There are things I can do. Who knows? I may have done something already. Remember what I said."

He grabbed her arm again, shoved her back against the car. Her heart still thumping, Hannah watched him as he walked out of the parking lot and turned down the sidewalk, his shoes hitting hard against the pavement. He was a vile and angry man. Cross him, and he fought back savagely. And Geraldine had crossed him.

Hannah picked up her scattered groceries, got in the car, and locked the door, her fingers trembling so hard she dropped the keys twice before she got them in the ignition. She pulled out of the parking lot and drove down the street, watching for Berger on the sidewalks, but she saw only two teenagers on bikes and an older woman walking a dog. Berger was gone.

By the time she pulled up to Perez's house, Hannah's fright had turned into anger at herself. She should have slapped Berger, kicked him in the balls, yelled for help, or done anything more aggressive than just standing there and cowering like a dog.

She sat in the car a minute, determining how much, if any, she should tell Perez. She decided to tell him, but not until later in the evening, not until he had a few glasses of wine. She didn't want the night ruined by him getting upset. Tonight was special. He was cooking dinner for her at his house for the first time.

After powdering her nose and putting on some lipstick, Hannah grabbed the grocery bag and walked up the stepping-stones that led to his door. His house was similar to hers, a Craftsman's cottage, only larger, with a fourth bedroom he had turned into a study. He answered the door wearing jeans and a white shirt with splatters of tomato sauce on the front. One of her favorite Jefferson Airplane songs played on the stereo.

He gave her a welcoming kiss, then took her bag and looked inside. "Good dessert."

"There's skillful cooking and there's skillful shopping,"

she said, trying to sound lighthearted. As she stepped past him into the living room, he wrapped his arm around her waist and playfully pulled her to him. She stiffened, the memory of Berger's grip fresh in her mind.

"What's wrong?" he asked.

"Sorry. I'm just tense."

He kissed her again, this time giving it more time and attention, and she felt a rush of pleasure. She was so contented in his arms, it made everything painful fade away, at least for a moment. She felt different with him than with any other man she had known. Being honest with herself, she knew that neither of her husbands had been that important to her. She couldn't remember why she had married them in the first place. She supposed she had loved them, or thought she had, but if she looked at it realistically, she had to admit that the entire male/female relationship scenario had never lived up to expectations. Now here she was at the age of sixty-one discovering a man whose kiss turned her to jelly, whose eyes made her heart do flip-flops when he smiled. She was falling in love for the first time in her life, and she wasn't comfortable with it. She hadn't told anyone of her feelings, not Kiki or Naomi, and certainly not him.

"We'll fix you up in no time," he whispered in her ear.

She walked with him toward the kitchen. The house interior was spare and masculine, with a few good antiques, dark oak floors, and a scattering of photos of his children and grandchildren. Passing the dining room, she smiled when she saw the table set with cloth napkins, candles, and a vase of flowers he had probably gotten from his neighbor. It was obvious he had put a big effort into the evening. She was about to compliment him, but was stunned by the sight of his kitchen. It was a train wreck. He must have used every pot and pan he owned, all of them on the stove or piled in the sink, everything covered with food. The counters were streaked with tomato sauce, splattered with bits of onion and mushroom and other foodstuffs she couldn't identify. Under the bright lights she saw he had tomato sauce in his hair, and she burst out laughing.

He looked puzzled. "What's funny?"

"You are. You said you'd fix me, and you already have."
Hannah pulled him to her and kissed him. Her next instinct
was to roll up her sleeves and start the cleanup, but she
fought back the hausfrau urge, thinking it would set a bad
precedent. They could clean up together, later.

Dinner ended up looking better on the plates than it had
on the kitchen walls. The pasta dish was a simple linguini
with tomato sauce and vegetables, and after seeing his
kitchen, there was no denying it was homemade. Hannah felt
guilty that when she had him over for dinner a few weeks
earlier, she had been busy that day with volunteer work and
had ended up serving him Thai takeout.

She forced herself to eat almost everything even though
she wasn't hungry. If it had tasted like stewed tennis shoes,
she still would have eaten it and pronounced it delicious, just
because he had gone to so much trouble. He had bought a
Jefferson Airplane CD and a bottle of nonalcoholic white
wine for her that looked like the real thing even if it didn't
taste like it. Yet she couldn't enjoy his attentions the way
she wanted to. Her mind was too full of David Berger. There
had been a desperation in him that frightened her just thinking about it.

She longed to tell Perez what had happened, to talk it over
with him, but he would overreact and she didn't want to start
an argument. She also didn't want him to know how much
investigating she had done over the past several days.

She watched him through the candlelight as he rattled on
about his jog that day, the heart-stopping beauty of his grand-
baby, the mountain in Russia he planned to climb, and some
new recipe for ravioli he had read in the newspaper. Funny
how some men mellowed so well with age, she thought.
Perez had surely broken women's hearts by the dozens when
he was younger. By his own account, his youth had been
wild. Now here he was, close to sixty-five and as comfortable
at home as an old cat, cooking dinner and fussing over grandchildren.

"You want decaf?" he asked as he pushed away his ice
cream dish. "It's instant."

"No thanks," she said. "The dinner was great."

"The sundaes were the best part, and you hardly touched yours. That's not like you."

"I'm just not that hungry tonight."

"You feeling okay?"

"I'm fine."

"You're not fine. What is it? Maybe I can help."

She gave in to an impulse. "Did you talk to Larry Morgan today?"

Perez leaned back in his chair and sighed heavily. "You won't relax until we have this conversation, so let's get it over with. Yes, Morgan called today. I'll tell you anything I ethically can."

She played it cool, taking a sip of her non-wine, not wanting to reveal her eagerness. She wondered if he knew her well enough to see through the act. "This relates to a lead I already know about. I gave Morgan information about Ron Gilman wanting to buy something from Geraldine."

"You mean her house," he said, apparently not realizing he was giving information away. He had drunk two glasses of red wine, and never would have made the slip if completely sober. One of the many perils of drinking the real stuff.

"Yes," she said, taken aback by his answer. She put her glass on the table. "Why did he want it so badly?"

"It turns out that Geraldine's property is zoned for commercial as well as residential use. Gilman owns the building next door, and he needed Geraldine's house so he could tear down both buildings and build a medical office. I guess the doctor business isn't as lucrative as it used to be. Gilman already had an HMO outfit ready to sign a lease on a build-to-suit basis, but he needed her property in order to have enough square footage."

"And she wouldn't sell?"

"It looks like at first she was going to. Gilman offered her a great price. I would have sold him my house and everything in it for that kind of money. But she got cold feet and backed out."

"How do the police know all this?"

"Gilman told them. Morgan called him in for questioning

today, based on the letter you turned in." Perez took a big sip of wine, watching her over the top of his glass. "How did you get that letter, Hannah?"

She realized that they both had unanswered questions on their minds that evening. "I found it," she replied, vague as a child who has done something naughty. She saw a slight throbbing at his temple.

"When? How?"

"You're changing the subject. Do the police think that Geraldine refusing to sell Ron Gilman her house was enough motive for him to want her dead?"

"Geraldine left her house to a school for homeless kids in San Francisco, and from what I heard, Gilman is already negotiating with them for the sale. It had to be important to him. There was big money involved in that HMO deal."

"But I thought Ron was wealthy. At least his wife was, and she must have left him a lot of money when she died."

"Either he spent it or the money was never there in the first place. There are lots of people in Marin living beyond their means. He told Morgan he was strapped for cash, and the bank records he turned over proved it."

Hannah knew that the only reason to check Gilman's bank accounts would be to help determine if he had paid Mendoza. Earlier she had thought Gilman might be high on the murder suspect list. Now he could be on top, since he had a motive as good as Berger's and access to Geraldine's high school picture. A golf ball-sized lump lodged in her throat. Kiki was home alone with him. Gilman had no reason to hurt Kiki. They were only having dinner. And if he really was the one who had hired Mendoza, then that proved he liked his murders committed long-distance. It wasn't like he was a homicidal maniac. Unless he had killed Mendoza. Hannah reminded herself that Berger was the number one suspect, at least in her mind, but the rationalizations didn't soothe her.

She tossed her napkin on the table. "I need to get home."

Perez's forehead furrowed with concern. "Why?"

If she told him the truth, he would only get jumpy and insist on coming home with her, and Hannah didn't want to cause a scene with Gilman. He was an old friend and there was only circumstantial evidence against him, at least that she knew of. She just didn't want Kiki alone with the man. Besides, she wanted to talk to him, and having Perez in the room would make that impossible.

"I'm not feeling well," she at last replied to his question, and it was the truth.

"Jeezus, was it the food?"

"No," she said, amused at his panic. "I have a headache, that's all." She got up from the table. "One more question. Have they learned anything new about David Berger?"

Perez stood up, his face clouded with worry. "Not much. They checked his personal and business bank records but didn't come up with any withdrawals that couldn't be accounted for. Bottom line, they can't find any evidence that connects him to Geraldine's murder."

"Maybe they're not looking hard enough."

Perez eyed her. "You know something. What is it?"

It was one of those times when alcohol would have been appreciated, but Hannah took a sip of nonalcoholic wine instead. She told him about her earlier visit to Hunters, Inc. and about Berger threatening her. Once she got started, it felt good to get it out, and she found herself wishing she had told him before. But the more she told, the more stressed Perez looked.

"What's your problem?" he blurted angrily after she had laid it all out. "Don't you realize we're dealing with people who kill?"

The intensity of his response took her off guard. She knew he wouldn't like what she told him, but she didn't expect him to yell. There was something about a man raising his voice that always rankled her, made her want to fight back.

"There's no harm in simply talking to people," she said, constraining her emotions.

"There *is* harm, Hannah. When men threaten you in dark parking lots, believe me, there's harm."

"Geraldine was my good friend. I have a right to know what happened."

"She wouldn't want you putting yourself in danger."

"I don't mind taking a few minor risks."

"These aren't minor risks!" Perez paused, put his hands on his waist, and closed his eyes to get control of himself. When he opened them, he seemed calmer. "I'm sorry I yelled. But you beat cancer, Hannah. Wasn't that enough risk for one lifetime?"

Hannah felt her blood rising. "People always tell me how I beat cancer, but I didn't beat it. You should know that. I wake up every morning wondering if today's the day it will come back. Surely your wife felt the same way."

"She never said so."

"That doesn't mean she didn't feel it." She lowered her gaze to the floor. *Nice work,* she told herself. *Bring up his dead wife.* How could she be so stupid? "The point is," she said gently. "I get tired of being afraid all the time."

"Sometimes fear is good, Hannah."

She knew she had hurt him. She could see it in his face, and it twisted her up inside, but she had to stand her ground. "These are my decisions, John, and not yours."

"Fine, great," he said, his voice back to high volume. "You go ahead and make your decisions, but you do it without me around."

The biting gruffness of his words stunned and insulted her. She grabbed her purse and jacket and moved to the door. "Now I've been threatened by two men today," she said, then walked out the door, slamming it behind her.

FIFTEEN

TICKED OFF, HANNAH BACKED THE Cadillac away from Perez's house way too fast and heard a soft crunch as she flattened the marguerites lining his driveway. Too bad, she thought, since it had taken her a whole day, with his help, to get them planted. Immature oaf that he was, he would probably think she had run over them on purpose.

Her eyes stung and she clenched everything inside her, too stubborn to cry. The planet would be an easier place to live if women could only self-procreate, she told herself. Men just mucked things up. They had no intuition, no ability to see beneath the surface. Instead of looking to the core of something, they stomped around barking out orders and making threats.

Her life had been going just fine before she met Perez, she concluded as she steered around the corner, giving Perez's house a last glance in the rearview mirror. She had gotten through her illness. She had interests, work, friends. She finally had control of her life and then Perez came along, and now look at her. She squirmed in her seat, her brand-new leopard-print underwear chafing. Kiki had talked her into buying it the week before, convincing Hannah that Perez would be highly appreciative. Now she planned to burn it.

Stopped at a red light, she calmed down a bit. On the other hand, he was only showing concern for her safety, and he wouldn't have gotten so angry if he didn't care for her. Yes, he definitely cared for her. Look at all the trouble he had gone to for dinner. He could be so thoughtful and kindhearted, yet he still had passion. He had bucketfuls of that.

As the light turned green, she gunned the engine. On the other hand, she wasn't going to let a man scold her like she was a schoolgirl just because of some pasta and a few romantic glances. Two husbands had tried to order her around and neither one had gotten as far as diddly, so why should things change now?

When Hannah reached her house, she saw Gilman's car in the driveway, blocking her from the garage. Typical male. She muttered another curse against the male sex and parked the Cadillac at the curb. She got out of the car but stopped before closing the door, feeling flutters in her stomach over confronting Gilman. She reminded herself that he was an old friend, that there was no direct proof of his guilt, and that even if there was, he had no reason to hurt Kiki. To be afraid was foolish, and she tried to tell her stomach that, but it wasn't listening. To hell with it all. She took a fortifying breath, shut the car door, and headed up the sidewalk.

Hannah was halfway to the house when she heard the rustling in the bushes. Her breath froze in her chest, her eyes searching the shrubs that grew in front of the house. At first she saw nothing, the plants nothing more than vague blobs of darkness. Then something moved. Blood rushed to Hannah's face. She saw a dark figure crouched behind the plants.

On another evening when she hadn't had a friend's murder on her mind, when she hadn't just had a fight with Perez and spent the past ten minutes reminding herself how she never had to take any guff from anyone, she might have run inside like a scared rabbit. But at that moment Hannah's blood ran hot, and whoever skulked in her shrubbery would feel the brunt of it. She stomped toward the figure and whacked it hard with her purse.

"Ow!" The figure stayed crouched behind the bushes, hands on head for protection. Hannah raised her arm to strike another blow, then, in the moonlight, noticed that the intruder's fingernails were painted bright red.

"Stop it, Hannah! Are you trying to kill me? That hurt!"

Recognizing the voice, Hannah lowered her arm. "Lillian, is that you?"

Straightening, Lillian rubbed the side of her head. "Obviously. I think you knocked out my earring. It's eighteen karat and came from Tiffany's."

"I'm so sorry," Hannah said, taking hold of Lillian's elbow and guiding her out of the plants and onto the walkway.

Lillian smoothed her dark blouse and pants that were oh-so-perfect for any fashionable prowler, then pressed her fingers against various points on her face. "If you've dislodged my chin implant, I'm suing."

"You were hiding in my bushes," Hannah said. "Explain yourself."

At first Lillian drew herself up, ready to hurl out a defense or insult, but apparently thought better of it. "I was going to look in the window, but you drove up and I panicked. So I hid," she said in a manner far from apologetic.

"Why look in my window?"

"To see what Ron and Kiki were up to, of course," she replied in a tone implying that it was a stupid question. "I heard from Ellie that Kiki is using witchcraft to get him. Is it true?"

"Lillian, you're too bright a woman to pay attention to such nonsense."

Silent a moment, Lillian heaved a shuddering sigh that ended in tears. "I'm making a fool out of myself, I know. But Ron and I have a relationship. I love him. I always have."

The stars must have been out of alignment and throwing everybody's love life out of whack. "Have you told him?" Hannah asked.

"Don't be ridiculous. Of course not. If I did, he'd run away. Men always run from me."

"That can't be true," Hannah said, giving Lillian a comforting pat. "You're a beautiful and intelligent woman."

"I know, I know. I'm gorgeous, educated, firm almost everywhere. You can bounce a quarter off my thigh muscles.

But there's something about me. I just can't hang on to a man." She sniffed, and Hannah rummaged through her purse until she found a tissue and handed it to her. Lillian blew her nose with finishing school elegance. "I shouldn't be so cowardly, peeking in windows." She held her hands close to her chest, fingers curled into fists. "I need to go inside and confront him." She stepped toward the porch.

"Please, Lillian, don't. We don't want another brawl like the one today."

"That was an unfortunate incident for which your sister is completely responsible. I'm feeling myself again. As you so kindly reminded me, I'm an intelligent, sophisticated woman with total self-control."

"There's a beetle in your hair," Hannah said, which sent Lillian squealing and bouncing until Hannah managed to remove the innocent bug.

"Thank you, Hannah," she said, patting her chest, still breathing heavily from the trauma. "I abhor insects. Anyway, I promise not to cause a scene, but I simply must go in, and you're not going to stop me. You can look for my earring while I'm inside." Lillian marched up the steps.

Hannah weighed her options. She could tackle Lillian on the front porch, which wasn't advisable since it was possible to knock fake body parts out of position, and no telling how many places Lillian had them. She decided instead to utilize the philosophy she gleaned from her hippie days in the sixties and just go with the flow. Whatever happened, happened. She followed Lillian into the house.

When Hannah walked into the living room with Lillian by her side, she noticed a man's raincoat tossed over the couch. She expected the lights to be dimmed to a romantic glow, but to her surprise the house was lit up like Safeway. She noticed Kiki's usual love nest accoutrements—red handkerchiefs over the lamps, shades drawn, the liberal aroma of musk oil, Nat King Cole on the stereo and Kiki's favorite erotic board game laid out on the coffee table.

Alerted by the rattling of dishes, both women turned toward the kitchen. Hannah saw two bowls of peaches and brandy sitting on the kitchen table, but no humans to con-

sume them. When Kiki appeared in the doorway, Lillian muttered "Holy Virgin Mary," in spite of the word "virgin"
hardly being operative. Kiki was swathed from chest to knees
in a fluffy pink nightie, the bottom trimmed in feathers that
made the hem stand out in a broad, even circle so that she
looked like a lamp. On her feet she wore pink satin heels,
each one topped with a feathery pom-pom. But Kiki's expression didn't match her vivacious outfit.

The pet pig, Sylvia, trotted in and halted at Kiki's feet,
letting out a worried snort. Hannah put her purse and keys
on the table.

"Oh, Hannie, I'm so glad you're home!" Kiki said, the
words ending in a sob. "I was just about to call you at John's.
Something horrible's happened!"

"Your Frederick's of Hollywood charge card's been can-
celed?" Lillian snapped.

Kiki heard the remark but didn't care. Tears in her eyes,
she threw herself into Hannah's arms.

"What is it, sweetie?" Hannah asked. "Is it Lauren?"

The back door slammed and Gilman entered the kitchen,
his face somber.

"I can't find her anywhere," he said. Kiki let out a moan
and clutched Hannah even harder.

"Find who?" Hannah asked, starting to panic. "Tell me,
please."

"Teresa," Kiki blubbered. "Teresa's been dognapped!"

There was a lull in the conversation while Hannah absorbed this strange and distressing news.

"How? What happened?" she finally asked, pushing Kiki
to arm's length.

"Well, I was going to let Sylvia and Teresa out so, you
know, Ronnie and I wouldn't be interrupted," Kiki said with
a choke and a shudder.

Lillian shot Gilman a scathing look.

"She was dressed like that when I got here. What could I
do?" he said to her.

Kiki continued, sniffling. "But I couldn't find Teresa. I
looked all over the house. Then I went outside and I found

a note taped outside the back door. Show it to her, Ronnie, honey."

Gilman stiffened at the word "honey." He pulled a small paper out of his shirt pocket and handed it to Hannah.

"Forget Geraldine if you want your dog back," it read. The letters had been clipped from a magazine and glued onto stiff white notepaper. Hannah's throat constricted, dread filtering through her. She considered few crimes worse than harming an animal, especially a beloved one that belonged to her. Her eyes moved to Sylvia sitting in the doorway, watching the humans with perplexed interest. All those treats Sylvia had begged and stolen over the past year had saved her from Teresa's fate. She was too fat to lift.

Feeling fresh anger, Hannah turned to Lillian. "What were you really doing outside just now?"

"You can't possibly think I kidnapped your dog," Lillian said, drawing back her shoulders in indignation. "Why would I?"

"To scare me off the investigation," Hannah said. "You're a murder suspect, remember?"

"You are, Lillian?" Gilman asked with what appeared to be pleasant surprise.

Lillian placed a reassuring hand on his arm. "It's just a misunderstanding."

Kiki punched her fists into her hips. "Like hell it is. You're a murder suspect, Lillian, big as day, everyone knows it. On the other hand, my reputation is unblemished."

Everyone shot her a look.

"To think I could harm Geraldine or anyone else is outrageous," Lillian said, looking from Kiki to Gilman and then to Hannah. "Is this what we've been reduced to, suspecting old friends?"

"I'm afraid so," Hannah said. "You and Ron are logical suspects, which the two of you very well know."

"What about Vera?" Lillian shot back. "If we're suspects, she is as well. She had plenty of motive for hating Geraldine."

"But Vera wasn't hiding in my bushes and *you* were," Hannah said. Both Kiki and Gilman looked at Lillian, who grimaced at that embarrassing fact being revealed. Hannah continued, "I want to inspect you both for dog hair."

Lillian spit out some air. "Are you insane?"

"Teresa shed enough hair each day to knit a sweater. Whoever took her would have hair on her, or his, clothing," Hannah told them.

"Good idea," Kiki said. "I'll search Ronnie." She headed for Gilman with her arms outstretched until Lillian grabbed her.

"I'll do it," Hannah said. She crouched down and examined his pants as politely as she could.

Gilman chuckled nervously. "This is absurd, but I'll humor you."

Hannah worked her way upward, inspecting his shirt. She found traces of Kiki's lipstick on his shirtsleeve, and Lord knows how it got there, but she found no dog hair. It was when she looked at the front of his shirt that she noticed a mark on his neck. It was a jagged scratch two inches long, reddened and slightly swollen. Remembering the hem of the raincoat she had seen that night and the raincoat now in her living room, she raised her eyes. When he saw her looking at him with such intensity, he glanced at Lillian.

"You couldn't possibly have found a dog hair on me," he said.

All eyes turned to Hannah, the kitchen silent except for Sylvia's low, anxious snorts.

"You were at Geraldine's last night," Hannah said. She couldn't be a hundred percent sure, so it was only educated fishing, but she saw him start to crumble. His face turned a few colors. He looked dumbfounded and scared.

"I wasn't," he said, fumbling with the words.

"Even in high school you were a rotten liar." Hannah picked up her car keys from the table and showed them to Gilman. He looked baffled.

"These made that mark on your neck," she told him.

He seemed to shrink, all his previous arrogance fading.

Kiki looked at him in bewilderment. "You said you got that shaving."

Gilman dropped into one of the chairs at the kitchen table.

"I haven't done anything wrong, not really, so why should I try to hide anything? I didn't know it was you, Hannah. It was pitch black in Geraldine's house. I just panicked."

"What are you talking about, Ron?" Lillian asked, but Gilman didn't answer. His eyes remained on Hannah.

"What were you doing there?" Hannah asked.

He straightened, regaining some dignity. "What you were doing there is another obvious question."

Lillian edged her way between them. "I want to know what both of you were doing in Geraldine's house with the lights off."

"Geraldine gave me a key to her house," Hannah said, directing the statement only to Gilman. "I had an idea about her murder. I was looking for some corroboration."

"And that was just what I was doing."

"I don't believe you," Hannah told him.

Lillian gasped. "How dare you?"

"This isn't the time to stand by your man, Lillian," Hannah said. "He wanted to buy Geraldine's house, and when she wouldn't sell, he got very nasty. The police know."

Anger flashed across Gilman's face. "Are you suggesting that I threatened her?"

"It's not a suggestion," Hannah said. "It's a statement of fact. The note you wrote proves it."

His shoulders slumped, and he pressed his hand against his forehead. "God, what a mess."

Hannah sat down in the chair opposite him. Lillian and Kiki stood a few feet away, looking confused.

"How did you get in so easily?" Hannah asked.

"She gave me a key about a month ago so I could look around the house. At the time she didn't realize I was going to tear it down. She never asked for the key back. Listen, I just wanted to get back that note I wrote her," he said. "I was afraid it would give the police the wrong impression. Which, thanks to you, it did."

"It's a logical conclusion," Hannah told him. "You were pretty angry at not getting what you wanted."

He lifted his shoulders. "I got a little hot when she backed out of the deal. Who could blame me? The HMO contract would have meant a million dollars' profit over five years. And you know why she backed out? She didn't want her garden destroyed. A million dollars down the drain to save some flowers and birds. It was all such crap. But I didn't have her killed. I had no reason."

"A million dollars strikes me as a good one," Hannah said.

"I didn't do it." He let out a rush of air. "And I couldn't risk being involved in a murder investigation. Not now." He stopped, his anger dissolving. "That sort of thing could scare a woman off."

Kiki and Lillian both stepped forward, bumping into each other and exchanging venomous looks.

"Nothing could scare me off, Ron," Lillian said quickly.

"He means me," Kiki said, pushing in front of her.

Gilman looked up at them with a combination of fatigue and annoyance. "I don't mean either of you. I'm in love with Ruth."

A chilly silence swept through the small kitchen, and Hannah said a silent *uh-oh*. She had the same feeling she got when she felt the first vague rumblings of an earthquake and had the panicked urge to grab the glassware and hold the paintings onto the walls.

"Who the hell's Ruth?" Lillian asked.

"She works at the hospital," he replied. "I know she's young, but I don't think age matters."

But on that point Gilman was sorely wrong, for on the faces of Lillian and Kiki it was quite plain that nothing mattered as much. To their sixty-year-old ears, the phrase "I know she's young" cut like a knife. Hannah remembered the pretty, dark-haired nurse she had seen at the hospital and again at Gilman's side at the funeral. And an older man courting a younger woman usually needed money, which gave Gilman an even better motive for wanting Geraldine dead and her real estate conveniently available.

Hannah looked at Kiki to see how she was faring under this brutal revelation. Her sister looked stunned and disappointed, but was holding up. Lillian, on the other hand, was on the verge of an explosion.

"You slept with me, you snake!" Lillian blurted. She

swung her arm back, then brought her hand hard against Gilman's face.

"So what?" he said, his palm against his stinging flesh. "I was doing you a favor."

"Oh, gawd!" Kiki sputtered, and in her pique, picked up one of the dessert bowls and dumped peaches and brandy on Gilman's head. Lillian burst into tears, her face buried in her hands. For a moment Kiki just watched her, her anger at the woman mellowing into sympathy until she finally wrapped a comforting arm around Lillian's shoulder.

"He's a bum. He's not good enough for either of us," said Kiki, leading Lillian into the living room, the former enemies now bonded by a common foe.

After tossing Gilman a kitchen towel, Hannah sat down across from him, eyeing him with distaste.

"Hannah, you won't tell the police about last night, will you?" he said, picking a peach slice out of his hair. "It will make things worse for me."

"I'm obligated to tell them," she said. "To be honest, I'm not in the mood right now to try and improve your situation."

He wiped his face with the towel. "That's right," he said with bitterness. "Always blame the man. The truth is, ever since my wife died, women in this town have been chasing me like I was a cash prize. So I decided to spread a little joy around. What would you have me do?"

"Keep your pants zipped," Hannah told him. "You knew you were leading on Lillian as well as my sister."

Looking petulant, he rose from his chair, retrieved his coat, and left. Once he was gone, Hannah cleared up the mess. Kiki ushered Lillian back into the kitchen and gave her herbal tea and a half-hour of ranting about men being no-good scums. By the time Lillian left, she had stopped crying and looked like she was feeling better.

When the sisters were alone, Kiki collapsed into a chair at the kitchen table. "What an awful night. Teresa's been kidnapped. Ronnie's in love with someone else."

"I'm so sorry about Ron. Are you okay?" Hannah asked.

"I guess so. So much for that silly love potion. To think

he was sleeping with Lillian. How come I'm the only person in this town not having sex?"

"You're not the only one. There's Lauren."

Too edgy to sit, Hannah paced the length of the kitchen. She wanted to console her sister, but she couldn't focus on Kiki's disastrous love life when her dog was missing. A dozen sickening possibilities crossed her mind. She stopped at the kitchen sink, pressing her hands against its edge, looking out the window at the dark garden. She remembered what Berger had said to her. "I may have done something already." A knot of worry lodged inside her. She would never forgive herself if something happened to her dog. Perez had been right. She should have stayed out of the investigation. But it was too late to undo it. "Kiki, sweetie, go change your clothes. We have work to do."

"But Hannah, it's after ten."

"We have to find Teresa. Go change. Get your purse. I'm going to need your help."

Kiki left, and Hannah looked up Harry's number and dialed it. "What are you doing?" she asked as soon as he picked up.

"Watching a rerun of *Cheers,* the one where Norm's got the big job interview. Who's this?"

"Hannah Malloy. You said you used to work on security systems. Do you still know about them?"

"Of course I do. I'm not brain dead."

"Do you still have some tools?"

"A few." There was a moment of dead air. "Why?"

"Because I have a job for you. Be ready in ten minutes."

$\mathscr{S}$IXTEEN

❧

"$\mathscr{L}$ISTEN, GALS, I'M HAVING SECOND thoughts about this little escapade," Harry said from the backseat of the Cadillac. He was dressed to the nines, with a black-and-white checked jacket, bow tie, and white buckskin shoes. "I assumed you were asking me out because you wanted my body."

"Only if we were doing medical experiments," Hannah replied, pressing on the gas pedal and moving into the fast lane. She wondered if Teresa's kidnapper was giving her plenty of water. Teresa had needed a lot of water ever since she was a puppy. Hannah imagined her pet tied up in some strange place, hungry, thirsty, and afraid. She gunned the car, surging through the traffic.

"Such a jokster," Harry said with a nervous chuckle. "But now that I know you're serious about checking out this security system, I'll admit to you, I'm a little concerned. You see, I've been retired a long time."

"Don't you worry. Hannah knows what she's doing," Kiki said, repairing her lipstick in her compact mirror. Hannah had insisted that she change her nightie to street clothes, even though Kiki assured Hannah that once Harry saw her sexy outfit, he would do anything they requested. Hannah was

more concerned that it would give him a stroke. Lillian almost had one when she saw it. Believing that in certain situations she knew better than her sister, Kiki had just put on
a long raincoat over the nightie and buttoned it to her neck,
with Hannah none the wiser.

Hannah pulled off the freeway and onto the road that led
to Hunters, Inc. In spite of Kiki's confidence, the truth was
that Hannah wasn't too sure at all about what she was doing.
She only knew that she had to find her dog, and David Berger
seemed the most likely candidate for dognapper. He had
practically admitted to it in the Hill Creek Grocery parking
lot.

"I'm not asking you to defuse a bomb, Harry. I just want
you to take a look at the security system and see if it's solid,"
Hannah said, expecting him to do much more. But he
wouldn't have come if she had told him the truth. He was
definitely the skittish type. Most men were when you got
right down to it.

"If all I'm doing is taking a look," Harry said, "then why
ask me to bring my tools?"

"Because it pays to be prepared," she replied.

"Prepared for what?" he asked, increasingly skeptical.
"There's something up, and don't think I don't know it. This
whole thing's funny, especially us starting out so late."

Snapping her compact shut, Kiki twisted around and
glared at him. "Why don't you pipe down?"

In the rearview mirror Hannah saw him shake a bony finger at her. "Listen, sister, just because one guy did you dirt
tonight, don't take it out on the whole male population."

Sneering at him, Kiki turned back around. "I never should
have told you about it."

He leaned forward in his seat. "You've been around the
block enough times to know that all men think with their
peckers."

"Could you not use that language?" Hannah asked. In the
mirror she saw him do a half-bow.

"Excuse me, madame. I should have said, don't you realize
that males perform cogitations substantially aided by their
love wands?"

Kiki giggled and Hannah stifled a smile.

"And when do we go to this great crazy bar you were talking about?" he asked with substantially more optimism. "The one with all the women."

Hannah and Kiki exchanged a secret look. At first Harry had been reluctant when Hannah asked him to go to Hunters, Inc., and she finally had to make up a story about a lively bar where they would go afterward. The problem was, she didn't know of any bars, and certainly none sleazy enough to suit Harry's gutter tastes. In her drinking days she had done her ladylike boozing at home.

"As soon as we're done," Hannah told him, hoping to drop that line of conversation. She drove past Hunters, and navigated the Cadillac to a spot safely down the street. After turning off the ignition, she rolled down the window, the cool night air washing over her face as she ran her eyes up and down the block. Every office building was dark, which made sense at that hour, but she couldn't help feeling a skin-prickling uneasiness, the way an animal sniffs the wind and knows something is out there. There was a strange energy around the place, like something was about to happen, and if you were smart, you would get far away from it.

"Bring your tools," she told Harry. She opened the car door and got out.

Muttering a string of complaints, he struggled out, a battered red metal toolbox in one hand, his cane in the other. Hannah offered to carry the toolbox for him, but he refused, looking insulted. Kiki and Harry followed Hannah down the sidewalk and into the Hunters, parking lot. The place was deadly quiet except for the freeway's distant thunder and the gentle sound of water lapping against the nearby shore. Hannah saw fog rolling in from across the bay, a cold gray cloud coming at them like smoke. She wished she had worn a coat over her dark slacks and sweater.

"Are you cold?" she asked her sister, knowing that Kiki hadn't changed out of the silly nightie because of the bits of pink fluff stuck to her coat.

"No, I'm all buttoned up," Kiki replied.

"It's spooky around here. Where the hell are we?" Harry asked.

"This is an office building," Hannah said, then stopped. "Your heels are making a racket," she said to Kiki. "We're trying to be stealthy, not dance flamenco."

"I'll walk softer," Kiki said, and began to tiptoe. "But I'm not taking them off." She elbowed Harry. "They make my legs look longer."

"You bet they do, dollface," he replied with a wink just as they neared the front door. Kiki gave him a big smile. Ever since they left home, Hannah had been amazed that Kiki wasn't more upset about the loss of Gilman. Now it occurred to her with wonderment that Kiki was transferring her hopes to Harry.

They continued around to the back of the building to see if someone had parked a car on the narrow concrete strip between the building and the bay.

"No cars anywhere," Hannah said with apprehension, "but I see a light in one of the back rooms."

"Probably just for security," Harry said.

"Let's take a look," Hannah said, switching on the flashlight she had brought. "And walk softly."

Kiki and Harry followed her to the lighted window, standing a few cautious feet behind her as she peered through the miniblinds. She remembered briefly seeing the room when she had visited the business a few days before. It looked a little like a kitchen, with a sink, Formica counters, and a linoleum floor. There was no trace of Teresa. Hannah turned and walked along the side of the building, moving the flashlight's beam along the wall.

"Now what?" Harry asked.

"We look for the security system," Hannah answered.

Kiki tugged on Hannah's sleeve. "How do you know they have one?"

"Just about every business has a security system," Harry told her. "There should be a sign somewhere giving the name of the company that installed it, or there could be an outside box."

Running her flashlight up and down the wall, Hannah

searched but couldn't find anything. They continued around the building's west side, at last coming upon a metal box, affixed low on the wall, that said Chapman Security Services.

Hannah looked at Harry and tipped her head in the direction of the box. "Check it out."

"What for?"

"To see if you could disarm it."

He held up one hand, palm outward. "Hold on, you didn't say anything about disarming any security system. This little outing was information only, you said. A little data gathering, you said. Then you were taking me to this great bar for margaritas you said were so strong they'd grow hair on my palms. You said nothing about doing anything criminal."

Kiki jabbed him in the ribs. "You want a ride home, buster? Do what she says."

"One guy dumps on you and we all have to pay," he snarled. "I'll take a look, but that's all. Hold the flashlight on it so I can see what I'm doing."

He put down his toolbox, got out a screwdriver, and put on his reading glasses, grumbling the whole time. After taking out the screws and removing the box's cover, he leaned over, bracing himself with his cane as he stared at a jumble of wires.

"Well, gals, I hate to be the one to break it to you, but this security system's solid as Gibraltar. Looks like we won't be getting arrested tonight. I know it's a disappointment." He put the screwdriver back in his toolbox and snapped the lid shut. "Time to catch that train to margaritaville."

He started toward the street, but Hannah took hold of his arm. "Can't you just cut one of those little wires?"

"For your information," he said sourly, "if I cut one of those little wires, the alarm will blare off like it's civil defense day."

Hannah's heart sank. She soon felt Kiki's hand on her arm. "Does this mean we won't be bringing our Teresa home tonight?" Kiki asked softly.

"Who the hell's Teresa? You have another sister?" Harry asked. He stepped closer, his eyes glinting with interest. "You know, I always liked that name. Is she single? You girls are a little pushy for my tastes—no offense—but this Teresa and I might get along."

"Come to think of it, the two of you would be uniquely suited," Hannah said.

"And she's in there?" Harry asked, cocking his thumb toward the building.

"She's been kidnapped," Kiki blurted.

"So why not call the cops?"

Hannah was about to explain that the woman of his dreams had four legs and fleas, when a sudden roaring sound crashed around them.

They all jumped, the noise thundering in their ears and growing louder. Hannah saw the strip of ground behind the building erupt into a cloud of dust.

"It's an earthquake!" Kiki shrieked, her voice barely audible against the noise. At first Hannah thought the same thing, since she knew from experience that earthquakes sometimes began with a roaring sound, but she didn't feel the ground moving. Then she remembered the expanse of concrete on the other side of the building.

Hannah put her arms around her trembling sister. "It's a helicopter!" she shouted. Hannah took Harry's arm and pulled him close to Kiki, motioning for them to stay put.

Keeping close to the wall, she made a dash to the back of the building and peeked around the corner. The staccato thunder pounding in her ears, she saw the helicopter's lights and the blur of its blades. She turned the corner, and with her back against the wall, sidled along the building until the helicopter was fully in view. She crouched behind a Dumpster.

Two men, one of them David Berger, stood outside the helicopter while a third man came cautiously down the steps, a large white box cradled in his arms. There was too much noise to hear anything, but from body language Hannah felt sure Berger was arguing with the man holding the box. After a few words were exchanged, he carried it into the building, Berger following, while the other man climbed back into the helicopter. Within a minute the second man hurried out of the building. He climbed back into the helicopter, the door shut, and the huge machine lifted off the ground. For a few seconds it swayed as if dangling from an invisible string, then it circled, heading back across the bay.

The helicopter's roar faded, leaving behind what seemed in comparison a cavernous silence. Hannah watched the machine's outline blending into the darkness until only its lights remained visible, and then those, too, disappeared into the encroaching fog.

Cold, Hannah wrapped her arms around herself. She felt a tap on her shoulder and jerked around, alarmed.

"What do you think was in that box?" Kiki asked.

Hannah frowned. "I told you to stay put."

"Hell, no, we're sticking together," Harry said shakily from behind Kiki. "That scared me so bad I almost wet myself."

"Keep your voice down," Hannah commanded.

"But what's going on?" Kiki asked.

"Gee, girls, let's put on our thinking caps," Harry whispered through gritted teeth. "They're delivering something via helicopter in the middle of the night. My guess is it ain't donuts. It's got to be drugs or worse."

Kiki let out a fearful squeak. "What could be worse?"

"Explosives, weapons," he said. "Stuff I want nothing to do with. Now, let's get out of here."

Hannah shook her head. "No, we can't. Not yet."

"Listen, sweetheart, my prostate can't take this much excitement," Harry told her. "Give me the keys and I'll come back for you later."

"You're right. You and Kiki go home," Hannah said, digging through her purse. She found the keys and dangled them in front of Kiki. "There's a pay phone at the end of the street. I can call a cab."

Kiki's expression was fretful. "You can't stay here alone."

"I have to get in there and look for Teresa. There's a chance they didn't lock the door."

Harry shook his head in confusion. "I'm missing something here. Why can't you just call the cops to get Teresa?"

"Because she's a dog," Kiki said.

He lifted his shoulders. "I don't see where looks have anything to do with it."

Kiki rolled her eyes. "A furry, tail-wagging dog that barks."

"All this for a dog?" he said with sneering disbelief. "You girls are nuts. Come on, we're going." After grabbing the keys from Hannah, he took Kiki's hand and pulled her, but she remained rooted to the ground.

"I can't leave you here, Hannie. Please come with us," she pleaded. "We'll call Detective Morgan about Teresa."

"He couldn't do anything about a dog, at least not tonight, and tomorrow could be too late. I'll be fine. You go home."

"I won't," Kiki said firmly. "I'm going with you. It could be dangerous."

"Which is exactly why I have to go alone. Please, Kiki, there's no point in both of us taking a risk, and I'll be able to maneuver better by myself." She took her sister's hand. "You can wait in the car for me. Then once I have Teresa, we can make a fast getaway. But if I'm not out in fifteen minutes, call Detective Morgan."

Kiki thought it over. If she went with Hannah, there wouldn't be anyone to call the police if her sister didn't come out of the building promptly, and she couldn't count on Harry.

"Okay, Hannah, but please be careful."

"Don't worry, I'll be fine," Hannah said, displaying a cheerful bravery she didn't feel. "Go that way so no one will see you. And be quiet. Tiptoe."

Harry, toolbox in hand, followed Kiki around the back of the building, toward the street and the car.

A lump of fear sat in Hannah's stomach as she walked cautiously around the building. Her plan was simple. Find the dog, then run like crazy. She noticed light shining from an additional window and thought it might be coming from Berger's office. A glimpse in the window confirmed it. He sat at his desk, reading the top page of a thick stack of papers. She didn't see Teresa. She made her way to the side door that Berger had used earlier. She tested the doorknob, her hand twisting it only a fraction of an inch, then a fraction more. When it rotated fully, she didn't know if she should count herself lucky or not. Carefully, she opened the door and slipped into a dark hallway.

Reminding herself to breathe, she pressed her back against the wall and stood there a second, considering her next step. Teresa had never been a good watchdog, and Hannah knew that if the animal was comfortably asleep somewhere, she wouldn't rush off to check out a stranger, but as long as the dog wasn't tied, she would come running if she knew it was Hannah.

She made kissy noises just loud enough for Teresa to hear. Nothing happened, no affectionate woof or soft sound of paws against the floor. She decided that if Teresa was there, she had to be locked in a room.

Hannah tiptoed down the hallway and cracked open the first door she came to. The room was dark, empty. She tried the next door and found herself in the lighted room she had seen through the window, the one with cabinets, Formica-topped counters, and a cabinet-style island in the room's center. But now there was an interesting addition. A white box, the one that had come from the helicopter, sat on the island. Only it wasn't a box at all, but a foam cooler. She wondered what was inside. Maybe drugs or explosives, as Harry had said.

She knew she should ignore it, continue her search for Teresa, and get out as quickly as possible, dreading to think what Berger would do if he found her. But as soon as she took one step down the hall, she halted, devoured by curiosity. One glance inside the box would yield critical information she could pass along to the police. Having hit upon the rationalization she needed, she went over and tried to lift the lid, but it stuck. She wedged her fingernails in the crack between the lid and the cooler's base. To her surprise, when she jerked the lid upward, it flew off with a loud squeak and fell to the floor. Hannah took one look inside the cooler and let out a yell. She was no doctor, but she knew what she was looking at. Wrapped in clear plastic and lying between two blocks of dry ice was a human heart.

She wanted to run, but before she got her breath back, the

door flew open, slapping against the opposing wall with a gut-wrenching *whack*. Berger glared at her, and every cell in her body froze. He stood between her and the door. There was nowhere to run. *Think, Hannah,* she commanded, but upon seeing the cold, murderous fury on Berger's face, the only thing in her head was a terrified jumble of noise.

"Get away from that," he said in a low snarl. Hannah darted to the other side of the small room. Berger breathed heavily, his eyes fixed on her, his face contorted with rage.

He lunged for her. She leaped sideways and he landed against the cabinets, his knees buckling. She moved for the door but he grabbed her leg. Her adrenaline pumping, she gave him a stiff kick, freed herself, and tried again for the door, but he scrambled upward and reached it first, slamming it shut. Now he had her trapped. He watched her for a moment, his breath coming in gasps. Hannah's fear became a roaring in her head. His hands would be on her in a matter of seconds.

With all the strength she had acquired from years of shoveling soil in her garden, she shoved the cooler at him. Much lighter than she expected, it flew off the table, missing Berger by a foot. The heart sailed out. Hannah and Berger stopped and stared at it, their eyes wide with horror as the heart hit the wall with a loathsome *splat,* the impact causing the plastic casing to split. For a long, sickening second the heart hung there on the wall, then it slid slowly to the floor, leaving behind it a bloody streak.

Berger looked so devastated that for a moment Hannah thought he might cry. Seizing the opportunity, she rushed for the door, but he recovered quickly. He grabbed her upper arm and tossed her back, her head hitting the upper cabinet's edge. Stunned, she collapsed to the floor. Through a haze she saw him move toward her.

"You just cost me a hundred grand!"

She barely heard the words through the throbbing in her head. Struggling, she rose from the floor and tried to back away, but she was trapped against the cabinets. She thought of Kiki and Harry waiting in the car. Would Berger find them out there and hurt them as well?

She threw herself toward the door. He grabbed her arm with one hand, jerking her downward, and in the next second they were both on the floor, his hands around her neck. She pulled at his fingers, but they were locked against her throat, tightly squeezing. All she could see was his sweat-covered face staring down at her, his teeth bared. She gagged, his hands choking off her air.

That's when she heard a scream, followed by a cracking sound. The next thing she knew, Berger had collapsed on top of her. Gasping, she twisted her neck, looking upward, trying to figure out what had happened. She saw Kiki standing in the doorway like some slumming avenging angel, with astonishment on her face, the pink nightie on her body and a large wrench in her hand.

SEVENTEEN

"I'M THROUGH WITH YOU GIRLS, you hear me? Don't call me again, ever. If the urge creeps up on you, take a cold shower," Harry said, hobbling back and forth in front of Hannah and Kiki. The sisters sat on the steps of Hunters, Inc., a blanket draped around Hannah's shoulders. He halted, pointing his cane at them. "Me, I like the kind of nights out with women where when you talk about bringing along the necessary protection, you don't mean adult diapers."

The fog had grown thick, lending halos to the blinking cherry lights on the squad cars parked on the street. There was an ambulance as well, needed for David Berger. A paramedic had examined Hannah and pronounced her all right except for some aches and bruising he promised would be worse by morning. But Berger had a serious concussion. *Couldn't have happened to a nicer guy,* Hannah thought.

Kiki gave Harry a scathing look and put her arm around her sister. "Stop being so crabby, or I'll tell people what a yellow belly you were in the face of danger. When you heard Hannah yell, you ran like a scared chicken."

"I was trying to get some distance so I could be objective," he replied. "I was right on the verge of asserting my manliness, but what could I do? You grabbed the wrench out of my toolbox and ran in there like your hair was on fire."

"Don't bicker. My head is throbbing," Hannah told them, holding her temples with her fingers. "The two of you should have stayed in the car like I asked you. You could have been hurt."

"It's a good thing we didn't. You could have been killed," Kiki said. She grinned proudly, the evening's crisis having left her strangely energized. "Did you see the way I hit him?" She punched the air with her fist. "Dang, it felt good to knock the poo out of somebody." Shaking his head, Harry looked at her like she was insane.

Hannah shivered with cold. Kiki had earlier offered her coat to Hannah, but Hannah preferred that it be used to cover up Kiki's nightie. Kiki had apparently been giving Harry a quick look at it when she heard Hannah's shout and ran into the building to save her.

Hannah managed a smile. "You saved my life."

Kiki waggled her hand. "Happy to do it, sweetie. And it's a good thing I didn't hit him harder. I wouldn't want to kill anybody."

"Glad you gals have some standards," Harry muttered.

Closing her eyes, Hannah moaned with fatigue as Harry and Kiki again began trading barbs. Thankfully, the sound of approaching footsteps interrupted them. Hannah opened her eyes and saw Detective Morgan coming their way. Novato wasn't his jurisdiction, but Hannah had had the Novato police call him as soon as they arrived. It was Morgan's case, after all.

"Mrs. Goldstein, Mr. Stanley," he said, "the other detective would like to talk to you again about what you saw outside the building. He's over by the squad car."

Still bickering, Kiki and Harry took off. Hannah looked up at Morgan, her eyes hopeful.

"There's no dog inside and no sign of one having been there," he told her. "Berger claims he doesn't have Teresa."

"He's lying. He has to be."

Giving his pants a tug over the knees, Morgan sat down next to her. "The problem is, we can't push him right now because of that blow he took to the head. It looks like he was running an illegal organ operation. One of the first officers on the scene saw a helicopter approach, then bank off. We're guessing that the first helicopter did the drop and the second was making the pickup, but the pilot must have seen the lights on our squad car and had a change of—" He hesitated.

"A change of heart?" Hannah said.

Morgan's baby face twisted into a frown. "We've got the county coroner here. He says that's what that mess is on the floor."

"That's what it looked like to me when it was all in one piece."

"Did you really throw it at that guy?"

"It was an accident."

Morgan moved his eyes straight ahead of him. "Maybe you don't want to hear this, but the coroner thinks the heart came from a child."

Filled with revulsion, Hannah closed her eyes. When she opened them again, she aimed them at the ambulance that held Berger.

"Are you okay, Mrs. Malloy?"

"I will be."

"At least things are starting to make sense. Your friend Geraldine must have found out what Berger was doing. He was probably part of a ring."

"Now I think I understand the link between those names, the ones on the paper I found at Geraldine's," she said. "They all needed organs. If they were children's names, that would explain why you had trouble finding them."

"They had rich parents, I guess," Morgan replied.

"Or they were so desperate for their kids' lives they'd pay anything. It makes me sick to think about it. All those people with such misery, and Berger making a profit from it."

"We should be able to locate his customers pretty easily and get what we need to convict him," Morgan said. "I'm sure if they needed organs, they had their names on the national waiting lists as well as working with Berger."

Hannah pulled the blanket more closely around her. She and Morgan watched as the ambulance closed its doors and took off with Berger inside. What was going on in her head was so disturbing she hated to form it into words, but she had to. "There's something else bothering me."

"What?"

"How was Berger getting the organs? I have an awful feeling that it wasn't voluntary. That's why Geraldine stayed after him, why she refused to give up."

"I'm not following you."

"If you can track down where that heart came from, I think you'll find that the donor was Asian. Thai, probably. And you couldn't ship an organ from overseas. It would take too long."

Morgan screwed up his face. "Are you saying that Berger brought the children over here, then murdered them for their organs?"

"How else? He used Hunters, Inc. as a front, a way to launder the money. It also gave him an excuse for helicopters landing on his parking lot, in case anybody ever asked. He smuggled the children in, then took what he needed."

"But donor organs and recipients have to be matched," Morgan said.

Hannah considered it a moment. "There are two ways he could have handled it. Find out ahead of time what organs and blood types he needed and then have a contact overseas find a child who matched. Or he could bring a healthy child over and then auction off what he could. A parent with a desperately sick child might not ask a lot of questions."

Morgan's gaze moved to his feet, his arms resting on his knees, his hands clasped. "What a lousy world." They were both quiet a moment. "Well, we'll get the feds involved and know soon enough." He looked again at Hannah. "But Geraldine Markham told the police months ago that Berger was importing animals illegally. Why didn't she mention body parts?"

"I think because at the time he really was importing animals. When the police investigated him and didn't find anything, Geraldine decided to keep after him on her own. After a while she realized that he wasn't importing animals anymore, that he had moved on to more profitable merchandise.

I think she must have known about it for months, but got the evidence, the list of customers, only in the last couple of weeks. She was ready to go to the police."

"So why did she want to get you involved?"

"Because this was a dangerous business and she was frightened. She knew I'd dealt with the police before and she knew of my relationship with John. She wanted moral support and some advice. She told me as much."

"But if she was afraid that Berger was trying to harm her, why didn't she just come to the police?"

"Listen, he threatened me a few days ago, but if I had come to you, what could you have done? No offense, but you couldn't have done much. And in her case, Berger would have just accused her of harassing him again. Her best bet was to get him put in jail."

Morgan drew in some air and let it out. "The problem is, unless Berger gives us details, we'll never know for sure exactly how it all happened."

"At least we know how she died," Hannah said. "She tried to stop Berger's illegal organ business, so he paid to have her killed. But it doesn't answer the question of who killed Mendoza."

They heard shouting from the direction of the street and looked toward the squad car. The other officer had left, and now Kiki was shaking her fist at Harry while he shouted something about women's brutality.

"I think they're actually enjoying themselves," Hannah said. "But I guess someone should break it up."

"I'll take care of it. You've already had your brawl for the night. I'll work on finding your dog, Mrs. Malloy, but in exchange I want your promise that you won't interfere anymore. I don't want you asking questions or even discussing the case with anyone."

"Trust me, I don't want to be involved. You have your man, anyway. Just, please, find Teresa."

"I'll try. I promise." Morgan stood up. Hooking a thumb in his belt, he turned and walked off.

Hannah remained on the step, her arms wrapped around her knees. She knew she should feel good about what had happened that night, but she only felt sad and alone. Now she knew what Geraldine had against Berger, and now he was in police custody. But Teresa was still missing, and Hannah had no idea if she was even still alive.

EIGHTEEN

ON MONDAY MORNING THE NEWS of Teresa's dognapping swept through Hill Creek, leaving behind tremors of disbelief and foreboding. Residents expressed shock while sipping nonfat cappuccinos, raged in front of the organic field greens at the Hill Creek Grocery, and could barely get their spiritual beings integrated during sessions with their transpersonal bodywork facilitators. By noon Hill Creek's population was so agitated there was an unprecedented rush on colonic irrigations, and the Sufi healing-breath retreats were suddenly booked up for weeks.

Murder was one thing. If a person killed another person, it was horrible, but you could attribute it to the offender's rotten childhood or hormonal fluctuations or genetically modified soy products. But to harm an animal was a deed no Hill Creeker could comprehend or tolerate, and by afternoon the citizens were ready to take to the streets with torches to track down the culprit.

The town bled sympathy for Hannah. Ramona at the dry cleaners didn't charge her for cleaning a silk blouse, and Paul at the gas station, having recently completed his men's experiential therapy weekend, burst into tears when Hannah confirmed the truth of the awful news. Randy at the Book

Stop gave Hannah a free espresso and said sadly, "Whoa, the world's like, a total scum bucket. Whoa." Such a steady stream of people came to her table and expressed condolences that at last she took her coffee outside to the plaza, where she could have a moment's peace.

Sitting on a bench, she found the plaza almost empty, for which she was grateful. The air felt cooler than usual, and she noticed a gray sky in the west behind the mountain. Indian summer was over. The rains would come soon. Having had little sleep over the past few days and still aching from her tussle with Berger the night before, she was exhausted and depressed. Discovering the truth about Hunters, Inc. and the motive for Geraldine's murder should have brought her satisfaction, but it had not.

She sipped her coffee and did her best to compose herself. She appreciated her friends' concerns about Teresa, but talking about her dog just made her want to cry, and she was more interested in finding Teresa than in sitting around feeling sorry for herself. All the sympathy meant that people considered the situation hopeless, and it wasn't. She wouldn't let it be. She intended to take action, only at the moment she didn't know what action to take. The only logical answer regarding Teresa was that Berger had her locked up somewhere. But if he wasn't talking, what could anyone do? And with Berger in jail, how would Teresa get food and water? If she was still alive.

"Aunt Hannah, I heard from Aunt Kiki what happened last night. I'm so put out with you!"

Looking up, Hannah saw Lauren trotting toward her, wearing a gray business suit, her briefcase in hand.

"I know, I know. It's my fault Teresa's gone," Hannah said, shaking her head with misery.

"I don't mean about Teresa. That's not your fault." Lauren took a place on the bench and set her briefcase on the ground. "I'm upset about Teresa, of course, but what's more important is that you took such a chance last night. You could have been killed. Aunt Kiki told me you almost were."

"But I'm fine."

"But you shouldn't be putting yourself in harm's way, especially at—"

"At my age? I'm as fit as you are. Maybe more so. When was the last time you exercised?" Lauren's idea of aerobics was to chew a Snickers bar very quickly, and yet she never gained an ounce.

"We're not talking about me."

"Detective Morgan asked me to stay out of the case from now on, and I agreed," Hannah said. "You obviously spoke to Kiki. Is she still at home?"

Lauren nodded. "On the phone, calling everyone she knows. Did she really give that horrible Berger person a karate kick in his privates?"

"She hit him on the head with a wrench. That's impressive enough. I don't know why she's embellishing."

Hannah took the last sip of coffee, both women gazing out at the plaza, sharing an uncomfortable silence.

"How on earth are we ever going to find Teresa?" Lauren asked.

"Morgan says he'll find her, but I don't know how he's going to do it."

"At least one thing is positive," Lauren said. "Kiki said the police are pretty certain that David Berger had Geraldine murdered."

"It had to have been him, but as far as I know, they haven't been able to tie the hit man's payment to him. And where did he get that old photo of Geraldine?" Hannah asked. "I doubt they've figured that one out yet."

A familiar whooping noise, followed by the jingling of bells, halted further conversation. The sound came from the direction of the strawberry tree, where they saw Naomi dancing around the tree's trunk. The jingling came from her Hopi war stick, a three-foot-long fat stick with feathers and bells attached at one end. She held it in the air as she danced, her knees lifted high so that she looked like a crazed drum majorette. Lauren waved, and when Naomi saw them, she stopped in mid whoop and rushed over.

"So glad to see you," Naomi said, breathless, the bells on the Hopi war stick jingling.

"What are you doing?" Hannah asked.

"Cleansing the tree of negative energy. It's getting droopier every day. I'm doing the Dance of the Spotted Eagle, but I'm having trouble getting in touch with Red Moon and I need his shamanic energy. He's still being obstinate. I've tried everything to coax him out—meditating, chanting. Last night I waved venison in front of my face, and still nothing. Now I think he's ticked off about having to work the 900 number, the insensitive oaf. He knows I need money."

Hannah found it bizarre that Naomi spoke of a dead spirit like he was her husband. "Perhaps if you just give him some time," she said, wondering if the next step was couples counseling.

Naomi pounded the war stick against the pavement, the clatter eliciting a terrified howl from a Chihuahua passing by with its owner. "Who has time? Not me, and certainly not you. I wanted to consult Red Moon regarding Teresa's whereabouts. He has a special affinity with animals, and I'm sure he could tell us where she is." Naomi exhaled with irritation. "If he wasn't such a Hopi pain in the butt."

"I appreciate your wanting to help," Hannah told her.

"Yes, well, I'm afraid my Red Moon problems are affecting more than just your terrible predicament. My 900 number was going so well, but I can't handle the calls without Red Moon's spiritual insights. I've scheduled transpersonal Reiki massage therapy this afternoon to see if I can get his juices going. The appointment's at one, which is just when my hours for the 900 number start. Kiki said she'd cover for me. She probably won't forget, but to be on the safe side, you could remind her. I'm going to forward my phone to your number."

"But how can Kiki handle your calls? Those people are expecting to speak with a psychic," Lauren said.

"She's just going to reschedule them for tomorrow. I'm sure Red Moon will be back by then. And if not, he's in big trouble." Naomi paused, staring at the top of Hannah's chest. "That's a nasty rash you have."

Hannah moved her hand to her chest but forced herself not to scratch. Her rash from the Zen mud had shown little improvement. "It's nothing," she said in a hurry, afraid that Naomi would do the Polka of the Dead Turtle or something else ridiculous to cure her.

"I've got some herbal cream at home that will fix it in a jiffy. I'll leave some on your kitchen table. Well, got to finish up on that tree." With a shake of the war stick, Naomi took off.

"That tree isn't suffering from negative energy," Hannah said to Lauren. "It's got some kind of fungus, I'm sure of it."

"You're probably right. Well, I've got to get to work now. I'm late." Lauren picked up her briefcase. "What are your plans for today?"

"I want to look for Teresa. It's killing me to sit here and do nothing, but I don't know where to start."

"Let the police handle it."

"But how can the police justify looking for my dog? They need to work on shutting down Berger's organ ring. I feel guilty even wanting them to look for Teresa, but you know she's like a child to me."

"Larry will do everything he can. He's a good man. You need to get your mind off things."

"You're right," Hannah said, fighting back tears. "I've got to distract myself. I think I'll go to the library and look into what's wrong with that tree. Then this afternoon I'm going to visit Geraldine's grave."

"Good." Lauren gave her aunt a kiss on the cheek. "I'll drop by tonight and fix you dinner if you're not busy. How about grilled salmon with mango salsa?"

"Perfect."

The Hill Creek library, within walking distance, was an old two-story building a few blocks from the plaza. It had been in the same sand-colored stone building since Hannah was a teenager and boasted a wide range of fiction and periodicals, relying on the main county branch to augment its smaller nonfiction selection. Pushing open the heavy oak door, Hannah stepped inside, feeling better just being near so many books. From the time she was a child she had loved libraries, finding them more spiritually uplifting than any church.

Gladys, the head librarian for almost sixteen years, sat behind a desk, staring at a computer screen, tapping the end of a pencil against her mouth. As soon as she saw Hannah, her eyes brightened and she hurried over.

"I have a new book on orchids you might want to take a look at. Just got it in," she told Hannah in a library whisper. "There's one close-up of a *Dendrobium burana* that just takes your breath away." Gladys clasped her hands in front of her breasts, a titillated blush creeping up her cheeks.

Hannah smiled, doing her best to feign polite interest, but she didn't much like orchids. Most of them were finicky and didn't bloom often enough. And to be honest, she found the blooms vulgar. She had always suspected that Gladys's fascination with them indicated some deep-seated sexual problems that, if properly analyzed, could keep a shrink in boat payments for years.

"I'll take a look later, Gladys. Right now it's tree diseases I'm interested in. I'll just go back to the gardening shelf."

The library had two shelves of gardening books, and Hannah was familiar with most of the volumes. She pulled out the thick tree encyclopedia, carrying it to one of the tables, where she sat down. Two teenagers in the throes of puppy love sat across from her, staring into one another's eyes and giggling. Hannah smiled inwardly, thinking that not much had changed since she had studied in this same library as a schoolgirl. She then focused on the book, flipping through the pages until she found the section on diseases. It didn't take long for her to figure out the tree's problem. Closing the book, she chuckled to herself. Amazing how people got an idea in their heads and then clung to it. Of course the Botany Club members had meant well, and if she remembered correctly, none of them had known much about trees back in high school, including her. There had been another teacher who had cosponsored the club with Geraldine back then, a Mr. Valentino, who had been fairly knowledgeable, but even he hadn't caught the simple mistake.

Hannah stole a glance at the teenagers staring dreamily at

one another, and she thought about Mr. Valentino. A gruff
and sour man, he had possessed beautiful, thick dark hair
and soulful brown eyes, and Hannah had a crush on him her
entire senior year of high school. He had remained in Hill
Creek the rest of his life and had died only the year before.
At his funeral his wife had said she wanted to donate his
books to the library, so Hannah helped her pack them up a
few weeks later. As Hannah placed the books in boxes she
had been amazed at all the poetry he had read—Dylan Thomas, Byron, Keats—the pages bent and marked from all his
readings. It had touched her that behind his harsh exterior
Mr. Valentino had possessed a romantic soul.

Ready to go, she rose a few inches from her chair, thought
of something, something incredible, then sat back down. Mr.
Valentino's books. There had been three large boxes of them
she had packed for his wife. Randy from the Book Stop had
delivered them directly to Gladys at the library.

Hannah pushed her chair back noisily, returned the tree
encyclopedia to the shelf, then hurried to the checkout desk.

"Five days late. That will be a dollar twenty-five," Gladys
informed the teenage boy standing on the other side of the
desk. She warily inspected him over the top of her reading
glasses, her lips puckered in disapproval. It was all for show.
Hannah knew there was nothing Gladys liked better than
collecting overdue fines, since the money funded new shelv-
ing. More important, the little library was Gladys's kingdom
and she mightily enjoyed wielding her power, never showing
mercy.

Hannah tapped her fingers against the countertop, waiting
impatiently as the boy fumbled through his pockets for
change. Finally he dropped a dollar and some nickels into
Gladys's hand and shuffled off.

"I need to talk to you," Hannah said.

Gladys smiled and arched an eyebrow. "You want that
orchid book?"

Hannah blinked. It was like she was pushing dirty pictures.
"No, thanks. Maybe later."

Gladys pushed her glasses farther up her nose, leaning
over the counter and staring at the base of Hannah's neck.

"You've got a rash. There's a new book on herbal remedies you can make at home, if you're interested."

"Thanks, but Naomi's making something for me. Listen, remember those books that Beatrice Valentino donated? It was about a year ago."

"Of course. We got them last winter."

"Did you unpack them?"

Gladys hesitated, looking guilty. "Well, no. I should have, but it's been so hectic around here. Just nonstop pressure with all the paperwork, and—"

"It's okay, I understand completely," Hannah interrupted. When Gladys wasn't discussing orchids with rapture, she was waxing on about the nerve-shattering pressures of running a small library. Gladys needed to get out more. "Do you still have the boxes?"

"Actually, I do. To tell you the truth, I knew they weren't anything the library could use, but I didn't want to hurt Beatrice's feelings. I was going to give them to the Salvation Army, but I was waiting a decent interval. I never even opened them."

Hannah's blood stirred. "Can I see them?"

"Why?"

"I'm researching something, and I think Mr. Valentino might have had a reference book I need."

Gladys gestured for Hannah to follow her. They went through the library office, then down a hallway. At the end of it, Gladys opened a door that led into a large storage room.

The dustiness made Hannah sneeze when she stepped inside. Cardboard boxes and stacks of books lined the room's perimeter, some piled so high they appeared on the brink of tumbling down. Others lay stacked on rickety-looking metal shelves.

"Sorry it's a mess," Gladys apologized. "It's turned into a junk room, and I haven't had time to clean it out. I'm just so busy all the time, with reshelving and new books coming in, and keeping up with—"

"It must be an awful lot of work," Hannah said quickly. "Do you know where Mr. Valentino's boxes are?"

Gladys surveyed the room, tapping her finger against her

chin. "Over here, I think." She picked her way through the piles to the far corner, dug around a minute, then called for Hannah's help. "Put these over there on the floor," she said, handing Hannah an armload of books. "Here they are. Three boxes in all. I've got to get back to the front. Will you be okay by yourself?"

Eager to be alone, Hannah assured her that she would be fine, and Gladys left. Stooping down, Hannah examined the boxes. Two were solidly taped, but the third box looked as if it had been disturbed, the tape loose at the corners. She tugged at the tape and it came off easily, proving that it had been removed before. With mounting excitement, she rifled through the books near the top, which included some paperback westerns, a crossword dictionary, and some old algebra textbooks. She pulled them out, laying them on the floor, then dug deeper. When she had originally packed the books, she had focused on the volumes of poetry and paid little regard to the rest. Underneath the next layer of paperbacks she found what she was looking for, a stack of decades-old Hill Creek High School yearbooks. Her pulse quickening, she sorted through them until she found the volume from nineteen fifty-five. After perusing the table of contents, she turned to the correct page and her breath caught in her throat. Geraldine's photo had been cut out. The job had been done hastily, the gap in the paper cut at an odd angle. Whoever had done it had been in a hurry.

So as not to disturb fingerprints, Hannah took the long scarf that topped her cotton sweater and wrapped it around the yearbook where she could hold it, then exited the storage room, closing the door behind her. When she got back to the main room, Gladys was behind the checkout desk, haranguing another teenager.

"I'm taking one of Mr. Valentino's books. Do you mind?" Hannah asked.

"Be my guest," Gladys told her, distracted with the prospect of securing another fifty cents.

When Hannah walked outside, the sun's soothing warmth didn't lessen the sick feeling inside her. There was no way Berger could have known about Mr. Valentino's books. It had to have been someone local who had slipped in the back hallway when Gladys was busy at the front desk and gone into the storage room. With Gladys's eagle eye it would have been too risky to try and get such a large book out of the building. Instead they had simply cut out the photo and slipped it into a pocket or handbag. Berger may have been Geraldine's enemy, but he couldn't have been responsible for her death. It was someone who had been to Mr. Valentino's funeral and knew the library, which included Vera, Lillian, and Gilman.

Hannah rushed to the Cadillac, her brain moving faster than her feet. When she arrived at the police station, she hustled up the steps, the yearbook under her arm.

"I need to see Detective Morgan," she told the uniformed woman sitting behind the front counter, "It's urgent."

The officer gave Hannah an appraising look, then checked her computer screen and banged a few keys.

"He's out," she said.

"What about the police chief?"

"He's out, too."

"Where are they?" Hannah asked, her tone atypically pushy.

"Not a lot of crime happens here at the station, so our officers don't hang out here much. Can I help you?"

Hannah apologized for her impatience and explained that she had evidence in Geraldine Markham's murder investigation. She laid the yearbook on the countertop.

Giving it a suspicious look, the officer excused herself, returning a minute later wearing rubber gloves. She turned the book halfway toward Hannah and opened it gingerly, as if she thought it might be a bomb.

"It's just an old high school yearbook," Hannah told her. "Look at page seventy-four."

When the woman saw the hole in the page, she let out an "Oh, gosh."

"It can't tell us exactly who the killer is," Hannah said. "But it narrows the field." At the officer's request, she filled out a statement describing where and how she found the book, then signed it. "Could you please ask Detective Morgan to call me?" The officer said she would.

Hannah drove home, and when she walked into the kitchen, Sylvia came up to her and nuzzled her leg. For a second Hannah looked around for Teresa, her heart sinking when she remembered the dog was gone.

She found Kiki perched on the kitchen countertop next to the wall phone, legs crossed, the phone receiver cradled between her ear and shoulder. Her face was makeup-free, a rare condition she referred to as "letting her skin breathe." Busily filing her nails, she nodded and said repeated "uh-huhs" to the person on the other end of the line.

"I think you're absolutely right, honey," Kiki said. "I'd kick his tush out in the street so fast he'd be a blur going out the front door. No, you'll be surprised at how good you'll feel. Men are like high heels. Easy to walk on once you get the hang of it." Kiki laughed giddily, then, noticing Hannah, she wiggled her fingers in greeting. "Absolutely," she said to her caller. "I'd take his shirts and underwear and toss them out on the sidewalk." There was a long pause. "Sure, burn them if you think it will make more of a statement. You betcha, honey. Any time. Bye-bye now."

"Who was that?" Hannah asked as she put her purse on the table.

"One of Naomi's hotline callers. Real nice girl who's having a heck of a time with her boyfriend. But I set her straight."

"I thought you were only supposed to reschedule the calls for tomorrow."

"I've tried, but some people want to talk so bad, they just won't take no for an answer." Kiki resumed filing her nails.

"What you told that last caller, it didn't quite sound like something a Hopi snake shaman would say," Hannah told her. After finding the yearbook she was in a heightened emotional state and needed activity, however trivial. She didn't especially want tea but put on the kettle anyway, just to do something with her hands.

"I don't think it matters, since I'm not making them pay. And the people who've called in the past hour just wanted

someone to talk to more than anything. I mean, you don't
have to be a Hopi snake shaman to figure out when a girl
needs to dump her deadbeat boyfriend," Kiki said. Hannah
had to admit that it made sense. "Somebody keeps calling
and hanging up, like they're nervous and keep changing their
minds, which is silly. Would you make me a cup of Lemon
Lift?" Hannah nodded. "I like taking the calls. People have
such interesting problems."

Hannah pulled the box of teabags from the cabinet. "Kiki,
we need to talk. I rushed home because there's been a development."

The phone rang before she could finish. Much more interested in hot line callers than she was in conversing with
her sister, Kiki grinned, recrossed her legs, and picked it up.
"Shaman journey. Let us tap into your mystical energy," she
said in a singsong voice.

As Hannah tossed two teabags in the teapot, she saw
Kiki's eyes widen, then narrow. Kiki twisted around, facing
away from her sister, then dropped her voice. Curious, Hannah edged closer.

"I'm wearing a dress with spaghetti straps," Kiki told her
caller, which was a lie. She had on an old sweatsuit. "Sure,
it's really tight." There was a pause. "Now don't be a
naughty boy." Another pause, this one longer. "I'll only
spank you if you're really—"

Hannah grabbed the phone. She listened a few seconds.
Her mouth dropped open. "You have a disgusting mind.
Same to you, mister. Who is this?"

"Hannah, what are you doing? That's Mr. Smith! He's
called three times today."

"He hung up." Hannah put the receiver back. "What a
disgusting weirdo."

Kiki slid off the countertop. "He was just lonely, Hannah."

"There's a good reason he's lonely. Why would he be
calling a psychic hotline and saying such things?"

Hannah saw her sister's mouth silently working, which
meant a truth, the unpleasant kind, was about to dribble out.

"Well, remember how Naomi is sharing the 900 number
with Walter's friend?" Kiki began, twisting her fingers. "I

think his friend's number is for sexy talk, and some of the calls have been spilling over into Naomi's time slot."

"You mean it's one of those hotlines for perverts?"

"Don't say 'pervert.' Some of them are really nice, and Mr. Smith's idea about the swing set wasn't that strange once you heard him explain it."

The phone rang again. Kiki made a move, but Hannah slapped her hand over the receiver.

"No," she commanded.

"But I promised Naomi. She won't be back from trans-personal Reiki for an hour, and you wouldn't want her to miss an actual client when she needs the money so badly."

The phone resounded against the kitchen walls, demanding attention.

"I'll take it." Hannah picked up the phone. "Psychic hotline. I mean shaman journey, or whatever." She listened a moment before her mouth formed an astonished "oh." "No, I wouldn't. For God's sake, get some therapy." She slammed down the phone.

"You didn't have to be rude," Kiki said. She slid off the countertop to attend to the whistling teakettle.

"The man should be arrested." Hannah sat down at the kitchen table. "I have another subject I want to discuss with you."

"You look so serious, Hannah. What is it? Has something bad happened?" Kiki turned off the burner beneath the kettle and then sat down across from her sister. Hannah told her about finding the yearbook and the missing photo.

"You realize what this means?" Hannah asked. Kiki's expression indicated she didn't. "It means that David Berger, regardless of his despicable business, couldn't have hired that hit man. It means that Vera, Lillian, and Ronald are still suspects. Very likely ones, by my estimation. I want you to keep your distance from all of them until we get this sorted out."

"But I was supposed to meet Lillian at the Book Stop this afternoon and then we were going shopping," Kiki said.

"Make an excuse."

"This is so awful, Hannie. First our friend gets murdered,

then our dog gets kidnapped, and now one of our friends could be a killer. What a week."

"Go take a nice bubble bath and get your mind off things," Hannah suggested.

"That would make me feel better," Kiki said. "You'll answer the phone?"

"I guess so. And when Naomi gets back, I'm going to visit Geraldine's grave. You want to come?"

"Yes, I do," Kiki said with a sniff. "It would give us closure. Closure's a good thing."

Kiki left for her bath. Once she was gone, Hannah put her head in her hands in despair. How could she have been so wrong? She had been certain that Berger had been responsible for Geraldine's death, and because of her mistake she, as well as the police, had wasted precious time.

Her hand involuntarily rose to her neck and she scratched her worsening rash. She noticed a jar on the table and knew it was the herbal cream Naomi had promised her. Opening it, she sniffed the grayish mess, then rubbed some on her chest.

The phone rang. Fortunately it was someone wanting actual psychic help, and Hannah took the woman's name and number and promised that Naomi would call back. Hannah then rang the police station and asked if Detective Morgan had returned. The male officer told Hannah that Morgan was still in Sacramento, at the forensics lab. Hannah hung up, wondering why the female officer hadn't revealed that simple information.

The phone rang again. "Shaman journey," Hannah said distractedly, thinking about how much better her rash already felt. Naomi's cream had worked wonders. The sound of a woman sobbing brought her attention back to the phone.

"I, I need your help," the woman said, her voice choked.

The woman sounded so upset, Hannah didn't feel right just taking her phone number. "I should tell you that—"

"I know something," the caller blurted. "About a murder."

Hannah's pulse quickened. "Whose murder?"

"I don't know what to do," she said through sobs. "I'm so afraid."

"The murder at the hospital?" The woman inhaled sharply, giving Hannah her answer. "Do you know something about Geraldine?"

"My God," the caller said, her shock audible. Hannah realized that the caller had mistaken her mentioning of Geraldine as proof of her psychic ability.

Hannah wanted to explain that she wasn't psychic at all, and that the woman should be calling the police with whatever she knew, but as soon as Hannah began, she hesitated. The woman's voice sounded familiar.

"What should I do?" the woman asked.

The woman's voice was too obscured by crying for Hannah to be certain if she recognized the voice or not, and she couldn't stand the suspense any longer. "Who is this?" Hannah asked.

She got a click and dead air for her answer.

NINETEEN

HANKIE PRESSED TO HER face, Kiki whimpered juicily when she saw the headstone marking Geraldine's grave, but Hannah took in the sight silently and without visible emotion. Geraldine's name chiseled in black granite and the smell of earth so recently turned brought only brief thoughts of her friend. It was another woman who filled her mind, the woman who had sobbed over the phone only an hour before. Who was she, and what did she know about Geraldine's murder?

Hannah's ears were acute, and she was good at remembering voices. If the woman had been speaking normally, Hannah might have placed her, but the woman's voice had been so thickened by tears that it was only an undertone Hannah had recognized. She had called again at the police station before they left for the cemetery, thinking that if she discussed it with Morgan, it might jog her memory, but he was still out.

Hannah closed her eyes, trying to re-create the voice in her mind, sorting out the sound and the woman's words, but her brain was like the dark jumble of her handbag, with her blindly feeling around unidentified objects. Sometimes she wondered if the few drugs she had taken in the sixties had killed critical brain cells, and the effects were only now displaying themselves. She made a mental note to research it on the Internet sometime.

Kiki blew her nose and then let out a shuddering sigh. "Why does Geraldine have a headstone and these other people just have little markers all bunched together? It looks like they got buried standing up."

Hannah squinted at her sister. Sometimes she thought Kiki was one taco short of a full combination plate. "They were cremated and then their ashes were buried," she explained, then added, "It's less expensive."

Kiki sucked in some air. "So this is how we'll end up since we don't have much money?" The damp hankie she pressed to her nose muffled the last part.

For a moment Hannah considered this, trying to think of a nice way to put it, and finally just shrugged and said, "Yes." Since they were children she had always done her best to soften life's blows for Kiki, but this was one she couldn't. "We're going to die one day, and there's not much we can do about it."

Thinking the issue put to rest, Hannah looked down at Geraldine's grave and closed her eyes to say a prayer, but was disturbed by the metallic rip and click of a pop-top. Opening her eyes, she saw Kiki take a swig of a canned margarita, the kind she liked to carry in her purse when she knew she would be confronting life's more stressful situations, like trying on bathing suits, renewing her driver's license, and confronting mortality.

"Yes, there is something we can do about it," Kiki said with grim determination. "We can have fun while we can. We can live life to the fullest."

"It was only a couple of nights ago that you danced at a strip club."

"Yes, but I barely remember it, so it doesn't count."

"I'll take photos next time."

Her lips curling up at the corners, Hannah conjured up the image of Kiki's dancing at the Poodle Dog and thought how much Geraldine would have enjoyed hearing the story. Then, for some reason, the image of Tulip, Lila Sue's daughter, came to her mind. She pictured the girl's face framed with thick black hair, her dark eyes against such lovely pale skin. Hannah's head popped upward. She knew the identity of the woman who had called the psychic hot line.

"Holy jeezus," she said under her breath.

"Let's not get religious, Hannah. I'm just not in the mood." Kiki took a sip of margarita. "Let's go." She looked down at Geraldine's grave and raised her can. "Here's to you, hon. I hope, wherever you are, you've got a young stud in one hand and a cold cocktail in the other."

"What a lovely sentiment. You start for the car," Hannah said, wanting a minute alone with her percolating thoughts. "I'll catch up with you in a sec."

Kiki patted Hannah's shoulder. "I understand, Hannie. I'll just take my toddy to the car and wait. Take all the time you need."

Hannah watched Kiki walk away, her high heels digging into the earth. The voice. Hannah thought she had identified it, but still, she couldn't be positive. She would have to hear it again, and she thought she knew how to make that happen. She turned to leave, but stopped and looked down at Geraldine's grave.

"I did what you wanted. David Berger's in jail," Hannah whispered. "If you could speak to me now, you'd probably say I'd done enough. But I haven't. I have to find out who wanted you dead. I have to know why."

Just then a thump reached Hannah's ears, and twisting around, she saw her sister in a heap about twenty yards away.

"Oh, spit. I broke my heel!" Kiki cried. Hannah hurried to her sister, and, grabbing her under the arms, hoisted her upward. "It must have caught on some grass. Look, it came clean off." Kiki looked down and grimaced. "Grannie-sucking-eggs, I fell on top of a dead man. Is that bad luck?"

"I can't remember you ever being on top of a man or under one when it didn't turn out to be bad luck. There's a sidewalk over there," Hannah said, pointing to the left. "Come on, I'm in a hurry. I want to go to the hospital."

"That's sweet of you, Hannah, but I didn't hurt myself."

"That's not the reason. I'm looking for someone."

"For Ronnie?"

"I can't say yet."

"You can tell me, you know. I'm your sister."

"Please, Kiki, don't harass me. It won't do you any good."

The women walked between the graves, Kiki limping alongside her sister.

"No kidding, Hannah, I think we should spring for a nice funeral plot. I don't want to be buried in a shoebox like a dead bird. I want something nice and roomy."

"We can't afford it."

"We can charge it, can't we? Look over there," Kiki said, pointing to a statue of an angel they hadn't noticed before. "We need something like that. So fancy and impressive." Kiki pulled Hannah in that direction.

"Hannah groaned. "I don't have time for this."

"Let's just take a look so you can see what I'm talking about. It's exactly what we should have. Really classy."

Figuring it would be faster to just do it and get it over with, Hannah let Kiki lead her over to a large fenced plot with a white stone mausoleum in its center, a winged angel standing at its top.

"I can't believe it. This is Vera's family plot," Kiki said.

"It *is* impressive," Hannah told her, increasingly impatient. "But we could never afford something like this. It's probably been in Vera's family for years. Can we go now?"

"You're right, it's really old," Kiki said, walking the perimeter. "That man died fifty years ago. His headstone's a little plain, but that must be his wife next to him, and she's got marble. Now that's class. Oh, and look at that grave, Hannah. That girl died so young. And it happened just six months ago." Kiki walked over to a polished granite headstone carved with a garland of flowers. "That must have been Vera's granddaughter. She was only ten. Poor little thing. It was so sad."

The girl's age grabbed Hannah's attention, and she looked at the headstone. It read Honoria Thompson. Something caught in Hannah's throat.

"You know how she died?" Hannah asked.

Kiki nodded. "I heard all about it at Lady Nails. The little girl developed some terrible heart problem and they couldn't cure it, and she died. It was real sudden."

"How come I never knew?"

"You don't come into the salon enough. Also, she lived in Oregon, I think. They flew her body back here because they wanted the whole family buried together. Which, of course, you can do when you have a nice roomy plot like this." Kiki looked down at the grave. "Honoria's an odd name."

"It's an old name. British, I think."

"I've never heard it before."

But Hannah had, only at the time she hadn't realized it.

Hannah knocked on the front door of a rambling, one-story ranch-style house on the outskirts of Hill Creek. It sat on a half-acre, the property flat and treeless, with the driveway running in a fashionable arc in front. When Vera's husband was alive they had enjoyed a good income, but the money had died with him.

There was no answer. Hannah pounded on the door with her fist.

She heard hurried footsteps. The door opened about a foot, revealing Vera dressed in a faded lavender cotton robe and terry cloth house slippers, her hair wet and slicked back. She didn't wear any makeup, and it surprised Hannah how old she looked without it.

"Hannah, how are you?" There was bewilderment on Vera's face. Hannah wasn't the type to drop by for a visit. Vera pulled the robe more tightly around her, retying the sash. "This isn't a good time. Could we meet for coffee later?"

"I'm sorry, Vera, but this can't wait."

Vera gasped when Hannah brushed past her into the large mirrored foyer. Hannah had been there several times over the years, and the decor was still the same, everything in off-white and French-looking fabrics. From where she stood she could see the living and dining rooms. The furniture was French provincial, whitish with touches of gold paint, a style that was once again chic, although Vera had bought the furniture years before.

Vera stared at her guest with amazement. "I'm sorry, Hannah, but I'm not feeling well. You'll have to leave."

Hannah laid her purse on a small table. "I want my dog. You have her."

Vera showed no response except to move slowly to the door and close it, the sound of the deadbolt clicking shut sending a jolt of apprehension through Hannah.

"What are you saying? I don't have your dog," Vera said calmly, turning to Hannah, her back pressed against the door. "Lillian called me yesterday and told me you were so upset over poor Teresa that you're acting a little crazy and accusing people of things, so I'm not going to be angry with you. But I have to tell you that I've got a terrible headache, and this isn't helping."

Vera's voice and mannerisms bore their usual gentle femininity, but Hannah saw a blankness in her eyes, like a shade drawn over a window so all you saw was colorless light, but nothing that went on behind it. Hannah wondered if it had been there all along and she had just never taken the time to see it. Vera was one of those timid, quiet people you never really looked at or listened to. It wasn't necessary. She always looked the same, sounded the same, spoke the same dull niceties. Hannah had a terrible feeling today would be different.

"I want to talk about Honoria," she said. At the mention of the name, Vera's face paled to a shade that perfectly matched the decor. Hannah went on. "I saw the grave. I know how she died. At Geraldine's funeral I heard you say 'You paid the price for honor' when you were looking into the casket. But I didn't hear you correctly, you were speaking so softly. 'You paid the price for Honoria.' That's what you said to Geraldine."

"You don't know anything," Vera replied. She was still in control, but the pitch of her voice had risen and had gained an unfamiliar edge.

"I know that Honoria died from a heart problem. She must have needed a transplant."

"I want you to leave my house."

The look on Hannah's face said there wasn't much chance of that. "You were Geraldine's best friend. When she suspected that Berger was selling organs, she must have told you. And you asked her to help you find a donor heart for Honoria. Is that what happened?"

Vera drew her hand to the top of her robe, her fingers clutching the fabric to her throat. "You haven't changed from the time we were in high school. Always butting your nose in everyone else's business, thinking you know everything."

"This *is* my business, Vera. You had our friend killed."

"If you really think that, then why are you here instead of the police station?"

"I wanted to talk to you first." Hannah moved closer, her hand outstretched. "I've known you over forty-five years, Vera. Since we were sixteen. Whatever you've done, you couldn't have been rational at the time. You're not a violent person."

Her eyes closing, her lips pressed inward, Vera ran her fingers through her hair, then she walked slowly into the living room, her slippers dragging across thick white carpet that wanted cleaning. She lowered herself onto the sofa.

Hannah followed and sat next to her. She knew she should hate Vera, but she didn't. All she felt was pity as she watched Vera staring down at her lap, smoothing the folds of her robe, her legs pressed together and angled like a girl at her first tea party.

"Tell me what happened," Hannah said softly. "You asked Geraldine to go to Berger to find a heart for your granddaughter?"

Vera lifted her eyes. "I didn't ask her. I begged. She had told me what Berger was doing, or at least what she suspected. I thought she would help me."

"Do you know how she found out about him in the first place?"

"Someone she knew in Bangkok called her a little over a year ago. He asked her to check out Berger. They thought he was smuggling live animals. But there was only so much

Geraldine could do. She went to see him a few times, watched what was going on at his office."

"When did she realize he was dealing with humans?"

"I'm not sure. Nine months ago, I think. She'd made a complaint about him when she thought it was animals, but the police came back and said he was a meat importer and that everything was legal. But she didn't believe it. She decided to find out for herself. After she investigated a while, she realized he wasn't importing animals anymore. That's why the police didn't find anything. She followed him for days, parked her car outside his office, went through his trash."

"And she told you all of this?"

"I don't think she intended to." Vera picked up a small fringed pillow next to her and held it close to her stomach, her body gently rocking. "She came over for dinner one night. She'd been on the phone that day with someone in Bangkok, someone she'd been working with for months, and whoever it was confirmed what she suspected, that Berger was bringing in children from Thailand and Burma. They bought the children like they were cattle, then smuggled them into the States."

"So Berger was part of an organized effort?"

Vera nodded. "Geraldine felt sure he was the contact in the U.S., the one who found the buyers. He only got an organ matched up to a donor every couple of months, and she never knew when it was going to happen. That's why it was so hard to get proof of what he was doing, and she knew that if she told the police without hard proof, he'd just get away."

And she finally found it, Hannah thought. The list of names was the evidence she needed, and she had been afraid to leave it unguarded at her house.

"Gerry was very down about the whole thing, and that night she drank too much wine. She said she needed to tell someone." Vera leaned toward Hannah until their faces were inches apart. "But you see, I knew the real reason she told me."

The intensity on Vera's face made Hannah uneasy. "What was that?"

"God," Vera told her. She had stopped her rocking motion and sat perfectly still. "It was God's will. I was never religious, but at that moment I knew it was all meant to happen. My little Honoria got sick only a month after that. When I found out she needed a transplant, I knew. So I told Geraldine I needed her help getting a new heart for Honoria."

"And she wouldn't do it."

"No." Vera's voice dropped an octave. "Berger would have cooperated. I would have mortgaged my house and gotten the money. But she said asking him for help wouldn't be right." Vera's fingers wrapped tightly around the pillow's fringe. "I pleaded with her. It was my grandchild, I told her, and she still refused." Vera's voice turned thick with bitterness, the pain heavy on her face. "The self-righteous bitch!" A ripping sound grabbed Hannah's attention, and she saw that Vera had pulled the fringe from the pillow's seam.

"Vera, I don't think you understand. If Geraldine had asked him for a heart, he would have asked his contacts to find some poor child with the right blood and tissue types. Then they would have brought the child to the States, and they would have murdered that child." Hannah put her hand on Vera's. "How could anyone justify destroying one child to save another?"

Vera jerked her hand away. "Because it was my Honoria's life. I've heard about children in those countries. Nobody wants them. They roam the streets like dogs."

Hannah drew back. "I know you're not that cold-hearted. Deep down you couldn't do it. Otherwise, why didn't you just call Berger yourself?"

"I would have, believe me, but I never knew his name or the name of his company. Geraldine wouldn't tell me. It was for my own protection, she said. That filthy cow! I didn't hear his name until you told me the other day at Lady Nails. But it was too late." Vera stood up. Her face crumbled into tears and she moaned in a way that sounded like the low wail of an animal. "I loved that little girl. She looked like me. Everyone said so."

"But Vera, to cause more death—"

Vera moved to a small table by the window. She picked

up a silver-framed photograph of a smiling child and stroked it with the tip of her finger. "Geraldine could have saved my granddaughter, but she wouldn't do it. She wouldn't even try. She deserved to be where she is. In the ground."

"What about going through normal channels for a donor?"

"Of course we tried that," Vera said angrily. "You know how many people are on lists in this country for donor organs? Sixty thousand. People die every day, waiting for something that never comes. For a child the odds are worse, and Honoria had very little time. Berger was the only hope. God meant for him to help Honoria. It would have been his redemption, but Geraldine stopped it."

Her eyes hot with tears, Hannah felt a swell of despair. She didn't want to know any more. The truth was too sad to hear, her friend's anguish too painful to watch. But if Vera wanted to talk, she felt she should let her. Vera might not be so forthcoming later, with the police. And there was still more that Hannah had to know.

"How did you find Mendoza?" she asked.

"Louis put in a new patio around the back of the house. We can take a look at it later. It's quite nice," Vera replied in a suddenly matter-of-fact tone Hannah found strange. The change in her voice was a small thing, yet it suggested to Hannah that Vera was no longer in control of herself. It dawned on Hannah that she was no longer talking to old sweet Vera who just happened to have made a terrible mistake, but a seriously crazy Vera who was perhaps capable of digging out her spleen with a potato peeler. Nervous, Hannah slid her rump to the edge of the couch.

After kissing the photo, Vera put it back on the table. "One day I caught him in the kitchen, going through my purse. I should have called the police, but I felt sorry for him. We got to know each other." She looked at Hannah with a sly smile. "We used to meet in the afternoons. I told him what had happened with Honoria, and he agreed with me that it was Geraldine's fault. He offered to pay her back. For a fee, of course. Louis did everything for a fee."

"Did Geraldine have any idea what you had planned?"

"Not at first. Louis tried to break into her house about a

week before she went into the hospital, and I know that at first she thought it was Berger."

"At first? You mean she realized you were behind it?"

"Of course she did. I told her. We had lunch, and over sandwiches I explained to her that I was going to make her pay the price for killing my granddaughter. She said, 'Oh, Vera, I understand you're overwrought. Oh, Vera, let's talk it out.' But it was too late for talk."

Hannah now understood why Geraldine put extra bolts on her door instead of going to the police. She was trying to protect Vera. Geraldine thought she could handle Vera on her own, but she had been wrong. Just like me, Hannah thought. She had a sickening feeling that for her, too, Vera would prove unmanageable. But she couldn't leave, not yet. She didn't have all the answers she needed, and most important, she didn't have her dog.

"Did you know Mendoza was going to kill her that night at the hospital?"

Vera shook her head. "I was as surprised as anyone. Louis was less than brilliant."

Just then a loud thump came from down the hall, like something heavy being hurled low against a door.

"Teresa!" Hannah called out. There was more thumping, this time wilder. Hannah ran down the hallway, found the door and opened it. Teresa jumped toward her, then fell backward. The dog was muzzled and her collar tied with rope to a bed frame. Quickly, Hannah untied the rope and removed the muzzle, a process made difficult by Teresa's wiggling. The dog covered Hannah's face with joyful licks, a clumsiness to her movements telling Hannah that the dog had been drugged. Hannah's arms were around the dog's neck, her face buried in fur, when she felt a metal cylinder against the back of her neck.

"You're not always right about everything, Hannah."

Letting go of Teresa, Hannah turned and found herself looking down the barrel of a gun with Vera attached to the handle.

"You see, I am violent," Vera said. Her face was wet with tears, but she chuckled, like she had just told a good joke.

Her heart knocking inside her chest, Hannah slowly stood, holding up her palms in front of her. "This can do you no good, Vera. Kiki knows I'm here."

"Kiki barely knows what day it is, when you get right down to it. She could think you were here, but she could have gotten it wrong. She's such a flake, as everybody knows."

"Let's leave my sister out of it."

"Excuse my rudeness. I know how sensitive you are on that subject. Let's talk about you and what people would say if you disappeared. They'd say you were such a nosy busy-body, that something bad was bound to happen to you sooner or later." She pushed the gun closer to Hannah's face. "Some people might say you deserved it."

"Put the gun down, Vera. I'll help you all I can. I understand what you've been through."

"You understand nothing. Neither did Geraldine." Tears spilled down Vera's cheeks and the gun started to shake. "The two of you never had children or grandchildren. You can't know what it's like to lose a child. But I can give you a taste." She turned the barrel away from Hannah and pointed it at the dog.

The realization of what Vera had in mind hit Hannah like a punch. "Don't you dare harm that dog," she said fiercely.

"Hurts, doesn't it? Capture this feeling, Hannah, and multiply it by a thousand, and maybe you'll get an inkling of how I felt about my granddaughter." Stiffening her arms, she held the gun closer to Teresa's head, preparing to fire. Teresa, tail wagging, looked eagerly at Vera.

A knock at the door startled both of them. Teresa let out a rapid stream of barks that resounded against the walls. Vera's eyes darted toward the living room, and within seconds Hannah had her hands on the gun's handle. She tried to wrench it away, but Vera held fast, cursing and kicking.

As hard as she could, Hannah shoved Vera against the wall while still hanging on to her. The gun went off with an ear-splitting crack, the recoil sending both women to the floor and the gun sliding under a chair. Vera and Hannah both grabbed for it, but Vera got to it first. Hannah heard a crash from the front of the house. Vera pulled herself up, the gun in her hand. Gasping for breath, she pointed it at Hannah's face.

"Put it down. Now."

Hannah heard Morgan's voice behind her. She didn't turn to look at him, the sight of the gun aimed between her eyes a more urgent attraction.

"Put it down," he commanded.

Vera glanced at him, then returned her gaze to Hannah. Out of the corner of her eye Hannah saw Morgan's gun aimed at Vera. It occurred to Hannah that Vera was probably going to shoot her anyway, that in a strange way Vera welcomed a witness to her final act of despair.

Then something happened. Vera's expression softened, her lips parted slightly. It seemed to Hannah that Vera's will had broken, that she was giving up. Relaxing her arm, Vera moved the gun's barrel away from Hannah. Hannah let out a groan of relief.

"That's right, Mrs. Brown. Now hand it slowly—" Morgan said, the words trickling off when he saw what Hannah now witnessed with panic. Vera moved the gun to her own temple and pulled the trigger.

TWENTY

꧁꧂

THE BUDDHIST PRAYER CHIMES RANG out feverishly as Naomi rushed through the front door of Lady
Nails, a gust of wind causing her pale pink caftan to float up
around her, enhancing her carefully concocted personal am-
biance of loving peace and harmony. But her pink turban
caught on a nail in the doorjamb, causing a distressing ripple
in these smooth waters. Reaching up to feel her now bare
head, Naomi discovered the turban hanging in the doorway
like a deflated party balloon. Detaching it, she repositioned
it on her scalp, then scuttled into the shop, her stuffed canvas
shopping bag swinging on her arm.

Composure regained, she smiled at the gathering of
women that included Hannah, Kiki, Wanda, a few other Lady
Nails regulars, and one interesting addition. Lillian sat, legs
crossed, in a chair near the front, idly turning the pages of
the latest *Vogue* while she waited for a pedicure and foot
reflexology treatment. Since the embarrassing mud incident,
she had avoided the Zen salon, preferring the more amiable
atmosphere of Lady Nails, where humiliating personal inci-
dents were not only accepted but encouraged.

Naomi surveyed the room and, when sure all eyes were
upon her, grandly swept her arm through the air like the Pope

blessing his flock. "*Hellooo,* ladies. What love and energy there is in the air this morning. I can hear the songs of the ancient ones giving our town their blessings."

Ellie looked up from Kiki's toenails, which she was painting a frosted pink. "How's the psychic hot line biz?" she asked with feigned innocence, the question causing the other women to suppress smiles.

"I've given it up," Naomi announced briskly with a dismissing flick of her hand. "It blocked Red Moon's communication pathways. Fortunately he's recovered, and I'm now devoting myself completely to our earth goddess ritual. It's going to be so transpersonally healing." She gave her chest a thump with her fist. "The terrible events of the past few weeks have been a cry for us to return to the purity of our more transcendent instincts, to dive deep, deep into that flowing river of our higher goddess selves."

Waiting for Kiki in the front of the salon, Hannah glanced up from her *Better Homes and Gardens* magazine, wondering if Naomi had practiced the speech before she left the house or if the New Age babble spilled out naturally. Practiced, Hannah decided, suspecting that Naomi's theatrical display was an attempt to repair her tarnished spiritual reputation. A week earlier an eighty-year-old organic gardening instructor named Jasper had called Naomi's hot line, hoping to communicate with his long dead mother. Unfortunately, Jasper called at the wrong time, and instead of a comforting chat with Mummy he received smutty suggestions involving nudity and certain vegetables. Even though after a brief and excited exchange the hot line worker assured the outraged Jasper that the suggested legumes were pesticide-free, Jasper contacted the police department. Within hours a police dispatcher, under a vow of secrecy, told his girlfriend, who, under a vow of top secrecy, told her tai chi instructor, who, under the strictest top secrecy, told her zhi neng healer, who just plain blabbed it. By the end of the day the whole town was chuckling at the story. Naomi convinced the police of her innocence, but only after she agreed to fifty hours of voluntary community service picking up trash along the highway. To further decrease litter, she had spent the previous day ripping down the flyers she had posted all over town, the flyers now made especially embarrassing by insensitive teenagers embellishing the words "psychic hot line" by scrawling "really hot" underneath.

"Where's Hannah?" Naomi asked. "Randy at the Book Stop said she came this way." Several fingers in various stages of manicures pointed to the wicker chair by the front window.

Naomi went over, waving a business card. "I found this woman you should call right away." She handed the card to Hannah. Hannah looked at it and wrinkled her nose. "Her name is Maya Eaglehawk Black Sky," Naomi said. "She's a holistic animal healer, and she can help with Teresa's healing process. She works by a laying on of the hands." Naomi punctuated the last part by closing her eyes and holding her hands, palms down, in front of her.

"I've been using her for little Zeno, I mean Uncle Marv," Wanda said from her chair, where she was getting a French manicure. "He wouldn't touch his dog food, and she did a soul attunement for him."

Shiloh looked up from Wanda's fingernails with an expression of vague awareness suitable for someone who had just awakened from anesthesia. "Wow. Does he eat his dog food now?"

"No, still only pastrami with a little Dijon," Wanda replied. "But the interspecies languaging she did was very empowering for him. I think reincarnation has been exhausting for the poor little thing, so I've decided that at least for a while I'm going to let him fully experience his dogness. He needs a rest from his financial counseling." This last part she said a bit stiffly, since everyone knew the dog's counseling had cost her and Naomi a couple of thousand. Hannah noticed Wanda avoiding Naomi's gaze.

"Well, Teresa doesn't need any interspecies languaging, whatever that is," Hannah said. "She's fine." It was happily true that Teresa didn't seem to be experiencing any ill effects from her incarceration, but then, although Hannah loved Teresa, she always suspected that the dog had a brain no bigger than a grape.

Naomi's face grew worried. "Perhaps Teresa is fine, but what about you, Hannah, dear? After that horrible ordeal. When I think what would have happened if Detective Morgan hadn't gone to your house looking for you that day. If Kiki hadn't told him you were at Vera's." Everyone in the salon nodded sympathetically. "I think you should reconsider my offer to have Red Moon assess your chakras."

Hannah put down her magazine. "Please stop worrying about me. I'm perfectly okay," she told everyone. In truth she was far from it.

Two weeks had passed since Vera's death, and Hannah still couldn't get the case out of her mind. The problem was that Vera had killed herself before solving the puzzle of Mendoza's murder. In some respects it seemed logical that Vera had killed him to cover up her involvement, but Hannah couldn't accept this neat ending the way everyone else had. She could see Vera paying to have Geraldine killed and then keeping a neat distance from the actual murder. But Vera driving a pair of scissors into someone? Maybe a drug addict would commit such a crime, but not Vera. And if Vera was brave enough to take such a risk, then why didn't she just kill Geraldine herself instead of hiring someone to do it? Hannah turned it over and over in her mind, trying to come up with a theory that fit the facts, but couldn't.

"We can't help worrying about you," Kiki said. "It's all so terrible, and to think you were right there when Vera blasted her brains out."

Hannah winced. "Kiki, please."

"Oh, sorry," Kiki said with sincerity. "But you have to admit, things around here will never be the same."

Throughout the shop heads bobbed in agreement. The sad events of the past days had cast a pall over Lady Nails. Geraldine's death had been horrible enough, but Vera's suicide struck a harder blow, for with Vera, a regular customer and fellow gossipmonger, one of their own had fallen. For the past few days Hill Creek's older women had flocked to Lady Nails with such frequency that there wasn't a chipped nail among them. Every chair in the shop was constantly filled, and Ellie and Shiloh had to handle the women on an assembly line basis. But no one minded waiting. They hadn't come for manicures anyway. They hadn't even come for gossip. It was commiseration they hungered for, reassurance that their narrow world was safe. Hannah wondered if it ever had been, when secrets seemed to lurk behind every smiling face.

"We'll soon have our energy meridians back in alignment," Naomi said with a forced brightness, wanting to lift the gloom. "I've been planning the dance for next week. We're going to be in a sacred circle formation. It's better for tapping into our ancestral collective consciousness. I'll be in the center, of course, leading us all."

She dug into her shopping bag and pulled out a wad of orange material. "I just picked up my shamaness tunic." With a flick of her wrist, she unfolded it, holding the gauzy fabric high in the air, displaying a floor-length dress with feathers and bells running along the neckline and down the front. "I borrowed it from an Apache medicine woman in Sausalito. See how it moves," she said, waving it back and forth. "You can just feel the mystic energy."

The women murmured approval. The plan was for them to participate in an earth goddess dance in the middle of the plaza that would honor Geraldine and, according to Naomi, forge a pathway into their authentic selves, and move them into sacred wholeness—which, translated into English, meant they would all have a real good time. All the Lady Nails patrons were invited, even those who hadn't known Geraldine, and the very mention of the dance put all the women in an excited twitter. The only exception was Hannah. She didn't much like the idea of dancing around in a public place, but after pressure from Kiki, she had reluctantly agreed.

"How come you get to wear the shamaness tunic?" Kiki asked, eyeing the garment with envy.

"Because I know the ritual," Naomi said. "I'll be leading the rest of you."

"But couldn't someone else learn the ritual and be the leader?" Kiki asked, her tone dripping syrup, thinking how good she would look in bells and feathers. "It might be more healing if one of us did that shamaness part," Kiki said. "Like me, for instance."

"Kiki could be right. The healing process would be enhanced by having a lay person perform the ritual," Wanda said, her own eagle eyes on the tunic. Watching this drama with amusement, Hannah guessed Wanda was thinking how to accessorize it with a Chanel scarf and an Armani handbag. Wanda continued, "Although I think it would have to be me. The tunic is too long for you, Kiki."

Kiki forced an accommodating smile that looked like it hurt. "I could wear my high heel boots."

"But *I* took a course last year from that Dzogchen meditation master," Lillian said, throwing her hat into the tunic ring. "His Holiness told me personally that I'm very centered. I could lead the dance better than anyone."

"I took that Dzogchen class," Wanda said tartly, "and I don't see where it would qualify you for anything. I sat in the lotus position on a hard floor so long my tush went numb."

"Now, ladies," Naomi said. "Your enthusiasm is so energizing, but my being Red Moon's physical vessel makes me the only choice for the shamaness role."

"I don't see why," Lillian said.

"Yes, this should be a democracy," Kiki chimed in.

Naomi's smile grew taut. "This is the spirit world. You don't get to vote."

Hannah decided she should intervene before the cotton balls started flying. "Ladies, it doesn't matter who leads the dance ritual. The important thing is that we honor Geraldine. And I don't think we should leave out Vera, in spite of what she did. I don't believe Geraldine would have wanted it."

"But Vera had Geraldine murdered," Wanda said. "Don't you think Geraldine, wherever she is, is pretty upset about that?"

"Poor Vera," Shiloh said. "Who would have thought she'd be responsible for two murders?"

Hannah stood up. "The truth is, the police don't know for certain who killed Mendoza. They're just accepting the simplest answer. It could have been Vera, but you were with her in the waiting room that night, Lillian," Hannah said. "Wouldn't you have noticed if Vera had left?"

"I took a sleeping pill," Lillian replied. "I was dead to the world until I heard Kiki screaming her head off. No one could have slept through that racket." She gave Kiki a conciliatory smile, now that they were, for the time being, best pals. "Of course, anyone would have screamed."

"All this negative talk is devitalizing my consciousness," Naomi said. "Let's focus on the positive. Hannah, do you have the pictures of Geraldine?"

To augment the earth goddess ritual, Naomi and Wanda were assembling a photo collage of Geraldine. The photos were going to be pasted artfully on poster board and placed in the middle of the dancing area, along with flowers and candles, to create a kind of altar. The only problem was, there were no photographs of Geraldine that anyone could find other than the yearbook photos, and those had disturbing connotations. To solve the problem, Hannah offered the old photos from Geraldine's box.

Hannah reached under the wicker chair and pulled a white envelope from her purse. "I almost forgot I had them." She took out the stack of pictures and held them in her lap, remembering with sadness the first time she saw them.

"Did you hear about Ron and that young nurse?" Lillian said, giving the words "young nurse" the same disapproving emphasis she would have used for "convicted felon." Other conversations, all less promising than this one, hushed. "He barely knows her, and he's taking her to Tahiti."

"No," Kiki said, the single syllable packed with a full range of emotions. All the women in the shop, mouths open, turned to Lillian.

"How do you know?" Ellie asked.

"I just saw them at the Book Stop. The two of them were sitting together, *cooing*." Lillian rolled her eyes with disgust. "Well, Ron was cooing. I said hello to them, which was no problem for me, since I'm completely over him." Lillian brushed a nonexistent speck of lint off her lap and recrossed her legs. "And he told me about the trip. They were just getting ready to leave to take the ferry into San Francisco to do some shopping."

"Shopping?" Kiki said.

"Ron said that Ruth, I believe that's her name, needed a few things," Lillian said, her voice laden with sarcasm. "They're going on to the airport from there. Men are so foolish. She's young enough to be his daughter."

"I hear women go topless in Tahiti," Kiki said, the image bringing a moment of contemplative silence from the other women.

"You mean, like, in the grocery store?" Shiloh asked.

"Probably," Kiki answered.

Hannah chuckled. "They only go topless on the beach."

"He could have a heart attack," Wanda said, her tone discreetly lowered, her eyebrow arched in a manner indicating the idea didn't offend her.

Hannah's eyes fixed upon the floor as the image of Ruth sharpened in her mind, a disheartening idea hardening around it. In the tumult of the past few days, Hannah had forgotten the psychic hot line call and the sobbing voice, but it now took on new importance. She sat up in her chair and hurriedly flipped through the photographs still in her lap. When she came to the last one, she muttered a soft "Oh, my."

"What, Hannah?" Kiki asked. "What are you looking at?"

Hannah said nothing. Taking the one photograph with her, she grabbed her purse and headed for the door.

"Hannah, where are on earth are you going?" Kiki asked.

Hannah stopped. "I just remembered an errand I have to run."

Kiki eyed her sister, then bolted up in her chair. "I'm coming, too. My toes are done."

A nail polish brush still in her hand, Ellie looked surprised at this news. "You're not dry."

Kiki didn't care. She scooped up her handbag and shoes from beneath her chair, the other women observing with wonder.

"But we need to work on the dance. I was going to have us practice sacred hand gestures," Naomi said with frustration as Kiki brushed by.

"And you still have cotton between your toes," Ellie called out. But Hannah moved much too fast for Kiki to dawdle, and she scurried behind her sister through the door, her thick wedgie sandals dangling from her hand.

"Hannah, I saw your face back there," Kiki said, struggling to keep up with Hannah's aggressive stride down the sidewalk. Wanting to save her pedicure, Kiki did a modified heel-walk, her cotton-swathed toes barely touching the ground. "You looked like you'd just seen Elvis."

Hannah didn't answer, her mind so focused that her sister's words were only a vague noise in the background. When they reached the Cadillac, she unlocked the doors and they both got in.

Kiki exhaled loudly as her sister started the engine. "Hannah, you tell me this instant where you're going!"

Hannah looked at Kiki as if only just realizing she was there. "To the ferry. I need to stop them. At least delay them."

Lips parted, head tipped sideways, Kiki stared at her sister with confusion. "Delay Ronnie and Ruth? Hannah, sweetie, we're all upset he's running off with a girl so young, but it's a free country."

"I want to talk to Ruth."

"Why?"

"There's something I need to ask her."

"What?"

"I can't tell you. Not yet."

"Are you not feeling well?" Kiki asked with concern. "You always try to be so strong, but it would be perfectly natural for you to feel a little depressed, with everything that's happened."

"I'm fine, trust me. Just get the ferry schedule out of my wallet and tell me when the next boat leaves."

Kiki picked up the purse and pulled out the wallet, her eyes staying on Hannah. "You ever thought of taking St. Johns' wort? My friend Barbara, she was so depressed she ate thirty-two Eskimo Pies in three days. Then she started on St. John's wort and she's down to only four pies a day. That's real progress."

"A miracle. I don't need antidepressants."

"But Hannah, honey, you're acting so strange."

Hannah couldn't tell her sister about the flash of insight that had hit her at Lady Nails. She couldn't tell anyone. She pulled into the traffic on Center Avenue, heading toward the freeway at a speed neither she nor the Cadillac was used to.

Kiki pulled the small folded schedule from Hannah's wallet, put on her reading glasses, and studied it. "The next one leaves in fifteen minutes."

"We have to hurry," Hannah said, pressing harder on the accelerator, barely making it through a red light.

"Oh, spit," Kiki said. "The cotton stuck to my polish, and I was so careful. Could we stop at the mini-mart and get some polish remover?"

Hannah glanced at Kiki's bare feet pressed against the dashboard, the pudgy toes tipped with fur. "They look good, like little mohair sweaters," Hannah said, having no intention of stopping for anything short of gushing blood.

Kiki examined her toes with fresh appreciation. "Hmm, I guess they are kind of cute." Her expression softened. "Listen, Hannah, I know what you're doing, and I think it's sweet."

Hannah gave Kiki a curious glance as she pulled onto the freeway. The term "sweet" hardly applied to what was on her mind.

"But you see, you shouldn't be mad at Ruth," Kiki continued. "It's not her fault. Ronnie is a hunk. Any woman would want him. And to tell you the truth, now that I know how mean he was to Geraldine over wanting to buy her house, I'm not interested in him anymore, so you don't need to do this for me." Kiki braced herself against the door. "Aren't we going a little fast?"

"If I don't rush, we won't make it. Let me get this straight. When you thought Ron might have had Geraldine murdered, he was still datable. But now that you know that he only acted rudely to her, you don't like him anymore?"

"Sure, it sounds shallow when you put it that way. The point is, I'm ready to move on. In fact, I was thinking that Harry Stanley's kind of cute."

Kiki fell back against the seat as Hannah gunned the engine and passed a sluggish car. She exited the freeway, pulling onto a busy four-lane road. Weaving through the heavy traffic, she drove two blocks and turned in to the ferry parking lot. As Kiki scrambled to buckle her sandals, Hannah pulled into a space with a screech of tires.

The women hurried out of the car. Hannah's flat shoes allowed her to jog across the paved lot toward the ferry building, a modern crab-shaped structure of concrete and Plexiglas, while Kiki kept up the best she could. When they got closer, Hannah saw with relief that the boat was still at the dock. A horn blasted. She quickened her pace.

"Hannah, wait up!" Kiki shouted just as Hannah reached the entrance. Kiki rushed toward her. "You know, I'm starting to understand what you're doing, and I've decided I like it," Kiki said, panting from the jog. "If every guy went for much younger women, then women our age would have to date ninety-year-olds. So I say, go ahead, give old Ronnie a piece of your mind. Let him have it."

Hannah had no time to correct this wrong impression. She grabbed Kiki's hand and pulled her inside the building while she searched the crowd.

"I don't see them. They must be on the boat already. I'll have to get a ticket." She headed for the ticket window.

"And leave me here?" Kiki asked, close behind.

"You're right. You should come, too," Hannah said over her shoulder. "I may need you."

"Good, because I want to be there when you do it. It's going to be a blow for older women of America. They're going to write this up in *Modern Maturity*."

Hannah approached one of the two ticket windows, bought two tickets, then she and Kiki moved to the back of the crowd heading up the gangway. Hannah soon felt a tug on her sleeve.

"Ronnie's over there." Kiki pointed to the ticket counter. Hannah saw Gilman fumbling with his wallet, two suitcases at his feet. He must have come in behind them. Not liking that he was alone, she looked around and finally found Ruth waiting by a bench not far from them. Gilman must have dropped her off before he parked the car so she wouldn't have to walk. The horn blew a second time, which meant the boat would soon be leaving. Hannah felt a nervous flutter. It was now or never.

"Kiki, I need you to do something for me."

"Sure," Kiki answered excitedly. "Anything."

"I want you to distract Ron while I talk to Ruth."

Kiki tilted her head to one side. "Wait a minute. You're supposed to let Ronnie have a piece of your mind, not Ruth."

Hannah took Kiki's hands in hers and gave her a penetrating look. "Do you trust me?"

Kiki concentrated a second, then nodded. "I get it. You're going to talk Ruth out of going, let her know what a mistake she's making. It seems extreme, though. Are you sure? Of course you're sure, or you wouldn't be doing it."

"There's no time for chitchat," Hannah said. "The boat's going to leave any minute. Think of some way to distract him."

With a lascivious smile, Kiki reached for the top button of her blouse.

"I said distract him, not send him screaming."

"Very funny. I'll take care of him, don't you worry." She gave Hannah a push. "Now go get 'em, baby. Go do whatever you're going to do. Do it for women over sixty everywhere." She hesitated, then held up one finger. "Just don't upset that little Ruth too bad, okay? Remember, we're all sisters under the skin."

Knowing she couldn't make that promise, Hannah moved toward her target.

Dressed in navy blue pants and a print blouse, Ruth waited near the gangway, the large blue-and-white passenger ferry visible behind her. She stood perfectly still, her face somber, and Hannah was struck by her loveliness. Ruth's delicate features, straight dark hair, and petite frame were as perfect as a doll's. Hannah glanced at the photograph she had in her purse, then again at Ruth.

Hannah called out her name. Ruth turned, the initial recognition on her face quickly changing to discomfort.

"Hello," Hannah said with feigned cheerfulness. "We haven't met formally. I'm Hannah Malloy, an old friend of Ron's. I just saw him by the ticket counter and heard all about your trip. How exciting. I've always wanted to go to Tahiti. I've got a dozen questions."

"It's nice to meet you, Mrs. Malloy," Ruth said hesitantly. "But we're in a hurry. We have to make this ferry."

"But that's just it. Ron asked me to get you on the boat. He had to make a phone call. You know how doctors are, and it's no trouble, since I'm taking the same ferry anyway."

Ruth looked worriedly for Gilman, a crowd heading up the gangway enclosing them. Hannah took her arm and steered her into the river of people to reduce the opportunities for escape. Hannah found it surprisingly easy to control her. Ruth seemed lost and unsure of herself.

With her best chatty senior citizen act, Hannah kept up a steady stream of questions about the Tahiti trip, which Ruth politely answered, her gaze always over her shoulder. Once on the boat, Hannah handed the uniformed man the two tickets she had purchased for herself and Kiki, keeping her hand on Ruth's arm, feeling the tension in the young woman's muscles.

It wasn't until Hannah and Ruth stopped at the boat railing that Hannah allowed herself to look back at the ferry building. Almost everyone was now on the boat, and Hannah easily found Kiki and Gilman, Kiki chattering away and Gilman looking annoyed, his eyes searching the waiting area for Ruth.

Ruth saw him. "He's going to miss the boat if he doesn't hurry."

Hannah saw Gilman start toward the boat. Kiki appeared frantic. She looked at the boat, then at Gilman. A few quick steps put her in front of him, and she let out a wail, then collapsed into his arms. The ferry horn blasted for the last time, the boat workers removing the massive ropes from their moorings and throwing them on the dock. Holding a slumped Kiki, Gilman looked at the boat, his face panicked.

Hannah saw Ruth wave to get Gilman's attention. He finally saw her, his expression morose.

Ruth gripped the railing as the ferry pulled a few feet away from the dock. "Can you see that? Some ridiculous woman passed out right in his arms."

Hannah bristled a bit. She thought "ridiculous" too strong a word for Kiki, but it wasn't the time to launch a defense of her sister. She saw Gilman pointing toward San Francisco and mouthing the word "taxi."

"What's he saying? Can you make out what he's saying, Mrs. Malloy?" Ruth asked, her anxiety growing.

"He's going to take a taxi, I think. Most likely to the ferry building in San Francisco. Don't worry. He'll catch up with you there."

The two women watched Gilman holding Kiki, looking like he wanted to drop her. Hannah saw Kiki open her eyes. When Kiki saw that the boat had pulled from the dock, she stood up and waved merrily to Hannah, with Gilman looking stunned at this sudden recovery. The ferry's engines kicked into gear and the boat glided through the bay's choppy water. Ruth turned to Hannah.

"You meant this to happen," she said, angry. "Why?"

"Because I loved Geraldine," Hannah said softly. "Almost as much as you did."

TWENTY-ONE

RUTH LOOKED AWAY AND FACED the water, its deep blue shining under the sunlight. They were near the front of the boat, where the wind tended to whip up; everyone else was on the more comfortable viewing deck at the rear.

Seeing the wretchedness on the young woman's face, Hannah felt her own resolve weakening. Sometimes it was better not to know the truth about things. Suspicions you could push to the back of your mind and pretend they didn't exist. Truth was in your face. For a moment Hannah considered walking away, but she ended up staying put.

"I barely knew Geraldine Markham," Ruth said. She was a lousy liar, and her voice broke. Her eyes followed a flock of squawking seagulls that tagged alongside the boat. As if they had all heard the same Godly command, the birds suddenly banked right, heading toward the Golden Gate and the open sea, and Ruth looked like she wanted to join them. *That's what she's trying to do now,* Hannah thought. *She's so desperate to fly away, she accepted the attentions of a man twice her age, a man she probably doesn't give a fig about.*

"There's no point in lying to me. I recognized you in one

of Geraldine's old photographs from Thailand," Hannah said.

Ruth looked at her, her eyes fearful and with the kind of wearied pain that usually takes a long lifetime to accumulate. Hannah's heart ached for her, but she pressed on.

"There was a photo of her with a young girl, the only one of her with a child," Hannah said. "It took me a while to make the connection because you don't look Asian."

Ruth's shoulders relaxed, and she smiled slightly, but there was no mirth in it. It was full of sadness and perhaps, Hannah thought, relief.

"I'm only half Thai," she said. "I don't know about the other half of me. American, probably. And I must favor him."

"You're beautiful. You were beautiful even back then."

"That's a time I don't like to talk about," Ruth said, her voice tense. The boat was picking up speed, the wind causing her hair to fly about her face. "I pretend I didn't exist until I came here."

"You have to talk about it. I know you killed Mendoza, but I need to know the rest. I'm going to help you all I can."

A little boy's delighted squeal shattered their solitude until his mother came and retrieved him. Her hand shaking, Ruth reached into her purse and pulled out a cigarette, put it in her mouth, and, shielding it from the wind with her hand, lit it with a plastic lighter. She saw Hannah's surprise. "I know. And a nurse of all people. Someday I'll stop. Today's not the day." She put the cigarette to her mouth again and inhaled. "Geraldine used to talk about you sometimes, Mrs. Malloy. She thought a lot of you."

"It was Geraldine who brought you to the States?"

"Yes." Ruth's eyes dropped away as she arranged her words. "I was a prostitute in the Patpong district by the time I was eleven. Not by choice. One night Geraldine and an Asian woman came into the back part of the bar and took out all the children they could, about five of us. They had bribed a policeman to help them, so the owner thought it was some kind of raid." She paused, lost for a moment in the memory, the cigarette burning unsmoked between her fingers. "I was so frightened. They took us to a house. I didn't cry, but I couldn't stop shaking, and Geraldine sat me down on the front steps. She didn't touch me. She just told me I was safe."

"After that, she brought you to California?"

Ruth nodded. "I lived at a church school in San Jose for a few months until I was placed with a Chinese family in South San Francisco. They were good to me, but I never forgot Geraldine. She was my savior. Can you understand what it's like to be a kid all alone and living in hell, then suddenly an angel comes and saves you?"

Hannah didn't. She couldn't imagine what such a childhood would be like. "And you kept up with her?"

"It was pretty one-sided. She didn't want a close relationship with any of the kids she helped. She wanted that part of her life separate, hidden away, but I guess in the end you can't do that."

"How did you end up in Hill Creek?"

"When I graduated from nursing school, I moved to Marin to be close to her. I called her every month or so. When I found out she was in the hospital, I couldn't believe it. It was my chance to do something for her. I made sure I got on her ward, and I think she was grateful for it. She told me she was. I planned to sleep at the hospital that night so I could be with her first thing the next morning."

"Does Ron know about your history with her?"

"No. He and I didn't even meet until Geraldine came to the hospital. He doesn't know her story and he doesn't know mine. I've worked hard to keep it secret. I know people here are supposed to be so liberal and open-minded, but they're no different from people anywhere. If they knew I'd been a child whore, they'd look at me differently."

Hannah didn't agree. People in Hill Creek would only feel kindness and sympathy, she felt sure. "And that night you walked in on Mendoza?"

Ruth wasn't half through the cigarette, but she tossed it over the railing into the bay. "I didn't plan it," she said, her eyes directed at the water. "I had no idea anyone wanted to hurt her. I went into her room to check on her, and saw him pull the pillow from her face. Something in me blew up."

"No one heard any of this?"

"There wasn't much to hear. I had the scissors in my pocket, and I struck him. It took him by surprise, and he just dropped. It was late. I was the only nurse on the floor."

"Did you hear my sister and me coming?"

"I just heard a noise at the nurses' station. I panicked and ran. Once I got down the stairs, I realized that I hadn't hit the Code Blue button. I couldn't believe I'd made such a mistake, but I was so scared. I ran back up to do it, and that's when I saw you go in the room."

"Why didn't you tell the truth to the police? The man had just murdered a patient. You could have claimed self-defense or that you were trying to save Geraldine."

"I wasn't thinking straight. All I could think was that if I told the police what happened, that I would have to tell about my relationship to Geraldine. Everything about my past would come out, and I couldn't stand the thought. People looking at me and whispering about me. And it's not like it would have brought Geraldine back."

The boat pulled up to the dock, hitting its edge sharply and bounding backward. The two women grabbed the railing, holding on without speaking until the boat stabilized.

"So now you know everything," Ruth said. "I'm not sorry I did it."

"I understand, I think. Geraldine had done a wonderful thing for you."

"It's more than that," Ruth said with new urgency. "I owed her a murder."

"Why would you say such a thing?"

"In Bangkok, once the police had their money, they took more money from the bar owner and told him where Geraldine had taken us. He showed up a day later. By then the other girls had already been taken to a boat, but there wasn't enough room, so Geraldine and I were still there. He tried to take me back. When he got physical about it, Geraldine shot him. She killed a man for me. It's right that I did the same for her."

The boat lodged against the dock, this time more gently.

Hannah saw a boatman throw a massive rope around a large iron mooring.

"Now, you can turn me in and be a hero," Ruth said. "I was thinking about turning myself in anyway. I guess this is fate."

Hannah felt a churning inside her. She knew she had to make a decision right then and stick with it. A crowd swarmed past them as people readied to exit the boat. Hannah and Ruth didn't move.

"Go to Tahiti," Hannah said quickly. "The police think Vera Brown did it, and I'll never tell them differently. I don't think they'll ever figure out the truth. There's no evidence against you."

Ruth gave her a questioning look. "Why would you protect me?"

"Because if I'd walked in that room and seen him, I would have killed him, too. So you see, I'm in no position to be your judge."

Ruth looked at her, not moving.

"Just go," Hannah commanded.

Ruth didn't thank her, but as far as Hannah was concerned, she didn't need to. Ruth moved into the river of people heading off the boat and onto the dock. In the crowd standing at the ferry building Hannah spotted Gilman, looking as anxious as a teenager waiting for his prom date. When Ruth reached the end of the gangway, she looked back at the boat. She caught Hannah's eye. Hannah nodded to her, then Ruth turned and moved on to a relieved-looking Gilman, and the two of them walked away.

"Maybe this is what you really wanted from me, Geraldine," Hannah said quietly to herself. "You saved her once, and you needed me to save her again." Hannah didn't feel any pleasure or even any satisfaction over what she had just done. She was only glad that at last it was over, and for her that was more than enough.

"Are you getting off the boat, ma'am?"

She turned and saw a young man in an orange jumpsuit looking at her expectantly. It crossed her mind that if the jumpsuit had a few rhinestones on it, Kiki would probably wear it out to dinner.

TWENTY-TWO

A HEADDRESS OF TURKEY FEATHERS balanced precariously on her head, Naomi stood regally in the center of the plaza, her eyes and arms raised skyward toward a higher wisdom. Her orange shamaness tunic had proven too small, and the fabric strained against her thighs and tummy, causing the feathers to poke out at forty-five degree angles so that she looked like a half-plucked chicken. But this misfortune was minor compared to her greater triumph, for the earth goddess ritual was going stupendously and had even attracted a crowd of coffee-sipping onlookers from the Book shop. At Naomi's bare feet lay a circle of stones and flowers, a poster board collage of Geraldine's photos standing in the middle. At Hannah's insistence a photo of Vera had also been placed there, not directly next to Geraldine's but a few inches away, leaning against the bottom of the board.

Playing to the crowd, Naomi shook her war stick and jogged around the makeshift altar, chanting Indian words and occasionally performing a small leap that was mimicked by the women who formed a circle around her. Then the women paused, and each raised one bare foot, balancing on their toes and raising one leg high above their heads, simultaneously emitting a loud hoot in emulation of the earth mother's cry.

It sounded more like a cry of severe abdominal distress, Hannah thought with a chuckle, watching from a bench at the edge of the plaza. She observed with satisfaction that her friends were having a ball. They hopped and swirled with grins on their faces, their pleasure heightened by the make-shift earth goddess costumes they wore. To eliminate the need for sewing, which none of them knew how to do any-way, they had tied sheets over one shoulder toga-style, then belted them at the waist with scarves, looking like an AARP chapter of vestal virgins. The polka dot fabric wasn't very goddess-like, but the sheets had been on sale dirt-cheap and not a strain on anyone's pocketbook. The fabric was second-ary, the priority being the delicious opportunity to dress up in costumes and make a public spectacle of themselves. This they had achieved to the hilt.

Kiki broke away from the group and pranced, arms wav-ing, over to her sister. "Don't be a stick in the mud, Hannah. Come and dance." Kiki performed a joyful hop, arms out-stretched and flapping, giving her the appearance of a hal-lucinating swan. "I feel so healed. I know that Geraldine is feeling very loved right now, looking down on us."

Hannah suspected that if Geraldine were watching, she was getting a good belly laugh. Hannah certainly was. Just then the dancers pivoted to move clockwise in the circle, half of them getting their directions confused and bumping into one another.

A cool breeze swept across the plaza, and Hannah pulled the sweater topping her toga more closely around her. The toga revealed part of her tattoo, and at the last minute she had thrown on the cardigan to hide it. She had shown her tattoo only to Kiki and John Perez, even though her friends knew it existed and always asked to see it. She wasn't sure why she kept it hidden. On the contrary, she often thought she should proudly display it, or at least a modest part of it, to show the world that the cancer hadn't beaten her.

The dancers let out another wild whoop, punctuated by a one-footed hop that caused Wanda to fall on her rather scanty tush. With assistance from Ellie and Lillian she was quickly uprighted and resumed dancing. Hannah wanted to join them, but felt silly being the only one wearing a sweater.

After giving the war stick a few more emphatic shakes and emitting her earsplitting cry of the eagle, Naomi knelt on the ground and touched her head to the pavement, concluding the first phase of the dance. The goddess ritual was supposed to be done all at one time, but none of the women could have their bladders jostled that long without using the bathroom, so it was decided beforehand that they would take a ten-minute break and then resume.

Their faces flushed, Naomi and Lauren came over to Hannah and Kiki, and squeezed next to them on the bench.

"The song of the ancient ones is on the wind," Naomi said, laying her war stick at her feet. "What joy and enlightenment. And the tree looks so much improved. My Dance of the Spotted Eagle really helped it."

"First of all, Naomi, I doubt there's any such bird as a spotted eagle. Secondly, the problem with the tree was fungus. I sprayed it with fungicide last week, which is why it's looking better," Hannah said. Naomi looked hurt, and Hannah regretted her bluntness. "But you were right when you said the tree told you that things weren't as they appeared," she added to soften the blow. "After going through the garden book, I realized that the tree wasn't the *Arbutus unedo* we thought we had planted back in high school. It's an *Arbutus marina*. The varieties are similar, of course, but still very different in the size of the leaves and flowers."

"You see, the tree did speak to me," Naomi said, her self-esteem restored. "The tree also told me that it was suspicious and afraid. Now I realize it wasn't referring to itself. It meant the humans."

The women all nodded in somber agreement. Hannah thought back on that afternoon. It was true that what Naomi had claimed regarding the tree had turned out to be uncannily accurate, as did so many of her psychic divinations. Many people in the Botany Club had turned out not to be what they appeared. It upset Hannah that she thought she had known her old high school friends, known them up and down, and never suspected what secrets they carried. The disappointment had taken a serious chunk from her general trust level.

A brassy "Hello, girls!" came at them from across the plaza. Harry Stanley limped in their direction, wearing a plaid sport coat a size too big for him and a red bow tie. Hannah's eyes widened with surprise, not at seeing Harry but at seeing Lila Sue at his side, her arm linked in his.

"You girls having a toga party without me?" Harry asked with a grin. "You remember Lila Sue, don't you?"

Hard to forget her, Hannah thought. "Nice to see you both." She introduced Lauren and Naomi.

"Harry, he taking me out on the town," Lila Sue said proudly, smoothing the front of her abundant red dress. "He gonna show Lila Sue a hot time."

Harry gave her a playful pat on the behind, and Lila Sue tittered with delight. "Yeah, being around you two gals made me reevaluate my woman situation," Harry said. "I decided I need a more quiet type of woman, somebody with old-fashioned values." He gave Lila Sue's shoulder an affectionate squeeze.

Hannah thought it would be in bad taste to remind him that Lila Sue owned a strip club and had her own daughter dancing there. Live and let live.

"Hey, you, girlie," Lila Sue said to Kiki. "You ever looking for work, you call Lila Sue."

Turning pink, Kiki watched with aggravation as Lila Sue and Harry said their good-byes and sauntered off.

"What did that woman mean?" Lauren asked.

"Nothing," Kiki briskly answered.

"Looks like another fish got away," Hannah said with a devious smile. She never thought Harry and Kiki were a match anyway. "Do you think it's your bait?"

"Oh, put a cork in it," Kiki said. "Darn him. Why does every other woman but me get the men?"

"If it makes you feel any better, John hasn't called me in almost two weeks," Hannah said. "He's still mad at me."

"He'll be back," Lauren told her. "He's too crazy about you to stay mad for long." Just then she took a gulp of air.

Following Lauren's line of sight, Hannah saw Detective Morgan, coffee mug in hand, standing on the Book Stop patio.

"Go talk to him, honey," Kiki said, giving Lauren a nudge.

"I can't," Lauren said. "I'm too embarrassed, especially with what I'm wearing."

"Don't be silly. Men love a toga," Kiki said with a certainty that comes only from direct experience. Hannah made a mental note to keep better track of the sheets. Blushing, Lauren shook her head.

"Too bad we lost the love potion we made for him," Naomi said. "I still don't understand where it went."

"Well, your herbal cream for my rash certainly worked," Hannah told her, trying to move on to a safer subject. "My rash cleared up completely once I used it."

Naomi gave her a puzzled look. "But I forgot to make that cream, I was so busy." She paused, then gasped. "You used Detective Morgan's love potion by mistake. So that's where it went."

"My God," Kiki said, eyes wide. "I wondered why Detective Larry was so anxious to see you that day you went to Vera's."

"Don't be ridiculous. Detective Morgan explained it," Hannah told her. "John had asked him to look after me, and when I left the yearbook with Geraldine's photo missing at the police station, he got worried."

"Then why didn't he just phone?" Kiki asked. "No, he rushed to our house, demanding to talk to you in person, and when I said you were at Vera's, he just took off like a rocket." She paused theatrically. "Like he was a man transfixed."

"It was the potion," Naomi said. "It had to be."

"So Larry's in love with you?" Lauren asked weakly.

"Of course not," Hannah said. "I'm old enough to be his mother or grandmother, and there's no such thing as a love potion anyway." She stood up. "It's time to finish the dance."

The break over, the other dancers were already forming a circle, and Naomi and Kiki hurried back to join them. Hannah and Lauren rose from the bench.

"Lauren, why don't you sit this one out?" Hannah suggested. "Detective Morgan just happens to be looking this way." She reached into her handbag, pulled out a small jar, and surreptitiously handed it to her niece. "Quick, rub some of this on your chest. You know I don't believe in that love potion silliness. On the other hand, it doesn't hurt to cover all the bases."

While Lauren slathered on the cream, Hannah slowly walked over to the dancers, stepping into the circle between Wanda and Kiki just as the dance began. She joined hands with her friends and followed their movements. She felt embarrassed at first, but after she performed a few hops and twirls, she found that her mood had lifted. Maybe it *was* cleansing, she thought. After a few minutes she had to admit that she felt happier than she had in days, as if the weight from the recent tragic events had been at least partially lifted.

Hannah laughed when she saw Naomi hop around the altar, shaking the war stick. Looking back at Lauren, she saw Detective Morgan sitting next to her on the bench. *Wonderful,* she thought, doing an especially high leap, her hands in the air. She had to start giving Naomi more credit. The silly love potion seemed to have some effect on Morgan, and the dance as well had something a little magical about it. She found herself feeling more at peace with the world, or at least with Hill Creek, and as she swayed and danced, she looked at the photos of Vera and Geraldine and hoped that, where ever they were, they had also somehow made peace.

"I say we just forget the sacred dance stuff and just shake our booties," Kiki said, breaking into a twist. "Speaking of shaking our booties, when are you going to call John and make up?"

"I'll call him tonight," Hannah answered. "I'll invite him to dinner, and if he doesn't want to see me, then I'll just have to live with that."

Hannah felt almost giddy, and didn't even mind so much that they were drawing a crowd. She noticed one of the women from her cancer support group standing on the periphery of the crowd, looking enviously at the dancers. Hannah waved her over and pulled her into the circle. Then, on an impulse, she took off her sweater and tied it around her waist, revealing the upper part of her tattoo. She saw the other women staring at the flowers and ivy imprinted on her chest and running up her shoulder, and she didn't mind. Let the world see it.

Mimicking Naomi's sounds, Hannah chanted to the earth goddess, tentatively at first, then louder. She was twirling and chanting when she saw John Perez standing at the edge of the plaza, a coffee cup in his hand, waving to her and wearing the most delighted grin.

EARLENE FOWLER

introduces Benni Harper, curator of San Celina's folk
art museum and amateur sleuth

❏ FOOL'S PUZZLE   0-425-14545-X/$6.50
Ex-cowgirl Benni Harper moved to San Celina, California, to
begin a new career as curator of the town's folk art museum. But
when one of the museum's first quilt exhibit artists is found dead,
Benni must piece together a pattern of family secrets and small-
town lies to catch the killer.

❏ IRISH CHAIN   0-425-15137-9/$6.50
When Brady O'Hara and his former girlfriend are murdered at the
San Celina Senior Citizen's Prom, Benni believes it's more than
mere jealousy–and she risks everything to unveil the conspiracy
O'Hara had been hiding for fifty years.

❏ KANSAS TROUBLES   0-425-15696-6/$6.50
After their wedding, Benni and Gabe visit his hometown near
Wichita. There Benni meets Tyler Brown: aspiring country singer,
gifted quilter, and former Amish wife. But when Tyler is murdered
and the case comes between Gabe and her, Benni learns that her
marriage is much like the Kansas weather: bound to be stormy.

❏ GOOSE IN THE POND   0-425-16239-7/$6.50
❏ DOVE IN THE WINDOW   0-425-16894-8/$6.50